Amber Sky

C.O.I.L.S of Copper and Brass Book 1

Claire Warner

Amber Sky

C.O.I.L.S of Copper and Brass Book 1

Published by Raven Press

© Claire Warner 2016
Published by Raven Press
ISBN: 978-0-9954631-2-7 – Paperback Edition
ISBN: 978-0-9954631-3-4 – Ebook Edition

Images designed by Freepik

Also by Claire Warner:

Night Flower:

The Black Lotus

Blood Orchid

Faded Rose (in progress)

Coils of Copper and Brass:

Amber Sky

Copper Temple (TBC)

Silver City (TBC)

Crimson: Short Story collection (in progress)

For Steve, thank you for your belief.

For Sarah, you've helped so much.

And strangely enough, thanks to a particularly dull day at the office, without which this book would never have been thought of.

Within the Coils of Copper and Brass,
there is a chance of freedom.

Anonymous (date unknown)

Chapter 1

It was November, and soot-laden fog obscured her progress as Taya strode along the busy street. A chill wind kept the smog moving and nipped at her exposed skin. She was grateful for the shifting whiteness: it kept away curious eyes, and gave her a sense of freedom. The Factory was ahead, belching clouds of smoke and steam into the air, choking the lines of workers that queued outside. She averted her eyes and kept going. Thoughts of the Factory led to thoughts of the Mine, and she could not allow that. The work site fell behind her as she began to move uphill, away from the choking smog of the Factory District, and toward the Mercantile District. The traffic thinned out as her feet carried her through the cold, whispering quiet. The crowds were lighter here and better dressed. In contrast to their well-heeled fashions, Taya looked like an old sack. Several threadbare garments covered her body, and a moth-eaten, woollen hat was jammed down on her chestnut-

coloured hair. Her boots were held together with twine, and stuffed with rags to keep the cold at bay. Despite her efforts to layer her ragged clothing, the wind still found its way to her skin, making her shiver. As she headed into the district, the fog shielded her from prying eyes and made her progress easier. Moving along the well-paved roads of the Merchant District with the elusiveness of a wild thing, she avoided the few traders that braved the cold, speeding up as she approached her destination.

The house was built from white stone, now discoloured from the ubiquitous soot. On the faded, cherry-coloured door, a brass knocker in the shape of a lion warned her off with what she fancied was a contemptuous gaze. For a long moment, she stared at the wood, wondering at the wisdom of what she was attempting. Lars and Cody could have been wrong, and this trip could easily land her in the cells. As the ever-present wind chapped her lips, she mustered her resolve. All other options had been exhausted, and this was all she had left. Taking a deep breath, she grasped the knocker with one shaking hand before letting it fall. For several moments, she waited on the doorstep, shifting uneasily from one foot to the other, nervous beyond thought.

The door creaked open, and a maid stared down at her with unconcealed distaste. Taya nervously wet her lips and opened her mouth to speak.

"No beggars." The maid spoke first, her voice shrill with strident condemnation, as she took in Tay's attire.

Confident in her dismissal, she moved to close the door.

"No, wait." Tay placed her foot in the hall, and leant forward. The maid stopped moving, distaste morphing into shock. "I need to speak to Darius..." Despite her best efforts, Tay's voice still shook. "Please." The woman stared down at her with disbelief, incredulous at her audacity to ask to see the Master's son.

"I don't think so." The woman began pushing the door shut, shoving Tay's fragile frame off the doorstep with its weight. Tay held her ground, trying to keep the door open.

"Please..." She pleaded once more, her voice echoing loudly in the hallway. Panic thrummed through her as she became aware of the spectacle she was creating. One complaint from any of the people on the street behind her and the guards would come. "I need to see him." It was a desperate, yearning plea, yet the maid was having none of it. The door jammed against her toes, and she winced. The maid was winning the battle, her far stronger, well-fed, bulky frame inching Taya closer to the street.

"What's going on?" A male voice echoed across the hall, and the maid stopped.

"It's this beggar, Sir." The woman held the door steady as she turned to face the speaker. "She wishes to talk to you." Her voice was sneering, only slightly mollified by deference to her master.

"Let me see." The man walked forward, and the maid reluctantly released her hold on the door. Tay's eyes

roved across a well-tailored, dark blue suit, which framed a lean body, and a cane of some dark wood laid carelessly in slender, elegant fingers. Casting her gaze upward, she stared directly into a pair of deep-blue eyes, which were alight with interest.

"I need to see you, Darius." She appealed directly to him, holding his gaze with silent entreaty. She ignored the scandalised tut of the maid as she took a step forward. "It's important."

Darius thought for a moment before he nodded. "Let her in," he said to the maid, stepping back along the hall. With a look of shock on her features, the woman stepped away from the door and let Taya into the house.

Heat enveloped her as she followed Darius' beckoning finger and stepped off the street. The maid closed the door behind her as she slowly crossed the hall toward a door on the left. Her eyes drifted across the panelled space, awed by the luxury she saw. Dominated by a sweeping staircase, the hallway was decorated in shades of gold and blue. A heavy chandelier, festooned with lights, swung from the ceiling, and it was blissfully, wonderfully warm.

"Come on girl." Tay's head snapped back to the doorway, and she almost tripped over her own feet, as she hastened toward the sitting room. A fire blazed in a large hearth, filling the room with a cosy light. Above the mantel, a gilt-framed mirror reflected her scared and lost face. Several comfortable-looking couches laid about the room, and a variety of expensive knick-knacks were

arranged on a wooden cabinet against the left wall. Intimidated, she looked around at the luxuriant surroundings and swallowed nervously.

"Warm yourself up." Darius indicated the roaring fire, and she stepped before it gratefully, feeling the heat radiate across her cold skin. "Emma." He turned to the maid. "Can you find me some old clothes?" With a sour look on her face, Emma nodded. As soon as she had left, Darius turned back to the room. "Now that she's gone," he said as he walked forward. "Why don't you tell me what you want?"

Taya bit her lip and fidgeted. What had seemed like a good idea in the safety of her home, now felt like insanity. She glanced at him, noticing the arrogant cast to his features and the surety of his gaze. He was handsome, she realised with a jolt. Beneath a shock of black hair, deep blue eyes stared out at her with disconcerting directness.

"My name's Taya, and..." She stopped, wondering how she could continue with her request.

"And?" he encouraged, noticing her hesitation. "I can't help you if you don't ask."

"My father has just been sent to the Mine," she said quickly, watching the realisation cross his face.

"I see," he noted softly, staring at her with interest. "And?"

"He already has a weak heart," she found herself saying. "The Mine will kill him."

"I fancy that's the idea," he uttered, reaching for a glass of amber liquid that laid on the mantel, and took

a sip. "What do you expect me to do about it?"

"You're the son of the Overseer," she argued, her voice becoming stronger as she attempted to argue her case. "They say you can get people released."

"Possibly." He took another sip and regarded her closely. "Who is he?"

Taya swallowed nervously, hoping that her gamble had paid off. If she were wrong, he could have a guard here within moments. "Caleb Emerson," she announced, fear rippling through every syllable.

"The saboteur," he whispered, understanding crossing his features. "He's a high-profile prisoner."

"He was set up..."

"I have no doubt," he answered, mockery rippling through his tones.

"It's true." She was angry now. "They pinned it on him because he was protesting at the ration reduction. He would never..." He held up a hand, and she stopped speaking, breathing rapidly with the sudden rush of emotion.

"All right I get the point." He fell silent, regarding her closely. For several long moments, he said nothing, his face creased in thought. Tay watched him with increasing impatience.

"Please." She moved to stand before him, her voice pleading as she stared at his face. "He won't survive, and his ration will stop. I have two siblings. We'll all starve."

"It's not as simple as that," he said finally, looking down at her. "Your father has been sent to the Mine to

die, you must know that." She glanced away from his gaze, unwilling to see the truth reflected there. "If I manage to get him released, my head is on the block."

"Then get him transferred," she pleaded, trying not to let tears flow. "Put him on a lighter duty, anything that will keep him alive."

"It's a big risk." He swallowed the last of the drink. "Particularly as your family..." He left the statement hanging, reminding Tay of her mother's death during an earlier rebellion.

"Please." She did not wish to beg, but she could see no other option. With her father incarcerated for a similar offence to her mother's, she would be barred from all but the most menial work. She had barely scraped together the rating for the job she had been doing, and her father's arrest had ended that employment. Any work she was eligible for would never feed the three of them. The fire popped, breaking the silence that had fallen between them.

"Alright," he said finally. "I'll see what I can do."

"Thank you." Relief flooded through her, and she stepped back, eager to leave the oppressive luxury of this room.

"Just one thing." She froze, sudden fear spiking through her. "What are you offering for my help?"

Tay's mouth dropped open in shock. He couldn't be asking for payment, they had never said that he would. "I thought..." she gabbled, feeling trapped by the room and her fears.

"You thought I did this out of the goodness of my

heart?" He gave a short, mirthless laugh. "Not a bit of it, this is going to be dangerous for me. What are you offering for my help?"

"I don't have..." She stopped speaking and stared up at the man, a desperate look on her face. There was nothing she could offer him, one glance at the riches around her told her that. She could feel her father's freedom slipping away from her, as a tense silence settled over the room.

For a moment, neither spoke, until Darius finally broke the quiet with a sigh. "If you have nothing to offer, then..." He started to walk toward the door.

"Wait." Sheer desperation moved her to intercept him. He stopped, looking down at her, a question in his eyes. "I can..." She stopped talking, unable to verbalise the mess of thoughts that were swirling around her head. Sure of what he wanted, she slowly moved her hand to the top of her ragged shirt and began to undo the buttons. "If this is what you want." Her third button slid open beneath her trembling fingers.

"No." He reached forward and caught hold of her fingers, stopping them from their work. Pushing her hands aside, he closed the shirt, doing up the buttons with careful motions. "That," he said, as she stared at him in shock, "is too cheap a price." He finished with the last button and stood back. "I certainly don't need to buy sex, and I would never take it as payment for this."

"Then what?" she asked, misery running through her voice. "I don't have anything at all." While she was

grateful that he had turned her down, her body had been her only bargaining chip.

"I'll tell you what." He moved back to the chair and sat down. "If I do this, then you have to owe me a favour. One that I can call in at any time."

"What kind of favour?"

"Don't worry, it won't be beyond your capabilities." He favoured her with a hard-searching look. "Well?"

She hesitated, unsure of agreeing to such a broad favour.

"I won't ask you to sleep with, kill or steal from anyone," he uttered, looking at her face with some interest.

"Okay," she whispered, looking at him with what could only be described as a frightened rabbit expression. "I agree." It wasn't an ideal situation, yet she had little choice. Her father would not survive for long down the Mine, and once he was dead, the rations of food and fuel would cease. The authorities were clever: even if you were sentenced to forced labour, the fuel and food payments were still paid to your family. Of course, they stopped on your death, and it was ensured that you died quickly. The authorities didn't believe in martyrs; they continued payment to seem generous, to claim that the guilty party was responsible for the starvation of the rest of the family. After all, should you die through chastisement, you have doomed those you loved.

"Good." He reached out and picked up a steaming cup of tea. "Here." He handed the cup to her and

retreated to the sofa whilst she drank in tiny sips.

"I have some clothes ready, sir." The maid returned to the room, her arms laden with garments.

"Thank you." He looked down at Taya and continued, "I think you had better take this one to the washroom and let her change."

"But sir..."

"Don't argue." His voice, though soft, cracked out like a whip. "I'm being charitable, not you." He looked over at Taya. "Go with Emma and get changed." His tone of voice had altered, becoming blander, yet somehow patronising. Tay almost bristled at the condescension, yet she knew that would be an unwise thing to do. He was clearly playing up the charitable act bit, and she couldn't jeopardise any future assistance.

Following the woman into the hallway, she was led to a closed door. Following the woman's direction, she struggled with the door handle and walked inside, her mouth dropping at the room she saw beyond. It wasn't a particularly large room, yet the tiling shone white and clean beneath the steady gas lamps, the toilet was familiar, but the sink had hot and cold running taps. Indoor plumbing was rare, and piped hot water even more so.

"Hurry up girl." The maid interrupted her train of thought, and she closed her mouth, accepting the bundle of clothing with a stunned expression.

"Consider yourself lucky that the Master saw fit to assist you," the maid commented, as she watched Taya remove her clean, but worn, clothing. Soon she was

standing in her underwear, exposing her skinny frame to the chill air of the bathroom. She avoided looking at herself in the mirror that rested above the sink, unwilling to see just how bad she looked in contrast to the richness of the room. The new clothing was of good quality and, more importantly, intact. As she drew the fabric over her skinny frame, she felt better, warmer, and a lot more human.

"It'll do, I suppose," the maid noted grudgingly. Pushing open the door, she led Taya back into the hallway.

"That's better," Darius' voice called from the end of the hall, and she stopped, staring with interest at the pair of boots he held in his hands. They were good quality, brown leather and barely worn. "Take these." He held them out, and she started, looking at them as though she had never seen shoes before. "They would replace those scraps of leather on your feet."

"Thank you." She took a step forward and slowly extended her arm, touching the smooth leather with wonderment.

"Just take it," he said with a touch of irritation.

"Thank you," she whispered, as she took the items from his hands. "Why so generous?"

"I can afford to be," he replied in an equally low whisper. "I'm afraid that's all I can do for you at the moment." He raised his voice as he walked back toward the parlour. "See the girl out Emma," he ordered over his shoulder as he left Tay in the hall, a bundle of clothes in her arms.

"On your way then." The maid seized hold of her arm and dragged her to the door. "And never let me see you plying your trade in here again. The Master will have none of the likes of you." Her fingers dug painfully into Tay's arm.

Tay did not protest as the other woman propelled her through the door and outside. The cherry-red door slammed shut behind her, and she was left in the street, the chill fog reduced somewhat by the new clothing. Carrying the new boots, she left the steps of the mansion and hurried down one of the side streets, hoping to find some place to change unobserved. She found a dry spot and hunkered down. The mixture of new and old clothing fell into an untidy pile as she removed the rags from her feet. Pulling on a new pair of socks, she reached for the first boot. She stopped, looking into the boot with confusion. Hidden within the leather was a small slip of paper. She removed it with shaking fingers and read the elegant script silently.

Meet me at the Webster Fountain at noon tomorrow. There are things we need to discuss.

She stood and leant back against the wall, unsure of just what she had gotten herself into. While Darius had shown that he was unwilling to use her body as payment, she still did not fully trust the man. Pangs of cold pinched her feet, and she remembered the boots she held in her hands. Slipping them on, Tay placed the

note into a pocket, collected her clothes and started to walk home. The fog had lifted a little as she traversed the Merchants' District, but her attire did not draw attention this time. Walking down the slope toward the Factory, her thoughts began to drift from her predicament and back to Darius. She had gone to him with little expectation, and purely on rumour. Her father's friends had mentioned his name at one time, and she had thought it worth the risk. She couldn't really say what she had been expecting, a rebellious son, a meek bookkeeper, certainly not the handsome man who had aided her. She walked past the schoolhouse and headed toward the Housing District. The houses were built in regular rows with minimal garden space, and a general air of hopelessness exuded from every one of them. Smoke drifted from each of the chimneys, contributing to the miasma and smog that permeated the air. She glanced skyward, looking for a hint of the mother-of-pearl sky amongst the cloud, yet she was disappointed as usual.

She turned left at the Ration Centre and walked on. What favour would Darius want from her? He claimed it would be within her capabilities, but how would he know? Troubled by her thoughts, she barely noticed that she had arrived at her house. Set at the end of a terrace, the small two-bedroom property promised partial respite from the raw weather.

"Lana? Roj? She called as she opened the door, stepping into the hall. "I'm back."

"Roj is still at school," her younger sister called as

she left the living room to stare at her. "Where did you get all that?" She indicated the bundle of clothing in her hands. "I thought you were going to talk to Darius."

"I did." Tay placed the clothes down on the table and began to sort through them. "He gave us this."

"And Father?"

"He can't get him released." Tay folded a warm sweater and placed it in a pile. "But he can get him moved."

"He'll still die though." Lana picked up the neatly folded sweater and examined it. "Why can't he free him?"

"Because he's high profile." Taya took the sweater from her sister's hands and placed it back on the table. "It's all he can do to get him transferred, particularly because of Mother." She folded the next item of clothing and gave a long sigh. The maid had clearly taken her revenge with the clothing: half of the pile was unusable. "We'll be alright, I'll be eligible to re-apply for ration soon."

"It's not as much as Father's claim."

Taya placed the thin, almost useless shirt on the table and counted to ten. "Don't knock it. This is the best option we have." She glanced at Lana's mutinous face and continued. "They arrested Father for sabotage, do you honestly think they will make it easy for him to be free?" She picked up another shirt and began to fold it quickly, nervous anger running through her.

"What's wrong?" Lana rested a hand on her sister's arm.

"It's..." Tay settled her hands on the table, trying to organise her thoughts. Her sister watched her for a long moment before she gave a huff of annoyance.

"Come on, out with it."

Tay glanced over at Lana and took a breath. "It's Darius," she said after a moment's pause. "He wants paying for his help." Lana's eyes narrowed with suspicion at her words, Tay noticed, and quickly continued. "He wants a favour."

"What kind of favour?" Lana's voice held volumes of distrust.

"I don't know." Tay admitted after a moment. "He didn't say."

Lana gave a huff of disgust. "Well, I think it's plain what he'll ask for," she muttered with a sneer that seemed wrong on her young features.

"No." Disagreeing with a shake of her head, Tay returned to the clothes pile. "I know he's not after that."

"How can you be sure?" Lana's eyes widened slightly as she stared at the slightly guilty look on her sister's face. "Tay?"

"I offered, okay," she announced finally, "and he said no."

"You offered?" Lana repeated with disbelief in her voice. "How could you?"

"I thought that was what he would want," she retorted with real heat to her voice. "I had nothing to trade for father's freedom and that was all I could think of."

"And he said no?"

"Yeah," Tay replied with a small smile. "He said he wouldn't take sex as payment."

"Well, you got away lucky."

"Not necessarily." Tay returned to the clothes pile and began sorting through it with greater speed. "Now I owe him a favour, and I don't know what it is. The other way, I would feel cheap, but at least it would be done." She finished going through the pile and handed an armful of clothes to Lana. "Now get those tidied away and come help me in the garden. We still have to see what we can salvage of the veg before winter sets in."

Lana took the offered clothes and headed for the stairs. Reaching the bottom rung, she turned to face her sister. "What was he like?"

"Darius?" Tay asked, a quizzical look on her face.

"Who else?" Lana leant back against the wall and waited. "All I know of him is what Father's friends said of him."

Tay thought for a moment, thinking back to the first time she had seen that handsome, arrogant visage. Unsure of what to expect, she had certainly not expected him. Close to her own age, with eyes so blue you could drown in them, Darius had been a surprise. Even without her nerves about asking for a favour, she would have been tongue tied anyway.

"Different," was all she said as she reached for the trowel and moved toward the back door.

"How different?" Lana pressed from the staircase. "Was he arrogant, ugly, a creep?"

"He certainly wasn't ugly," Tay finally replied as she pressed the latch on the door. "And he's not a creep." Pushing open the door, she began to head into the garden. "Younger than I expected."

"Go on." Lana placed the pile of clothing in her arms on the steps and followed her to the door.

"It wasn't that exciting," Tay answered, sucking in a breath as the frozen air hit her skin. "I just wasn't expecting the man I met."

"Tay..." Lana whined as she pulled another jacket about her shoulders and followed her outside.

"Why is Darius so important?" Tay asked as she reached the first row of vegetables and began to dig.

"Because of what Father's friends said about him."

"Oh?" Tay dug a small, stunted carrot from the ground and placed it in a metal pail. "And how would you know what they said?" She glanced up at her sister and nodded to the ground.

"I listened." Lana knelt down in the dirt and began to dig. "They said he had his own agenda and I thought..."

"Thought what?"

Lana sat back on her heels and looked at her older sister. "That he wanted you to be part of it; whatever it is."

Tay stopped digging for a moment and stared at her sister. "Well, I doubt that," she said finally. "Father didn't exactly include me in his schemes so, I don't know how much help I can be."

"But what if Father has some plans hidden and he

wants us to find them?" Lana's voice rambled on excitedly as she reached back into the dirt to pull forth some more of the sorry-looking vegetables. "What if he's part of the resistance?"

"Lana," Tay snapped out in a sharper voice than she intended. "Don't talk about things like that out here." She nervously glanced over her shoulder at the fences that ringed the garden. Lowering her voice, she continued. "What if someone's listening?"

"Why would anyone be listening?" Lana questioned, rolling her eyes at her sister's paranoia.

"Get on with your chores," Tay muttered as she began digging in the ground with fresh determination.

"Alright." Lana acquiesced in a bored tone as she jabbed her trowel into the hard ground. "I think you're crazy."

"Really?" Tay stopped digging and raised an eyebrow at her sister. "How did they know about Father?"

Lana stopped digging, and her face fell. "I hadn't thought of that," she whispered. "You think one of our neighbours?"

"Let's not talk about this now." Tay threw another two carrots into the pail and stretched. "Just get on with it."

Their fingers were numb by the time they finished, and the light was fading. "Time to get back in," Taya announced, shivering as another gust of icy cold wind blew across her skin. "Roj will be back soon, and I need to pick up the ration for today." Wrapping a cloth about her fingers, she picked up the freezing-cold, metal

pail before she headed back toward the house, and the relative warmth it supplied. There would be time later to ponder her meeting.

Chapter 2

Tay left her home the following morning to a clear amber sky. The strong winds the previous night had swept the sky of fog, leaving a sharp, dry cold in its place. Smoke drifted from the chimneys of the houses lining the road, the grey-white vapour curling into the clear air like clouds. Huddled against the cold, dressed in her father's old coat, she looked like a lost child. Beneath a concealing wrap of old rags, her new boots warmed her feet, and a new jumper kept the worst of the chill at bay. Frost rimmed the edges of the puddles on the main thoroughfare, and she swore at the sight. With the onset of ice and frost, it became more imperative to keep the fire stoked at home. Ration only provided the bare minimum of coal for a week, and it certainly wasn't enough to heat the house and cook. As the winter deepened, she began to wonder about joining the scavengers at the depot. It was dangerous to steal from the supply lines, but she might not have any other

choice.

Not for the first time, she wondered what life would have been like if their mother hadn't died. She skirted the puddles, her thoughts elsewhere. Her memories of her mother were patchy and coloured by time. If she thought hard enough, she could almost see her face. Tarin Emerson had been killed during the food riots, two years after Roj's birth, and like all of those present at the riot, her family had suffered the rating loss. A man loomed ahead of her, and she ducked to one side, apologising for the near miss. The authorities had almost cleared that blot from the family records, and then her father had been arrested. She kicked a pebble across the frozen road and kept going. Had it not been for her mother's rebellion, they would have been living a comfortable existence.

Passing the Ration Centre, she avoided the group of guards that lingered beside the entrance, and hurried on. Thankfully, the cold seemed to have dissuaded them from their usual game of harassment, but their eyes followed her as she moved off down the road. Protected by the authorities, the guards became tyrants, assuming duties that were beyond merely keeping order, and she avoided them as often as she could. Rating for guards and Ration Centre workers was generous and came with accommodation in the more salubrious areas of the City. As a consequence, guards tended to have an increased desire to maintain the system, and they were enthusiastic in their duties. Her mind flashed back to the morning of her Father's arrest. They had woken to a

loud banging on the door and immediately realised the danger. There was no guarantee that the guards would have stopped at merely arresting their target, and they had all heard the horror stories. As the door splintered with the force of the blows, her Father had shunted all of them into the attic. In the cramped and freezing crawl space, they had watched their father being dragged from the house. Despite his lack of resistance, he had still been severely beaten, and the house turned upside down. Thankfully, the route to the attic was concealed, and the guard had failed to find them. For an hour, they had huddled together, too terrified to move as their home was torn apart. Once they had smashed what they could, the guards finally left, and Tay walked downstairs. There hadn't been a single thing left unbroken, and the front door hung drunkenly from its hinges. Swallowing back her tears, she had immediately called the numbers that her father had drilled into her memory.

The train station came into view and broke her from her daydream. Once immaculate, it's façade was now coated with soot and factory pollution. She had been told that there had once been regular passenger traffic between their community and others, even as far as the City, but she had never seen such a thing in her lifetime. The only trains that left the station these days were either supply wagons or transport for the nobility and their guards. Travel wasn't forbidden, but it was prohibitively expensive, and there was little reason for people to leave the area. When actual money was scarce,

it wasn't wasted on travel. She stopped to watch the train being loaded for a few moments, wondering whether she could just clamber onto one of the carriages and run far from the mess of her life. The breeze picked up and ruffled her hair, distracting her from her musings. Shaking her head free of thoughts of escape, she continued to walk, hoping to reach the park before the meeting time.

Moving away from the stockyard, she walked along the broad, weed-choked avenue toward the park that laid in the exact centre of town. The park was usually an oasis of greenery in the squalid misery of the surrounding areas, but at this time of year it was barren, the green stripped from the trees. There were only a few visitors to the park on this cold morning, and she crossed the frosted grass without interacting with another soul. Moving past the ancient play equipment that was decaying on the southern edge of the now disused flower garden, she hurried toward the fountain that stood in the middle of the park. Set in a shallow pool, worn with age and soiled with years of soot, the fountain depicted two figures clutching a ball. For a moment, she stared at the sculpture, wondering about their significance.

"I'm glad to see you came." She whirled about at the voice, heart increasing its pace as Darius moved closer to her.

"I almost didn't," she whispered, struck again by the attractiveness of the man before her. Dressed for the weather in a thigh-length, black woollen coat, his hair

concealed by a dark grey trilby he exuded the same confidence he had displayed the day before.

"Understandable," he replied, falling into place beside her. "You don't know anything about me."

"Why did you..." He placed his fingers to his lips, and she stopped talking, waiting as an elderly couple walked past them. A bitter wind ruffled her hair, and she shivered, drawing the coat further about her shoulders. Wordlessly, Darius removed his gloves and handed them to her. With trepidation, she slowly reached her hand out.

"They don't come with any strings," he said with a hint of impatience.

"How can I be sure?" she retorted as she took the offered items, and slid them onto her hands. The gloves still retained the heat from his hands, and she closed her fists, absorbing the welcome warmth. "Thank you," she whispered.

"That" — Darius tucked his hands into his pockets as he spoke — "isn't a problem."

"Why did you want to meet me?" Despite her best efforts, her voice trembled, and she hoped he would pass it off as a reaction to the cold.

"Your father," he uttered in soft tones, "is a high-profile prisoner."

"Yes," Tay answered, a feeling of dread coursing through her blood, "I told you yesterday."

"Indeed, you did." He walked forward, and casually placed his hands on the top of the fountain wall, leaning forward as he stared into the murky, stagnant

water.

"Are you telling me that you can't move him?" Tay whispered, fear racing down her spine.

"No." He turned around and faced her. "I keep my promises. I just have to ensure that you will fulfil your end of the bargain." His eyes bored into hers, the dark blue gaze almost as cold as the air around them.

"I will," she assured him, trying not to take a step back. "You have my word."

He gave a small chuckle. "But how can you repay me if I can't find you?"

"You could tell me now how I can repay you," she suggested, wondering just what he had in mind for repayment. Certainly, there was nothing material she could offer him.

"Not just yet," he replied, dismissing the idea with a cavalier wave.

"I don't understand," she protested, nervousness giving way to irritation. "What do I have that I could possibly offer you? Why can't you just tell me and get it over with?"

"Because I don't need the favour right now," he answered, watching her increasing impatience with a lazy smile.

"Then I can just tell you where I live," she offered, wondering briefly why she was volunteering this information, when he could discover it easily through his contacts. "And you can visit when you want me to repay."

"Too risky for me to make the trip," he retorted,

staring out across the wintry landscape. "But I have a solution." A pair of deep blue eyes connected with hers. Tay grew still, sure that he was about to name his price. "I believe you have need of a job." Tay started, unsure of what she had just heard. "The house next to us has a vacancy for a scullery maid," he continued, oblivious to the look of shock on her face.

Tay froze for a moment, waiting for his words to make some kind of sense. "Why?" she found herself asking as the silence stretched uncomfortably between them.

"It solves my problem," he answered. "I need to be able to contact you without too much difficulty."

"How will I get the job?" she asked, too stunned to think of anything else.

"Don't worry about that." He leant against the edge of the fountain. "The Frazers use Carfax Domestics to hire their staff, and Carfax Domestics will send the next person on their list." He gave a small shrug. "It's child's play to hack the system and add you."

"Why would you go to such trouble?" A chill breeze tugged at her hair. "Why can't I just promise to come to see you?"

"How often do you think I can see the same beggar at my door before my staff begin to question?" A wry smile crossed his face. "I don't trust them enough to not call the authorities."

"Alright." A sense of unreality settled over Tay as she began to process just what had just occurred. Absolutely none of the scenarios she had envisioned had given her

this possibility. "So, if I do this, will I have to live at their house?"

"You will." He was watching her carefully, as though he expected her to panic.

"What about my brother and sister?" Her voice grew stronger as thoughts of her siblings began to swarm through her mind. "I can't just leave them to fend for themselves."

"How old are they?" he asked mildly.

"Lana is fifteen and Roj is ten," she answered with a crisp finality. "They're not old enough to draw father's ration." She folded her arms across her chest, challenging him. "You can't expect me to just leave them."

"I'll see what I can do about them," he said, pushing himself away from the fountain's edge. "But I can't promise anything." He adjusted the scarf around his neck as he spoke. "Nevertheless I'll expect you at the Frazers' tomorrow."

"Now, wait." She stepped forward and placed her hand against his chest, stopping him from walking away. Angry at his assumption that she would obey him without question, she continued, "I never agreed..."

"You want your father safe?" She froze at his words, her objections abruptly cut off by the threat in his voice. He glanced at her hand on his chest, and she removed it, unnerved by the cold glint in his gaze.

"What?" Tay felt her heart sink as she tried to process just what he had said.

"I have just signed a transfer order," he continued,

his eyes not leaving her face. "It ordered your father removed from the coal face and sent to work in the administration building." His voice was low, threatening and she stepped away from him, unnerved by the coolness in his eyes. "He is as far away from the danger of the Mine as he can possibly be." He took a step toward her, closing the gap between them. "If that transfer is scrutinised, my head is on the block." His voice was almost a whisper now, and she could feel the darkness behind it. "As I told you yesterday, I do not stick my neck out for nothing." His hand reached up and came to rest on her shoulder. "I should think you would be willing to endure some hardship to pay me my due."

"But..." Her voice was a breathless whisper as he backed her to the edge of the garden.

"I said I would see what I could do." He loomed over her, his fingers gently resting against her collarbone. "I will try to arrange something concerning your siblings." He released her. "I can't make promises, but either way, I want to see you at the Frazers' tomorrow morning." He stepped back and began to turn away. "If you don't show up, I may rescind that transfer." He looked back at her. "Do you understand?"

"Yes," she uttered, misery in her voice. "I understand."

"Good." Darius flipped the collar of his coat up and turned back to the path. "The Frazers' will expect you at eight, wear the new clothes I gave you." And with that, he walked away from the fountain and headed back

through the park.

Tay watched him walk into the distance, her heart thumping painfully in her chest. The weight of his words settled heavily on her mind, yet her skin tingled from the contact of his fingers. She had the distinct feeling that she had just struck a deal with the devil. Darius could potentially talk her into anything by holding her father's fate over her head. Bowing her head, she stared down at the overly-large gloves that still covered her hands. For one moment, Darius had appeared to display a soul, but his threat burned her to her very core. She would have to go to the Frazers' house the following morning and hope that he would hold up his end of the bargain. Picking herself up from the frozen ground, she began to walk home, dread weighing down every step.

The kitchen fire had burned down to ash when she finally walked through the doors of her home. Stepping into the kitchen, she added another handful of coal to the dying fire and used the poker to stir it into life. For a moment, she stayed still, watching the flame lick the edges of the fresh coal, as the fire began to burn once more. The amber and gold flames danced before her eyes as she allowed her mind to drift back to the meeting. What on earth could he want so badly that he would insist on her taking a job at the house next door? She sat down on the chair before the fire and nibbled

her lip, running scenarios through her head. He didn't want her for sex, of that she was fairly sure. She had given him the perfect opportunity, and he had turned her down. Granted this could be an elaborate ruse, but she didn't think so. He had seemed sincere in his denial of her. She pushed a strand of hair away from her face and began to think about the job. In some way, she could see it as a blessing. She would never have obtained such a position without the assistance.

Schooling was mandatory to the age of sixteen, and ration could not be paid to those underage. Promising students were removed from local schools at a young age and re-educated at the prosaically named, but restrictive capital city of Riverton. Once educated, and a lot older, these students would return to be the area's doctors and engineers, with the appropriate money and privileges. Students left in local education had few options once school ended. The Factory was the primary employer in the area, but the rations paid were tiny and barely enough to sustain a family. The merchants in the district fared better; they were paid in actual money, making it easier for them to trade with other settlements and cities. Merchant families were dynasties, handing their businesses to their children and grandchildren and increasing their wealth through marriage. Service to the wealthier families was considered more stable than factory toil and far less demanding, as it not only came with an increased ration and accommodation, but they also paid in money. As such, these jobs were in high demand and rare. You

could only obtain these jobs if you were taken up by an agency, and they usually recruited straight from the school system. Biddable pupils with little or no trouble on their school record were placed on the list of potential staff. Without an agency's acceptance, there was only the Factory, or even worse, the Mine.

If she were in a charitable mood, she would attribute his actions to some altruistic impulse on his part, but she was far too concerned about his motives to believe that. The kitchen door opened, sending a freezing gust of air through the tiny room.

"Is everything alright Tay?" Roj walked through the door, his hair tousled from the weather outside. Tay stood up, schooling her expression into one of calm unconcern.

"Everything's fine," she replied with a smile. "Why don't you shut the door." He closed the door and walked across the kitchen. Tay watched him with concealed worry as he sat down at the table. Despite the ragged layers that bulked out his frame, her brother was thinner than she would have liked. "Something to eat?" she asked as she moved to the pantry and drew out a small joint of salted beef and several puny carrots. Closing the door on the pitifully small selection of food, she turned back to the table and began to slice the meat into bite-sized chunks. "Take your coat off and start on the potatoes."

Roj nodded as he pulled his outer coat from his body and hung it next to the fire. Walking across to the pantry, he picked up a handful of the misshapen

potatoes and began to wash them.

"So how was school?" she asked, trying to find some normalcy in amongst the mess that their lives had recently become.

"The same," he replied, scrubbing the clods of dirt from the stunted potatoes as he gingerly held them beneath the jet of icy water from the tap. "Andrew Hazleton got docked ten points for graffiti." He sliced the washed potatoes in half and placed them into a pot. Picking up a couple more potatoes, he continued, "They're saying he won't make the list."

Tay glanced over at her brother. Making the list was a significant advantage. It showed that you had the mental capacity for engineering or science and that meant a transfer. She shook her head at the Andrew Hazleton's idiocy. She would have killed to be able to make the list.

"Where are you?" That was a more important question. With Andrew losing the ten points, it was likely that those further back in the rankings could move forward. Not that she particularly liked having to dance to the tune of the leadership, but starving for ideals seemed stupid. If Roj made the list, the authorities could ignore the negative rating imposed by their father's arrest. It didn't often happen, but gifted students had the chance to be elevated beyond their family. Though, with a mother dead in the food riots and a father arrested for sabotage, it was highly unlikely. She placed the meat into the pot and added some water.

"Fifteen points below," her brother answered, picking

up the last of the potatoes. "Is that all there is?" he asked, looking at the empty tray.

"Unfortunately." Tay placed the pot on the stove. "Potato grubs ate half the crop." Her lip set in a thin line as she began slicing the carrots. Adding the slices to the pot, she reached back into the pantry for the small bowl of pearl barley. The pantry was depressingly bare. Ration for the Mine was even less than ration for the Factory, and the Centre was very on the ball when it came to allocation. With the poor harvest, they could starve before the spring. Placing the last of the carrots into the pot, she came to a decision. She would have to take Darius up on his offer. It was that or starve. As the stew began to bubble, she hoped that she was making the right choice.

Chapter 3

Tay stood in the kitchen of the Frazers' house and waited for the housekeeper to arrive. Still cold from the bitter conditions outside, her fingers tingled from the warmth of the kitchen. The itch beneath the skin intensifying as the blood returned to the numb digits. She stood awkwardly by the door, her eyes taking in the sights and sounds of the room with wonder. A large stove heated the space and provided scalding hot water. A long table dominated the room, it's wooden surface scrubbed clean and laid with pots, pans and other utensils. Against the walls, cupboards loaded with food and other items commanded her vision. When one of the cooks opened the pantry, she stared with open wonder at the sight of the fully stocked shelves. Controlling her desire to drool, she shuffled her feet and looked down at the well-scrubbed, tile floor. As she waited for the housekeeper, she thought back to the previous evening and the conversation with her siblings.

Lana had been sceptical of the plan, as she expected, but Roj was surprisingly encouraging. He had pointed out that as Tay's rating had been badly affected by their father's arrest, the best opportunity she could hope for was Line Operative at the Factory. Correctly summarising the dilemma, he noted that even if she couldn't stay with them, her new employers couldn't stop her from visiting or drawing ration. Encouraged by her brother, Lana had reluctantly admitted that as they spent so much time at school, there wasn't an issue with them being home alone for too long.

"Besides" — Lana had said, toward the end of the conversation — "If you go to the Factory, you will be away just as much."

That was the end of the discussion and, armed with her siblings' approval, she had made the journey this morning in the cold.

"Ahh. Here we are." Tay looked up as the bustling form of the housekeeper reached her side. "Carfax just confirmed your appointment." She waved the typed piece of paper like a banner. "I understand you have ration responsibilities?" Tay nodded, wondering just how much clout Darius really had. "You are released from duty every Thursday afternoon so that you may collect ration."

"Thank you," Tay stuttered out, wondering just what that piece of paper said.

"Of course you are still expected back on Friday morning." The housekeeper slid the piece of paper back into her pocket. "Well, now that's out of the way, we're ready to go." Turning back to the kitchen, she beckoned, "Come with me."

Tay picked up her satchel and followed the other woman as she led her across the room.

"Now, your duties are simple," the housekeeper called as they reached a door. "Washing dishes and pans," she recounted as they walked into a plainly decorated, narrow hallway. "The laundry, and lighting the kitchen fire." Moving quickly toward the stairs, Tay had to hurry to keep up with her. "That means you have to be an early riser." Tay nodded as she tried to keep pace with the long legged woman. Almost tripping up the next flight of stairs, she tried to follow what the woman was saying next.

"I don't expect you to have anything to do with the family," Tay heard as she steadied herself with the bannister, "and there's no reason at all for you to be in the main house." She moved up another flight of stairs. "If I find you in any of the family rooms, you will lose this position." The woman stopped abruptly and glared down at her. "Do you understand?"

"Yes," Tay breathed finally, stunned by the sudden antagonism in the woman's voice.

"Sometimes, the Master or any of his family will visit the kitchen." The housekeeper turned and continued up the next flight of stairs. "When they do, I expect you to stay in the scullery unless specifically asked for."

Tay nodded, stumbling up the next flight of steps with inexplicably clumsy feet. They reached the top step and the housekeeper turned right. Leading Tay along the narrow corridor and past several closed doors, they finally stopped in front of the last door on the left.

"In here." She removed a heavy key from the bunch at her side and unlocked the door. The room beyond was small and cramped-looking. A small window tucked into the eaves provided minimal light and revealed a small bed, a nightstand with a cracked pitcher and bowl, and a single chest for her clothing. Spread across her bed were two uniforms of rigid gabardine and cotton.

"Now" — The housekeeper turned about and handed her the key— "This is your room." Tay shoved it into a pocket, the heavy piece of metal banging into her leg as she let go. "Get cleaned up and make yourself presentable, then come back downstairs to start work."

Tay nodded and glanced back at the uniform. The material was sturdy and considerably warmer than the clothes that she was currently wearing.

"Wait." She called as the housekeeper turned to leave the room. "What do I call you?"

"Mrs. Mitchell," she called back over her shoulder as she walked through the door, and closed it behind her, leaving Tay standing in the middle of her room. For a moment she stood still, staring at her new bedroom. The room was cold and impersonal. The iron-framed bed looked hard and uncomfortable, and the window provided only a bare minimum of light, but she had accommodation and the potential to earn money. She

crossed to the bed and climbed onto its starched surface, using the height to stare out of the window to the frozen yard below. She caught her breath. Standing in the garden below, the now familiar figure of Darius looked up at her, a tiny, knowing smile playing about his lips. She drew back sharply and closed the curtains, wondering just how he had managed to get her employed. Her father's friends had said that he could transfer people but had mentioned nothing about his other skills. Not for the first time in two days, she wondered what she had gotten herself into with the Overseer's son.

Climbing off the bed, she looked down at the uniform. Slowly, with shaking hands, she removed her threadbare garb and quickly washed. Drying herself with the rough towel she discovered in one of the drawers, she dressed quickly, the chill air of the bedroom raising goosebumps on her skin.

Once fully clothed in the cumbersome uniform, she pulled on the pair of shoes and headed back down the stairs to the kitchen. The room was a hive of activity as she shyly walked through the door.

"Ah, there you are." A short, dumpy woman walked toward her, flour was dusted all over her apron, and her hands were covered with pastry. "I'm Meg, the assistant cook." She looked down at her messy hands and shrugged. "I would offer to shake but..."

"Don't worry about it," Tay replied, smiling at the other woman. "I'm Taya, but people usually call me Tay."

"Good to see you." Meg walked past her and picked up a pitcher of water from the side. "I'd start on the breakfast pans if I were you," she continued, as she moved back to the large basin sitting in the centre of the table. "And be quick about it."

"Right," Tay replied as she walked past the table, and toward the scullery door.

"They're on that side," Meg called just as she entered the room. Tay turned back to the kitchen and the pile of pans that were stacked on the worktop nearest the stove. An embarrassed flush flooded Tay's cheeks, as she moved to pick up the grease-encrusted pans. Stacking them easily within her hands, she moved back into the scullery and set them in the sink.

"So where did you come from?" Tay jumped as a voice sounded from somewhere behind her, and she whirled around. Another girl walked out of the corner and stood before her. Dressed in the same black and white uniform she was wearing, the girl's heart-shaped face smiled at her from beneath a fringe of strawberry-blonde hair.

"Carfax."

"We're all from Carfax," the other girl answered in a slow, slightly mocking tone. "I meant, where do you live?"

"Oh" — Tay flushed slightly — " I'm from Westford." She gave the name of her street, hoping that it matched the information on her transfer. The other girl said nothing as she processed the information, but a mocking, slightly supercilious smile curved her lips.

"Really?" she asked, her voice revealing volumes of meaning in that one small word. Tay gritted her teeth and tried not to look at the ground. Westford did not have the best reputation in the city, and it was clear that this girl was not impressed by her address. "Where do you come from?" Tay threw the question back at the other girl, unwilling to be cowed by her.

"Larkway," the other girl replied, naming one of the areas in the city closest to the Merchants' District. Larkway was slightly better off than some other parts of the city. Its population were mainly servants of the merchant houses, and as such, they assumed a superior air to the rest of the slum. It was evident from the girl's tones that she considered herself a cut above Tay and her humbler surroundings.

"Really?" Tay replied in almost the exact tone that the other girl had used, watching as an annoyed scowl creased the other girl's features. "How absolutely fascinating." She added the sarcasm with an almost vicious glee, watching as the girl's face reddened slightly.

"Are you going to wash those?" The girl nodded at the greasy pans in Tay's hands. "Or do I have to tell the cook you're shirking on your first day."

Tay watched as the girl glided past and gave a shrug, more irritated with the other girl than upset.

"Do you need help with the taps?" the other girl asked, a sneering note entering her voice. "I know you probably don't have running water in Westford."

"I'm fine, thank you." Tay struggled to keep her temper as she reached out to turn on the taps. The

water gurgled through the pipes and began to empty into the sink, steam rising from the hot water tap as it did so. Reaching down for the thick bar of dish soap and scrubbing brush, she set to washing the greasy pans. "Don't you have your own work to do?" she called back over her shoulder, ensuring that her voice was loud enough to be heard in the kitchen. She was rewarded by the girl's guilty flinch and near run from the scullery.

Left alone in the quiet of the scullery, hands submerged in warm, soapy water, she could finally relax and think. Darius had been watching for her, and he had known which room she would been given. That was strange enough on its own, but how could he hope to claim his payment if she was to be kept hidden? She quickly washed the breakfast pans and dried them. Stacking them carefully in her arms, she left the kitchen and fell headlong over the girl's foot. The resulting crash reverberated about the kitchen, and all eyes turned to face her.

"Clumsy thing, isn't she?" the other girl quipped as Tay picked herself up, her elbow bruised from the fall.

"You tripped me." She rounded on the blonde, who affected a look of total shock.

"I wouldn't," the other girl answered, feigned innocence shining through her face.

"Pick those up" — Meg ordered as she crossed the kitchen to confront the pair of them — "and then wash them again." She looked across at the blonde. "You can get on with the silver, Lora." Lora gave a meek nod and rushed across to the other side of the kitchen, leaving

Meg to stand over Tay as she slowly picked up the pans. As the last pan settled into place, Meg spoke. "I don't need trouble in my kitchen." Tay started to explain, but Meg overrode her words. "No backtalk," she ordered in a sharp rebuke. "You're the new girl here, and you need to learn your place."

Tay swallowed the words that were gathering on her tongue and nodded dumbly.

"Now get back to the scullery," Meg ordered, "finish those pans and then start on the laundry." Tay nodded, feeling her cheeks flush with repressed anger as she hurried back into the scullery and returned the pans to the sink. The scullery door closed behind her, but not before she heard Lora give a snort of laughter as she spoke to one of the other kitchen hands.

In the relative quiet of the scullery, she examined her elbow, wincing at the sight of the bruised and reddened flesh. Turning on the cold tap, she held her arm beneath the ice-cold flow of water, hoping to numb the pain. Turning off the tap, she leant against the sink and tried to calm down. She had met girls like Lora before, and she had never failed to get on their bad side. Perhaps because she bit so readily whenever they started to poke at her, or maybe they saw her as an easy target. Either way, punching the girl in the face would not deal with the problem here. She glanced up and stared at her distorted reflection in the pots. Her eyes were bright with unshed, angry tears, and her skin was flushed. Reaching down, she ran the cold tap again and washed her face. She would just have to grin and bear it.

Throwing the pans back into the sink, she added more hot water and began to scrub, wondering all the time what she had managed to get herself into.

Chapter 4

The week passed in a blur of new names and back-breakingly hard work. The labour never seemed to stop, and each night she stumbled into bed in a haze of complete exhaustion. The rest of the kitchen staff ignored her or barked orders at her, and she spent most of her days in silence. Lora was also becoming a problem. Barely a day went by without her performing some petty act of bullying. Scrubbing brushes would be taken and hidden in the pantry, buckets of dirty water would be 'accidentally' kicked over, and she would find black socks hidden in the lights laundry basket. So far she had managed to keep her temper, but it was becoming harder and harder to look the other way. The only saving grace was the food; plentiful and doled out three times a day, it helped focus her desire to remain calm. Biting her tongue at each childish action, she waited for her first free afternoon, and trip home.

Thursday, when it finally arrived, dawned bright, yet

frosty. The typically amber-coloured sky was lit a pale gold when she finally drew back the thin curtains to her room. The bright colour lifted her mood, and even Lora's pettiness could not dampen it. After lunch, she returned to her room and dressed in the sturdy boots and warm clothing that Darius had provided for her. Placing her maid's clothing into the laundry, she headed down the stairs to the back door.

"Going to see your kids?" Lora called out through the open kitchen door. "Do they even have names or are there so many that they need numbers?"

Tay gritted her teeth and refused to answer. Pulling open the back door, she walked out into the crisp winter air with a sigh of relief. Picking up the pace, she hurried toward the back gate and swung it open, heading out onto the frozen street with a spring in her step.

The frost crunched beneath her feet as she headed through the alley and out onto the street. She glanced to the right and regarded the front of Darius' home. It was as imposing at it had been the first time she saw it. Not for the first time, she wondered just what he wanted from her. A flicker at one of the windows caught her eye, and she stopped, peering through the glass with interest. Darius stalked across the room and stopped just before the fire. She couldn't completely make out his features, but she could tell that he was acutely upset. Tay continued to watch as he turned to face the door and started to speak, his hands gesturing wildly in time with his words. Curious, Tay glanced at

the doorway, and the girl standing there. The girl's head was bowed, and her hands were clenched before her, in misery or anger, Taya couldn't tell.

"What do you think you're doing?" She jumped as an outraged voice sounded in her left ear. Turning to face the source of the voice, she bent her head at the sight of the elderly woman before her. Dressed in an expensive-looking woollen coat, the woman advanced on her. "How dare you spy into the homes of your betters?"

"I'm sorry," Tay apologised quickly, trying to back away from the woman. "I didn't mean..."

"Outrageous," the woman continued, reaching up to prod Taya in the chest with the handle of her cane. "I should report you."

Taya felt her stomach sink, and she gulped back the plea that was rising to her lips. "I'm sorry," she mumbled again. "I was just curious and I..." She gave her a small, piteous sob. "I won't ever do it again."

"Hmm." The woman gave a small huff, mollified slightly by her expression of remorse. "Very well. I'll overlook it this time, but if I ever catch you peeking through windows again..."

"You won't," Tay gabbled, eager to be away. "Thank you." Gratitude and relief flowed through Tay's voice as she stepped back. The window was still in her field of vision, and she almost stopped walking. Darius had finished speaking and was now standing at the window, staring directly at her.

"Get away with you before I call the guard," the

woman prodded her again with her cane, and Tay winced as the heavy wood connected with her shin. Out of the corner of her eye, she could still see Darius, his eyes fixed on the pair of them.

Ducking slightly to avoid his scrutiny, and to forestall any further aggression from the woman before her, she backed away and all but ran from the scene.

Moving from the relatively clean streets of the Merchants' District, she crossed back into her home region with something akin to relief. The streets were full of people moving to and from the Factory, and she navigated the crowds with ease. As she walked through the familiar streets, she felt a lessening of the tension she had been carrying all week. In the grander surroundings of the Frazers' house, she had constantly felt on edge and lost. At least here she knew the dangers and pitfalls. Rounding the corner, she walked into the small square that laid before the Ration Centre. A sprawling building, half warehouse and half military stockade, it had one entrance. Wide enough for only one person at a time, the door, and the queue lined up before it, was watched carefully by at least a dozen guards. All of the guards carried weapons, and most seemed eager for an excuse to use them. The queue began at the door and reached around the block. Walking past the waiting crowd, she reached the last place and stepped into line. Ducking her head to avoid unnecessary scrutiny, she waited as she had done every Thursday for the past six months. As so many times before, she reached into her pocket and carefully took

hold of the two small tokens that nestled within. One was familiar, the battered surface testament to the years of service to her family. Her father's token laid beside her own, bright, shiny, new disc. The two tokens were precious, each indicating that she was eligible to draw the required ration listed in their tightly packed grooves. If she were to lose one, the Centre staff would not release the ration she was entitled to.

The line shuffled forward slowly, and she thought back to her first trip to the Centre. It had been raining, a gentle, drenching drizzle that sank through each layer of fabric she wore. Her father had just been arrested, and as was usual, his token had been passed to her. With the hit to her rating from her father's arrest, Tay had been ejected from the minor post she had managed to secure. Luckily, she had already finished school and could draw her father's ration. If all three of them had still been school-aged, they would have been left to starve.

The line took another pace forward, and she ran her fingers over the metal discs in her pocket. The ration promised would keep her siblings in sufficient food and fuel for the following week, if she was able to get away with convincing them that she was entitled to it. She took a deep breath as the line moved closer to the door. Thoughts of what could happen if they didn't believe her raced through her mind, and she bit her lip until she tasted blood.

"Go in." She looked up in surprise at the door guard, so lost in thought, she had not noticed the man

before her enter the building. Clenching her fist around the tokens, she walked into the building. The room beyond was small, with walls the colour of pea soup. A long counter ran along the far wall, with three assistants at each post. On the right-hand side of the room, there were three closed doors, which she averted her gaze from. The door on the left led to the warehouse and hopefully her ration. She walked forward, toward the empty chair, a sick feeling twisting her insides. The woman behind the desk had a tight, pinched face, and unsmiling eyes behind a pair of spectacles. Impatiently, the woman beckoned her forward. Sitting down, her eyes flickered over the objects that laid on the desk before her. A brass typewriter and telegraph machine sat next to the token reader. A small stack of labels laid in a neat pile on the edge of the desk. An elegant fountain pen laid beside a sheaf of blotting paper. The woman reached into a drawer, removed some paper, and, picking up the pen, began to write. Tay swallowed back the cluck of irritation as the woman ignored her, casting her eyes over the rest of the room as she waited.

"Token?" The woman's words startled her, and she reached into her pocket with nervous, fumbling fingers.

"Two?" A quizzical look entered the woman's stern features as she took hold of the metal discs.

"I'm drawing two rations," Tay explained in soft, apologetic tones as the woman placed them into the reader. Tay tried to look unconcerned as the small needle flicked across the surface of each of the discs in turn, reading the details of her rations. The large, brass

machine burst into life, and a long strip of paper began to chatter forth. Printed with her name, job role and selected other information, this narrow strip of paper confirmed her entitlement to draw her father's ration, as well as her own. Tearing the paper free, the woman began to read. Tay, looking on with fear, watched the woman's eyes flick between each line of text.

"Emerson?" Her eyes flicked up to meet Tay's, and a frown creased her features. "How did you manage to draw a servant's ration?" Tay froze in fear as the woman glanced at the guards stationed at the sides of the room. With quick steps, two of the guards moved into place on either side of her and caught hold of her upper arms.

"What's wrong?" Taya tried to sound unconcerned, but her voice came out as a small squeak. She should have known that the Centre staff would recognise her family name. The woman did not answer but nodded to the guards. Tay felt her stomach sink as they pulled her upright. "I haven't done anything," she called out as they dragged her across the floor, hands clamped about her upper arms like steel. The few other patrons of the Centre stared down at the floor, ignoring her panicked voice and expression. Struggling vainly against their grip, Tay was dragged toward one of the small interrogation rooms. The guards pushed her through the door, into a small, claustrophobia-inducing, room. Rough hands thrust her into a chair, and she cried out as her elbow smashed against the arm. Both guards ignored her squeal of pain as they took positions on

either side. Bulky, and solid with muscle, the guards discouraged any effort to escape. She swallowed nervously as she looked at the empty chair before her. Why had she not anticipated this? The Centre Controllers would know her father's name and realise that she wasn't entitled to the position that she now held.

"She's not bad-looking," the guard on the right noted, his voice packed with leering innuendo as he leant over her. Self-conscious, she hunched forward, trying to hide from his ogling gaze. "Don't be like that." He drew closer to her, and she shuddered. "You and I can be great friends." His fingers slid across her shoulder and began to reach downward. "Treat me nice, and your detention will be paradise. I may even be persuaded to petition for lenience on your behalf."

"Knock it off Marlon." The Centre Controller entered the room and slid into the chair opposite. "She's not under your control yet." Marlon stood bolt upright, and Tay felt her insides lurch as thoughts of the Mine seared through her. If she were sentenced, Lana and Roj would starve in her absence. With neither of them able to draw ration, they would have to resort to begging, or worse. She watched the woman place a file on the table, unable to stop her hands from trembling. "Now" — the woman flicked open the folder and began to leaf through the pages — " Your father, Caleb Emerson, was sentenced to the Mine for activities against the common good," the woman recited in a flat, monotonous tone. "As such, the rating for his

dependants would have been reduced. With that reduction" — she lifted her head and stared at Tay — " none of you would qualify for service within a noble's home."

"I made rating," Tay whispered, hoping that Darius had made her alibi rock solid. "You can check." She took a deep breath and tried to find some confidence. "The agency has my record, and I was cleared." Tay locked her fingers together and tried to hold her hands still. "I'm only sanctioned for scullery work, nothing more." This, she was taking a gamble on; she had no idea of what Darius had written in her file, though she wished she had thought to ask. Her fingernails dug painfully into the palms of her hands as she tried not to fidget.

"It's an irregularity," the woman continued, giving no sign that she had accepted or even heard her explanations. "Keep her there whilst I check." She stood and left the room.

"Where were we?" The guard returned to her side and placed his hand back on her shoulder, slowly rubbing his fingers across her body. "A bit skinny," he commented, as she gritted her teeth and tried to remain still. "That's a good girl," he whispered as his hands dipped lower, stroking down her side to the top of her thigh. Her fingernails sliced into her palms as his fingers began to wander across her upper thigh. "See we're going to be great friends." His fingers reached her inner thigh, and she finally snapped. With a cry, she pushed herself backward, away from his wandering

hands. There was a bang; she and the chair hit the floor in a heap of flesh and wood. Pain ripped through her skull as the back of her head smashed into the ground. The guard smiled and reached down for her. She smacked at his hands as she tried to scurry away, her head throbbing from the contact with the ground. The wall quickly pressed into her back, halting her progress. The second guard caught hold of her upper arms and dragged her upright. Forgetting her earlier decision to remain cooperative, she attempted to break free, elbowing him in the stomach as she did so.

"That wasn't very smart of you, girl." A choking gasp escaped her lips as he slammed her into the wall, the force of the blow driving the air from her lungs. "You'll have to obey us when you get to detention." Her head was rocked violently to the side as he raised his hand and slapped her hard across the face.

"Marlon! Darrow!" The voice of the Centre Controller echoed from the door, bringing all movement in the room to a halt. "Put her down." Tay slumped back against the wall as Darrow released her, raising her hand to cradle the throbbing bruise on her cheek.

"She was troublesome," Marlon argued as Darrow moved back into position, assuming the benign pose he had maintained throughout Marlon's groping.

"I'm sure." Tay thought she detected mild mockery in the woman's voice.

"We have the authority to deal with difficult prisoners," Marlon argued, his face turning red with

frustrated anger. "Just let us take her." Tay leant back against the wall, watching the argument with increasing concern.

"Nothing would give me more pleasure." Tay trembled as the woman shot her a venom-filled look. "Unfortunately" — she closed the file before her — " she's not yours to manhandle." The woman pointed back to the chair, and Tay gingerly walked across the room, avoiding the incredulous stares of Marlon as she did so.

"What?" Marlon turned red with anger, striding across the floor to tower over the Centre Manager. "But you said..."

"She's cleared," the woman answered in a calm, unruffled tone as she handed the discs back. "She's entitled to the ration." Relief flooded through Tay as the words penetrated the shroud of panic surrounding her. "I'm not sure how" — the woman glanced down at Tay, and a calculating look entered her eyes — " but all the records are in order."

"Can I go?" Tay winced at the tremor that ran through her voice. "If everything's clear?" Marlon looked down at her, and she swallowed nervously, hoping to escape before the guards created another reason to hold her.

"Yes." The woman closed the file and waved her toward the door. "Your ration is waiting in the usual place."

Tay got to her feet, and controlled her desire to run from the room. Moving out into the main part of the

Centre, she walked through the left door and into the warehouse. A set of steel bars ran along the right-hand side of the room, closing the racks of food to the supplicants that came through the door. A bored clerk took possession of her ration ticket and began to call out numbers to the workers on the shelves.

As she waited, the door banged open and Marlon and Darrow sauntered into the room. Shuffling forward, she attempted to ignore them as two, wheeled crates were pushed to the centre of the room. The clerk stamped the ticket and nodded, giving her leave to take the ration. Taya secured a set of straps to each of the wagons, mindful of the guards' scrutiny. There was a bell tone and the side door opened. Tay glanced back over her shoulder and suppressed a shudder at the cold rage on Marlon's face. As calmly as she could, she dragged the heavy wagons out of the building. The door did not close immediately and she knew that they were watching her.

Shuffling past the lines of gaunt-faced workers, she did not stop until the Ration Centre was almost out of sight. Darius had kept his word and managed to securely embed her into the system. Had he not done so, she looked back at the stockade with a shudder of remembered fear. Thoughts of Marlon and Darrow rippled through her mind, and she shook her head, trying to dispel the memory. Bracing the straps against her shoulders, she started the trek home.

The noise of the wheels against the cobbled streets bounced off the surrounding walls, and she became

more vigilant. It was not unheard of for groups of scavengers to mug those carrying rations. To give the guards their due, they violently discouraged such theft, but it did not dissuade the hardened or desperate. A wheel jammed into a pothole, and the weight of the trolley nearly pulled her over. Nervous and conscious of the deepening shadows, Tay crouched in the dirt, trying to free the trapped wheel. A whistle sounded off to the left, and she looked up. In the distance, she could see several figures silhouetted against the sky, and her heart beat even faster. Another sharp tug and the wheel jerked free. With the panicked thud of her heart hammering in her chest, she started to run, fear lending her the strength she needed to drag the trolleys. Another whistle, this time to the left, galvanised her to further speed. She rounded the final corner to her home, looking at the thin tendril of smoke from the chimney with increasing cheer. The whistles became running footsteps, and she pushed more energy from her aching legs. Reaching the front door, she wrestled with the key, expecting to be attacked at any moment. Her hair whisked across her face, as she finally unlocked and pushed open the door.

"Tay." Lana threw her arms about her as she dragged the wagons across the threshold. "You're back."

"Don't sound so shocked." Tay forced a chuckle, driving the unpleasant scene in the centre to the back of her mind. She reached back and slammed the door, pushing the bolts home, before she turned to her sister and returned the hug. "It's good to see you," she

whispered, taking as much strength as she could from the embrace. Even with the door closed, she could still hear the catcalls and whistles of the gang.

"Aren't you going to talk to me?" She turned as Roj walked in from the kitchen.

Tay smiled and, without letting go of Lana, drew him into the hug.

"I missed you guys," she whispered, feeling the final traces of tension drop away in the warmth of their embrace.

"Let's get this stuff away," she noted, pulling away from the group, as she tried to hide the gleam of happy tears from her siblings.

"Sure." They moved apart and began to unpack the wagons one at a time.

"Medicine." Lana held up a small, brown, glass phial and peered at the label. "It's for grazes, burns and cuts," she noted with wonder as she gingerly transferred the item to the cupboard.

"New clothes," Roj crowed as he pulled a small, shrunken package from the box. Tearing open the top of the parcel, they watched as the smooth wrapping expanded to almost twice its size, revealing a complete set of winter clothes for each of them. Roj took the new clothes upstairs, as Tay carefully folded the clear, slippery fabric that had been the package. She could never understand how the package shrunk its contents, but all deliveries of new garments came in such wrapping. She placed the bag into a drawer and began to dig through the wagon again.

"Money." Lana picked up a leather pouch and peered inside. A gleam of gold reflected the light, and Tay stopped what she was doing to stare at the small pile of coins.

"Oh my..." she sighed, looking at the gleaming gold with awe. "Place it behind the loose brick in the fireplace," she ordered as she began to work out what she could afford to buy. As Lana moved to obey, Tay reached back into the wagon and began to remove the carefully packed food items. Meat, butter, flour and a large sack of potatoes. Walking into the kitchen, she loaded them onto the shelves, filling the cupboard for the first time ever.

A knock sounded at the front door, and Tay moved back to the hall. Undoing the bolts, she pulled open the door to reveal two men. One was tall with straw-coloured hair poking out from beneath a thin woollen hat, the other was stocky, with thinning hair shaved down to near stubble. Both wore the rough garb of the Factory, the ragged, thin fabric barely keeping out the cold. Her heart sank slightly as she recognised the pair of them. Lars and Cody, both friends of her father and deeper in the resistance than she cared know to about.

"Tay." Lars stepped forward, his voice pleasant. "Can we come in?" Beneath the mass of hair, a pair of green eyes stared out from a prematurely lined face.

"Sure." Tay stood back, and let the two walk past her into the hallway. Before she shut the door, she glanced back out into the street, checking for anyone watching. Satisfied that no one was paying attention, she closed

the door and returned to her visitors.

"What's all this?" Lars asked, pointing at the wagons.

"Ration," Tay answered shortly as she pushed past them, and entered the main living room. "Why are you here?" she asked as they followed her in and sat down on the sagging couches.

"I take it you got to see Darius," Cody noted, nodding back in the direction of the wagons.

"Yes," she replied, sitting down on one of the other chairs with a growing sense of dread.

"So where does the second box come from?" Lars asked, glancing toward the hall in curiosity.

"She works in a merchant house." Tay's heart sank further as Roj poked his head around the door and spoke.

"Really?" Lars cast a quick glance at her and turned back to face Roj. "How did she manage that?"

"Darius got her the job," Roj answered absently as he returned to the wagons. "She's been working there a week."

"That's interesting," Lars noted as he turned to face Tay. "What happened?" he asked, a strange smile on his face.

"Nothing really," Tay answered, disliking the knowing look that now crossed Lars' face. "I did what you said." She stood up, trying to find some confidence. "I went to Darius and asked him to help father."

"Then why are you at a merchant house?"

"It doesn't matter why," Cody broke into their

conversation. "She's now in a position to help."

Tay felt her stomach roil at his words and she took an involuntary step backward. Cody and Lars were more than her father's friends. They had been deeply involved in the campaign for better accommodation, rations, clothing, and it was only by a fluke that they hadn't been picked up by the authorities along with her father.

"What do you mean?" she asked, her voice a breathy whisper, hoping that he wasn't suggesting that she join their doomed revolution. Her mother had died, and her father's small involvement had already landed him in the Mine. Much as she hated the authorities, Tay was not looking to follow either of her parents to disaster.

"Information," Lars replied. "You're in the perfect place."

"I wash dishes," she retorted. "I can't even look at the family, let alone find out state secrets."

"Don't you want to change things?" Cody raised his voice as he stepped closer to her, idealistic fervour shining from his face. "You can't be happy with the way things are."

"By doing what?" she hissed back at him, angry at the righteous spiel flowing from his lips. She had heard this rant before, and it had cost her both parents. "Writing a petition?" Derision dripped from every syllable. "Or do you plan to sabotage the supply train for real?" Lars glanced down at the floor, cut to the quick by her words. "It won't work because no one is willing to stand with you."

"Well you certainly aren't," Cody snarled down at

her, and she took an involuntary step back. "Your parents would be ashamed of you." He cast a glance toward the wagons in the hall. "Selling yourself to the Overseer's son for a few extra grams of flour."

Tay reacted without thinking, slapping him hard across the face.

"How dare you." Her voice was low, too angry for much volume. "My mother died for this rebellion, and my Father went to the Mine for you." She advanced forward and raised her hand again. "You let him take the fall for a plot that you were in up to your necks." Taking a deep breath to control her voice, she continued. "You are quite happy for me and my siblings to starve once my Father dies, how dare you assume what my parents would want."

"Cody." Lars took a step forward, and placed a hand on his arm, drawing him backward. "This isn't the way we do things." Cody drew a breath, and reluctantly stepped back. Lars watched him back off before he glanced back to Tay. "I understand how you feel."

"I doubt it."

"But," he overrode her, "we can't continue on like this." He waved at the shabby surroundings and paltry fire. "We're starving and dying by inches." He walked forward, intensity in his gaze. "The rating system is skewed, you have to see that."

"But what can we do?" she whispered, unable to deny the truth of his statements.

"There's more of us than you think," he continued, his voice soft and coaxing. "We can change the system,

redistribute the wealth."

"It'll be impossible."

"Then help us." He leant toward her, a plea in his blue eyes. "We can help you."

"How?" She wanted to believe him, wanted to hope that there could be something better for them than the life they currently led. Both her parents had shared that dream, and it had taken them away.

"Find the Coils of Copper and Brass."

Tay nearly laughed at his words. The Coils of Copper and Brass were a fantasy, an old fairy tale told to children, and certainly nothing to pin dreams of freedom on.

"They do exist," Lars continued to speak, recognising the look of amusement on her face.

"I'm sure they do." Lars winced at the derision in her voice. With two quick strides, she returned to the hall and flung the front door open. "You two, get out now."

Lars and Cody glanced at each other before Lars nodded in resignation and they walked to the door.

"I mean it." Lars turned back to her just at the door. "The Coils exist, and they will help us win."

"Get out!" she shouted, her patience finally exhausted by their visit. "I don't want to see either of you here again." Reaching past Lars, she held the door open, wafting an icy cold breeze down the hall.

Cody took one look at her furious face and ducked past her into the street. Lars stayed for a few moments more, a beseeching look on his face.

"Please listen, Tay," he whispered softly, staring at her intently. "You can help us."

"Goodbye." She stepped back and closed the door in his face before leaning forward and resting her forehead against the cold wood.

"What was that all about?" Lana walked in from the kitchen, concern etched on her face.

"They wanted me to spy for them."

"Yeah, I heard that," Lana interrupted, coming to a stop beside her. "But that's not what I meant." Tay turned and leant back against the door, looking at her. "What I want to know is" — she took a breath — "what are the Coils of Copper and Brass?"

"Didn't you ever hear Father speak about it?"

"No." Out of the corner of her eye, she noticed Roj enter the room and lean against the balustrade opposite.

"Oh..." She glanced at the pair of them and lowered her head. "Okay..." She hadn't expected to talk about this myth, particularly after a visit from Lars and Cody. She relocked the door and headed back into the sitting room. Roj and Lana followed her in, closing the door and stoking up the fire.

"It was really Mother's story," she said, settling down into the armchair and tucking her feet beneath her. She took a breath and started to recount the tale in a sing-song tone of voice. "Long ago, when the sky was blue" — Roj gave a small snort of laughter at that idea — "the founders created the Coils of Copper and Brass." Both Roj and Lana leant forward to hear the tale, and for a moment she forgot she was talking to her

siblings. In that instant, she travelled back several years, back to her childhood, and her mother's voice softly describing the story that she had never given credence to. It had been her favourite tale from childhood, and she had loved some of the more outlandish aspects, such as the sky being blue. Yet as she had grown, she had put aside all thoughts of that story, even when she encountered it as a legend within one of the books in the school library. It provoked far too many sad memories.

"Tay?" Her head snapped up at Roj's questioning voice. Shaking her head free from dark recollections, she began again.

"Back when the sky was blue" — Lana shifted into a more comfortable position and listened intently — " a sickness fell across the land, poisoning the air and water." She settled into the story, letting her words weave a spell. "Our founders saw the coming destruction, and they saw the solution. They would come to a place free from poison." Roj sat down at her feet and leant against the chair. "So they did." She shifted her position, allowing Roj to climb onto her knee. "To do this, they created the Coils of Copper and Brass. The Coils turned the sky amber, and kept us safe." She took a breath and glanced at her sister; Lana was staring at her with rapt attention. "For many years, everything was fine, but then the sickness came, and the only salvation was the Coils." Roj's eyes flicked to hers, and she could see the excitement behind them. "But the Coils had been lost. A group set out to find them..."

"Did they succeed?" Roj asked, almost bouncing up and down with excitement.

"Of course they did, stupid," Lana interjected with scorn. "Otherwise we wouldn't be here."

"Don't be mean to your brother," Tay said absently.

"But what happened?" Roj asked.

"After undergoing a dangerous journey, the seekers finally recovered the Coils, and used the power within them to cure everyone." There was considerably more to the story, but Tay didn't want to delve into the more lurid parts. "Everyone healed and grew stronger. But the Coils disappeared. After that, we discovered the secrets of steam, and better harvesting techniques."

"Is that why Lars wants to find them, to make everyone stronger?" Lana asked, snuggling into the back of the chair as she spoke.

"Yes," Tay replied, remembering what her mother had told her. "It's been said that the Coils are the key to freedom."

"How, though?" Lana mused, her voice sleepy. "What are they and what do they do?"

"Nobody knows what they look like," Tay replied, "Mother only said that they were very powerful, that they could cure sickness and even turn the sky blue again."

"Then why didn't they use them before?" Roj asked, his forehead creasing in confusion.

"And the noble families?" Lana spoke up from her position by the fire. "I heard my teacher say that they arrived about the same time."

"She's right," Tay confirmed, wondering how Lana's teacher had managed to tell that bit of the story without getting arrested. "The noble families seized control of the capital and imposed their control. Some said that they had learnt the secrets of the Coils, as their power base grew extremely quickly. And the rest is history."

"So, if they have the Coils," Roj asked, his voice brightly curious. "How can us having them, save us?"

"Because nobody really knows if the nobles do have the Coils," Tay explained, much as her mother had done all those years ago.

Both fell silent for several moments, digesting her words carefully. "So..." Roj began, his face screwed up in earnest. "If we find the Coils of Copper and Brass, we will be free?"

"That's the theory," Tay agreed, wondering if she had made a mistake in telling them the story. "There's no evidence that it's true," she insisted, worried by the eager look on Lana's face. "No one has ever been able to prove that they exist."

"But if the families have them, then they may have hidden them," Roj continued, his imagination clearly fired by the thought of such a thing.

"And Lars seems to believe they exist," Lana chimed in. "You could do what he asks?"

"And then what?" Tay snapped back, tired of the speculation. "What do you think is going to happen?" She tried to hold back the angry tears that threatened to spill down her face. "It's just a tale and not true." She

waved toward the wagons that laid in the hall. "Now finish putting away the rations so I can start on dinner." There was a moment's silence before they both nodded and stood up. Tay leant back against the chair and closed her eyes, wondering why she felt so defensive. It was purely a fairy tale; a pretty little fable of hope for children. She had spent her childhood listening to her mother recite it, so why did Lars believe in such a thing? There was a rattle from the hall as Lana pushed one of the empty wagons into the cupboard under the stairs, and Tay opened her eyes.

Pushing herself from the chair, she headed to the kitchen and began to prepare the evening meal. As several chunks of meat sizzled in a pot on the stove, she turned to the large, new sack of potatoes, removed three and headed for the sink.

Cold water gushed from the tap as she began to scrub the thick clods of mud from the tubers in her hand. "Why are you so angry about this?" Lana's voice interrupted, and she stopped moving to glance across at her younger sister. With a peeler and several carrots held in her hands, Lana looked almost domesticated. Tay nearly made a point of mentioning it but decided against it.

"I'm not angry," she replied, returning the potato in her hand to the stream of icy-cold water. "I just think it's foolish to put such trust in an old fairy tale, that's all." She scrubbed vigorously, trying to cover her agitation with industry.

"It's because of Mother, isn't it?"

Tay slammed the potato down and whirled about to face Lana. Her sister stared back at her, curiosity and concern etched onto her face.

"I know that it upsets you Tay, but..."

"It has nothing to do with Mother," Tay snapped, picking up the potato once more and scrubbing it with excessive zeal. "It's a tale, a fairy story told so that we will believe that something will change things."

"You don't think that we can change what's happening?"

"No I don't." She finished with the first potato and placed it in a pot of cold water. "Even if Lars and his friends manage to overthrow the families, what will happen then?"

"It's something to try," Lana retorted as she finished peeling the first of the carrots and started on the next. "Don't you think that freedom would be worth it?"

"Freedom." Tay gave a snort of derision as she continued to scrub the potatoes. "All that's going to happen is a lot of death, destruction and starvation." She threw the second potato into the pot and picked up the third.

"But we're already starving," Lana argued. "The guards already act as they please, so..."

"Don't talk about things you don't understand." Tay threw the last potato into the pot and turned to stare at her sister.

"Okay." Lana slammed the peeled carrots down on the counter. "I'll talk about what I understand." She drew a knife out of the drawer and began to chop the

carrots with heavy, irritated gestures. "I know that you're scared of doing anything because of Mum and Dad."

Tay froze in the act of placing the pot on the stove and stared at Lana, her voice dropping open in shock. "I'm not scared," she argued, wondering when her younger sister had begun to sound so adult.

"Yes. You. Are." Lana punctuated each word with a heavy blow from the hand holding the blade. "Mother left us, and died for the cause, and Father got sent to the Mine. You're scared that you'll be picked up next." She picked up the handful of carrot pieces and placed them in a bowl. "You're afraid that Roj and I won't manage without you."

"You won't manage without me," Tay argued as she finally found her voice. "You know that neither of you can draw ration yet." She placed the pot of potatoes on the stove, and turned back to her sister. "If I get arrested, you two will starve." She stared intently into Lana's eyes, trying to make her understand.

"No, we won't."

"Really?" Tay asked, her patience nearing its limit. "And what do you intend to eat if ration is withheld?"

"We have the garden," Lana insisted, waving the knife around in her agitation. "And we can get help from Cody and Lars."

A sharp bark of laughter escaped Tay's lips. "Oh that's rich." A small sprinkle of salt went into the pot. "They didn't even offer to help when Father was arrested. They only sent me to Darius." Tay slammed the lid down on the pot of potatoes and began to busy

herself with the rapidly browning meat. "They could let you starve." Her voice was soft, anger muted by fear. "You're too young to be involved in this." She turned the meat over and whispered. "I don't want to lose you as well."

"I'm not a child anymore," Lana insisted, matching her tone to Tay's. "I'll be able to draw ration next year." She returned the knife to the chopping board and began to fill a smaller pan with water. "I'm not going to get a good placement, and we'll still starve."

"No you won't," Tay replied, "but you certainly will if I get arrested."

"But aren't you fed up with this?" She gathered the small heap of carrots and threw them in the other pot. "Living to the tune of the ration? And then there's Darius." She dropped the knife on the counter. "You know he will be asking for his favour." Stepping closer to a now silent and wondering Tay, she continued, "You can't protect us forever, and if you do as Lars and Cody want, then we may not have to live in fear." Silence reigned in the kitchen as Lana finally finished speaking. The water in the pans started to simmer as Tay stared at her younger sister, impressed not only by her passion but by her maturity.

"I'll think about it," Tay conceded, turning back to the stove and dinner. "Now get your homework done while I finish tea."

"Alright." Lana moved toward the door. As she reached it, she turned back. "Please think about it Tay." Her voice was soft, pleading, and Tay bit her lip. "We

need more than this." She left the kitchen, leaving Tay alone with the simmering pans of food, and her thoughts.

After checking the meat, Tay leant back against one of the kitchen counters and stared up at the ceiling. How could she think about joining the revolution? The consequences for her family if she were caught would be unthinkable. She chewed her lip in thought as she removed the meat from the pan. It wasn't that she liked the system — far from it, she hated the guards and the quotas — it was just that there wasn't anything she could do about it. She wasn't a soldier, she knew nothing about activism. All she was trying to do was keep her siblings alive. Stirring a couple of tablespoons of flour into the meat juices, she began to make gravy, struggling with the thoughts that would not leave her.

"Why does she have to be right?" she muttered as she returned the meat to the pan and checked on the potatoes. "But I just can't abandon them." And there was Darius to consider. She still had no idea as to his plans or what he would ask her to do. Rubbing the bridge of her nose, she tried to come to some kind of decision.

Chapter 5

Tay walked back to the Frazers' house the following morning with a heavy heart and tired eyes. The conversations of the previous night had not managed to resolve themselves, and she had spent a good portion of the night wide awake and worrying. She had easily said no to Lars and Cody, but she was concerned about her sister. Lana had shown far too much interest in the workings of the revolutionaries for her to be comfortable with. She had drummed into Lana that neither Lars nor Cody were allowed in the house when she was not there, but she felt that the warning had fallen on deaf ears. Lana was clearly enamoured with the idea of rebellion. She walked down the alley and out into the square, her mind still focused on Lana.

"Good morning." Tay jumped as Darius fell into step beside her. He was dressed for the cold in a long woollen coat. Beneath a warm-looking winter hat, deep blue eyes stared down at her. "Did you have a good

evening?"

"Yes, thank you," she answered as she dropped her gaze to the floor, flustered by his regard. "How did you manage to fix my ration allowance?"

"I have my ways," he replied in soft tones.

"Well, I just wanted to thank you." They walked in awkward silence across the main square, their feet crunching on the frosted ground.

"It wasn't anything." She chanced a look upward only to look away hurriedly as Darius stared back at her. "You needed time to see your family," he finished, as her gaze slid back to the ground. She looked at the cobbles, the fountain, anywhere but toward his face. Darius seemed comfortable with the quiet, yet Tay's mind was a whirl of questions. The people in the plaza appeared to pay them no mind as they passed, yet Tay was convinced that they were marking her every move. Uncomfortable with the lengthening quiet, Tay opened her mouth once more.

"What is this favour?" she asked, hating the whiny note to her voice. "Can you just tell me?"

Darius came to a stop in the shadow of the fountain and turned to face her. Caught by surprise, Tay's momentum carried her forward for a few startled paces before she too came a halt. She turned back to face him, heart racing with anticipation.

"You will know soon," he whispered. Tay moved closer, finding it difficult to hear.

"I don't understand." Tay stared up at him, her face flushed from the cold and emotion. "What can I do for

you?" He made to speak, but she overrode him. "You're the Overseer's son, you have access to wealth that I can only dream about, what could you possibly need from me?" Her fingers played nervously with the key to her room.

"You'd be surprised." The wry tones rippled between them, and a strange shudder flowed down her spine at his voice. "Are you unhappy with your current placement?" His eyes flicked down to her trembling hands as he spoke.

"No." She replied. "I just..." Her fingers twitched involuntarily, and she dropped the key. Darius gave a small chuckle and bent down to retrieve it.

"Why are you so nervous?" he asked, as he returned the key to her hands. "I'm not going to hurt you."

"How can I be sure about that?" The words escaped from her lips, relieved to finally fill the air between them. "I don't know what you want, or what you could ever need. I'm just a servant."

"Nobody is ever 'just' anything," he replied with some heat to his voice. "And it is certainly not my intent to hurt you." A long sigh escaped his lips, and he seemed to come to a decision. "All I will tell you now is that I need you to stay within reach."

"Is that all?" Confusion settled over her as she struggled to work out his motives.

"No." The clock in the square began to chime the quarter hour, interrupting her question before it could be voiced. Darius glanced up at the clock face. "But we certainly can't talk about this at the moment." He

turned back toward the square and began to walk. "Otherwise work will be wondering where you got to."

Tay looked at the time, panic replacing annoyance as she realised her lateness. Matching her stride to his, they continued to walk across the square in silence. As the Overseer's house came into view, Darius moved away from her side with barely a glance in her direction.

"You'd better go in." His voice drifted across her ears, and she tore her gaze away from the looming house to glance over at him. He was striding toward the front entrance of his home with the air of someone on business. Satisfied that he was no longer looking her way, Tay moved to the left and began to walk toward the Frazers' home.

"Darius." A woman's voice called through the frosty air, and Tay's head whipped round, trying to locate the source. Dressed in the trappings of nobility, the girl, for she was close to Tay's age, moved down the steps of Darius' home and rushed into his arms. Embarrassed by the affectionate display and conscious of the passing time, Tay turned away from the sight and walked down the set of stairs into the kitchen.

Warmth settled over her chilled body as she walked into the steamy kitchen.

"Ahh good, you're back," Meg called as Tay removed her outer coat, and placed it in the cupboard with the rest of the outerwear. "Can you go through the dressers and thoroughly clean the dinner service?" At Tay's quizzical look, she explained, "The Frazers are hosting a dinner party for the Overseer and his family tonight."

"Are you sure she's not going to break anything?" Lora called from the other side of the kitchen table. "You know how clumsy she is."

Tay's face reddened, yet she stopped herself from launching herself toward the other girl. It seemed as though the evening's freedom had not improved the girl's disposition toward her.

"Give it a rest Lora," one of the other kitchen maids piped up from the other side of the room. "She's done nothing to you."

Tay flashed a grateful smile at the other girl as she walked toward the first dresser and the array of plates that laid within. Opening the heavy, wooden doors, she picked up the first stack of plates, and carefully turned around, fully conscious of Lora's tendency to aid her clumsiness.

"Do you need any help?" The friendly kitchen maid stepped to her side and, without waiting for an answer, reached into the cupboard and picked up a second stack of plates.

"Thanks," Tay whispered as they walked across the kitchen toward the scullery.

"We're not all like her, you know." She leant back against the scullery door and pushed it open. "I'm Annabeth, but most people just call me Beth." She held the door open as she waited for a response.

"Tay." Walking through the open door, Tay placed the plates on the kitchen side. "I haven't seen you here before."

"Oh, you wouldn't have." Beth placed her stack of

plates on top of Tay's and smiled. "I've just spent the last few weeks working in the Overseer's house."

Tay stopped in the process of turning on the tap, and raised her eyebrows. "Can you do that?" She picked up the slab of dish soap and shaved several flakes from it. Throwing the soap shavings into the sink, she turned on the tap.

"Oh yes" — Beth replied as she dug a second cloth out of a drawer and began to wash the plates — "we do it all the time. If you've got a good record, you can be sent to help them out." She placed the first plate onto the draining board and started on the second. Tay leant past her and began to dry. Her mind was whirling, it seemed too much of a coincidence that she would be placed into a position where she could end up serving in Darius' household. She had assumed that he wouldn't wish her to.

"So does this happen often?"

"Often enough," Beth continued. "Usually when they're short-handed."

"Hoping to get an invite over there?" Lora's sharp tones echoed through the kitchen, and both girls stared toward the door.

"So what if I am?" Tay snapped back, forgetting her desire to remain calm.

"A gutter brat like you?" Lora gave a vicious chuckle. "You've got no chance."

"And yet, I'm here," Tay replied, playing to the lie with airy abandon. She washed the next plate and continued. "I guess I must be doing something right if

I" — she stressed the word — " can get a job here."
Placing the cloth down on the side, she threw a quick,
mocking smile at Lora. "Or is it just not that
challenging to find a place in this household?"

Lora turned a shade of crimson, and took a step
forward, only to be stopped in her tracks by Beth.

"Just leave it," Beth advised. "I'm sure you've got
work to do."

Tay watched with no small sense of satisfaction as
the other girl stalked out of the kitchen in a huff. Beth
waited for the door to close before turning to face Tay.

"Well, she's gotten her knickers in a twist." Tay gave
a snort of laughter, as she turned back to the stack of
dishes. "Let me guess," Beth continued, "she's been
picking on you since you got here?"

"Yeah." Tay reached into the hot water and grasped
the next plate. "She always seems to be around when I
have a clumsy accident."

"Oh, she's good like that." Beth brought the next
stack of plates over to the sink. "But general bitchiness
aside, she's relatively harmless." Tay raised an eyebrow.
"Okay, harmless is probably stretching it a little, but if
you stick up for yourself, you should be fine."

"It's not her that I'm worried about."

"Don't worry about Meg, she's sharper than she
looks..."

"Are you two going to natter all day, or do you want
to do some work?" Meg's voice echoed through the
room, and both girls jumped. "Things must have been
too easy over there," she commented as she walked into

the scullery, a fresh stack of plates held in her hands. "You seem to have gotten a little lazy."

"Sorry Meg," Beth apologised as she picked up the next plate and began to dry it with increased alacrity.

"Well, chop to it," Meg continued as she settled the plates on the counter. "The breakfast service will be coming back to the kitchen soon, and I want all of these plates cleaned and ready before it does."

"Yes Meg," both girls chorused as they returned to their work.

They had very little time to converse after that. Dinner for so many people required the complete dinner service which had been held in storage. Once that had been washed, the breakfast plates and pans swamped the small scullery. As the day wore on, the jobs continued to pile up. The noonday meal passed in a blur, filled with a seemingly never-ending supply of dirty crockery. As the sky beyond the window darkened, Tay was finally able to stop and rest. Drawing her body upright from the sink, she rubbed her tired eyes and stretched. Her back and neck were aching, and her fingers were rubbed raw.

"Right, my girl," Meg called as she walked in from the main kitchen. "Get upstairs, wash and change into your spare uniform." She picked up one of the pots and placed it into a cupboard. "You're needed to serve tonight."

"Really?" Startled at the words, Tay glanced toward Meg with some confusion. "But you said..."

"I know what I said," Meg snapped as she began to

chivvy Tay toward the door. "But the Master and Mistress are hosting a party, and they've invited more people than usual." She gently pushed Tay out into the kitchen. "We need the serving staff," she finished as she shut the scullery door behind her. Tay opened her mouth to speak, but the sight before her drove the thought from her mind.

The kitchen was full of staff, steam and activity. The cook and her assistants were barking instructions at several of the younger housemaids, directing them in the creation of a magnificent feast.

"Out of the way." One of the other housemaids, laden down with a bulky tray of appetisers, rushed up to them, heading for the larders on the other side of the room.

"Go on then." Meg urged as Tay looked at the organised chaos in shock.

"Right." Tay headed for the staircase door and away from the bedlam behind her. Rushing up the stairs, she headed for her room, a prickle of unease running along her spine. Stepping over the threshold, she closed the door and leant back resting her head against the rough wood, wondering just how she was going to handle tonight. Serving did not particularly bother her, but she remembered what Meg had said earlier about the Overseer and his family coming to dinner.

Thoughts of facing Darius in a social setting roved through her mind as she slowly pushed herself away from the door and began to undress. There was no suggestion that he would reveal anything about their

association, but that wasn't a given. Thoughts of what could go wrong flowed through her head as she washed and dressed into her fresh uniform.

Adjusting her hair into what she hoped was a tidy style, she opened her door and walked out of her room, almost hitting Lora as she did so.

"Watch it," Lora snapped as Tay muttered an apology and locked her door. She slid the heavy key into her apron pocket and began to head back along the corridor. "I bet you'll be as clumsy as this tonight." Tay gritted her teeth and walked faster, hoping to reach the company of others before she snapped and punched the girl. "What do you think will happen to you if you spill red wine over the guests?" Tay pushed open the door to the stairwell and began to head downstairs, cheeks flaming red with suppressed emotion. "No, really," Lora badgered as she followed her down the steps. "What do you think will happen?" Tay's hands clenched into fists as she tried to clamp down on her anger. "Will they sack you?" Her voice was light, almost friendly but the words ate into her brain like poison. "Will you starve if that happens?" Tay came to a stop as she struggled to keep her temper. "What about your brats, they'll starve as well, won't they?"

"What is your problem?" Tay turned and snarled at the other girl, pleased that she had managed to avoid slapping her. "We're exactly the same."

"No." Lora stood above her, and she loomed slightly as she leant forward. "You managed to take this job from someone who worked hard for it."

"I..."

"Yes, you did," Lora interrupted, her face creased in anger. "I know one of the teachers at the school, and she said that she couldn't understand how you could have gotten a job here." Tay felt her stomach drop, and she stared at the other girl in shock. "She said that your grade wasn't high enough."

"She could have made a mistake," Tay ventured, hoping that her voice did not betray her fear.

"Doubtful," Lora continued, dislike in every line of her face. "She was very sure." She leant in and peered closely at Tay.

Unable to move backward because of the stairs, Tay stayed put and tried to brazen it out. "I should be here." Tay squared her shoulders and attempted to invest some confidence in the lie. "I have the tokens that prove it."

"But how did you get those tokens?"

"I don't have time for this." Tay turned on her heel and began to walk down the stairs. "I've got work to do." She strode down the stairs, and headed toward the kitchen, trying to keep control of the panic that was thrumming through her. Stepping back into the organised chaos, she looked for Meg and discovered her standing beside several trays of small appetisers.

"Take one of these and pass them around," she instructed as she reached up and brushed a speck of dust from Tay's uniform. As Tay balanced the large, silver tray in her hand, Meg finished with, "Just smile and say nothing, when the tray is done, come back the kitchen for a refill."

"Yes Meg," Tay managed as she headed toward the door that would lead her into the rest of the house. Pushing open the door with her hip, she moved into the empty hallway and walked toward the muted sounds of the party.

"I'll find out." She almost jumped, having forgotten about Lora following her. The other girl moved past her, throwing the comment back over her shoulder as she did so. "However you managed to do it, I'll find out." Lora reached the door at the end of the hallway, and depressed the handle. "You and your brats will be working in the Mine by the time I'm done." On that final threat, she pushed the door open and walked out into the glittering party beyond.

Tay bit her lip and followed, remembering to plaster what she hoped was a convincing smile on her face. The Frazers' hallway was large, and expensively decorated in shades of white and gold. Several portraits lined the walls, and various vases and expensive-looking knick-knacks were arranged on several small, spindly tables and counters. The hall was carpeted, and at least two dozen, well-dressed members of the upper-crust mingled within. Moving with a grace and confidence she did not feel, she lifted the tray and began to walk among the crowd. Hands covered in jewelled rings and bracelets reached out to remove the small scraps of food from the tray, ignoring Taya completely.

"They had the nerve to stop the motorcade," a loud, aggressive voice carried over the crowd as Tay meandered through the throng, "waving their placards

and shouting slogans." Tay glanced up at the speaker. The man was tall; lean with sharp features, and for a moment she stopped moving. This was the Mine Overseer, and Darius' father. Tay had seen him on several occasions during her lifetime, the last time was during her Father's trial. Taking a deep breath, she continued to cross the floor, hoping that her nerves wouldn't get the better of her. She moved closer, taking note of the traits he shared with Darius as she did so. Like his son, the Overseer was handsome, and several women clustered around him, fluttering like butterflies in their bright dresses. Tay moved closer, the tray growing lighter with each step, as she approached the man who enslaved so many. Sneaking a fleeting glance, she clamped down on the shudder that threatened to travel along her spine. That handsome, strong-jawed face held eyes that were as cold as the grave. Glancing away from that callous gaze, she continued to hand out appetisers, listening all the while to the conversation going on around her.

"So what did you do?" A woman dressed in lilac, cooed the question, her face alight with curiosity and desire as she looked up at him.

"I had the guards shoot them." He replied before taking another sip from his glass.

Tay almost stopped moving; stunned by the dispassionate delivery of the news. Around her, she felt the mood of the crowd shift, become slightly nervous as silence descended in the aftermath of the Overseer's words.

"You shot them?" The woman in lilac spoke again, her voice breathless with shock.

The Overseer looked at her, and then out at the rest of the crowd, before throwing back his head and laughing.

"Of course not," he said, laughter making a mockery of their horror. "I had them arrested."

There was a beat of shocked silence before the woman in lilac gave a bark of stunned laughter. As though a dam had burst, the small group broke into chuckles of obvious relief. Darius' father joined in with the merriment, his rich baritone a strange counterpoint to the cruelty she could see in his eyes.

"Bring those over here, girl." His gaze landed on her, and she repressed the small shudder of fear that rippled through her. Putting on her best smile, she moved through the small group and held out the tray. "Thank you." He reached out to pick up the morsel, and glanced up at her face, recognition flaring in his dark eyes. "Don't I know you?"

Tay shook her head, hoping to escape his scrutiny. The Overseer could not have recognised her. Granted, she had been in the gallery during her father's trial, but surely he could not have recognised her from that. A flinch rippled through her, as he leant forward to stare at her face, his fingers reaching up to grip her chin. "Hmm," he mused as she squirmed beneath his touch, trying to find a way to get free.

"Father," Darius' voice echoed over the space, and the Overseer dropped his hand from her face. "Why are

you molesting Frazer's staff?"

The Overseer pointed at Tay's features. "I recognise her." Tay took a deep breath and tried to relax as Darius gave a sigh and walked forward.

"And what do you want me to do about it?" Darius responded, looking up at his father with a raised eyebrow. "I don't tend to notice maids."

"Take a look at her face," his father insisted, oblivious to the group surrounding them.

"This is hardly the..."

"Do it." The words snapped out, startling the assembled group, and cutting his son's words off in mid-sentence. Darius gave a small sigh of resignation and reached out. Tay took a breath as his fingers lightly gripped her chin, and lifted her face to the light.

"There's something familiar," he conceded with a grudging sigh, "but I can't think of the resemblance." He let his hand fall, and turned back to his father. "Leave the girl alone, Father, she's trying to do her job." Tay took a small step back, grateful for Darius' presence.

"Maybe you're right." The Overseer waved his hand in a dismissive gesture. "You can go." Taking the opportunity, Tay fled from his presence with relief.

Trying not to run across the floor, Tay retreated to a corner of the room and leant against the wall. It was possible that he had recognised her from the courts, he could even have noted her resemblance to a known member of the resistance. The chatter from the room swamped her senses, and she closed her eyes. It took several deep breaths to calm her whirling thoughts.

"Are you alright?" Her eyes snapped open at the muffled question, and she stared in consternation at Darius' back, as he concealed her from the room.

"I think so," she replied in shaking tones. "What was that all about?"

"He was playing with you," Darius answered in soft tones. "Trying to shake you up." He shifted his weight slightly but did not turn round.

"Then I'm glad I don't work for him." Tay took another breath, and looked down at the empty tray in her hands, remembering just what she was supposed to be doing. With a sigh, she pushed herself free from the wall and began to walk away. "I've got to go," she said, eager to leave the opulent surroundings and intimidating company.

"Don't let him frighten you," he said, as she drew level with him. "That's what he wants."

Tay gave a firm nod but did not answer. With quick, light footsteps, she returned to the kitchen to refill her tray. Loaded down with a fresh platter of appetisers, she stepped out into the party and continued to serve. Thankfully, Darius and his Father were nowhere to be seen. Relaxing a little more, she stopped thinking about the unpleasant encounter from earlier and began to focus on her job. The night passed swiftly in a parade of trays and drinks, and she finally fell into bed with a sigh of relief early in the morning.

Chapter 6

A hand shook her from the depths of a deep sleep. Jolted awake, she stared blindly about her. The room was dark, and there was little noise from the rest of the house. Confused, she opened her eyes and focused on the darker shape above her.

"What is it?" she muttered, sleep slurring her words, as she began to drift back into its warm embrace. The hand shook her again, keeping her awake.

"You're going to the Overseer's house." The words seized her attention like a slap to the face.

"What?" She rubbed the sleep from her eyes and reached out to the candle on her side table. Lighting it with nervous, trembling fingers, she finally looked at the shape above her.

"Lora?" She stared at the other girl in confusion.

"Who else?" the other girl snapped back, pulling back from the bed with a grimace. "I can't believe you're getting to go over there." Her voice was low,

bitter, and full of barely suppressed rage. "You've only been here five minutes."

"I didn't ask for it." Tay pushed herself upright and glowered across at the other girl. Lora's antagonism burned away the last vestiges of sleep. "I don't want to go over there." The air in the bedroom chilled her skin, and she wrapped the covers about herself, trying to keep warm.

"Of course you don't," Lora sneered, her face filled with disgust. "I saw you talking to the Overseer at the party. Quite a little charmer aren't you?"

"And you're a bitch, but I don't harp on about it all the time." Cut to the quick by Lora's insinuations, Tay hardly stopped to think as her reply sizzled across the space between them. Lora blinked, the retort stunning her briefly, before she reached across the bed, and slapped Tay across the face. Pain flared across her cheek, the blow stunning her momentarily. A tense stillness settled between them before Tay moved. Barely thinking about the consequences, she returned the blow. Lora's head snapped back as Tay's hand struck her across the face. As the other girl reached for her, Tay briefly considered that she was making a mistake, but she couldn't stop herself. It was three o'clock in the morning, and she was tired, irritable, and scared at the thought of going to the Overseer's home. As they tussled, Tay briefly wondered if the altercation would get her out of going.

"Get off!" Lora's fingers raked through her hair, tugging at the brown strands until her scalp burned

with the pain. Fighting back but hampered by the cocooning bedcovers, Tay scratched at Lora's face, her nails drawing a thin line of blood across her cheek. Tay's head slammed against the wall, sending a dizzying wave of pain through her. She felt some of her hair tear free, and fresh agony seared through her scalp. "Get off me." Levering herself away from the wall, she caught hold of Lora's reddish locks. Her fingers slid through the other girl's hair, exerting as much pressure as she could.

"Ow... you crazy bitch," Lora snarled, as her eyes started to water with the pain. Releasing her grip on Tay's hair, Lora drew her fist back and punched her solidly in the face.

Tay felt her lip split from the blow, and blood dribbled from the cut. She held on, pulling a small clump of hair from Lora's head.

"Stop!" A new set of hands entered the fray and dragged the two apart. Tay took several deep breaths, as Beth pulled Lora off the bed and dumped her on the floor. "What the hell are you two doing?" she demanded as she pinned Lora to the ground. "Do you want to get Meg in here?"

Tay stopped moving and settled down, breath coming in harsh gasps as she tried to calm down. Lora struggled futilely against Beth's arms for several moments, before finally giving up and slumping down onto the floor. Red scratches stood out livid across her neck and face, a testament to their fight.

"Now," Beth addressed the two combatants, as they

both calmed down. "What the hell is going on?"

"She broke into my room," Tay started, unwilling to let Lora get the first word in.

"She called me a bitch," the other girl complained, holding her hand to the bleeding scratch on her face. "And look what she did to my face."

"You bloody well deserved it," Tay called back, her voice increasing in volume once more. "You're damned lucky, I didn't knock your block off."

"Tay," — Beth stood and laid a calming hand on her shoulder — "calm down."

"And this is the kind of girl that the boss wants to send to the Overseer's house," Lora interjected with some heat. "I bet she offered all kinds of promises for that."

Tay started forward, only to be held back by her friend. "Is that what this is about?" Beth asked, holding Tay in place, as she cast an incredulous look at the pair of them.

"She's going next door when they go to the capital," Lora complained, anger running through her voice. She stood up and adjusted her clothing. "How could they ask for her?" She sneered the last words as she picked her shawl up from the floor and pulled it around her shoulders. "I don't think she should go," she continued. "She's violent." Drawing her shawl closed, she walked up to the cloudy glass of the mirror and inspected the damage. "I think I'll tell Meg about it," she announced with an airy wave, as she began to walk to the door. "She'll be out of here by the end of the week." She

reached the door, only to stop as Beth caught hold of her wrist.

"No you won't," Beth muttered, as she pulled her back into the room.

"Why the hell not?" Lora sneered, tugging her hand free with a yank. "You certainly can't tell me what to do."

"Maybe not," Beth continued in silky soft tones, "but you can be damned sure that I can get you the sack."

"What do you mean?" Lora retorted, turning to face the other girl with bemusement. "I haven't done anything wrong."

"Oh? You think so?" Beth smiled. "You're out of bed." She glanced over at Tay. "And in another girl's room." Lora took a step back as realisation slowly creased her features. "What do you think Meg will say about that?"

"She had no right to attack me," Lora muttered, the heat taken from her voice by Beth's threat.

"You woke her up," Beth said, confidence oozing through her words. "Maybe you were stealing."

"I wouldn't," Lora snapped back with some returning heat.

"But that's what we'll say," Tay added, catching on to Beth's meaning with glee. "After all" — she assumed a piteous manner — "I woke up, and there was someone in my room, going through my things, and I just reacted." She managed a credible sob. "I didn't realise it was Lora."

The clock ticked loudly in the sudden silence as Lora absorbed their words. Tay watched the other girl's face, waiting for her to speak, and wishing that she was still fast asleep.

"Alright." Lora finally spoke, angry reluctance flowing over every syllable as she faced both girls. "I won't say anything." She secured her shawl about her neck and headed for the door. "But this isn't over." And with that, she left the room.

Tay waited until her footsteps had faded into the distance, before settling back onto the bed with a sigh of relief.

"Are you alright?" Beth kicked the door closed and sat on the edge of the bed, turning to face Tay with a look of concern.

"Yeah." Tay tucked the edge of the covers beneath her chin and started to relax. "I don't know what's gotten into her."

"Being given the opportunity to serve elsewhere can lead to more responsibility, more money," Beth explained patiently. "She thinks she should have the opportunity."

"Well, good for her," Tay snapped back, irritated by the petty politics that dominated the kitchen. "She can go in my place for all I care."

"You're not looking forward to it?" Beth asked. Tay rolled her eyes at the obvious question. "Why not?" Beth tucked her feet beneath her as she attempted to keep warm.

"Many reasons." Tay glanced at the shivering girl and

drew back the covers on her bed. "Here" — she beckoned
Beth forward — " get in and keep warm." The other
girl's eyes flicked down to the offered place and
hesitated. "Come on," Tay continued with mild
exasperation. "I can't talk to you if you're that cold."
Beth gave a small smile and slid into the bed. Tay drew
the covers back around them, feeling warmer almost
immediately.

"So why?" Beth continued, her voice muffled by the
covers. "Afraid of the Overseer?"

"Yeah," Tay nodded, unwilling to tell Beth about
Darius, and the deal she had made.

"Don't worry about him," Beth continued, her voice
reassuring but sleepy. "He won't bother you."

"But why would he pick me?" Tay asked, worry
teasing the edges of her voice.

"I dunno." Beth turned to face her. "Maybe he
thinks you're pretty."

Tay gave a bark of sharp laughter, the humour
diffusing the tension slightly. "Sure he does," she
responded.

"But you are," Beth continued, "I could understand
him wanting you around." As Tay continued to stare at
her following these words, Beth continued, "but I don't
think that's it."

Silence fell between the pair of them as Tay struggled
to tear herself from the thought of the Overseer finding
her attractive. Even if he had not arrested her father, she
would still be scared of him. One look at those eyes
told of the darkness that laid within. "Do you have any

family?" she found herself asking, trying to tear her thoughts away from the Overseer, and her upcoming role.

"A brother," the other girl replied, her voice heavy with sleep. "Our parents died in the food riots three years ago."

"I'm sorry." Tay wished she could take back the question. Many families had been torn apart by the riots.

"Don't be," Beth replied. "It's not your fault."

"Were you already working here?" Tay asked.

"Yes." Beth rolled onto her back and stared up at the ceiling. "Luckily my parents weren't actually involved in the rioting." Beth took a breath. "Which is why I didn't lose rating."

Silence fell once more between them, and Tay wondered if she had fallen asleep.

"Tay." Beth turned her head and looked at her. "How did you get this job?" Tay froze, and as she frantically looked around for an excuse, Beth continued, "because while Lora is a stuck-up bitch, she isn't wrong about you."

"I..." Shivers that had little to do with the temperature raced down Tay's spine.

"I've heard of your family." Tay felt as though she had been punched in the gut. "With your mother's record and your father arrested, you shouldn't have this job." Beth raised herself up on her elbow and stared across at her. Tay opened her mouth, then closed it again, unable to find a credible lie. "I won't tell

anyone," she continued, "but be very careful." She moved closer and whispered. "If they find out, it won't be the Mine as punishment." Her voice dropped. "They'll kill you."

Tay began to shake, all her fears racing to life, as Beth pushed the bed covers aside and got up. "If you ever want to talk..." She left the sentence hanging and pulled her robe tighter about her shoulders. "You know where I am." She then turned and left the room, closing the door quietly behind her.

For a long moment after Beth's exit, Tay stared at the door, dread flowing through her veins. Beth knew her background, and despite her reassurances, Tay couldn't be certain of her intentions. Leaning over, she blew out the candle and laid back in the darkness, terror at the thought of her ruse being discovered, keeping her awake.

Chapter 7

Tay barely had any time to talk with Beth the following morning. Her eyes were dull from worry and lack of sleep. Thoughts of being discovered had plagued her dreams and kept her awake. Concern at Beth's motives gnawed at her insides. Lora, she didn't worry too much about, but Beth actually knew her history. Despite the other girl's friendly demeanour, she knew nothing about her.

"Come here, girl," Meg called from the other side of the kitchen, as Tay put the last plate into the cupboard. Flinging her cloth to one side, Tay crossed the kitchen to stand before the older woman, holding her hands behind her back as she tried to still their nervous twitching.

"Yes?" she answered, grateful that her voice did not shake.

"Well you obviously impressed somebody last night," Meg began, her voice tinged with disapproval.

"Oh?" Tay tried to act curious, as though she did not know what was coming.

"Indeed." Meg's mouth twitched, apparently unimpressed by Tay's efforts to seem surprised. "You've been asked to work with the Overseer's family when they go to the City."

"Why me?"

"Why indeed?" Meg looked her up and down, disapproval in each line of her face. "You wouldn't have been my choice." Tay wondered if she should be acting upset at the news, but decided against it. She really wasn't that good an actor. "But they make the rules. You'll be going over there later today."

"Thank you, Meg," Tay replied, more from a need to fill the uncomfortable silence than for any other reason.

"So" — the other woman straightened up and continued — "you're to finish cleaning the scullery and pack your spare uniform. They'll be here for you in the next hour."

"Yes Meg." Tay bobbed a curtsey and turned away. "Barely been here ten minutes and you're already being afforded privileges," Meg grumbled as Tay walked away. "Don't let it go to your head."

"No Meg." With light steps, she hurried away from the older woman and began to finish scraping down the scullery counters.

"You're going then?" She started and looked up at Beth. The other girl's arms were full of clothing for the laundry, and her face was placidly concerned.

"Yes." Her voice was awkward, still nervous from the

conversation the night before.

"Are you..." Beth hesitated for a brief moment. "Are you worried about me saying anything?" There was a pause, and Tay stared fixedly at the buttons on Beth's blouse. There was a small sigh, and Beth stepped forward. "Don't worry about that," she whispered. "I won't turn you in."

"Slacking off again." Lora's voice sounded from nearby, and they both glanced up. The other girl was watching them, hatred simmering in her eyes. "I don't know, Beth," she continued, walking closer. "You've only known her five minutes." Beth drew in a breath. "What will your girlfriend say?" A vicious anger gleamed in Lora's eyes. "Trying to get another one of the maids into bed." She shook her head with mock dismay. "It's a shame the new girl doesn't know how you operate."

Tay raised her head to stare at Beth, confused by the direction the conversation had taken. Beth looked straight at her but did not answer. Her mouth opened, then closed, as though someone had stolen her power of speech. The redhead shook her head slightly, before she turned on her heel and walked from the room with quick, agitated steps.

"Beth?" Tay moved to follow, but her arm was seized by Lora, and she fell back.

"Enjoy your time over there, bitch," Lora whispered into her ear as Tay tried to drag herself free. Beth reached the end of the corridor and vanished through the door.

"Taya!" Meg walked back into the room as Lora released her arm. "What are you playing at?" The older woman crossed the floor in a rush. "Get upstairs and get ready."

"I'll take her," Lora replied brightly as she reached out and recaptured Tay's arm.

"Fine," Meg responded in a resigned tone of voice. "Just hurry up."

Unable to protest as Lora bundled her out of the room, Tay walked up the stairs with short, angry strides. Reaching her room, she dragged her spare clothes from the cupboard and began to pack. As she stuffed the clothes into her small case, her mind kept returning to Beth's stunned, slightly hurt look.

"Get a move on," Lora's voice echoed from the door, and Tay shot her an annoyed glance.

"Why did you do that?" Tay asked as she closed the lid and began to drag it out. "What was the point?"

Lora gave a small, victorious smile, and declined to answer. As Tay lumbered down the servant's staircase, she was acutely aware of Lora's presence. Not that she thought the girl would try to hurt her but, Tay took a deep breath, it wasn't completely outside of the realms of possibility. They reached the back door, and Tay's eyes searched the kitchen, hunting for Beth's red locks. She didn't know precisely what to say to the other girl, but she needed to talk to her.

"She's not in there," Lora replied, smiling at the consternation on Tay's face, as she opened the back door, and waved her toward the street. "And you'd

better get going, or Meg will have your hide." Tay glanced back to see Meg standing at the kitchen door, ensuring that she left.

"You're a real piece of work," Tay snapped back, her voice contemptuous.

"And you're a mannerless gutter rat," Lora replied in a quasi-pleasant voice. "You took a job from a friend of mine who should have been next on the list at Carfax." Tay flinched back from the hate in the other girl's face. "You shouldn't be here, or over there"—Lora nodded in the direction of the Overseer's house— "and sooner or later, everyone will know it." She placed both of her hands on Tay's back and shoved her hard. The sudden movement sent Tay stumbling down the steps, dropping her case as she tried to maintain her balance. The kitchen door slammed shut, leaving her alone in the snowy alleyway. Picking up her trunk, she cast a long look back at the kitchen windows, but she could see no sign of Beth. There was only the alley, the snow and the door to Darius' home. A heavy sigh escaped her lips as she crossed the passageway and stepped up to the door of the house opposite. Knocking on the heavy wood, she waited for an answer. For several long moments, she stood in the alleyway, waiting for the kitchen door to open.

Chapter 8

It had started to snow, and she shivered as cold, wet flakes settled onto her bare arms. Lora had not given her any time to put on a coat, and she shuddered as the frigid air raised goosebumps on her skin. She knocked again before wrapping her arms around her body, trying to keep warm. Time seemed to stand still as she stood there waiting. It was quiet and still within the alley, and ever thicker flakes of snow began to drift down from the leaden sky. She knocked for the third time and shuffled her feet, wondering why she had been asked to arrive when the rest of the household seemed to be away.

Reaching down, she picked up her case and started back across the alley, unwilling to wait in the snow much longer.

"Taya." She turned at the sound of her name, and looked up at the now-open door. Nervously she headed for the entrance and warmth. Stepping over the

threshold, she stopped at the sight of the empty kitchen. The hearth was lit and its warmth washed over her chilled skin, but no staff worked at the tables. Apprehension washed over her as she took another step forward and looked across the echoing space.

She jumped slightly as the kitchen door clicked shut. Whirling around, she came face to face with Darius, moving out of the shadows. "What's going on?" She could not help the nervous tremor that entered her voice. She took an involuntary step backward, heart rate increasing with each passing second.

"Nothing to be worried about," Darius answered. He stopped several paces from her, clearly attempting to put her at ease.

"Then why?" She stopped speaking as he took another step closer to her.

"Come with me," he said, holding out his hand. Swallowing nervously, she moved to his side and gingerly took his hand. He led her through the servants' corridors, and out into the main body of the house. With increasing fear, she followed him up the central staircase. Beneath his fingers, her skin grew slick with sweat as scenarios chased themselves through her mind.

"Where are you taking me?" she asked, her voice a pathetic whisper as he drew her along richly decorated halls.

In answer, he placed his hand on a door handle and pushed open the door. "In here," he said, his voice taut with some unnamed emotion.

"No." Mustering courage from somewhere, she

stopped dead and pulled her hand free. "Why am I here?"

"Not for sex," he clarified with wry humour. "Though it would make it a lot easier if you were."

"I don't understand." Confusion tinged with relief rippled through her as she searched his face for answers.

"Oh, for heaven's sake Darius, tell the girl." A feminine voice echoed from the depths of the room, and Tay took an involuntary step forward, looking into the room with curiosity. Standing next to the bed was a young woman in a bathrobe, her dark hair hanging loosely about her shoulders. It took a moment for her to recognise the woman who had flung her arms about him earlier.

"This is my sister." Darius walked to stand beside Tay. "I need you to take her place."

Tay froze, her eyes swivelling from his sister to Darius so quickly she could have gained an injury.

"What?" she asked, her voice a horrified whisper. For a long moment, she tried to speak, but her words tumbled out in a flood of confused babble.

"Well done Darius." The woman walked forward and placed an arm around Tay's shoulders, leading her into the room, and sitting her down on the bed. "Here, drink this." A glass of something warm was placed in her hand. She drank it down, feeling the liquid burn all the way to her core. "He shouldn't have sprung it on you like that."

"But" — Tay finished choking from the burning taste of the brandy and stared at the pair of them — " how

can I replace her, and why?"

"Lyana is due to attend court to meet her betrothed," Darius stated, the words sending jolts of fear through her. "She won't be able to attend, so I need to send someone in her place."

"How can I pretend to be your sister?" Tay retorted, staring up at him as confusion gave way to anger. "We don't look anything alike." She got up from the bed. "This is utterly ridiculous." She waved a hand at the other girl. "If she doesn't want to go, can't she just pretend to be sick?"

"I can't," Lyana replied, misery flowing through her voice. "Father would want to know why I can't go."

Tay glared at Darius, shrugging her shoulders in query. "Lyana is pregnant," Darius answered the unspoken question. "And Father would kill her if he knew."

"I don't understand why it has to be me."

"Because you owe me," Darius replied, the words sending ripples of panic through her. "And you can do this."

"But someone will notice," Tay begged, her voice quietly pleading. "I don't look at all like her."

"You think?" Darius held out his hand and led her to the mirror. After a moment, Lyana left her place and joined them. Tay stared up at the three of them reflected in the glass, and her stomach sank as he began to speak. "You're the same height, and while it's true you don't have her features, your hair and eye colour are a match."

"But no one's going to believe this," Tay whispered, desperation leeching through her voice. "I can't pretend to be her."

"No one in the City knows us well. You're there to attend a function and sign some papers," Darius explained. "And that's all."

"Please," Lyana whispered, tears hovering on the edge of her voice. "Father can't find out about my pregnancy."

"It'll take one week to reach the City," Darius explained, "and Father is currently engaged at the Mine for the foreseeable future, so it falls to me to make the introductions."

"But surely this betrothed of hers will notice that I'm not the girl he's supposed to marry," Tay argued, trying to find some way of making them understand the idiocy of what they were attempting. "I can't get away with this."

"You can," Darius reassured, turning her away from the mirror to stare into her face. "You won't be expected to talk to him, only to make an appearance." His hands settled onto her shoulders, their warmth cutting through the numb sensation that the conversation was producing.

She hesitated, waiting to protest once again. The idea was the highest level of recklessness. Faced with this plan or deliberately spying on her boss, she would prefer to spy, at least then she could get away from the lion's den. In the City, miles away from her home and in unfamiliar territory, she could not hide or run. She

glanced into Darius' face and swallowed at the implacable look that had settled over his features. No amount of pleading or reason would make him change his mind.

"I'll be with you" — he spoke quietly, and she was certain she heard reassurance in his voice — "every step of the way."

"It'll just be until I can get this dealt with," Lyana uttered, adding her own brand of pressure.

"What about my family?" she asked.

"Your sister will be given temporary access to draw ration," Darius replied his voice back to its usual business-like tones. "After all, you will be in the city as additional staff."

Tay stepped back, and sank down on the bed, holding her head in her hands.

"I can promise that I will do everything I can to ensure that you are not exposed."

Silence echoed through the plush bedroom as both siblings waited for an answer. In Tay's head, visions of being discovered played on a never-ending loop with each outcome even more terrible than the last. But if she did this, then her deal with Darius would be finished. After what seemed like an age, she raised her head.

"Okay." Her voice shook slightly as she gave her answer. "Now what?"

"Now you get washed, manicured and dressed appropriately," Lyana replied, stepping forward to sit down next to her on the bed. "And thank you."

Tay glanced across at the other girl. "I didn't really have a choice," she retorted as she stood up and moved back toward the door. "Where's the bathroom? I suppose I'd better get started."

Darius stepped out of the way and pointed across the hall at the door opposite. Refusing to look at his face she strode past him into an expensive, tiled bathroom. A tank stood above the large, claw-footed tub, promising hot water, and several bottles of bath oil and fragrance sat on the shelf near the door. The room was larger than her lounge, and she began to undress with nervous, shaking fingers. As her clothes fell to the floor, the door opened. Lyana walked in, a thick robe hanging over her arm.

"Here," Lyana said, placing the gown over the back of the radiator. Reaching past Tay's partially unclothed form, she turned on the bath taps and added a stream of oil from one of the bottles. The scent of rose drifted into the air as the water began to froth. "I know this is going to be hard" — she picked up Tay's uniform and placed it on a chair — "but I am grateful." She turned on the cold tap and drew her fingers through the steaming water.

"But I don't know what to do," Tay whispered as she looked down at the rapidly filling tub. "Or how to behave."

"I wouldn't have asked if there were any other way." Lyana sat on the edge of the bath and smiled at her. "Darius will help you."

Tay snorted with derision, wondering how she could

trust the man who had put her in this position.

"He will help," Lyana assured, as she tested the water. "He wouldn't want you to be harmed."

"How can I believe that?" Tay replied as she watched Lyana turn off the taps.

"Because he's a good man." She stood up and headed for the door. "Have a long soak," she advised, "and then rejoin me in the bedroom." She depressed the door handle, and began to leave. "We'll make sure everything's fine." Opening the door, she walked out into the hall, leaving Tay's stunned and mildly frustrated form in the centre of the expansive bathroom.

As the door closed, Tay sat down on the edge of the bath. Alone in that steamy, luxurious bathroom, she gave full rein to her fears and doubts. There were so many things that could go wrong. No matter how many assurances Darius and his sister provided, it was still a huge risk. It would only take a chance meeting with someone who knew Lyana, and the entire deception would come crashing down. She knew that she would bear the brunt of any punishment, and shuddered at the thought. There was no known statute for impersonating one of the nobility, but she was certain that the penalty would be thorough, exacting, and aimed at dissuading others. She leant back and trailed her hand through the deliciously warm water. If she were sensible, she would refuse, but she couldn't run the risk that her father would be returned to the Mine. There was also her appointment with the Frazers' to

consider. Would Darius maintain her cover if she refused? Closing her eyes, she allowed her head to fall back, accepting her decision with reluctance, and a gnawing sense of dread. The rest of her clothing fell to the floor, as with decision came action. If she had to go through with this charade, she might as well enjoy the perks. The warm water cocooned her and she drifted into a soft haze of rose scent and bubbles. Ducking her head beneath the water, she obscured the tears that had begun to slide silently down her face. Despite her resolve, she could not stop the fear that she had signed her own death warrant. Not for the first time, she wished she had never heard of Darius.

Fifteen minutes later and feeling a lot warmer, she stood up from the bath, dried herself off, and wrapped herself in the warm robe. Hesitantly, she opened the door to the hallway and peered outside. Relieved to see that Darius was nowhere in sight, she crossed the landing and entered Lyana's room.

"Feel better?" Lyana asked, watching as she crossed the threshold.

"Yes... thank you." Tay winced at the timidity in her voice, but it could not be helped. She felt intimidated, not only by her surroundings but by the thought of what was to come.

"Don't be so worried." Lyana stepped around the bed and closed the door, before placing a concerned arm about Tay's shoulders. "By the time I'm through, even my father will be convinced you're me."

Sceptical, Tay allowed the other girl to lead her to the

dressing table. Sitting before the gilt-framed mirror, she stared at her reflection. Beneath a ragged mop of wet hair, a pair of hazel eyes glared back at her. Reaching into a drawer, Lyana pulled out a comb and began to gently tease it through the damp, unruly mess. As Lyana worked, Tay used the time to examine the girl she would be impersonating. Despite having the same hair and eye colour, their features weren't particularly similar.

"Now..." Lyana continued to speak as she drew the comb through her dark locks. "You're going to the City for the annual betrothal ball." Tay winced as the comb tugged at a particularly tough knot. "It's a masked event." The knot continued to resist Lyana's ministrations and Tay hissed with pain. "So no one will see your features." Tay closed her eyes in relief as she processed the other girl's words. "All you will need to do is register." The knot finally gave way, and the other girl continued to draw the large-toothed comb through Tay's hair.

"What will I need to do to register?" Tay asked.

"Sign my name." The comb was sliding easily through the wet locks now, and Lyana stopped brushing. Reaching forward, she drew a slim, dark green bottle from the desk, and poured a generous amount of oil into her hand. Lyana worked the substance through Tay's hair before picking up the comb again.

"Well, I presume you mean your name," Tay noted, as the scent of almond and honey drifted into the air.

"Of course." Lyana's movements were sure and smooth. "It won't be as bad as you think." She finished

combing and wrapped a large towel around Tay's head. "Go sit near the fire, and I'll sort out your clothes."

Tay shuffled across the room and sat down before the gently crackling fire. The heat radiated across her skin, keeping her warm. Behind her, she could hear the sound of cupboards opening, and the subsequent rustle of fabric.

"So what will you be doing while I'm at this thing?" Tay turned her head as several objects landed on the bed. Her eyes widened as a small stack of clothes began to pile up on the white coverlet.

"Getting this sorted out," Lyana replied with a heavy sigh. "I can't keep the baby, my father would kill it on sight, and possibly me too."

Tay stared at the other girl, stunned by the matter-of-fact manner in which she spoke.

"Really?"

"Yes." Lyana sighed and sank down onto the bed. "Without hesitation."

"But you're his daughter," Tay whimpered, horrified by the picture that Lyana was painting with her words. "How could he?"

"I'm not his daughter." The words were too calm, almost flat, as her fingers played with the hem of the dress in her hands. "I'm only an asset." In the stillness that followed, Tay could hear the crackle of the fire behind her, as Lyana stared blankly ahead.

"You see, Darius is the heir and a boy." The words were whispered, and Tay could hear the fragile calm that surrounded her begin to chip and break. "His path is

easy." Clenching her hand into a fist, she continued. "Mine is laid out through marriage." She finally turned her head to stare at Taya. "I'm to link our family to another and increase our influence. If I jeopardise that" — Taya swallowed at the sight of crystalline tears in her eyes — " he will kill me." With those final words, her façade cracked, and her head fell forward. She stared at her knees, shoulders shuddering as the tears made their way to the surface.

Startled by the sudden outpouring of raw emotion, Tay got up from the chair and crossed to the bed. Gingerly, she reached out a hand and hesitantly stroked Lyana's shoulder. Lyana continued to cry as Tay sank down onto the soft mattress and slid her arm around Lyana's shoulders. There was a moment's awkward silence as Tay gently patted the other girl's upper arm, feeling strangely uncomfortable.

"Tay." A choked sob fell from Lyana's lips before she fell against Tay's body, crying for all she was worth.

"It's okay," Tay soothed awkwardly, unsure of how to proceed. True, she had calmed her siblings before, but this felt strange. She should feel angry at the girl for making her risk everything she held dear, but she only felt pity. She had not thought of what it could be like for those born into privilege, beyond thoughts of envy.

"What about the father?" she asked gently. "Could he not..."

"No," Lyana interrupted and pushed herself upright. "He's useless." Anger rippled through her words, and Tay could hear the pain behind them. She remained

quiet, wondering if she should ask for details.

"You'd better get dry." Lyana stood, locking her emotions back away behind a mask of calmness and competence. "I'll sort you out an outfit."

"Okay." Tay stood up from the bed, and returned to the warmth of the fire, wondering just how she could pull this off. Settling back down into the chair, she toasted quietly as Lyana worked behind her, moving items from the wardrobe to the bed. Her hair was nearly dry beneath the towel when she was finally called back to the room. Turning back to the bed, Tay's face dropped at the array of clothes laid out on the bed. Splayed over the coverlet was more clothes than she had seen in her life. Thick wools, furs and silks in different colours and shades beckoned to her with their lustre. She reached out a finger, and gently stroked across one of the fox furs, its soft warmth sliding across her skin like a whisper.

"So, what do you want to wear?" Lyana's voice broke into her thoughts, and she looked up at the other girl, bewildered by the choice before her. "No problem." Lyana reached into the pile and drew forth an outfit. She laid it across the back of the chair and beckoned her toward the small dressing room.

Tay followed her, wondering why she had left the outfit. Lyana led Tay to a chair in the centre of the dressing room, and she sat down. As she opened her mouth to ask why she was there, the other girl removed the towel from her nearly dry hair and began to brush through it.

"We need to sort your hair," Lyana said, pre-empting her questions as she drew the brush through the newly clean locks. She finished brushing after a minute and opened a nearby drawer. Returning to Tay, she pinned some of the hair to one side and continued to comb. There was a snip, and several strands of dark hair fell to the ground.

"What are you doing?" Tay whirled round, narrowly avoiding a cut from the pair of scissors that Lyana held in her hands.

"Cutting your hair," Lyana replied mildly. "Don't you remember?"

"But I didn't..." She faltered at the sight of the long strands of hair that laid on the floor. "How much will you be cutting off?"

"About two inches."

"I see."

"Think of it this way," Lyana said with a smile, "your hair needs a cut, and you need to look more like me." She unfurled a strand of her own hair from the braid that wrapped her head, and showed it. "See." Tay looked at the hair, its dark strands only a few inches shorter than hers. "It won't be that bad, and it will regrow." She pointed to the front, and Tay turned back, her fingers tensing with each snip of the scissors.

"There." In no time at all, Lyana stepped away, and gave her a mirror. Tay reached out and took hold of the gilt-framed item. With trepidation, she stared down at herself, before drawing in a long, surprised breath. Her once ragged, bluntly cut hair had been trimmed to just

below her shoulders. Two feathered strands of hair framed her face and gave her a light, more sophisticated look.

"It's incredible," she said, handing the mirror back to the other woman. "I wouldn't have thought you would know how to do this type of thing."

"Why?" Lyana placed the mirror back in a drawer and began to clean up the pile of hair that had pooled on the floor. "Because I'm a noble?"

"Yes," Tay answered, slightly embarrassed at herself for making the observation.

"My mother thought it necessary for me to learn a skill." She began to place the excess hair into a bag. "My father disagreed but" — she gave a tiny smile — "mother managed to convince him that hairdressing was a usual skill for the nobility." She affected a high-pitched, snobbish tone. "After all, finding a decent hairdresser is so taxing." She got up from the floor and beckoned Tay to follow her. "My father is a skinflint at heart, and the appeal to his wallet caught his attention." She lead Tay back into the bedroom and pushed her back into the chair.

"Now what?" Tay asked, trepidation flooding through her, as Lyana reached for a small bag on the dressing table.

"Now we sort out your makeup." She opened the small pouch and began to apply creams and lotions to Tay's skin. By the time Lyana was done, Tay's body felt stiff and uncomfortable from being sat in the chair for so long. As Lyana indicated that she had finished, Tay

stood up, only to be handed a pile of clothes.

Taking the small stack from the other woman, Tay began to dress, pulling on the unfamiliar garments with difficulty.

"So how come you have so many clothes if your father is a skinflint?" Tay asked as she pulled on a cotton blouse.

"He's only frugal in private," Lyana explained as she helped Tay into the next layer of clothing. "We have minimal servants and hire extra if there is to be an event. To the other nobles, we're as extravagant as they, but we don't have personal staff; only a few maids, a housekeeper and a butler." Lyana handed her the last piece of clothing, and then stood back. "There," she announced, satisfaction running through her voice. "I think we're done." She walked over to the door and pushed it open. Stepping out into the hallway, she ushered Tay before her until they reached another door. Without waiting to knock, Lyana pushed open the door and entered the room.

Darius' bed chamber was large and plainly decorated. Cream walls and dark wooden furniture gave the room an austere look. Darius was laying on a large, four poster bed as his sister strode into the chamber, dragging Tay behind her like some parcel.

"What do you think?"

Darius propped himself up and looked across at them, his eyes slowly travelling across Tay's form with appreciation.

"Not bad," he said finally, the admiration in his gaze

sending a flush to Tay's cheeks.

"She doesn't quite look like me," Lyana noted critically.

"Put a mask on her, and she'll be fine," Darius replied, standing up from the bed, and walking across the floor. He stopped just shy of them. "Turn around." Tay slowly moved to obey, too used to obeying instructions to question. "From the back, she could be you," he said to his sister, almost ignoring the girl beside her. "It'll work."

Tay turned back to the front and shuffled uncomfortably as Darius walked back to the other side of the room.

"So now what?" she asked, her voice trembling slightly as she thought of the deception they were asking her to perform.

"Now we spend the next week teaching you how to become my sister," Darius replied as he leant nonchalantly against the wall.

"I see..." Tay took several deep breaths and tried to calm down. This was as bad as Lars asking her to spy, and far more likely to end in exposure. As she looked across at Darius, a question bubbled to the surface, one that she feared to ask, for she did not know what she would do with the answer.

"What is it?" His eyes were fixed on her face, and she swallowed nervously.

"Did you know that this would be the price of your help?" she asked with some hesitation.

"Yes," he answered, sending waves of fury through

her.

"Then why didn't you say at the time?" she demanded, anger finally suppressing the nerves.

"Would you have backed away from the deal?" His question was mildly curious, and she stopped, thinking back to that conversation.

"I don't know," she admitted finally, bowing her head slightly as she considered his question. Would she have backed down? Considering that the other option was starvation, she would have to say no. Though she would have liked to know what she was getting into. Her thoughts drifted back to Lars and Cody, knowing that they would insist that she take this opportunity to spy.

"Then there's no problem," Darius said as he returned to the bed and sat down. "Good job with her by the way," he called across to Lyana. "She looks similar enough to not garner a second glance."

"She won't be seen for long," Lyana confirmed, watching as Darius laid back on the bed and relaxed. "We'd better get on with it then," she said, noting the dismissal in his stance. Backing up to the door, she pushed it open and beckoned to Tay. "Let's go."

"Wait." Tay walked up to the bed and stared down at him, idly noting the tautness of his muscles beneath his shirt. He opened his eyes and stared up at her, and she was struck by the bright blue of his gaze.

"Can I have time to let my sister know?" Darius pushed himself up and glanced across to his sister. "She needs to know that I won't be here to collect ration,"

she snapped, frustrated by their hesitancy. "Look, I'm going to do this, but I need to let my family know, just in case I..." She stammered to a halt. "Just in case I don't come back."

"Very well," Darius said, settling back against the bed with a sigh. "Just don't take too long."

Tay stepped away from the bed and followed Lyana out into the hall. They closed the door to Darius' room and walked back along the corridor in silence. Reaching Lyana's room, the other girl stopped at the doorway and faced her.

"You will come back?" she asked, a whisper of fear in her voice.

Tay nodded, wondering why she agreed to return. She could run from the situation, take her siblings and... she stopped thinking. She could indeed flee, but it would be temporary. She had no doubt that Darius would withdraw his bargain if she left. There was even the possibility that he would turn the authorities onto her. Despite his calm, almost friendly demeanour, she had no delusions of his altruism. With his admission, he had declared his determination to save his sister, and he would look unfavourably on any effort to ruin her. Following Lyana into the room in silence, she changed out of the fancy clothes and back into her work garb, the fabric scratchy and uncomfortable after the luxurious feel of Lyana's clothing.

"Tay." Lyana took a hesitant step forward and clasped hold of her hand. "Thank you for doing this." Tay looked down, focusing on the pale, unblemished

hands that held hers as she tried to formulate a response.

"My hands." She declared as the impact of seeing those fingers blazed into her mind. "They're worker's hands." She held up her own fingers and displayed the roughened calluses, reddened skin and chipped nails that were the lot of a scullery maid's life. "They'll notice."

"Not if you wear gloves." Lyana smiled as she pulled a thin pair of kidskin gloves from a dresser drawer.

Tay gave a small snort of laughter at Lyana's practical suggestion, and she drew the gloves onto her hands. "You've thought of everything," she quipped lightly as she looked down at her concealed fingers.

"Of course," Lyana replied with a chuckle. "Though you'd better take those off if you're going to your home."

"Oh." Tay gave a start and removed the gloves. Placing them onto a table, she turned back to the room, and Lyana.

"I know it'll be difficult," Lyana said, watching the colour drain out of Tay's face with some sympathy. "But I do thank you."

"Yeah..." she replied, walking toward the door. "I hope you realise just how bad a position I'm in." Her voice was flat, the anger strangely muted. "They could kill me for this."

"I know you're assuming most of the risk" — Lyana reached her side — "but I trust my brother to keep you safe." Her fingers squeezed Tay's upper arm reassuringly.

Tay picked up her cloak and stepped through the door. Moving through the empty house, she reached the kitchen without seeing another soul. Pushing open the heavy door, she moved into the alley, trying not to give in to the panic that was pulsing through her.

Chapter 9

Tay walked through the front door of her house and froze at the sound of masculine voices drifting from the direction of the kitchen. Carefully, she reached out and picked up a cane that stood by the front door. The kitchen door was closed and the voices continued from within. Hesitantly, she approached the door, cane shaking lightly in her grasp in preparation for confrontation with the intruders.

"Are you certain?" She stopped at the sound of Lars' voice, and fury replaced caution. A loud bang echoed through the house as the door smashed against the wall. Lars and Cody stood within the kitchen, talking with a stunned Lana who was sitting on the edge of the kitchen counter.

"What the devil are you lot doing here?" Tay demanded as she brandished the cane in what she hoped was a threatening manner.

"I invited them." Lana hopped down from her perch

and walked toward her older sister.

"And I didn't want them here." Tay glanced across at Lars, who had the decency to look abashed. Rounding on her younger sister, she continued. "You're inviting people in behind my back?"

"You would have said no." Lana ignored her sister's anger as she walked forward and poked a finger at her sister's chest. "You don't want to do anything." Her voice echoed through the kitchen, full of righteous fury. "You know Father would have wanted us to help."

"That still doesn't..."

"No, Tay," Lana protested, "I'm fed up with it. I'm fed up with the lack of food, the bullying from the guards, the slavery to the Ration." Her voice spilled forth, like a river that had burst its banks. "We need to make changes. You know that."

"Lana..." Lars stood and held up his hand. With an effort, Lana stopped speaking. "She wants to help," he explained, as though he thought Tay could not understand.

"She's still a child." Helpless, frustrated fury, snarled from her lips.

"If you would help us" — Lars glanced across at Cody — "then we wouldn't need to use her."

"Blackmail." Tay almost smacked him with the cane, disgusted by his words.

"No" — Lars gave a small smile — "practicality." He nodded at her. "You could provide us with excellent information." Cody nodded with agreement. "With that information, we would be more accurate with our

targets." He glanced across at Lana. "Besides which, your sister asked us if she could help."

"And you didn't think to say no?" It was only through supreme self-control that Tay did not smack him with the cane. "She's only fifteen."

"She'd only try to do this herself," Lars continued, his voice the very soul of reason. "And at least this way I will be able to keep an eye on her."

Tay lowered the cane a fraction, but didn't release it. Intellectually she knew what Lars said was true, that he couldn't stop her sister from doing anything dangerous, but it still rankled.

"Okay, fine." Defeat mixed with anger flowed through her voice, as she gave in to the inevitable. "I'll help." She winced as Lana enthusiastically threw her arms around her. "If..." She focused on her younger sister. "If you keep out of trouble."

"I will," Lana promised fervently, fervour shining from her face.

"Good," Lars said, stepping forward to face her. "So here's what we want..." He stopped speaking as Tay raised her hand.

"Whatever you wanted me to do, you'll have to change it," she said, watching their faces shift expression as she spoke. "I'm going to the City," she announced before they could speak. "I've been picked to go with the Overseer's family," she said, debating whether to explain just how she would be going to the city, and deciding against it. "That's why I'm home now." She reached into her pocket and handed over the two

Ration tokens and the special dispensation disc. Lana looked up at her in shock as she palmed the three discs. "That disc will allow you to draw my and Father's rations."

Lana's mouth opened and then closed, as though she could not ask the questions that were clearly forming in her mind.

"How did you get to go to the City?" Lars asked, staring down at the dispensation disc with disbelief.

"I'll tell you how..." Cody spoke for the first time, the accusation in his voice as clear as a bell.

"Cody," Lars warned, turning from his scrutiny of the disc to face the other man. "Give it a rest."

Cody closed his mouth, but he still stared at Tay, scorn etched over his face.

"So when are you going?" Lars turned back to Tay, his voice gentle.

"Today," she replied, trying to ignore Cody and his antagonism. "I got leave to deliver this."

"Alright." Lars stood back and gently ran his fingers across his upper lip in thought. "Here's what I want you to do."

Fifteen minutes later, Tay left her home and returned to the Overseer's house, her heart beating much faster than normal. As if she didn't have enough to handle. Lars had asked her to investigate the corridors of power. She could have refused the job, but if she had, there was

every possibility that her sister would attempt to join the rebels in her stead. As her footsteps echoed on the cobblestones, she wondered how she had managed to end up mixed up in all of this. If only her father had not been involved with the resistance, then she wouldn't have been forced to seek Darius' help. She walked past the Ration Centre, avoiding the gaze of the guards as she hurried along the road. No, all she had to do now was survive pretending to be Darius' sister and manage to steal the delivery schedules from the transit office. The thought chilled her, and she moved faster across the snowy ground, hoping for some miracle to get her out of the mess she had gotten into.

Chapter 10

"No, not that knife," Lyana's voice snapped through the still air of the dining room. Tay, in the process of selecting what she thought was the main course cutlery, dropped the offending object with a clatter. "And don't just drop the silverware."

Tay glanced up at her task-master; the last few days had been an endurance trial. Lyana had proved to be as harsh a teacher as she'd ever known, and the array of information that she needed to learn was beginning to make her head swim.

"So which knife is it?" Sitting at the table, dressed in Lyana's less-than-comfortable clothes, Tay hoped that some miracle would prevent her travel to the City. The only positive point about the experience was Darius' absence, and even that didn't help the feeling of disorientation. There was too much to learn and not enough time to learn it.

She still had to perform her scullery duties, to keep

up appearances, and cram lessons in the hours she was meant to be asleep. Even her sleep was disturbed with morbid musings on what could go wrong. Exhaustion was rapidly becoming an issue, but Lyana gave her no quarter in the lessons, drilling her endlessly on each point of etiquette. As a consequence of the taxing regime, comments about her capability had begun to circulate in the kitchen. Since her arrival she had broken three plates and knocked over a stack of pans. Tay could only hope that any reports of poor performance didn't make their way back to the Frazers and affect her normal role.

"That one." Lyana's voice softened at the look of tired bewilderment on Tay's face. "Just remember, outside in, and you'll be fine."

"It's just..." Tay picked up the correct knife and began to eat. "It's all so..."

"New," Lyana interrupted, finishing Tay's sentence for her. "Just relax, and it'll come."

"It's easy for you to say," Tay muttered. "You don't have to learn a lifetime of etiquette lessons in three days." A sigh whistled from between her lips. "This isn't going to work."

"It will." Tay tried not comment on the desperate sound to Lyana's voice.

"Is it going well?" Darius poked his head through the open door. A glance passed between him and his sister, and he walked into the room. "Don't worry, I'll help you." The words were gentle, softer than she had expected from him. As he sat down at the table and

helped himself to a plate of food, Tay looked up from her dinner and stared at him. While Lyana could almost be called friendly, she still did not know what to think about Darius.

"Well?" Lyana asked, after a moment of watching him chew.

"Well, what?" He reached out and picked up a glass of wine.

"Is Father occupied?" A nervous quaver entered her voice. "I thought you were checking."

"He won't be back for a while," Darius confirmed, after taking a sip. "According to Carson, he's been taken out of the district and the earliest estimate for him to return is about a month." He nodded over at Tay. "More than enough time for us to get this done."

"So..." Tay's voice squeaked. She swallowed and started again. "We'll be going tomorrow?"

"As planned." Darius took another bite. "So I would see your family tonight" — he glanced down at the table — " just in case." Tay stopped chewing, the food turning to sawdust in her mouth. On the other side of the table, Lyana threw her a sympathetic glance. Darius took another forkful of food, before pushing his dinner aside and standing up. "And get some sleep tonight." He shot another glance at Lyana. "I'm going to need to talk to you."

"Go see your family." Lyana pushed aside her own plate of food. "I'll see you when you come back."

They walked out of the room, leaving Tay alone at the makeshift dinner table in Lyana's room. A sense of

dread settled over her as she contemplated the next few days. It had become easy to lose herself in the training and the food. She took another forkful, not quite willing to allow thoughts of the days ahead to affect her appetite. Now that the journey to the City was only a day away, she could barely keep still. Nervous and agitated, she finished her meal and headed back upstairs.

Tay walked into the room she had been given and changed back into her regular clothing. Her fingers shook as she did up the buttons on her coat, and she bit her lip. More than anything, she wished she did not have to do this. Moving to the door, she left the room.

She headed along the corridor, only to stop at the sound of Lyana crying. Carefully, she pushed open the door to Lyana's room and stopped at the sight of Lyana in Darius' arms. Tears streamed down her face, as she wept against her brother's chest. Darius looked at Tay over the top of his sister's head, and she was startled at the raw agony she saw there. Aware she was intruding on a private moment, she stepped back out of the room and headed downstairs, her emotions in tatters. She liked Lyana, despite the gulf in their backgrounds, and she hated to see her in pain, but at this moment in time she was far too worried about the trip to the City. This charade they were asking her to play could mean her death. Tay pushed open the kitchen door and headed off down the street.

"So you're pretending to be a noble?" Lars sat in her mother's chair and raised an eyebrow. "That's why you're going to the City?"

Tay nodded, unsure if she had done the right thing in telling Lars this information. Thankfully, Cody had not accompanied him to the house, but mistrust still festered between them. Spilling Lyana's secrets had been the hardest, the noble girl seemed to trust her, and this felt like a betrayal.

"That's great news." Lars jumped up, a smile creasing his features. "As a noble, you'll have far more access than any servant."

"I doubt I'll have that much," Tay muttered, reluctance in each syllable. "But I can try."

"That's all I want." Lars reached into a bag and drew forth a brass contraption. "This will plug into any of the archive devices in the City." He placed it in her hands, and began to point at different parts of the mechanism. "We want the supply routes and guard schedules. I'm certain you'll have access."

Tay examined the recorder carefully, sceptical of Lars' claims. "That's if I can get away from Darius," she noted, remembering his job as chaperone.

"I don't think you'll have a problem there," Lars contradicted. "I'm sure you can be resourceful."

Tay sniffed in derision, still unconvinced of the ease of her task. "And what about my siblings?" she asked, placing the device into a pocket. "I barely trust you to keep them safe, I don't trust your friend at all."

"I understand, Cody is dedicated..."

"Dedicated?" Tay gave a bark of laughter. "He's accused me on two separate occasions of sleeping with Darius, despite the fact that you both sent me to the man." Tay paced the room, agitation and nerves turning into anger. "There was every possibility that was going to be his price. So knowing that, you sent me there, and then Cody attempts to make me feel cheap." Another scornful chuckle ripped from her lips. "Whatever your excuses for his behaviour, I don't ever want him to come here again, understand?"

"Yes, yes, of course," Lars promised, attempting to mollify her. "Just get this done and that's it, we can do the rest."

Tay pursed her lips but stayed silent. There was only so much she could say before it became repetitive. Showing Lars out of the house, she moved up the stairs to her siblings' bedroom, for potentially her last night with them.

Chapter 11

The train carriage was unlike anything she had ever seen. Drawn by a smoking locomotive, the carriage that belonged to the Overseer was painted royal blue with gold accents, and lace curtains hung over the windows prevented people from seeing in. Standing on the platform, dressed in the elegant travelling gown that belonged to Lyana, Tay looked every inch the lady. She took a cautious breath, and the soot and smoke nearly made her cough.

"Come on." She felt Darius' fingers grasp her elbow, and she allowed him to walk her forward. "Delicate steps." His voice was a muffled whisper, as he guided her toward the steps. There was a click as a footman opened the door. Taking a fortifying breath, she stepped aboard.

Passing the footman with a brief nod, Tay moved through the panelled hall and into the main car. The space was beyond luxurious. Instead of rows of seating,

the carriage had been turned into a lounge with a dining table beyond. Across the back wall, she could see the dark shape of a bar, and a small bookcase laid on the opposite side. Taking another step, her feet sank into the thick carpet that covered the floor, and she swallowed nervously.

"Come on." Darius drew her into the room as the door shut behind them. There was a hiss of steam, and the train began to move. Tay dropped into a chair, suddenly unsteady on her feet.

"We will be arriving in the City late tomorrow," the footman informed them as he entered the room.

"Thank you." Darius sat in the chair opposite and picked up a paper. "Can you fetch us a coffee and" — he looked over at Tay— "a hot chocolate."

"Indeed sir." The footman left the room, and Tay felt some of the tension lift from her shoulders.

"See," Darius uttered, his voice soft. "Don't worry."

"I wish I could," she replied, sinking down into a chair, and trying to relax.

"I'll keep an eye on you," he assured, and she looked up into his face, startled at the sincerity that she saw there.

"What's the City like?" she asked, disturbed by the gentleness in his eyes.

"Full of fog," he answered, settling back into the chair and relaxing. "But beautiful in a way." His voice became distant as he recalled the memories. "The buildings are a lot grander than those back at home, and the main Palace..." He stopped talking as the

footman returned, and handed over two steaming cups. Tay's chilled fingers wrapped about the white porcelain, and she sniffed the chocolaty concoction, relaxing with the rich scent.

"The main Palace?" she prompted as the servant walked out of the room.

"It's surrounded by parkland and gardens," he continued, his voice strangely soothing. "The main building is only three stories high and made of golden stone. Inside" — he paused and looked at her — " it's fully heated. Our apartments are on the southern edge of the Palace and overlook the ornamental gardens."

"We're staying at the Palace?" Tay managed to keep the squeak of fear from her voice, but shock permeated her words all the same.

"Yes." A sympathetic gleam entered his gaze as she assimilated the new information. "They're private." What could have been reassurance rippled through his tones.

"There's a swimming pool in the basement," he continued. Tay stayed silent, the fear keeping her on edge. "You'll like it." She thought for a moment, finding it strange that he would concern himself with her likes. She stared down at the swirling chocolate, allowing her thoughts to drift ahead to the City, and she shifted uncomfortably in her seat.

"Lyana." She dragged her gaze away from the cup and looked up. Darius' eyes were fixed on her face and she was surprised by the concern she saw there.

"What will I have to do?" She took another sip and

tried to calm down. "I won't have a maid." She seized
on the least of her worries, trying to forestall thinking
about the more difficult things she would have to
attempt. "Won't they find it strange that I don't have a
maid?"

"You will have one," he said, understanding creeping
into his voice.

"Won't they know that I'm not her?"

"There's no reason for them to." He placed the cup
he was holding onto a nearby table, and leant forward.
"For all intents and purposes, you are Lyana James."

"But..." She couldn't help it, the doubts and fears
seemed to stack up against her, and her hands started to
shake. "I don't..." She despised herself for the plea she
heard in her voice. "What if...?" She couldn't finish the
sentence, fear choking her before she could.

"It's alright." He stood and crossed the room in
several long strides. Crouching down, Darius' gentle
gaze reassured and calmed. "You can do this."

"How do you know?" she whispered, nerves stealing
the power from her voice.

"Because anyone who had the guts to visit me at my
home, and ask for her father's life, has enough courage
to manage this." A hand reached out and removed the
cup before it spilt. Placing it down on the nearby table,
he reached out and caught her shaking fingers. "Now
relax," he murmured, a soft note that was somehow
comforting.

Tay took a deep breath and nodded, allowing his
voice to reassure her. The tremors in her fingers began

to diminish, bolstered by his confidence and support. She attempted a watery smile as she reached deep within herself for the strength to keep going.

"That's better." He released her fingers and moved back. "Come on." He held out his arm as he reached his full height. "You'd better see your room." After a moment, she reached out and caught hold of his lower arm, feeling the muscles beneath the soft fabric of his shirt. He drew back and pulled her upright. The train's motion swayed beneath her feet, leaving her almost clumsy as she joined him. Suddenly shy, she removed her hands from his arm and waited. Gently, courteously, his fingers encircled her upper arm.

"Remember," he whispered as they headed toward the back of the carriage, and two sets of doors, "that this is not new to you. Granted, we are not the most cosmopolitan of families, but we have had our share of parties." He came to a stop before the doors and looked down at her. The motion of the train rocked them and almost without meaning to, they moved closer together. "There's no need to baulk at courtesy." He whispered before stepping back and turning to the doors. She released a breath as he led her forward, and pushed open the door on the right to revealed a small but exquisite-looking room.

The room was panelled in a warm, golden wood and plush red carpet covered the floor. Beneath the window, a small desk stood, and built into the wall on the right was a bed. A nightgown was laid across its crisp surface, a long confection of lace and satin.

"Yours," he said, releasing her arm, and allowing her to walk into the small room. She stepped forward, wonder flooding through her at the sight of the cabin, and for a moment all fears about being discovered faded. She stretched her hand out, and ran her fingers over the nightgown, marvelling at its silky feel.

"There's more clothing in the wardrobe," Darius continued, moving over to the panelled wall and pressing a small switch. The wall slid open to reveal the dresses beyond. Her mouth dropped open at the sight, and she reached into the cupboard to draw one of the dresses free. Her fingers slid over the rustling, deep burgundy taffeta, and for the first time, she relished being Lyana James. Thoughts of wearing this dress, and others like it, chased through her mind, and a smile came to her lips.

"You have a beautiful smile." She dropped her hand from the dress, and stared up at Darius, having forgotten that he was there.

"Thank you," she replied, unsure of how to take the compliment.

"A maid will be assigned to you in the City," Darius continued, not missing the sudden tension that straightened her back. "And none of them know what my sister looks like." He backed up to the door. "Dinner will be served at six if you want to spend the rest of the journey here." He reached for the door and began to walk through.

"Darius..." He stopped and looked back at her, a question in his eyes. She took a breath, and closed her

mouth, unsure of what she wanted to say. "Nothing," she clarified, shaking her head.

"You don't have to be concerned," he said, his eyes fixed on her face. "I won't let you be discovered, there's far too much at stake for that." And with that enigmatic statement, he turned back to the door and walked through, leaving Tay to stare after him in shock.

The door closed behind him and left her alone in the cabin. Running a nervous hand across her upper lip, she paced over to the window and stared out at the landscape beyond. The sky was almost gold today, and the view from the moving train was as clear as a bell. In between clouds of soot-filled smoke, Tay could see what laid beyond the Factory, and her jaw dropped open in disbelief. Once past the wall that surrounded her home, the fields began in earnest, and the sight of those wide-open spaces made her head spin. From the tracks to the horizon, the fields stretched out in all directions, the furrows filled with scraggly-looking plants choked by weeds. On a distant field, she could see the distinctive shapes of livestock, and in the midst of it all, a large farm with several outbuildings.

As her gaze drifted across the fields, she saw several teams of workers tilling the frozen ground, watched over by guards in warm towers. For a moment, shame rushed through her, she had forgotten about the farming communities. Despite being free of the Factory, they did not have a better life, with their existence dominated by quotas. As she watched, one of the workers stretched and glanced up toward the train. For an instant, her

gaze looked with the woman on the ground, and Tay stepped back at the hostility she sensed. She turned away from the window and sank down onto the bed, her fingers nervously plucking at the bedspread.

Darius' last words flowed through her mind, and she focused on them with some concern. What stakes could he be talking about? True, the stakes for her were quite high, and he was concerned about his sister, but she somehow knew that he was referring to something else. There was also the scene she had witnessed the day before. Lyana had not even referred to any issues. Granted, Tay was not one of her closest friends, but it could be something she should be aware of. Secrets within secrets. Tay was surrounded by them, Darius and his sister; Cody and Lars. They seemed so interested in Darius' motives, but they had been the ones to send her to him.

"What else does he want?" There was an answer to that whispered question, but she dismissed it as soon as she thought of it. As he had said in their first meeting, he had no need to pay for sex, and he didn't strike Tay as a man who would go to such lengths to obtain it another way. With his looks and almost arrogant confidence, he would be certain to entice any woman he chose. No, she was sure Darius had another plan in mind.

Stressed and tired from the last week, Tay closed her eyes and began to doze. Memories of her mother flooded her thoughts, and for the first time, she focused on the stories that her mother had told. Tales

of life before the nobles, of the Coils, and other ephemera had dominated her youth, and she had always dismissed them before. With Lars' interest, she had been forced to re-examine the role of those stories. The Coils had never been history as such, but on reflection, they had also never been discussed in open surroundings. Any discussion of the Coils occurred in closed rooms with people you trusted. As she drifted into the clarity that sleep sometimes brought, she wondered why she had never noticed that before. Sinking into a heavier slumber, her thoughts drifted, finding different memories, darker memories. Tears slid from her eyes as she remembered a recent argument with her father. He had wanted to explain his reasons for rebelling, and she had not understood. When he had been dragged from their house, Tay had almost felt vindication, hollow though it was. Rebellions and riots never did any good. She rolled onto her side, and clenched her eyes tightly shut, trying to still her troublesome mind. Several deep breaths and her thoughts began to clear, allowing her to find enough peace to sleep.

She woke some time later. The sky was darker, and long shadows stretched across the room. With a sigh, she pushed herself off the bed and flicked the small switch that turned on the light. In the cool glow of the bulb, she stared at herself in the mirror. Her hair, which had been curled and pinned into the latest style, was lightly mussed from her doze. She wore a long skirt in heavy green twill, a matching jacket, and beneath it all, a fine cotton blouse in white. With the small, pillbox

hat pinned to her hair, she had to admit that she at least looked the part of a wealthy lady. Tugging at the hairpins, she dragged the hat from her head to reveal the cleverly pinned, and elegant-looking, hairstyle. Her brown locks had been teased into ringlets, and secured with silver-tipped hatpins to the crown of her head. For a long moment, she stared at her reflection, noting the richness of her dress with a strange mixture of envy and frustration. Any one of the pins adorning her hair would feed her family for days. Turning away from the mirror, she removed the green jacket and placed it on the back of the chair.

She reached beneath the bed and drew out the small attaché case that had been left for her. Placing the small box on the bed, she crossed the room, and turned the flimsy lock on the door, giving her some small measure of privacy. Taking a deep breath, she turned back to face the box. It laid on the crisp bed sheets like a sleeping tiger, and she watched it for a few moments, as though concerned it would harm her. Shaking her head to clear it of worrying thoughts, she hesitantly stepped forward and undid the latch on the small case. A tray of various cosmetics met her eyes as she lifted the lid, but she paid them no attention, as she reached to the top right-hand corner, and pressed twice. There was a click, and the deep cosmetics tray lifted free to reveal a large, metal disc. Gingerly she reached her hands forward and picked up the item. Lars had given her a brief tutorial on how to use the recorders, and while it seemed simple enough, she still hadn't worked out how she would gain access to

them. Despite her assumed parentage, she doubted that she would be allowed to visit the records office, and it was even less likely that she would be there for long enough to steal the shipping records. Running her fingers over the notched edge of the disc, Tay pondered her options, which were depressingly few. Not for the first time, she wondered why she had agreed to spy for the resistance, and whether it could be managed at all.

There was a sudden jolt, and the train screeched to a halt. Tay fell forward, the disc dropping from her hands as she landed on the bed, her knees stinging painfully as they collided with the wooden bed frame. Silence settled over the carriage as she began to pick herself up. The luxurious cabin now felt oppressive, more of a trap than it had been before. With careful fingers, she lifted the disc from the floor and returned it to the box, fumbling the cosmetics back into place as shouts sounded from other parts of the train.

"Lyana." Darius' voice echoed through the door as he rattled the door handle. "Are you hurt?" Tay had to give him some credit, he sounded genuinely concerned.

"I'm fine," she called back as she shoved the case back under the bed. Standing up, she walked back toward the door and popped the lock. Casting a quick glance at the bed, she reassured herself that the box was out of sight before she opened the door. Behind Darius, two of the train guards waited with weapons in their hands.

"What's going on?" she asked, as Darius curled his fingers about her upper arm.

"We think rebels," he replied carefully, as he drew her into the hallway. Tay felt her stomach clench at his words. It was unusual for rebels to attack the transports of the nobility, but not unheard of. "We should stay in the parlour, just in case," he continued, guiding her along the corridor.

"But how?" she asked as he pushed open the door, and took a spare weapon from one of the men.

"They would have blocked the line," he answered tersely, as he indicated that she sit behind the bar and out of sight. "It's easy to do out here."

Tay slid to the floor, blocking out the fear with the sound of his words. "Surely the guards..." She almost chortled to herself at the thought of expecting help from that quarter, but the hope was there. She was currently dressed as a noble and as such, her chances to escape unscathed had dropped.

"It's hard to guard out here." Darius rested his back against the wall of the bar. "There's too much space for a sufficient presence." He nodded at the window. "The farms and warehouses can be guarded effectively, but once out in the countryside, the train is reliant on the guard it carries."

"So" — she disliked the tremor that entered her voice — "what's going to happen?"

Darius glanced down at her but did not answer, leaving Tay to imagine what fate could be in store for them. Silence settled between them, stretched taut with unspoken fears and secrets. Resting back against the cabinet, Tay tried to keep her hands from shaking. After

a moment, Darius moved forward and sat down beside her.

"It's alright." His voice was soft, gentle and reassuring as he reached out and took hold of her hand. She almost flinched at the warm pressure of his fingers but controlled the impulse, conscious of the watching guard. "Nothing's going to happen to you." Tay glanced up at him, confused for a moment by his manner. He winked at her and continued, "Don't worry about it, sis." With those words, Tay understood, he was reinforcing the image the guard had of them as siblings, and she had a role to play.

"Easy for you to say." The joking tone was forced, but the guard could interpret it as nerves over the situation. "You're holding a gun."

"Do you think I'm daft enough to hand you a weapon?" Teasing tones rippled through his voice. "You're far more likely to shoot me than any intruder."

"Well, you'd probably deserve it," she joked back, encouraged by the familiar notes of sibling teasing. If she relaxed, she could almost pretend that he was an older brother.

"And that's why you don't get a gun," he finished, as a door swung open behind them. Darius stood up and faced the newcomer. "Well?" he asked, and there was no trace of the humour in his voice as he stared at the guard.

"We've checked the obstruction."

"And..."

"It was a fallen tree," the guard clarified, staring

straight at the lapels on Darius' shirt. "No sign of rebel activity, and the train staff are clearing it from the track as we speak."

"Excellent." Tay looked at Darius, impressed at the crisp, curt notes of command that infused his voice. "Is that all?"

"That's all sir."

"Good, then get on with your work." Darius dismissed the guard with barely a glance, and held out his hand to Tay. "See," he continued in a lighter tone, "there was no need to furnish you with a weapon." Tay gave a watery smile as she took hold of his hand, and he helped her to her feet.

"You two can go as well." Darius nodded at the remaining guards and waited for them to leave. As the door clicked shut, Darius released his hold on her hand, and strode back to his chair. Settling back against the cushions, Darius regarded her carefully.

"Sit down," he suggested as a loud whistle screeched from outside of the train. Tay took an involuntary step forward as the train jolted into motion, and she caught hold of the bartop to steady herself. With careful steps, she crossed the carriage and dropped into one of the chairs. The engine picked up pace, and soon they were flying through the landscape at much faster speeds than before. Tay chanced a look out of the window, only to be disappointed at the high embankments that laid on either side of them. With nowhere else to place her gaze, her eyes returned to Darius.

"Does this happen often?" she asked, more out of a

need to fill the uncomfortable silence than for anything else.

"More often than you think." Darius reached out and picked up a slender book from the table before him. "Here." He beckoned her forward, flipping open the book as he did so. Tay leant forward and stared down at the line drawing in front of her.

"What is it?" she asked, looking at the curious shapes and notations that covered the double page of the book.

"Haven't you ever seen a map before?" She shook her head as he traced his fingers across the surface of the page, following a line in bold, shaped like a ladder. "This is the railway," he said, his voice soft and instructional. "The Factory and its surrounding district are up here." Tay followed the direction of his finger to the large dot at the top of the ladder. "All of this is farmland." He swept across the map, indicating the terrain to either side of the track, from the Factory southward. "And here" — Tay looked down at the section of map labelled 'Borderland' — " is the area we're currently travelling through."

Tay reached out and drew the map closer, staring at the landmarks and locations that she had only heard about. The City laid on the far-eastern edge of the map. The Factory and Mine were in the Northernmost section. Several other settlements were dotted about the landscape in a haphazard fashion.

"And as you can see, we're quite a distance away from help," he finished, watching her face as her eyes scanned the book before her.

"Is that the forest?" She pointed to the light green shading that edged the map close to the city. Darius nodded, and Tay thought back to the scant lessons in geography that had been given at her school. The forest surrounded the country, save on the western border which opened to the sea, and no one knew what laid beyond. Her fingers timidly reached out and, when Darius made no protest, settled against the page. "Do you know what's beyond?" she asked, her voice almost a whisper.

"No." he answered just as softly. "Only the King and his top advisors know what is beyond the Forest."

"Do they know about the Coils of Copper and Brass?" Tay mused, lost in contemplation of the map before her.

"You mean the fairy tale?" Her head jerked upward at the sharpness in his voice. He was staring straight at her and, as she met his eyes, he shook his head.

"Yes," she replied, taking note of his warning. "I guess I'd like to believe it was true." Her eyes found the window again, and she continued, "I can't imagine a blue sky."

"No" — Darius reached forward and closed the book — " I can't either." Quiet descended between them, leaving only the clatter of wheels on rails. With a sigh, Darius settled back against his chair and closed his eyes. Taking advantage of his inattention, Tay took the opportunity to cease her contemplation of the world beyond the train window and regard Darius with nervous curiosity. Why had her question about the

Coils rattled him so much? She had never considered the tale anything other than a fairy story related to her by her mother, and his reaction troubled her.

"Why don't you sleep?" She jumped as his eyes snapped open and fixed on her. "It's been a disturbing trip so far."

"I'd rather stay here," Tay answered, unwilling to return to her cabin just yet. "I can't sleep during the day," she lied. Though the thought of sleeping through the remainder of the train journey appealed to her, she couldn't risk losing the opportunity to discover fresh information. "You were talking about the forest..." she prompted, delaying his efforts to feign sleep.

"I don't know much about it," he replied, bringing his fingers to rest beneath his chin as he leant forward. "It's one of the few places that's only accessible to the royal family, and select members of the Clockwork Temple." A stray strand of hair fell in front of his eyes, and he brushed it away with a careless gesture. "Information is very scarce concerning the forest."

Tay turned the information over in her mind. Her teachers had known little about the woods, it was generally assumed that the merchant families had full and exclusive access, which Darius had effectively denied. It was entirely possible that he had lied, but she didn't think so.

"Are any of the rumours true?" Curiosity won out over nerves as she asked one of the questions that raced through her mind. Rumours abounded about the forest, they ranged from the mundane, with tales of great

wealth, to the ludicrous and stories of monsters. To her knowledge, no one had managed to confirm any of the claims made about the woods, They were as big a mystery as the Coils of Copper and Brass.

"Which ones?" His eyes fell on hers, and she was startled by the sparkle of humour she saw there.

"Monsters?" She decided to start with the most ludicrous claim.

"Ahh, yes." An amused chuckle escaped his lips. "That's the story we were told as children."

"So is it true?" she pressed, her nerves forgotten as she joined in the laughter that spilt from his mouth.

"Not that I've seen, but" — he forestalled her next question with a raise of his hand — "I wouldn't put it past the King."

"Is he that bad?" She sobered slightly with the thought of the next few days in royal company.

Darius did not answer, but she caught the look he levelled at her and swallowed nervously. Tendrils of fear coiled about her as she focused on the next few days, and the small measure of hilarity between them died.

"I didn't mean to upset you." Darius' voice interrupted her train of thought, and she looked back at him. "Will you be alright?"

She nodded, determined to not let him see too much of her fear.

"In any case," Darius continued, "it'll be dinner soon, and we can continue this conversation later."

Tay nodded as she recognised the clear dismissal in his voice. What she wished to discuss clearly laid in the

realm of those secretive conversations that were only to be discussed in absolute privacy. She stood and walked toward the rear of the carriage and her cabin. The rest of the trip promised to be strange, stilted and awkward, filled with topics that she was forbidden to discuss. As she fell on the bed, she once again wondered why she had agreed to this charade.

Chapter 12

Snow drifted across the platform as she stepped down from the train, and into the hustle and bustle of the crowded terminal. As the servants unloaded the luggage they had brought with them, Tay stared about in wonder. Unlike at the station near the Factory, people here swarmed across the surface of the platform, moving briskly from one train to another. Porters and servants were in evidence, but the biggest crowd were those of the merchant class. Women in small, pillbox hats carrying umbrellas mingled with aristocratic-looking gentlemen, and harried-looking Centre workers.

"Don't get lost." Darius caught hold of her hand and drew her away from the train. Several porters trailed behind them, lugging the heavy suitcases and trunks toward the station's exit.

"I had no idea there were so many destinations," Tay whispered, her eyes wide at the sights and sounds around her.

"This is the hub for the country." His fingers tightened on her arm as he led her from the station and onto the main street. "Trains go from here all the way to the sea." Bitingly cold winds swept across her skin as they walked toward a small building just outside the station. Horseless carriages moved along the road, the noise and smoke reminded Tay of the Factory, yet these carriages ferried the wealthy from place to place. Across from the station, a large building dominated the skyline, and Tay stared in disbelief at the heavily ornamented spires that seemed to brush the sky. Used as she was to buildings of only two or three stories, the sight of a twenty story construct boggled her mind, and it took all of Tay's self-control not to stare in fascination.

Despite Tay's tendency to stare at everything she saw, they reached the waiting area in no time and stepped out of the bitter wind. Darius immediately walked to the counter on the other side of the room and requested a taxi. Tay, feeling dwarfed by the experience, sank into one of the comfortable chairs. A fire burned brightly in the hearth, and the room was deliciously warm in contrast to the weather outside. A quiet servant placed warm drinks on the small side table, and Tay sipped carefully as Darius returned to her side.

"So, how long are we going to be here?"

"Not long." A gust of wind rattled the windows as Darius picked up his own cup and took a drink. "Long enough to finish our drinks, then head to the Palace."

Liquid slopped over the edge of the cup, scalding her fingers, as his words forcibly reminded her of her task. Several small tremors rippled through her body and shook her fingers. The cup landed back in its saucer with a loud clunk, as Tay shakily set it down.

"We're going to the Palace now?" A scared squeak escaped her lips, and Darius raised his eyebrows at her.

"Of course," he answered calmly as he placed the cup into its rightful place. "You need to be settled before the ball."

"Give me a moment." Tay stood, and tried not to race across the room toward the toilets. She pushed open the door and headed for the ladies. Her heart thumped like a hammer in her chest, and she felt sick. The door to the waiting area opened behind her, and with several long strides Darius caught up to her. As the door swung closed behind them, his fingers dug into her shoulder and turned her to face him.

"Look at me." She raised her head, her breath catching as she looked straight into the intense blue of his eyes. Time stopped for a moment as he looked down at her, gaze softening as he took in the panic in her eyes. "It will be fine." Gentle and reassuring, his voice drifted across her ears, and she craved to hear more. "You won't be abandoned."

"But..." The door opened behind them, and she choked back the words, conscious of who she was pretending to be. "I don't know the court," she managed, almost choking with the weight of the lies on her tongue.

"All you need to know, I'll teach you." Approval at her quick-thinking shone in his eyes, and he smiled. He dropped his hands from her shoulders and handed her a handkerchief. "I have as much riding on this as you do." A soft reminder of his own danger drifted between them, as she reached up and took the square of white cotton.

"Do you promise?" Much as she didn't want to, Tay needed the reassurance that only he could give.

"I do." With that simple statement, he stepped away from her and nodded back at the waiting room. "Shall we go back in?"

Tay hesitated for several long moments before she nodded and headed back toward the waiting area.

"I understand your worry, sis," Darius declared as they walked over the threshold, and back into the room, "but you'll be fine."

"I know," Tay forced herself to answer, as he pulled out her chair for her, and she sat down. Sipping the remnants of the rapidly cooling drink, Tay spent the rest of the time in deep thought. Darius was an enigma, the menace and power that he wielded were easier to deal with than this gentle reassurance. The memory of his fingers pressed against her upper arms lingered in her mind, and she cast a covert glance over the top of her coffee cup at him. With his face hidden behind a large paper, only his hands were visible, with those fine-boned fingers that had gripped her upper arms with such strength. When the door opened to announce the arrival of the taxi, she dragged her eyes away, strangely

troubled by the thoughts that had begun to run through her head.

The taxi had no horses hitched to the front of its dark green and brass chassis. A liveried footman from the waiting area held the door, and she climbed inside, grateful that the real Lyana had covered this aspect of ladylike behaviour in her week of training. The door closed as Darius took the seat opposite and with a jolt, the vehicle began to move. She stiffened at the strangely smooth motion, and stared out of the window, watching the streets go by in a blur of snow and colour. The City was larger than she could ever have dreamed. Shops, homes and businesses began to blur into one as the minutes passed.

"There's the academy over there," Darius interrupted her train of thought, as he pointed to the left-hand side of the road. An ornately carved, stone building rose up from a crowd of smaller ones, its gates padlocked shut. "Term starts again in March."

"So far ahead?" Tay asked, interested despite herself as the main gates drifted out of sight.

"With all the social events through the winter, it isn't viable to keep it open."

Tay craned her head to stare back at the forbidding structure, she had heard many tales about the Academy. Unlike the people in the Factory area, the children of the Merchant set were educated at the Academy. It took students from four to twenty-one and trained them in the ways of power.

"Do you still go?" She glanced up, curious as to his

actual age.

"I've got a year to go," he said, causing Tay to glance up at him in interest. He was only two years older than she was. They drove away from the campus, and soon they turned onto a broad, yet strangely empty boulevard. The buildings on either side of the road were large and set in tree-filled grounds.

"Palace District," he answered her unasked question, as they travelled past mansions that could house half of Tay's street. As with the station area, the streets here were populated by the wealthy. Even though snow fell heavily over the City, the rich and famous still paraded themselves as they preened in warm, expensive furs. The taxi pulled up at a stop sign, and Tay stared out of the window in disbelief.

"It's freezing," she declared in shock. "Why are they outside?"

"To show off." Darius moved and sat beside her. "You should know that feeling sister." Tay flicked her eyes at him, but he ignored her as he began to point out the different families and their most pertinent secrets.

"The Palace is just ahead," the taxi driver called over his shoulder, and both Tay and Darius fell silent as they approached a set of tall and wide double gates. As the taxi drew to a close, a man dressed in the garb of a soldier walked out of the gatehouse and approached the vehicle.

"I'll do the talking." Tay nodded, as the driver wound down the window and let a flurry of snow drift

into the carriage.

Darius leant forward and began to talk to the guard, as Tay let her eyes wander. The gate was set into an even taller, deep, wall that stretched off into the distance on either side. Beyond the gate, a long road led out of sight through the largest park she had ever seen. Snow-covered trees and hedgerows were dotted across the vast expanse, and she was reminded of the farmland they had travelled through to get here. Stunned by the space before her, she barely noticed when the guard shut the door and waved them through.

The driveway was long and sweeping. On either side of the road, snow-covered fields laid in an unbroken line to the edge of a forest. Stunned by the quiet, and sheer beauty, Tay said little as the carriage rolled toward the large, imposing building in the distance. Made of a golden stone, the building was a large, square, three storey structure with turrets on each corner. As they drew nearer, Tay pressed her nose to the cold glass, struck dumb by the magnificence before her.

They came to a halt before a large set of double doors. Several porters rushed out of the building to remove the trunks from the back of the taxi. Still petrified by the building before her, Tay said little, as Darius took hold of her arm and helped her exit the vehicle. The building loomed above her, and she shrank back against Darius' arm, intimidated by the structure.

"This is Lloyd." He indicated a slender man dressed in a dull grey suit. "He's been assigned to run our staff while we're here." Tay suppressed a wild giggle as the

man bent into a deep bow. "He'll make sure that our stay runs smoothly."

"This way sir, miss." Lloyd led them up steps swept free of snow, to the main door which remained closed.

"How do we get in?" Tay asked, shivering as another blast of bitterly cold, snow-laden air buffeted them.

"Like this miss," Lloyd replied, as he reached into a pocket, and removed a small, elegantly carved fob watch. With his thumb and forefinger gripping the edges of the watch, he reached forward and pressed it into a small indentation that laid on the side of the door. A click sounded, and he began to rotate the small brass case, first to the right and then to the left.

"It's a combination," Darius whispered at Tay's look of curiosity. "No keys, just the fob watch and a memorised set of rotations."

"I see." As Lloyd continued to turn the watch, Tay's thoughts drifted back to Lars and Cody. How could they have thought it would be easy to steal information from the Palace? As the watch clicked from right to left, Tay began to wonder how she would be able to seek out any information, if all of the doors within the Palace were locked in this fashion.

The clicking noise stopped, and Lloyd straightened up. Pressing his palm against the door, he gave a gentle push, and the door swung noiselessly open. Grateful for the opportunity to escape the wind, Tay followed the man inside, only to stop in stunned wonder at the sight of the hallway beyond the door.

Criss-crossed with wrought iron, a vaulted glass

ceiling arched over their heads and bathed the hall in natural light.

"How do they keep it clear of snow?" Tay asked in a hushed whisper, as they followed the servant toward a set of double doors.

"Spiders." Lloyd answered before Darius could, and he pointed to the wall, and what Tay had assumed were decorative brass plaques. Arranged at regular intervals, the plaques were, on closer inspection, large, eight-legged mechanical spiders. "They can be tasked to perform several roles," Lloyd continued, as Tay leant in closer to have a look, "not the least of which is keeping the roof clear of snow."

"Oh." Tay took a closer look at the still objects, the kernel of an idea forming in her mind as she stared at their articulated bodies.

"Lyana." Darius' voice drew her from her contemplation, and she followed them deeper into the Palace. With each step, her sense of wonder at the decadent surroundings grew. Thick carpet absorbed the sound of their footsteps, and elegant glass lamps were attached to the walls at regular intervals. Each of the tables in the hall was made of a lustrous, honey-coloured wood, and exquisitely decorated. On the walls, several large paintings captured her interest. Landscapes met her vision, and she leant in closer, following the image of coastline and harbour with fascination. Stepping back from the seascape, she turned to stare at the richly coloured canvas behind her. Intrigued by the picture, Tay walked closer and peered at the painting. A

white tower, gleaming in a painted shaft of sunlight, stood against a backdrop of dark, densely packed trees. Fascinated, Tay moved closer, tracing the lines of the picture with her eyes. A wide river flowed parallel to the tower, and off into the woods.

"Lyana." With a jolt, she turned her attention back to the room, and the waiting Lloyd and Darius.

"Sorry." With a last look at the canvas behind her, Tay followed the other two through the doors and into the room beyond.

"Our apartments are through here," Darius said as he led the way through the long, panelled room. Their feet sounded loudly against the polished, wooden floor, but Tay did not notice, too enthralled by the mother of pearl inlay to the panelling.

"So what's this room used for?" Tay asked as she tore her eyes away from the marble statues that graced each alcove.

"This is one of the ballrooms," Lloyd answered again, as he hurried beside them. "It will be in use tomorrow."

Tay stared up at the chandelier that hung from the centre of the room and tried not to gape at the number of lights attached to it. Lloyd led them through the room and out into another hallway, which was as quiet as the rest.

"Here." They stopped before a set of elegantly carved doors, and Tay watched in interest as Darius reached for a button set into the side of the door. There was a bell tone and the doors slid open to reveal a small, box-

shaped room. Lloyd entered the room and turned back to face them. "Miss." He stepped aside and waited.

"What is this?" Tay took a step back, unnerved by the sight before her. "I thought we were going to our apartments."

A sound that could have been a stifled chuckle escaped Darius' lips, and he leant forward.

"This is an elevator, sister dearest," he said, with what could only be described as brotherly condescension. "You remember, we discussed them."

"Oh." Tay turned bright red and clasped her hand to her mouth. Darius and Lyana had indeed mentioned an elevator, but she had forgotten that conversation in the excitement and wonder that the trip had inspired. "Of course." She attempted a dismissive laugh, but it was clear that it fooled no one. If Lloyd were anything like the servants at the Frazers' home, her faux pas would spread through the kitchen like wildfire.

"Please." Lloyd indicated the room for the second time, and she walked forward with trepidation, Darius following close behind her. Once all three stood within the small space, Lloyd reached forward and pulled the two sets of doors closed. The light from the hallway beyond was replaced by the dim light that emanated from a glow-ball light that was attached to the wall. Tay felt uncomfortable as the small room darkened, completing the illusion that they were standing in a coffin. Her mind supplied the unhelpful thought as Lloyd pressed the second of the three buttons beside the door. There was a shudder, and the elevator began to

move. Tay jumped, the sensation of travelling upward vaguely unpleasant, and she gritted her teeth in an effort to remain calm. With agonising slowness, the elevator moved between the floors. Tay clenched her hands at her sides, breathing long, steady breaths in through her nose. The enclosed space seemed to heighten her senses. In the awkward stillness, she could smell the cologne that Darius used. The musky, slightly spicy scent filled her nostrils, and she closed her eyes, clinging to the scent as a distraction from the stale elevator air.

There was a clunk, and they came to a stop. Tay opened her eyes, as Lloyd pulled open the door.

"I know the way from here," Darius said as he took hold of her arm, and escorted her back to the hallway. Without a backward glance, Darius led her along the dimly-lit hall, and toward the door at the end.

"Here we are." Darius stepped into the large room, and she stopped in shock. A large window dominated the right-hand wall, overlooking the snow-laden gardens. A fireplace sat on the opposite wall, a coffee table and two sofas laid out before it. Several paintings adorned the walls, their rich colours warm against the pale walls. A deep pile carpet laid on the floor, and Tay stepped out of her boots so she could wriggle her toes in the warm expanse. A large bookcase stood next to the fire, and Tay ran her fingers along the spines of books bound in leather and gold.

"Your rooms are through there." She raised her head as Darius spoke, and took note of the direction he was

pointing. "Your maid has been sent up and should be waiting for you."

"Thanks." Nervous once more, she turned to face the door he had indicated, and she stepped through into a smaller living room. A large stove sat in the middle of the chamber, bordered by two, curved, high-backed sofas. Bookcases lined the walls, and her estimation of Lyana etched up to a notch. Another door laid on the left-hand wall, and she walked toward it, dread in every step.

Chapter 13

The door swung open before she could reach it, and a figure walked in from the other room. Tay stopped moving, shock freezing her in place. Stunned into silence, she could only gape in disbelief.

"Surprised?" A cheeky smile creased Beth's features, as Tay slowly sank into one of the chairs, too stunned to think.

"How?" she stammered out eventually, as Beth moved to stand beside her. "How do you..." A peculiar rushing sound filled her ears, and she leant forward, placing her head between her legs as she tried to control her breathing. The sofa sank a little as Beth sat next to her.

"It was Lars' idea." A hand reached out and gently patted her on the back.

"How do you know Lars?" Tay was struggling to understand. The unreality of the situation made her head swim, and panicked thoughts of discovery whirled

through her mind. She moaned and pressed her hands to her face.

"He's my older brother." Beth slid her arm across Tay's back. "He said you might need help."

"I don't understand." Tay lowered her hands and stared Beth in the face. "Why does Lars need me to spy for them?" Anger bubbled within her. "They already have you in the house. Why do I have to do this?" Beth's hand dropped from her shoulder. "I'm already stuck doing this thing for Darius, why do I have to do this as well?"

"Tay, I didn't know he got you involved."

"But you knew about my parents." Tay pushed herself out of the chair. "You knew about my situation." Beth reached out a hand toward her, but she slapped it down. "Why do I have to do this?"

"Because Darius didn't ask me," Beth answered. "And when I found out, I told my brother I'd have to help you."

"Help?" Tay snapped back. "Or to make sure I do my job?"

"Help," Beth repeated firmly, as she handed Tay a handkerchief. "I'm sorry he put this on you, but it's done now."

Tay dabbed the angry tears from her eyes and paced across the floor.

"So what about Darius?" she asked, as a troubling thought occurred to her. "He knows you work next door..."

"It's fine," Beth interrupted.

"How?"

The door to the wardrobe opened, and Beth began rummaging through its contents. "He trusts me," was her only answer as she began to pull garments free. "Come on, we have to get you ready for dinner."

"Dinner?" Sudden terror filled her voice, drowning her concerns about Darius. "You mean I have to go down and meet people?"

"Yes." Beth removed a robe from the cupboard and placed it on the bed. "Now come on, you can't do your job if you're stuck in your room."

"But that's not what..." Anger flared into life as Tay whirled on her heel, and strode back toward the main suite.

"Darius." Throwing open the door, she stalked toward him, noting his flinch with a hint of satisfaction.

"Is there a problem?" he asked, the mild question fuelling Tay's anger.

"You're damned right there is," she snarled back, pacing the room with the energy of a caged tiger. "Why didn't you let me know that I had to go to dinner this evening?"

"Didn't I?" he asked, his voice deceptively mild.

"No, you bloody didn't," Tay snapped back, anger making her voice sharp. "You only said I had to go to the damned ball." Her hands closed into fists. "You never said anything about a dinner."

"You can handle it." He opened a nearby cupboard, and drew out a dark green bottle.

"Don't give me that," she retorted. "You said I had to sign a document, not socialise." Ragged breaths escaped her lips as she tried to stave off angry tears. "This isn't going to work."

"It will work," Darius replied, pouring a glass of wine. Placing the bottle back in the cupboard, he turned to face her. "Because you will make it work." He took a sip, and settled down onto one of the chairs. Taking a look at her mutinous face, he gave a sigh. "I thought you could turn it down, but apparently you have to attend." He took another sip. "You won't meet your betrothed; it's for women only and these girls are infrequent guests." Standing, he walked over to her and held out the glass. Tay ignored the proffered drink, rage still bubbling through her.

"I was beginning to think you were different," Tay said, her voice almost trembling with emotion.

"When did I ever give that impression?" he replied, after a moment's pause. "But this is something you have to attend." He returned his glass to the table. "If I could get you out of it, I would, but I can't, and you have a job to do." His voice grew cooler, almost glacial in tone. "So, get on and do it."

"Fine." Tay whirled round and stormed through the door to her suite.

Beth turned as she stalked back in through the door. "What happened?"

"Don't ask," Tay snapped back, as she bent down and pulled the boots off her feet. Flinging herself onto the couch, she tried to gather her wits. "I shouldn't be

at this dinner," she complained, her words echoing slightly in the large room. "If they see me too clearly..." Shuffling forward, she pulled the coat from her shoulders and dropped it to the floor.

"No one will have met his sister," Beth replied, as she picked up the discarded boots, and placed them next to the fire, where they began to steam from the heat. "And none of the suitors will be able to meet you before the ball." Before Tay could move, Beth picked up the coat and hung it on the stand in the corner. "So, don't worry about that." She reached out a hand. "Just try not to say too much."

Tay sighed once before she allowed Beth to drag her upright and usher her through the door into the bedroom.

"Wow." Tay stopped moving, and briefly forgot her arguments with Darius and Beth, as she walked into a brightly lit bedchamber. Decorated in deep reds and warm gold, the room was rich and inviting. Heavy red drapes hung at the windows that graced the north and east walls. A subtly patterned, deep gold paper lined the walls, giving the room a welcoming glow. On the floor, a carpet in the same shade as the curtains welcomed her stockinged feet.

"Nice, huh?" Beth led her past the large, ornate bed and pushed open the door on the west wall. "What do you think of the bathroom?"

Tay poked her head through the door, and her jaw dropped at the sight of the room beyond. Larger than the bathroom at Darius' home, a tub big enough for

three laid in the centre. Ornate glass and brass lamps arced out from the walls to light the room.

Tay glanced over at Beth, her mouth struggling with the words to describe the luxury she saw before her.

"I know," Beth said, as she walked past her, and turned on the taps. "And back near the Factory, we can only hope to get enough to stay alive." Steam drifted into the air as the bath began to fill. Beth turned back to face her. "I'm sorry for Lars, I don't know why he made you do this."

Tay sighed and sat on the edge of the bath. "I'm not angry with you." Her fingers toyed with one of the bottles. "I just feel used for no reason at all."

"Look, I'm going to help you survive this," Beth continued. "I don't want anything to happen to you." She reached out a hand. "Friends?"

Tay swallowed, before reaching out to clasp Beth's hand. "Friends," she replied, pushing the anger far from her.

"Okay." Beth pointed back to the bedroom. "Let's get you ready. Come on, get your clothes off." Tay glanced over at her and raised an eyebrow. "Well, you're hardly going to take a bath dressed, are you?" she argued, as she took hold of Tay's hand, and led her back to the bedroom.

"Fine," Tay answered, as she began to undo the buttons on her blouse, "but I get to undress myself, I'm not completely comfortable with someone else doing it." A chortle escaped Beth's lips, and Tay glared at her. "Now what?"

The other girl shrugged. "Maybe now you're uncomfortable." She smirked as she picked up the blouse that Tay had dropped to the floor. "But I'm fairly sure that you'll meet the right person, and be begging them to tear the clothes from your body."

"But that's entirely different." Tay stepped out of her skirt and scowled at the other girl as she divested herself of her undergarments. "Having someone else undress me as though it's a normal thing makes me feel like an incompetent baby." Naked, she walked into the steam-filled bathroom and looked down at the tub.

"You're not that." Beth reached into a cupboard and removed two thick towels before she tested the water. She dried her fingers on her skirt, and tapped the edge of the bath. "Hop in."

Tay bathed as Beth hurried about the room, picking out her clothing for that evening.

"I still don't understand how you managed to get assigned to me," she called through the door, "and you never mentioned that Lars was your brother." She lifted her hand from the water and marvelled at the steam that drifted from her skin.

"I didn't know you knew him," the answer came back. "But when I mentioned your name..."

"...he thought of sending you here." Tay reached out and seized hold of the bar of soap. "But how did he manage it?"

"Don't know." The bathroom door opened, and Beth walked back in. "I have to assume he has contacts that I don't know about."

"I see." Tay ducked her head beneath the water, trying to focus her thoughts. The sick, unsettled feeling still rippled through her body and she sat back up, water streaming down her face. For a moment, quiet reigned in the bathroom, broken only by the gentle splash of water. Tay's thoughts chased through her head, flashing between Darius, Lars, her family, and strangely, the last conversation at the Frazers'.

"Beth." Beth finished arranging a set of towels and turned to face her.

"What is it?"

"What did Lora mean?" With all the strain of the past few days, she still hadn't forgotten Beth's speedy retreat.

Beth stilled and nervously wet her lips. "She...err..." Her voice trembled slightly. "I have a girlfriend," she uttered eventually, the words stuttering slightly as they reached the air. "And Lora's managed to ruin friendships for me by revealing that." Tay turned the information over in her mind as Beth took an involuntary step back. "Look, I wasn't a friend for any reason other than friendship. I don't fancy every girl I meet." The words almost tripped over themselves in their bid to make themselves heard.

For a moment, Tay didn't speak, weighing the information in her mind. Did it make that much of a difference, especially considering the utter mess the rest of her life was in.

"If you want another maid..."

"No." Tay's voice echoed across the bathroom,

startling them both with its volume. "I can't do this alone." She clambered out of the bath and reached Beth's side. "I don't care what Lora says." The water ran from her body and pooled on the floor. "She's an unpleasant cow, you've been nothing but a friend, why would I do what she wants?"

Beth gave a small smile and wordlessly handed her a towel. Tay dragged the soft fabric across her body as Beth returned to the other room.

"I'll get your clothes ready." Her words echoed slightly as Tay finished drying and reached for the nearby robe. Tugging the robe closed, she returned to the bedroom, thoughts of the conversation disappearing as she faced the small stack of clothing that was lying on the bed.

"Am I going to have to wear all of this?" she asked as she stared down at the small pile in horror.

"Not all at once." Beth lifted the first dress from the mound, and held it against her. The gauzy confection of lace and organza was ice blue, and Tay shot Beth a quizzical look. "Okay, not that one." She placed the dress back on the bed and turned to the next outfit.

Half an hour passed as they moved through outfit after outfit, more than once Tay insisted that they stop and pick a dress, but Beth was adamant that she find one that was perfect for her first night in the Palace.

"It's not as if I mean to stay here," Tay protested, as a perfectly serviceable dress in dove grey was thrown back on the bed. "Why are you going out of your way to make me memorable?"

"Because if they're noticing your clothing" — Beth muttered as she rooted through the pile — "they won't notice you." A crow of triumph passed her lips as she picked up a dress in deep crimson. "Here we are."

"Red?" Tay's fingers stretched out and touched the fabric with nervous fingers. "Isn't that a bit bright?"

"Not with your colouring." Beth tugged the dress out of Tay's hands and pushed her into a chair. "Now sit still as I do your hair and makeup."

"How do you know how to do this?" Tay asked, as Beth set to work. "Aren't you a scullery maid like me?"

"One of the perks of being sent to the Overseer's house," Beth explained, through a mouth full of hairpins. "You learn to do lots of different things."

After what seemed like an age, Tay sat in an uncomfortable chair as Beth applied makeup and then combed, teased and pinned her hair into place. With each uncomfortable, and sometimes painful, tug at her hair, Tay drifted further away from the room, as her thoughts wandered to Lars and Cody. They had been very clear that they had no authority to transfer people from their assigned positions, which was why she had to see Darius about her father. Granted, she had never had an unshakeable belief in their trustworthiness, but with Beth's arrival, the little faith she had, disappeared in a cloud of suspicion.

"Now for the dress." Shaken from her thoughts, she stood and allowed Beth to dress her in the vivid, jewel-rich tones. "Stand up straight." She glanced over and scowled at Beth, but her shoulders pressed back at the

command. A hiss of pain escaped her lips as Beth drew the dress tight at the back. "Stop being a baby."

"One more word," Tay warned. She had to be here, but she was damned if she were going to take much more ordering around.

"There." Beth stepped back and pointed at the mirror. "Take a look."

Set into the side of one of the wardrobes, and etched in gilt, the full-length mirror gleamed slightly in the light. With a sigh, Tay stepped forward. Her image swam into focus, and she took a step back, startled at the reflection she saw before her. The slightly timid house maid had vanished, replaced by some richly dressed stranger. The deep crimson dress fitted in all the right places, and the rustling taffeta held a glossy sheen which glowed beneath the lights. Small clusters of jet and crystal were stitched across the bodice and full skirt, and they glittered as the light struck them.

Tay slid her fingers across the fabric before turning her attention to her hair. The dark locks had been twisted into a mass of corkscrew curls and pinned to the crown of her head beneath of jet and silver fascinator. Her makeup had been lightly applied, and her face almost vanished beneath the magnificence of the dress.

"Oh." Barely able to speak, she turned back to face Beth. "I look..."

"Beautiful," Beth answered, a slight hint of regret in her voice. "And not at all like yourself." She walked forward and brushed an imaginary bit of dust from the back of the dress. "Now you'd better get going." She

stepped back and jumped slightly as Tay flung her arms about her.

"Thank you." Now that the costume of nobility had been donned, she felt somewhat better about the whole situation. Despite the slightly underfed cast to her appearance, the dress altered her entire façade. Visions of immediately being denounced as an imposter began to fade as she stepped back, and headed for the living room. She pushed open the door and stopped at the sight of Darius sitting in one of the chairs. As the door swung open, he jumped to his feet. Tay was gratified to note that his mouth opened slightly in shock as he took in her appearance. A moment of stunned silence fell over the pair of them as each regarded the other. Darius had also dressed for dinner, and Tay ran her eyes across his elegant garb in stupefied appraisal. He had been handsome before, but now, she closed her mouth as she realised that she was staring.

"Do I look okay?" she asked, nervous with the silence that fell over the room.

"You look..." He paused for a moment, and she could almost see his mind working as his gaze slid over her. "...the part," he finished lamely, before he turned and headed for the door. "It was a good choice." He depressed the door handle, and opened the door. "Shall we?" He held out his arm and gestured to her.

Tay swallowed nervously and glanced back at Beth. The other girl flashed an encouraging smile. Tay took a deep breath, before she walked across the floor, and joined Darius in the corridor.

The door closed quietly behind them, and they walked in an uncomfortable silence toward the elevator.

As the elevator door closed, she turned to face him. "Now what?"

"You eat dinner," he replied, his voice maddeningly calm. "Quietly and with no fanfare."

"What about the others?" Questions and fears rose up to strangle her, and she wished she could talk more freely.

"What about them?" He looked down at her and modified his tone. "Talk if they talk, answer questions if asked. The tables are also mixed, so you may be seated next to someone of a higher rank." The elevator door opened, and faint sounds of music and conversation drifted toward them. Darius stepped out into the hall, but Tay hesitated, nerves freezing her in place. "I'm sorry, I couldn't get you out of it." At his apology, Tay felt some of her anger melt away. "It'll be fine." He held out his arm and nodded encouragingly. "I won't be too far away."

Slowly and with reluctance, she stretched out her fingers and took hold of his arm. Together they walked down the corridor in silence. Tay's fingers shook as they gripped his arm, and she was grateful for the makeup, as it hid her pasty and terrified face.

"There you are." Darius stopped by a wide, closed door and let go of her. She felt her hand drop to her side with something akin to loss, and she looked up at Darius, wishing that he would remain with her. The thought of navigating the social whirl beyond that door

was more than she could bear. "I'll be next door." And with that, he left her there.

Tay dithered on the threshold, wondering if she could feign some sudden illness. From beyond the heavy door, she could hear the sounds of laughter and conversation, and panic rose within her.

"Don't just stare at it." Tay jumped at the sound of the voice, and turned to face the speaker. A girl in a long dress of fuchsia and black walked toward her. "Open the door," she continued, as she drew level.

"Sorry I'm just a little nervous," Tay said, trying to control the quaver in her voice. She reached out and pushed the door open. The girl swept past her and walked sedately into the room. Tay followed slowly, taking in a room packed with more nobility than she had ever seen in her life. At each of the circular tables sat groups of young women, dressed in their finest.

"Your name, Miss?" Tay jumped and turned to face the smartly dressed footman by the door.

"T...Lyana James," Tay said, almost fumbling her assumed name in a hurry to speak.

"This way." Seemingly heedless of her slip, the footman led her to the other side of the room, and one of the smaller tables. Five other girls sat at the table, and they regarded her curiously as the footman smoothly pulled out her seat and she sat down. "Would you like a drink, Miss?" he asked, after he had placed the napkin on her lap.

"Water please." Ignorant of the choices available to her, she went with the safest option. The footman

nodded and stepped away, leaving Tay to the curious stares of the other women.

"So" — Tay turned to face the speaker, a young woman with jet black hair and dusky skin — "where are you from?"

"I'm Lyana James. My father's the Overseer of the Manufacturing sector." Her answer had been drilled into her by Lyana, and later on, Darius. Snobbery, they had explained, ran deep within the nobility, and making mention of the Factory would certainly not endear her to any of the others.

"How fascinating," one of the other girls noted, with a too-sweet smile. Tay felt heat rise to her face at the implied insult but managed not to respond. "I'm Talia Winnick. My father leads the Clockwork Temple." Tay swallowed as Talia spoke. The Clockwork Temple was responsible for all of the gadgets that maintained life. It designed lighting, token readers, and other wonders that she had only ever heard about. In the hierarchy of nobility, The Clockwork Temple was second only to the King. "I've heard so much about the Factory," Talia continued, with a nasty smile. "Can you tell me all about it?"

The rest of the girls at the table leant forward, vicious anticipation in their eyes. Tay felt her palms grow sweaty as she struggled to come up with a response. If this had been the Frazers' kitchen, she would have had no trouble in formulating an answer, but here in this strange nest of vipers, she felt lost. Talia smiled broadly as the silence lengthened, and colour

rose in Tay's cheeks.

"There's not a lot to tell," she said finally. "It's a Factory, it makes goods." The waiter appeared at her elbow with a tall glass of water, and she sipped it gratefully. "It doesn't tap dance or anything, so why are you so interested?" Talia's face reddened slightly at her words, and she opened her mouth to speak.

"I'm Amira." Another girl spoke, interrupting the impending tirade. "My family deals in the trade in exotic goods."

"Nice to meet you." Tay smiled, and with that, the rest of the table began to talk. The other three girls, Annetta, Cara and Linnett, were the younger daughters of landowners from the South Western provinces. By the time the first course had been laid on the table, she had made an enemy in Talia, a friend in Amira, and was cautiously optimistic about befriending the other three. The second course had been served and eaten when the sound of a gavel striking wood caused all conversation in the room to stop.

"Good evening." A tall woman stood up from one of the larger tables and addressed the room. "I am Matron Caline." There was a brief murmur from the room at the sound of her name. "I maintain the dignity of this household, and its affairs." Dressed in tones of grey and black, the matron certainly looked the part, and Tay watched with interest. "Tomorrow, the betrothal ball will be held." An excited chatter rose but with one wave of her hand the noise stilled. "And at that time you will flirt, dance and amuse yourselves to your heart's

content." She stopped speaking and glanced about the room. "However" — silence followed, as her piercing gaze landed on each table in turn — " until that time, you have no need to be seen alone in the company of a man you claim no relation to. Your parents have placed you into our hands, and they expect certain behaviour." Her eyes landed on Tay's table, and the group shivered at the severity in her gaze. "So woe betide any that is discovered in places they should not be. You have your apartments, and amusement can be found in other areas of the palace. Keep to these areas, and we will have no problem. Stray from these rules, and the penalties for disobeying will be severe." Speech exhausted, the woman sat back down and conversation slowly resumed.

"I've heard of her," Amira noted, after taking a sip of wine. "Last year she found the Winterson heir with the Rosen heiress, and she sent them both packing." She lowered her head, and everyone leant forward to catch hold of her words. "Both lost their betrothals."

"I heard that she's the reason the Princess is not attending this year," Linnett butted in, her voice alive with gossip. "Apparently she was caught in a compromising situation with her tutor."

"Well, I heard..."

Tay tuned out the gossip and focused on the newly arrived dessert; a warm chocolate cake with ice cream. Their talk was petty, full of dresses, dances and betrothals, and she could not feign interest in such things. All of her life had been concerned with the difficulty of finding food, and worry about the future.

In contrast, worrying about finding the right pair of shoes seemed childish. She took a forkful of cake and chewed thoughtfully, content to let the conversation drift past her.

"So, what do you think?" She jerked out of her thoughts as Linnett spoke to her. Her head snapped up from the swirling pattern of chocolate and ice cream, and stared about her. All of the other girls were staring, their eyes fixed and waiting for an answer.

"Err..." She stammered slightly as she struggled to recall anything from the conversation. The only thing she remembered concerned the matron, and talk had certainly moved past that. The other girls shifted slightly in their seats as the silence lengthened. She wracked her brains for an answer, but nothing occurred, and before the silence grew too uncomfortable, she asked. "What about?"

"The Prince," Cara said with incredulity. "What do you think?"

"I..." Once more, the sensation of feeling trapped rose in her, and she swallowed, trying to get her emotions under control. "I haven't met him yet," she uttered, hoping that she would be let off the hook to continue with her thoughts.

"Well, I haven't met him," Amira butted in, "but I have seen him."

"And?" A small chorus surrounded her announcement, and all of the other girls, Tay included, leant forward to hear more.

"He's very handsome," Amira said, with a sigh. "And

funny." She rested her back against the chair and continued. "He came to open a new mill on my father's estate."

"So"—the group moved even closer— "details."

"He's got the most wonderful eyes," Amira gushed, as she revelled in her place, at the centre of attention. "And he seems to be laughing all the time."

"We want to know about his body," Linnett groaned, exasperated by the sentimentality that Amira seemed to display. "Is he..." She mimed something with her hands. "You know...?"

Amira blushed slightly and lowered her gaze. "Yes," she whispered as the small group around her gave genteel giggles of appreciation.

"Well, come on," Cara prodded, "tell us more. What's he like?"

"What about his voice?" Linnett interrupted and poured herself another glass of wine. There was a slight slurring, giggling quality to her voice. Tay reasoned that she had conquered tipsy, and was now racing toward being drunk.

"Screw his voice," Annetta called out, the sound of her voice carrying further than their small table, drawing looks of disapproval from the rest of the room, Matron Caline in particular. Giggling like a naughty child, she covered her hand with her mouth and tried to stifle her chuckles.

Tay felt the energy of the group wash over her for a moment. Despite the wealth they wore, it was little different from the gossip that reigned around the

Frazers' kitchen table at the end of a long day. The cook would brew a large pot of tea, and they would sit at the long wooden table, chatting and gossiping as they polished off the remnants of that day's cake. For one strange moment, she wondered if she could call these women friends, even privileged as they were. The conversation moved beyond the Prince, and they began to talk about the other men that would be at the ball. Tay followed the discussion with a little more interest, but less enthusiasm, as she suddenly remembered her task.

"Don't you have a brother?" Talia broke into her thoughts, and she looked up from the coffee cup.

"Yes," she answered finally, controlling the squeak in her voice as she readied herself to answer questions about Darius.

"Isn't he betrothed to Kaylin Amstead?" Linnett asked, with a thoughtful expression.

"No," Cara replied. "You're thinking of Rogir Tamstein. Darius James is the handsome one."

Tay felt a jolt of shock at Cara's words. True, she did consider Darius attractive, but it hadn't really occurred to her that he had made an impression elsewhere.

"He's not betrothed yet is he?" Talia pressed on with the questioning, as though none of the others had spoken.

"I don't think so." Tay cringed at her wishy-washy words. She had to be making the worst impression on this small group of people, and she struggled to find some confidence. "He hasn't said anything about it."

"He is going to be at tomorrow's ball?"

"Yes." Tay managed to inject some surety into her voice, as the group broke out into excited giggles at her words.

"You'll have to introduce me," Cara demanded, as Amira chuckled next to her.

"Of course." Tay felt mildly annoyed at the way the girls whispered and giggled, as they each asked pointed questions about Darius and who he would dance with.

The sound of the gavel struck again and the hall fell silent as the last of the crockery was cleared away. Matron Caline stood once more, and smiled across the crowd, a slow smirk that did not meet the eyes.

"Thank you for your attendance." And with that, she swept out of the dining room and away.

"Nice to meet you." Amira smiled as she pushed her chair back, and made ready to leave.

"I think we should meet for breakfast tomorrow," Linnett called, as she dragged a lemon-yellow shawl about her shoulders.

"Breakfast will be served in your rooms," Talia interjected, with a sneer. "Didn't you read the itinerary?"

"Alright then," Linnett continued, unruffled by Talia's mocking tones. "We'll meet in the library before lunch." She glanced at Talia. "I believe lunch is a communal affair."

"Deal," Annetta replied, as she picked up her small clutch bag and started to head for the door. "Tomorrow at eleven?"

There was a general nod of assent as the group stood up from the table and made ready to leave. Tay followed behind them, acutely aware of the limitations of her knowledge. The thought of attempting further conversation left her cold. They walked out into the hallway and headed for the main staircase and elevators. The babble of noise felt strangely comforting as Tay followed the crowd and away from the dining hall.

Chapter 14

Tay made her way back to her chambers with some relief. The meal had been exquisite, but she couldn't take any enjoyment from the evening. Despite her concerns about her cover, the indulgence displayed by every member of that room had sickened her. They dined well, on fine plates and in heated rooms, wearing jewels that could feed her family for a year, and still, they complained. She pushed open the door to her chambers, and walked toward the curtained windows, dropping her bag on one of the chairs as she did so. Pushing open the heavy fabric, she stared out across the grounds. Shrouded in snow, the grounds stretched away into the darkness, and the burning desire to escape once again filled her mind.

"Tay." She turned away from the scene as Beth walked in. The curtain fell from her hand and hid the vast expanse beyond. "Do you want to get out of that?"

Tay looked down at her dress and nodded. Beth led

her back into her room and began to unlace the garment as Tay stared off into space.

"Has Darius come back?" she asked.

"Not yet." Beth removed the pins in her hair, and it tumbled down around her shoulders. "Are you worried?"

"No." She stepped out of the dress and dragged on the long, soft robe that had been laid on the bed. "I just..." She hesitated, trying to work out her thoughts. She may have survived this dinner, but she didn't fancy her chances during the luncheon or the ball. Darius could at least reassure her that she was managing her cover, or give her further pointers on behaviour. "I just want to talk to him."

"Okay." Beth picked up the dress and returned it to the wardrobe. "What are you going to do about your research?" She shot Tay a meaningful glance.

"I think I'll go down to the library tonight," Tay replied, remembering her other task with a sinking sensation. "Not right now but in a couple of hours. Hopefully the place will be empty."

"Just be careful," Beth continued, as she tidied the pots on the dressing table. "I don't want to see you arrested."

"I'll be fine," Tay lied, as she placed a comforting hand on Beth's back. "Remember," she continued, with a confidence she didn't feel, "I'm a noble." She left the bedroom and sank into one of the chairs beside the fire.

"That's what I'm worried about," Beth said, letting

her hand fall to her side. "Do you know what happens to nobles who turn traitor?" Tay shook her head, fear at Beth's words insinuating its way down her spine.

Beth opened her mouth to speak, but a knock sounded at the door, making the pair of them jump.

"Lyana?" They relaxed slightly at the sound of Darius' voice, and Beth left her side. She shot a questioning glance in Tay's direction, and on her nod, opened the door.

Still dressed in his ball finery, Darius strode across the room and came to a halt beside her chair. Behind him, Beth allowed the door to close and walked back across the room to stand in the corner.

"May I join you?" Tay lifted her head and nodded, unsure of her voice. Beth's words still rang through her head, jangling her nerves. As he settled himself on the chair opposite, that strange mixture of nervous anticipation and comfort rushed through her.

"Did you have a good evening?" Softly spoken words interrupted her thoughts and reminded her of the conversation at dinner.

"It was different," she replied, attempting a smile. "The girls at my table seemed alright."

"That's good." He glanced over his shoulder at Beth. "You can retire, Beth," Darius noted as he leant back into the chair. Beth bobbed a curtsey and left the room. Without Beth's presence in the corner, the room seemed smaller, more intimate, and a tense silence flowed between them. Tay chanced a look at Darius. His eyes had closed, as he rested his head against the back of the

chair. Once more, she found her eyes tracing the lines of his face.

"Something interests you?" She jumped. He had spoken without opening his eyes.

"I wanted to ask..." Dismayed at being caught staring, she jumped onto the first explanation that came to her head. "Is this your betrothal ball as well?" His eyes snapped open and fixed on her. "I mean," she stammered out, "they asked me all these questions at the dinner, and I didn't know what to say."

Darius gave a small laugh and leant forward. "I would have thought my sister would have schooled you in the matters of the court."

"She did," Tay replied, with a bite to her voice. "But she never mentioned your status."

"Is it that important?"

"Yes," she answered, with a surety that she did not realise she possessed.

"I'm not," he replied softly, a strange, soft look in his eyes. "I was due to be engaged last year, but it fell through."

"What happened?" As soon as the words passed her lips, she wished she could take them back. They hardly knew each other, and despite the charade they were engaged in, they were not siblings. Tay held her fingers tightly clenched in her lap and tried not to fidget, uncomfortable once more in his company.

"Her parents found her someone better." Her head lifted at his words, and she regarded him carefully. If he were upset, she could not tell.

Quiet settled between them, broken only by the crackle of the fires. Tay missed the sound of the clock in her room, its monotonous ticking would have alleviated much of this oppressive silence.

"Are you to be betrothed this year?" She finally broke the silence to ask the question that was burning within her. "Or are you just here to chaperone me?"

"I'm only here to chaperone," he confirmed, a smile creasing his lips. "I'm not on the betrothal lists this year."

"Why not?" Interested, she leant forward, eager to hear what he had to say.

"I asked not to be."

"And why is that?" A nonchalant shrug rippled across his shoulders, but he did not speak. Tay felt her curiosity increase at his vague answers. "Were you upset about the failed betrothal?"

A chuckle echoed across the room; a rich, warm sound that made her flush.

"I don't have a failed love affair behind me," he said, amusement rippling through each of his words. "Though it's interesting that you seem to think that."

"No... I just..." Tay waffled, face warm with embarrassment. "I'm curious."

"About my love life?" Another chuckle and he raised an eyebrow. "Any reason?"

"Like I said," she stammered quickly, "the questions at dinner, these girls asked me things."

"About me?"

"Yes." Her voice was soft, tremulous with nervous

tension. "They're interested in you."

"And what did you, as my doting sister, say?"

"That I didn't know and I would ask."

Darius stood and walked toward the fire, staring into the flames, caught in deep thought. Tay watched for several moments, trying to control her embarrassed blushes. She hadn't meant to pry so obviously, but, she looked down at her robe and shuffled uncomfortably, he was such an enigma. Beyond the desire to handle any future conversations, she wanted to know more about him.

"I was passed over for betrothal because of my father's position," he said finally, his voice free of humour for the moment. "But I was glad of it." Tay controlled the urge to interrupt, and waited impatiently for him to continue. "My betrothed lived in the Clockwork Temple, and she felt that she could do much better than the son of a minor noble."

"I don't quite understand," Tay replied, lost in the intricacies of courtly life.

"We're a fairly minor house," Darius explained, as he returned to his chair and sat back down. "While we look after the Factory and the Mine, we do not own them." A wry smile crossed his lips. "I assure you that in the grand scheme of things, we're nothing special."

"Tell that to the families in the slum," Tay retorted, remembering the fear that his father inspired.

"Point taken." Fingers steepled beneath his chin as he stared at her. "May I ask you something?"

"Depends on what it is," Tay replied, a leaden weight

settling on her chest as she anticipated his question.

"Why were you not already in employment?" The question startled her somewhat, and she straightened up in her seat. "After all, you are of age."

"My work ended when my father lost rating." Hands twisted in her lap as she thought back to the day after her father's arrest. She had been working in the Seamstress Shop on Station Road, a small, but reasonably paid appointment, and one she enjoyed. The owner of the shop, Mrs. Carsby, had called her into the office and two Guards from the Ration Centre were standing there. She bit her lip as she remembered the fear they had inspired, and she closed her eyes.

"Tay?" His voice slid across her skin like silk, and she took a deep breath. Opening her eyes again, she continued to speak.

"The guards asked for my ration disc, which I handed over, and then" — she wet her lips with her tongue as the memory threatened to swamp her — "they wanted to go through my pockets. One of the guards held me still as the other searched me." Darius stiffened in his seat but said nothing, waiting for her to finish. "Luckily Mrs. Carsby spoke up for me." The older woman had stood up from behind her desk, and demanded they stop. "She said that I wasn't a criminal, and even if I was, they had no right to paw at me like animals, and she threw them out."

"You couldn't keep on working," Darius noted, a strange expression crossing his features as he spoke, "without your ration disc."

"No." Tay took another breath, trying to banish the dark thoughts that had begun to flow through her mind. "Mrs. Carsby wanted to keep me on, but the ration law prevented it."

"I…"

"So there's your answer," Tay interrupted his words, unwilling to hear any pity or sympathy from Darius' lips. "And now I'm going to bed." She stood up and began to walk away, feeling the familiar prick of tears at the back of her eyes. "I'll see you tomorrow."

"Tay." She heard the creak of his chair as he stood up and began to follow her. She increased her pace, the door to her bedroom promising a safe place to nurse her old, wounded feelings.

"Why won't you to talk to me?" She stopped at his voice, and half turned.

"Because you're one of them," she answered, a bitter smile on her lips. "And I'm here because you could destroy me and my family." He had the decency to bow his head as she continued. "And even if you don't betray me, someone else could, and out of the two of us, I'm the one who'll face the worse punishment." Her fingers rested against the wood of the door, and she pushed, eager to leave his company and the strange mixture of feelings that he aroused. Pushing open the door, she stepped across the threshold and closed the portal behind her. She leant back against the wood and closed her eyes, half hoping, half fearing that he would attempt to continue the conversation. She heard the click of the door to her suite and sighed. With quick

steps, she crossed the room and slid into bed. A quick adjustment to the clock at her bedside and she settled back for a few hours of potentially sporadic sleep.

Chapter 15

Sure enough, when the alarm chimed three hours later, she was alert and ready to begin her nighttime jaunt about the Palace. As quietly as she could, she drew on a dark robe and thrust the small brass recorder into a deep pocket. Taking a clockwork torch from her belongings, she headed for the door. The fire had burned low in the grate, and shadows clustered in the corners of the room. Before she left the safety of her chambers, she wound the torch and switched it on. The door opened quietly into the main suite, and she walked across the empty space on tiptoes, hoping that she would not wake Darius. The door to the hallway opened easily, and she moved quietly into the corridor. The steady white-blue beam cut through the shadowy darkness, and she headed for the steps she had seen earlier, wishing to avoid the noise of the elevator. The air was still and somehow heavy as she traversed the dark corridors, hoping that she would pass undetected.

The clock in the hall struck three as she finally descended the stairs. She navigated the space quickly, the light of the torch illuminating a path along the hallway. The spiders hung on the wall, grotesque in the pale blue light. Taking a breath, she reached out and caught hold of the first spider she reached. It lifted easily from the wall, and she cradled its scratchy, articulated form awkwardly.

With even more care, she continued to walk through the halls. She encountered no one, and despite the fears still eating at her, she began to relax. With painstakingly slow movements she pushed open the door to the library wing. There was more light here, several of the lamps were lit, and she moved even slower. The doors to both the library and records room stood open, and the sound of voices echoed from the second door. She stopped, trying to find the courage to proceed.

Her fingers firmly gripped the edges of the spider as she edged closer to the door and the voices beyond. There were at least two people in the room, she could tell that much from the conversation. With nervous, shaking fingers she wound the spider, hoping that the sound of the clockwork wouldn't draw attention. As the key ticked slowly, she felt the mechanisms in the legs twitch, and she sped up, occasionally glancing toward the door as she tried to quickly, but quietly, wind up the appliance. A voice sounded close to the door, and she stopped, breath hitching in her throat as she flattened herself against the wall, thoughts of discovery running through her mind. Prickles of unease ran

across her skin as she held her position, unwilling to move and possibly draw attention. Time ticked by as she waited, praying that whoever stood on the other side of the door would stay within. The voice grew quieter, as though the speaker had moved away, but before Tay could breathe a sigh of relief, the legs of the spider twitched again. She glanced down and watched in horror as the construct slowly began to unfurl itself. One of the legs extended outward and a clacking sound echoed out across the empty hallway.

"What's that?" a voice echoed from beyond the door, and in panic, Tay dropped the spider.

The mechanical creature whirred again as another leg extended outward, and found the floor. Tay did not wait to see any more and darted across the hallway through the open library door. Sounds of movement echoed from across the hall, and she dove behind the library door and pressed herself against the wall. A desperate prayer echoed through her mind as she heard people enter the hallway.

"How did that get there?" the first voice asked, curious, yet suspicious at the same time.

"Search the hall," the other voice replied, and she flattened herself against the wall even more as she tried to hide. She could see it was pointless, the door would be the first place they looked. Visions of being dragged off in chains ran through her mind, and she closed her eyes.

"I'll check the library." She bit her lip as she stifled the whimpers of panic that threatened to fall from her

mouth. A shadow moved through the door, and she crossed her fingers, praying for a miracle. Any moment now the guard would check behind the door, and find her. She squeezed her eyes shut as the door began to move.

"Is there a problem?" The door stopped, and Tay opened her eyes as a new voice echoed across the library. A young man stood up from one of the high-backed chairs before the fire and looked directly at the guard before him. He could not have failed to miss her, he had a clear view of her cowering form. She waited for him to point her out to the guard, and she began running through a set of painfully thin excuses for why she was out of her rooms.

"Someone set off a spider," the guard began.

"That was me." Tay started, and stared at the young man in shock. He was studiously avoiding looking at her, but she had no idea why he was covering for her.

"Sir?" The guard, evidently confused, stared at the other man in wonderment.

"I was experimenting." He stood up and walked across the room, keeping the guard's attention. Tay watched him approach, her heart in her mouth. He moved like a cat, with quick, fluid movements that barely made any sound. Dark haired with almond-shaped eyes and fine-boned features that made him look fragile, but there was nothing fragile in his gaze. He wasn't particularly tall, but something in him drew her attention, and she could not tear her eyes away.

"Of course, Sir," the guard answered, as he bowed

and moved to leave. "Will you require the spider brought to you?"

"No." Tay thought she saw his eyes flicker in her direction, but she couldn't say for sure. "I'm done with it."

"Very well." The guard turned and exited the study. The young man walked forward and slowly but firmly closed the door.

"Late night prank?" he asked. His voice was crisp and somewhat sharp, yet it wasn't unpleasant.

"Yes." Tay jumped on the offered explanation, as she tried to moderate the relief in her tone.

"At three o'clock in the morning?" A ripple of what could have been laughter flashed through his voice, and she bowed her head. "I don't buy it." He turned away from her, and returned to his chair.

"I couldn't sleep." The words spilt out without too much thought, she couldn't let this man know her reasons for roaming the castle. "I thought I'd play with one of those spiders, but when it startled the guards, I panicked."

A shrewd gleam settled across his features, and he peered at her. "And acted like a thief?"

"Yeah..." The reply hesitantly fell from her lips, and she winced inwardly at the knowing smile that crept across his face. "I mean... I was trying..." Her words stammered to a halt as he looked at her.

"Alright, don't strain yourself." He sat down and picked up one of the books on the table before his chair, dismissing her with that simple movement.

"Why are you here?" Tay asked finally, recovering from the shock enough to throw the question back to him.

"I couldn't sleep." A smirk slid across his features as he mirrored her earlier answer. "Reading sometimes helps."

Tay took several halting steps forward, and stared down at the stack of books before him. Most of the titles were obscured, but some made her pause and think.

"You're reading history?"

"No, maths." He flipped over a page, and stared at the print, undoubtedly attempting to ignore her.

Annoyance at his flippant, sarcastic manner began to supplant the nervous fear from earlier, and she answered almost without thinking. "You don't have to be rude about it."

"Then you shouldn't state the obvious." Only partially paying attention to the conversation, his words were muffled.

Tay hesitated, conscious of both his patience and the weight of the apparatus in her pocket. By rights, she should head back up to her room, but the small pile of books before the man called to her. The history taught in the Factory school was minimal, and reduced to a list of what was owed to those in power. The chance of reading a possibly accurate history was a powerful draw, and she didn't want to leave.

"Can I join you?" she asked, her voice nervous but excited at the same time.

He glanced up and stared at her quizzically. "You're in your dressing gown," he noted, with a raised eyebrow. "And I'm fairly certain that you're breaking some code of conduct."

Tay glanced down at the dark robe with a flush of embarrassment. "I won't tell if you don't," she hedged, with an effort at a conspiratorial smile.

A slow smile creased his features, and he laughed. "Fine." He indicated the pile of books before him. "Knock yourself out." He then returned to the book before him.

Tay took a couple of steps forward and sank into one of the other chairs. Like the armchairs in her room, the seat was well sprung and comfortable. She reached out, picked up one of the thickly bound books from the table, and began to read. A comfortable silence settled over the pair of them as they both lost themselves in the history that laid before them.

Chapter 16

"Come on." A hand shook her awake, and she jolted upright as a heavy book slid off her lap to land with a thump on the floor. The man stepped back as she dragged herself to her feet, and stared about her in consternation. "It's nearly six," he noted, with a small smile. "You dropped off."

Tay glanced up at the clock in the corner of the room, and almost choked at the time displayed on its face.

"I've got to get back to my room," she announced unnecessarily, as he retrieved the fallen tome and returned it to the table.

"And without being seen?"

She nodded, wondering how she could have fallen asleep so readily. "Can you...?"

Another quick grin flashed across his features, and he smiled. "Of course." He beckoned her to the corner of the room, and pressed down on a small knot hidden

in the floor. A door in the panelling slid open, and the tunnel beyond led off into the distance. "Just follow that, it'll take you to the second floor."

"Thank you," she whispered, as she pushed past him, and ducked into the passageway. Cobweb and dust free, it was clearly in frequent use.

She took several paces down the tunnel before she heard him call from the other end. "What's your name?" Tay stopped moving and stared back over her shoulder. The door was still open, and he was leaning against the frame, a curious look on his face.

"It's Maria," she lied quickly, unwilling to provide him either her real name or her alias. Despite the strangely companionable few hours she had spent in his company, she did not wish to draw too much attention to herself. Turning on her heel, she continued to head down the tunnel and back to her rooms.

True to his word, the tunnel opened out onto the second floor, and she turned onto her landing with relief. Quickly, she rushed along the corridor and pushed open the door to the suite.

"What the...?" She froze and stared out at Darius who was sitting at a newly added table, clad in a dressing gown. For a moment, neither said anything, both too stunned to speak.

"What are you...?"

"I went for a walk."

They spoke at the same time, stopped, and Darius indicated that she should continue.

"I woke early," Tay explained, unwilling to go into

the events of the night. While she was convinced that Darius had something to do with the rebellion, she wasn't willing to trust him with her secrets. "And I wanted to take a look round." She attempted nonchalance, hoping that he would buy her rapidly constructed lie.

"Like that?" he asked, nodding at the dressing gown that covered her form.

"Yes." A rapid nod to confirm the tale. "I didn't expect to see anyone."

"I see," he noted, a small smile playing about his lips. "And did you?"

"Did I what?" she asked, flustered as she always was by Darius' presence. She had expected a more intensive interrogation or at the very least a demand for an explanation. This calm, questioning manner confused her, almost as though he cared little for her night-time excursion.

"See anyone?" He reached forward and poured himself a cup of tea, seemingly disinterested in her answer.

"No," she answered, far too quickly, and she bit her lip, expecting him to call her out on her obvious lie.

"That's alright then." He set the pot of tea back down on the table and picked up his cup. "Breakfast?" he asked casually, after he took a sip of the steaming liquid, eyes fixed on her nervously twitching form.

"In a minute," she replied, moving toward her rooms with rapid footsteps. "I'll need to get dressed." She reached the door and depressed the handle.

"You'll need to improve before tonight," he said, as she pushed open the door and prepared to step into the room.

"Pardon?" She turned back, puzzlement on her face.

"Lying," he answered calmly, a concerned look on his features. "You're awful at it."

"I..." Tay stammered, struggling to find an answer for him.

"I need you to be better than this." His voice was still calm, yet he stared at her with an intensity she found unnerving. "My sister's future depends on it." With that said, he returned to the repast before him and began to attack it with gusto.

Tay stared at him for a long moment. "I'll try to be better," she whispered, before turning toward the door and walking into her quarters.

"Where the hell have you been?" Beth rushed forward and flung her arms around her. "I came up to wake you and" — she indicated the rumpled bed with a wave of her hand — " I thought something had happened to you."

"I'm sorry." Tay rested her head against her friend's shoulder, as she tried to sort out the events of the night. "I had something to do for Lars." She pulled out of Beth's grasp, and sat on the bed, disappointment running through her as she realised her failure.

"And did you?" Beth reached into the wardrobe and drew out a simple dress in royal blue, before placing it on the bed.

"I tried," Tay replied. "I couldn't get to the office."

She reached into her pocket, feeling for the brass recorder. A troubled frown crossed her face. "I'll have to try again later." She searched the other pocket, a sickening feeling running through her.

"What's wrong?" Beth asked, watching Tay root through her pockets with concern.

"Where is it?" A raw note of panic ran through her voice as she checked her pockets for the second time.

"What?" Beth looked on with concern as Tay jumped off the bed and began to rummage through the sheets. "What's wrong?"

Tay could not answer, too distraught with the loss to formulate a sentence. The search of the bedding proved fruitless, and she began to pace the floor, peering for a gleam of brass in the vibrant red of the carpet. Beth watched in shock as Tay whirled round, and headed for the door, anguish written in every angle on her face.

"Tay." Her hand whipped out and snagged her by the arm, pulling her to a stop. "What is it?"

"The item your brother gave me is gone," she whispered, the shock robbing her voice of any volume. "I dropped it."

"What?" Beth took hold of her upper arms and guided her back to the bed. "Just sit down and tell me what happened." The bed sank beneath her weight as Tay sat on the soft surface and began to chew her fingernails. "Stop that." Beth gently removed Taya's fingers from her mouth and sat before her. "Now tell me what happened?"

Tay rubbed incipient tears from her face and took a

deep breath. "Your brother gave me a recording device so I could copy the shipping records." Agitated, she stood up again and began to pace across the floor.

"Where did you leave it?" Beth let her pace, but her voice was tinged with concern. "In the records room?"

"No, no" — Tay stopped pacing and shook her head — "I never got into the records room." She closed her eyes and steeled herself for what was to come. "I heard the guards, so I hid in the library."

"So you dropped it there," Beth interrupted, sure that she had solved the problem.

"I think so." Tay covered her face with her hands and sighed. "But it's worse than that, I saw someone in there when I hid... If he saw it fall..."

"Is everything alright?" The door swung open, and Darius poked his head into the room. "I heard raised voices."

"Everything's fine," Tay began, only to be cut off by Beth who faced Darius directly.

"She dropped the recorder in the library." As Tay stared on in shock, Darius turned to face her, a visibly frustrated look on his face.

"Was anything on it?" he asked, his voice mild.

"I don't unders..."

"Was there anything on it?" he asked again, overriding her words with some impatience.

"No." Tay glanced from Beth to Darius in confusion. "I didn't get the chance to use it."

"Well that's a blessing at least," he uttered, as he sat down on the bed. "Tell me what happened?"

"Why should I?" Tay replied, anger finally winning out over confusion. "What's your part in this? I thought you just knew her through her working at your home?" Darius began to interrupt but she kept going, fury fuelling each word as the sense of betrayal began to deepen. "What else are you keeping from me?"

"Alright, so we've lied a bit."

"A bit?" Tay threw a furious look at Beth, who had the decency to appear ashamed. "Was this all a set-up?" She thought back to the week with his sister, and beyond. Had they all lied to her? A sick feeling rushed through her body, and she sank into a chair, holding her head in her hands. "Your sister?" She glanced up in pure loathing as another thought occurred. "My father?"

"No." Darius shook his head as he reached out a hand toward her. "Your father was a good friend of mine."

"You claimed not to know him." He drew his hand away as Tay slapped at his fingers.

"Not true," Darius corrected. "I downplayed my association."

"But you still let me believe that I had to pay this debt." Horror flowed through her voice. "Why make me go through this if you would have helped my father anyway?"

"Because I couldn't just tell you about my association," he replied, his rich voice comforting despite her rage. "I didn't know how it stood with you; Caleb never mentioned that you were involved." Tay

raised her head and looked into his eyes. "People know that I can fix certain things, but they all know I don't do it for free." He glanced skyward and continued. "If I hadn't asked for the favour, it would have been out of character."

"He wasn't going to ask for it," Beth replied, "until Lyana."

"So Lyana is pregnant?"

"She is, and I did need someone to take her place."

"He would have used me," Beth interjected smoothly, "but I don't look anything like her."

"But why did your brother ask for those files when he" — she pointed at Darius — " could have gotten them?"

"I'm being watched," he replied simply. "They know that someone in the nobility is aiding the rebellion, and I'm under suspicion."

"Why couldn't Beth?"

"Because my brother never asks me to spy for him," Beth replied. "He wants me to stay under the radar as much as possible."

Tay took several deep breaths as she tried to reconcile this new information. "So you just decided to use me for your own ends?"

Beth winced at the anger in her voice. "No... We just..."

"Why couldn't you just tell me?" Tay's gaze fell on Beth and Darius in turn, and both looked away. "I wouldn't have been involved in this shit if I had known..."

"Yes, you wouldn't be here," Darius retaliated, his voice sharp. "I apologise for misleading you, but it's done now. Make no mistake, you're in as deep as we are."

Tay took a deep breath as the implication of his words hit her. "You would turn me in?"

"No." Beth reached her side and glared at Darius. "No, we wouldn't do that."

"But you are guilty by association," he noted quietly. "They won't care that we tricked you into this, with your parent's records and the falsification of the ration records against you." Tay felt her stomach lurch as he spoke.

"They'd..." She couldn't finish the sentence, thoughts of the Mine, and worse, raising an ugly spectre in her head.

"We won't let it come to that," Beth reassured, casting a disapproving glance at Darius as she spoke.

Tay barely heard the words, still fixated on their betrayal, and the thought of being incarcerated. Lifting her head, she glanced across at Darius, and he flinched at the raw hatred on her face.

"No." He softened his voice, apology coating each word. "We will keep you safe."

"How thoughtful," Tay finally replied, her voice snarling out from behind clenched teeth. "You've managed to snare me into this, and now you expect me to trust you?"

"Tay..."

"Get out," she ordered, anger making her voice

sharp. "Leave me alone." Darius stared at her for one long moment before he bowed his head and turned to go.

"Both of you." Tay turned her gaze to Beth and waited.

"I'm still on your side." Tay barely lifted her head at her words. "I wasn't lying all the time, I'm your friend."

"And I only have your word for that."

"I guess I earned that," Beth murmured, as she walked toward the door. "I'm sorry for lying to you." Tay looked away, unwilling to find any forgiveness for the pair of them. Beth followed Darius to the rooms beyond. The door shut behind them, and Tay threw herself across the bed, large tears of anger streaming down her face.

Chapter 17

The tears had long dried by the time she plucked up the courage to leave her bedroom and face the world beyond. The small sitting room was empty, yet she could hear voices coming from the main suite. Taking a deep breath, she laid a hand on the handle and opened the door. Darius and Beth stopped talking as they watched her enter the room. A hard knot of emotion almost choked her as she looked across at their faces. Though she had wanted to, she had never really trusted Darius, but Beth, her mood dropped further as she looked at the girl she had considered a friend. It was Beth's betrayal that hurt the most. With Darius, she had always known that he had some other agenda, and his betrayal, while hurtful, was not a surprise.

"Are you...?" Beth's voice petered out as she took in the look on Tay's face.

"Well, what do you want me to do?" In a tone leeched of emotion, her question whipped across the

room, and they both winced at the dead note to her voice.

"Who was in the library with you?" Darius asked, his voice the same steady calm that it had always been.

"I don't know," Tay replied.

Darius expelled a long breath of air, troubled by her words. Beth opened her mouth to speak, but Tay deliberately turned away, ignoring her. Beth closed her mouth as disappointment flooded her features.

"I'll deal with this," Darius said, noting the chill silence between the two women. Beth nodded and left the room, a wounded expression on her features as she did so. Darius waited for the door to shut fast before turning to face her.

"Don't be so hard on her," Darius noted. "I'm the one who lied the most."

"But I expected you to," Tay shot back, her voice raw with anguish. "Not her."

Darius nodded and stepped back to the table where a fresh breakfast awaited. "She wasn't totally lying." He poured a cup of tea, and returned to stand before her. "Not about being your friend or caring." He took a sip of the steaming liquid and continued. "You expected me to lie, I'm not sure how I should take that."

"I've always known you had an agenda," Tay argued, wondering just what it took to shake that insufferable calm. "I always expected some form of betrayal, you lying isn't a shock because in my heart I knew that you would."

"Then why did you agree to my terms?" She stared

up into the icy blue of his eyes. "Why did you put yourself on this path?" With a nod of his head, he indicated the door that Beth had gone through. "Her brother told me that you didn't want to join, that you were happy to struggle through on the barest possible existence, with your life in the hands of those guards." He took a deep breath and kept going. "If you are so desperate to remain 'safe'" — he framed a set of quote marks with his fingers as he continued — " then why even bother?"

"Because they'd imprisoned Father, and I couldn't let that go."

"Sure you could." Her eyes narrowed as he spoke. "Lots of people in the Factory let that happen. They take the hit in rating, and their family struggles on the barest of life's essentials. You could have managed the reduction in ration, particularly if your sister got a job." The cup was placed on a nearby table. "All you had to do was give in and knuckle under." She took a deep breath, as the flood of words continued to assail her. "Why didn't you?"

"Because I didn't want them to win," Tay finally shouted, provoked to answer by his needling jabs. "And they've won so often that I can't let them win again." Without realising, she stepped closer to him as she faced him down. "You don't know what it's like to stand on a knife edge all of your life, knowing that some small slip will destroy you."

"Don't I?" She winced at the bitterness she heard in his voice. "I saw my father send my younger brother to

the Mine for daring to suggest better working conditions. Everyone here" — he indicated the building with a wave of his hand — "believes my brother is dead, but I saw my Father throw him into bondage." Tay took a step back as the words poured forth. "You find him terrifying, but you don't live with him." He took a step closer. "You want to talk about living on a knife edge, try keeping your rebellion sympathies from a man who would sell his own mother for higher status." Tay froze, mesmerised by the intensity in his face and voice. "At least you could keep your head down on the streets and be yourself at home." He stopped talking, and visibly tried to get his emotions under control.

"Darius... I..." She tried to say something, anything that would ease his pain. For the first time since she had met him, she saw through his mask of calm indifference.

"If I could have left you out of this, I would have." He continued to speak, his voice reverting back to the calm, languid tones that she had become used to. "This business is hard enough without involving someone reluctant." She watched as he stepped back from her, and returned to his chair at the table.

"I don't need your sympathy or understanding." A steady hand picked up a fresh cup from the table. "I just need to know if I can trust you to do this."

Tay looked down at her feet, at the swirling patterns on the carpet. Expectation hung in the air between them and she wished she could refuse this role she had to play. Her thoughts flickered back to her home, to the

faces of her father and siblings. Even if she had never wanted to join the rebellion, she couldn't let her sister take the same route to self-destruction that her parents had.

"My Father." Darius' head twitched in her direction. "How did they find him?"

"I think we have a traitor," he answered, in those same quiet tones. "Or at the very least a leak." He took another sip from the cup of tea and regarded her thoughtfully. "Whoever it is, doesn't seem to know about me."

"That's lucky for you." Sarcastic tones greeted his statement, and he raised an eyebrow.

"Do you think I enjoy seeing people like your father go to the Mine?"

"I wouldn't know what you like," she grumbled, pain driving her words.

"Would you try to find out?"

She was spared from answering as a loud tap sounded from the main door. Darius beckoned her forward and pointed at the breakfast table. Tay got the point and sat down at the place which had been laid for her. The delicious scent of bacon, egg and sausage assailed her nostrils, and her mouth watered. Despite the frustration of this morning's argument, her appetite had not been affected. She lifted the cover on the plate before her and began to eat as Darius opened the door for the visitor.

"Kail." He nodded at the newcomer and returned to his chair, picking up a piece of toast from the rack. Tay

glanced up at Darius' decidedly neutral tone, and froze as her eyes connected with the man before her. Rail thin yet muscular, the man filled the room with nervous energy, which brought a sense of unease to her already rattled senses. Like many of those she had seen in the castle, he was well dressed, and several expensive items made by the Clockwork Temple adorned his person.

"Darius." Nodding, Kail returned the greeting and moved to stand before the fire. "I've come to see if you're still listed for the sleigh race this morning." His voice was steady but cold, the lack of emotion sending a chill about the room. Tay swallowed her mouthful of bacon and glanced at Darius, noting the taut set of his shoulders as he spoke.

"Of course." Neutral, bland tones laced his voice. "I'm looking forward to it." The barest hint of a sneer rippled from his lips, and Tay resisted the urge to raise an eyebrow at the suppressed hostility she could sense from him.

"Of course you are," Kail answered, before he turned his gaze to Tay. "And is this your sister?"

Darius nodded, his face blank, yet Tay could feel the tension radiating out from his seemingly impassive form. "Lyana" — he waved a hand across at the other man"this is Kail." Tay reached forth a slightly unsteady hand. "His father runs the Guard." It took all of her self-control not to pull her hand away as the impact of what Darius said struck her.

"Delighted." He lowered a pair of dry lips to the skin on the back of her hand and gently kissed.

"It's a pleasure," she replied, trying to control the shiver of fear that slid down her back.

"So, I'll see you at the stables?" Kail stepped back and addressed Darius.

"Wouldn't miss it for the world," Darius replied, managing to mask his disinterest in the activity.

"Good." Kail stepped back to the door and opened it. "In an hour and a half then." Nodding once more to Tay, he stepped through the door and out into the corridor. Darius continued to smile politely as the door swung closed.

"What..." Darius held up his hand and stopped Tay from speaking. He drew a finger to his lips and pointed at the door. Tay nodded with understanding and focused back on the plate before her.

"It might be fun to race," Darius continued. "Though after my performance last year, I'm not holding out much hope."

"You raced last year?" Tay asked, helping him to maintain the fiction of bored nobility.

"Yes." He stood up and took several small steps toward the door and stopped. "I came fourth, after Kail."

"Do you think you can beat him this year?" As she approached the door, she lowered her voice slightly.

"I can try." Darius leant closer to the door. "Hopefully this year I'll win."

From the other side of the door, they could hear the sound of retreating footsteps. For several moments more, they continued their conversation, waiting for

Kail to leave. As they heard the distant sound of the lift, Darius breathed a huge sigh of relief.

"His father runs the guard?" Tay's voice said weakly, as she returned to her seat.

"That's what I said." Darius ran a distracted hand through his hair.

"Is he the one watching you?"

"One of them." Another breath whistled through his lips, and he visibly got his emotions back under control. "I'm not saying be paranoid but..."

"...be careful." Tay finished his sentence as she reached down to finish eating her now cold breakfast.

"Exactly." With a glance down at the timepiece on his wrist, Darius stood up. "I am sorry for the deception." Dropping his napkin to the table, he reached out for the jacket that hung on the stand in the corner of the room. "But you already agreed to steal the information, so" — with a shrug, he drew the coat about his shoulders — "you'd better get on with it."

Tay watched him leave the room without saying a word. She dropped her fork onto the china plate and pushed herself upright, heading for her suite.

Several dresses were still draped across the bed and chair, remnants of the aborted morning. The clothes on the bed were rumpled, creased from her earlier crying fit. Tay carefully picked them up and laid them over the back of a chair.

"Try the blue." Beth's voice sounded from the door, and she turned to face her friend. "You'll look good in that." Light steps carried her across the floor, and she

picked up a simple but richly coloured dress in royal blue. She folded the dress over her arm and approached Tay, her face filled with apology.

"When did you know?" Tay asked, as Beth began to arrange the dress layers. At Beth's look of incomprehension, she clarified. "About me having to steal these records?"

"Not until Darius discovered that Lyana was pregnant," Beth answered, as she held out the first layer of petticoats. "Before then, I didn't know how involved you were."

"Why couldn't you tell me?" Tay turned, and Beth began to lace the back of the dress. "Didn't you trust me?"

"Did you trust me?" Beth said, as her fingers deftly tied the dress shut. "Did you tell me about your father? About Darius?"

"No..."

"Well then" — she finished lacing the dress and reached out for the set of matching shoes — " we both lied, and it was for necessary reasons." Tay held out her foot, and Beth laced the first shoe. "But I can say that there will be no lies after this."

"Don't make promises you can't keep," Tay said, as Beth finished with the second shoe. "So now what?"

"Now you go down to the library and hope that you find that recorder," Beth responded, as she began to tidy away. "With any luck, no one has spotted it."

Chapter 18

In daylight, the library seemed different to the shadowy, dangerous place of the night before. As she walked into the book-filled space, she was relieved to note that nothing appeared out of place or disturbed. Pretending to read the spines of the books, she moved through the library toward the front of the room. The curtains that had covered the large windows were now drawn back. The same snowy landscape that she saw from her window stretched out before her. Stopping for a moment, she stared out at the seemingly endless grounds. Could she run? Thoughts of escape running through her mind, she was tempted to open the windows. Her fingers hovered over the window latch, itching with the desire to fling it open. It was a hopeless dream, she knew that. Even if she could escape unscathed, there was nowhere for her to go. A resigned sigh escaped her lips, and she returned to her examination of the room. The books that had been laid

open on the tables last night had been cleared, and the sick sensation rose once more in her gullet. She forced herself to move slowly as she hunted through the library for the missing recorder. With every step she took away from the seats, she felt her stomach lurch. There was little chance the recorder had fallen so far away. With diminishing hope, she found her way back to the fireplace. The tunnel's entrance held her attention as she seized on the hope that the recorder had fallen out within the narrow passageway. She ignored the little voice that pointed out the tunnel's frequent use.

"Hello again." She glanced up at the voice and stared as the young man from the night before walked closer.

"Do you live in this library?" Her words slid from between her lips, stunned into speech by his appearance.

"No. Do you?" He threw the question back to her with a smile.

"No." Tay glanced down at her feet, troubled by his teasing manner.

"You look like you're looking for something," he noted, in the same teasing voice. Tay froze and tried to school her expression into something bland. "Something you dropped?"

She opened her mouth and shut it again just as quickly. The last thing she wanted to do was indicate how much she needed the recorder.

"It's a nice little recorder," he continued. "I wonder why you'd need it this morning?"

"It's my brother's," Tay answered, thinking quickly. "He loaned it to me, and he'd be furious if I lost it."

"Who's your brother?" With languid grace, he moved to one of the chairs they had been sitting in the night before. "Maybe I could pass it along to him."

"He's not here." Tay wished she could have had more time to concoct a better story, but she couldn't give him Darius' name, particularly when she had lied about her own. "I can take it back."

"You seem a little jumpy."

"And you're a little nosy for someone who hasn't given their name," Tay shot back, deciding that aggression would be the best route at this point. "Besides which, that recorder is not yours, and I've asked for it back, so would you mind?"

"Fair point." With a smirk, he reached into his coat pocket and drew the recorder from within. Sounds of movement could be heard from the library entrance, and he handed over the instrument. "Call me Talon," he said, as she pushed the recorder back into her pocket. As the noise from the doorway grew louder, Talon stepped back. Several of the girls from the night before breezed into the room, their chatter disturbing the peace. Talon pressed the button for the tunnel and quickly walked out of sight.

"Lyana," Annetta called across the room, and Tay reluctantly went to join them.

"So have you heard about the sledge race?" Amira spoke excitedly, as they sat around one of the circular tables that were dotted about the room.

"Yes," Tay answered quickly, and blushed as they all looked at her. "It's being held in approximately" — she

glanced down at the timepiece that she had been given — "an hour."

"What do you say, girls?" Cara spoke to the group. "Do you fancy going?"

"In this weather?" Amira pointed out of the window to the snow-laden sky. "It's far too cold."

"Chicken," Cara retorted, as she turned from the window and stared across at Tay. "What about you Lyana?"

"What?" Tay had been staring across the room at the hidden door, thinking about Talon and his strange manner.

"Are you going to the race?" Cara spoke in slow, measured tones.

"I, err..."

"Oh come on," Annetta called, her voice jollying and enthusiastic. "You've got a brother in the race, you should cheer him on."

"I don't know." Tay hated the hesitancy in her voice, but she could not help it. If it were down to her, she could watch the race with ease, but as things stood, she couldn't risk it. She had taken a massive gamble meeting the girls here. The more contact they had, the more likely her ruse would be discovered. She tried to tell herself that what could happen to Lyana would be none of her concern but that didn't sit well with her.

"Lyana." Annetta drawled her name with frustration. "Don't be such a spoilsport." She indicated the other girls around her. "Everyone else is going."

"Even Amira?" Tay pointed at the other girl.

"She said it was far too cold." Tay noted.

"She was just kidding," Cara insisted. "You're coming with us, aren't you?"

Amira gave a sigh and nodded. "Just let me get hold of something warm."

Cara then turned to face Tay with a smug grin on her face. "See."

"Alright." Unable to find any more excuses, Tay agreed.

"Excellent." Annetta swept past her and walked back to the door. "See you outside in an hour."

Silence settled over the small group as Annetta swept out of the room. For one long, uncomfortable moment, they looked at each other without saying a word.

"I don't really want to go," Amira said finally, as she sank into one of the soft chairs beside the fire. "It's going to be cold out there, and I bet it's going to start snowing."

"Then why did you say yes?" Cara asked, her fingers picking up a candied sweet from one of the jars on the table. "You could have gone back to your room."

"And miss everything?" the other girl retorted. With a sigh, she stretched her feet out toward the fire. "We might actually get to see our betrotheds before the ball tonight."

"I thought they kept the candidates out of the race," Linnett called.

"No." Resting a hand on the back of Amira's chair, Cara tugged on the other girl's plait. "They relaxed that rule last year."

"I guess everyone will be outside," Tay noted, as she tried to keep the tremble from her voice.

"And they'll serve spiced wine," Cara continued, her fingers teasing the feathers from Amira's headdress as she spoke.

"Stop that." Amira stood and moved away from Cara's fingers. "That took an hour to put in, I don't need you shredding it."

"It looks awful." Another feather fell from her fingers and drifted to the floor. "Feathers don't suit you in the slightest, I'm doing you a favour."

"I could do without this kind of favour." Amira slapped at Cara's hands and pushed her away. "Go and bother someone else."

"Fine." A sigh of exasperation escaped her lips as Cara moved away and sat in the other chair. "I offer my fashion expertise, and I'm cruelly rebuffed."

"You're not the one left with a headdress that looks as though a bird's pecked at it," Amira retaliated, as she removed a small mirror from her bag and examined the damage. "I'm going to have to go and get my hair redone."

"What's the point?" Cara continued in. "You'll be wearing a hat outside."

"It's the principle of the thing." With a grimace, Amira tucked the remaining feathers across the bald section of the headdress. "I look like a plucked goose."

"Oh for heaven's sake, here." Cara picked up the handful of feathers and began to repin them to the fascinator.

"Do you know if Talia's joining us?" Tay asked, remembering the unpleasant girl from the night before.

"She'll be there for the race," Cara noted, after a moment's thought. "Are you missing her?" A rich vein of laughter flowed through her voice as she spoke.

"I was actually hoping that she'd come down with something unpleasant," Tay replied, answering the amusement with some of her own.

"No such luck," Amira broke into the conversation. "I heard..." She stopped speaking as her eyes took in the clock on the mantel. "Time to go I think." As Cara voiced her disapproval, she pointed at the time. "The race starts in just under an hour, and I'll need to get dressed." Amira smoothly got to her feet. "I'll see you all out there."

"I'd better go too," Cara noted, and followed Amira from the room. Tay waited for a few moments more, allowing the others a head start before she too left the library.

As she made her way back to her room, she focused her thoughts on the man who had called himself Talon. Not for one moment did she think that Talon was his name and the obvious subterfuge made her uneasy. Despite the aid he had given her, she could not trust that he was harmless. When she could barely trust those who maintained her secret, it was even harder to trust others. This trip had become much more than she had anticipated and she could barely wait to return to the drudgery of the Frazers' and a life that did not promise an early death. As she pushed open the door to her

chambers, she resolved to find the information and get out of this nest of vipers before she got bitten.

Chapter 19

Snowflakes drifted from the leaden sky to land in white blobs on her hat and eyelashes. Tay blinked and brushed the cold flakes from her face as she walked across the courtyard toward the small crowd of people and horses that were gathered at the other end. A freezing wind whipped across the landscape and drove the snow in faster flurries as she left the relative shelter of the Palace courtyard.

Dressed in a long, dark blue woollen skirt, blouse, light jacket, heavy coat and cloak, Tay barely felt cold as her leather, fur-lined boots stomped over the snow-laden ground.

"You made it." Amira reached her side and gave her an awkward hug. "Damn it's cold." The other girl wore similar clothing, but in dark red. A pair of thick mittens covered her hands, but she still shivered.

Tay felt toasty in her layered garb, much more clothing than she was used to for the ravages of winter.

"Are they still going to race?" The wind continued to build as the snow began to fall faster. "It looks like we're heading for a blizzard."

"It never gets cancelled." Tay and Amira turned as Talia walked toward them, resplendent in white wool and fox fur. "Don't they teach you anything down the Mine?"

Stung, Tay opened her mouth to retaliate but stopped as Amira stepped on her toe. "Is your cousin racing today?" she asked, as Tay looked at her in shock.

"Of course." Talia almost pushed Tay out of the way as she moved forward to stand next to Amira. "He's got a shot at the title this year." With a poisonous smile, she turned to face Tay. "And he's certainly not going to get beaten by a minor noble from the back end of nowhere."

As those words echoed through her mind, Tay glanced up to see Darius walking out of the stables toward the waiting sleighs. As her eyes roved over the group of racers, she caught sight of Kail. He was standing by his sledge, watching Darius with an unflinching stare. Memories of Darius' warning flashed through her mind, and Tay shuddered, visions of being caught racing through her mind. With a sweet smile at the look of fear on Tay's features, Talia leaned over. "Your brother has no chance whatsoever." She leant in further and Tay fought the urge to step back as the girl invaded her personal space. "I heard something interesting yesterday." A light, teasing tone rippled across Tay's ears and she shuddered at it.

"Did you?" With supreme effort, Tay forced herself to keep looking at Talia's eyes as she tried to channel calm to her voice. "What was it?"

"I heard that your brother's betrothal was declared void last year." A hiss of breath escaped from Amira's lips, but the other girl did not speak up. "I wonder why that was?" Leering tones rippled through the snowy air. "Did he do something he shouldn't?" The innuendo could not have been more overt if she had painted it across the Palace wall. "Is that why he's not pledging this year?" Another step and Talia was almost breathing on her. "Did he disgrace himself?" Hazel eyes pierced hers, and Tay almost stopped breathing at the viciousness she saw in them. "Can't you speak?" One white-gloved finger prodded her in the chest. "Are you a mute?"

Tay could hear Amira muttering something incoherent behind her, but she paid no attention. Her focus was on Talia and the needling jabs she was throwing her way. She was certain that it was not done for ladies to brawl, or she would have slapped the girl straight across her smug, superior face. The insults were meant for Lyana, yet Tay could not take snide comments about Darius' character. Despite her lack of trust for him, Tay knew that he was a gentleman. Even given carte blanche to abuse his position, he would not do so. She took a breath and answered Talia with distaste.

"I find your questioning distasteful and crude," Tay answered, surprised by the chill condescension that

fuelled her voice. "Are you an heiress to the Clockwork Temple or a dock worker?" She glanced over at Amira, who gave an encouraging nod. "I believe girls of our standing should not gossip like servants. I'm certain Matron Caline would be devastated to learn that one of your stature is bringing the name of a noble house into disrepute." A thin smile drifted across her features. "Should we ask her?"

The smirk dropped from Talia's lips. "No." She stepped back, affecting submission. "I apologise for my manner." A would-be apologetic smile creased her features. "I did not sleep well last night, and it has affected my temper."

"I completely understand," Tay replied, relishing the look of panic that she saw in her eyes. "I'm sure I'll forget the whole thing when you're gone."

Talia took the hint and backed off, almost slipping in the rapidly deepening snow. As the girl moved out of earshot, Tay gave a sigh of relief and turned to face Amira.

"Well done," the other girl grinned, blinking as a large snowflake landed on her lashes. "Though don't think you've won. She's Clockwork Temple. They're unfailingly nasty, and her cousin..." She stopped speaking as one of the servants stepped up and handed each of them a tin cup of steaming liquid. "Oh thank heaven," she uttered, as she lifted her cup to her lips and downed the contents. "Drink up," she urged, as Tay sniffed at the strong-smelling beverage. "It'll warm you."

The drink was warming as she downed the fruity, but

undoubtedly alcoholic drink. It was a little more than a swallow or two of liquid, but it burned slightly as it slid down her throat. A warming sensation began to spread through her body, staving off the incipient chill. Following Amira's example, she downed the rest of the cup and handed it back to the servant.

"Nice?" Amira asked as she returned her gloved hands to her pockets.

"What was it?" she asked, licking her lips to capture the remnants of the drink.

"Warmed sloe gin."

"It was very nice," Tay noted, the warmth still spreading through her body. "So" — with the lingering taste on her tongue, she returned to their earlier conversation — " what were you saying about her cousin?"

Amira cast a quick glance around the courtyard before she moved in closer. "I heard he managed to stop a betrothal last year." At the blank expression on Tay's face, she clarified, "There are only two ways to end a betrothal." Her voice dropped even lower, as though she were afraid of being overheard. "Either the family can instigate a block, or the family is accused of a transgression. Her cousin supposedly got the Carson family demoted because they rejected his proposal." She downed the last sip of her gin. "I pity the girl who gets betrothed to him."

"He's at the ball?" Tay squeaked, wondering if Darius knew about his attendance.

"Hey." Amira's answer was lost as Annetta and the

rest of the group reached them, little cups of warmed sloe gin in hand.

"We thought you weren't coming." Amira smiled, as they approached, the conspiratorial nature of their conversation disappearing as the others joined them.

"You left us alone with Talia," Tay chuckled, feeling a strange mixture of relief and kinship as the group of girls reached them.

"I bet that was fun," Annetta noted, with a smile before she downed her sloe gin in one swallow. "Are we late?"

"No, they're still getting ready." Tay nodded at the racers. The horses had been hitched to the sleighs and were now pawing at the snowy ground. Darius had already climbed into his fragile-looking vehicle, ready to begin. "Though you've only just made it." She stopped talking as Kail walked toward Darius' sledge. The snow filling the air swirled between them, and Tay blinked, unable to see the scene with any clarity. They spoke for several moments, the wind and distance preventing any chance of eavesdropping.

"He's another one to watch," Annetta noted softly, nodding at Kail. "He's high up in the guard, no noble status, but apparently he's in the lists this year."

"Which I didn't think was allowed," Cara muttered, her words almost swallowed by the mouth of the cup. "I thought the guard were separate."

I don't think we should stand here." Amira's voice broke into their conversation, with overly bright enthusiasm. "It's cold, and I can barely see."

"Over here," Cara suggested, as she led the small group into the lee of the large stone wall that surrounded the courtyard. "Out of the wind, the temperature increased slightly, but the snow still covered their clothing in ever increasing patches of white.

"They should really put up a shelter for spectators." Tay turned as Linnett joined them, her dark plaits hidden by a deep, cowled hood.

"It's been suggested," Cara noted, with a wry grin, "but as it's not really a spectator sport..."

"They're about to set off." Amira interrupted the conversation with a note of excitement in her voice.

The sledges were now in a line, facing the gently sloping ground of the gardens. A lone man clad in yellow walked in front of the pawing horses and stood on a box almost within touching distance of the racers. Words spilt from his lips, but the wind tore them unheard to the sky. In his hands, a large yellow flag fluttered, eager to be free. Tay felt the excitement of the group grip her, as the man held the flag aloft, the bright material whipping in the frigid air. Anticipation gripped the crowd, each member staring intently. A few heartbeats passed, as the watching audience collectively held its breath, snow forgotten as they waited impatiently for the race to start. Tay fixed her eyes on Darius' sleigh, nerves wrapping around her throat like a scarf. The man's arm moved, the flag becoming a yellow blur against the snowy landscape. The race had begun.

As soon as the flag dropped, the horses moved, dragging the sledges across the snowy ground as each

driver vied to be the first to leave the start. Darius touched the whip to the back of his horses just the once, and they were off, their hooves striding through the snow with only minimal slippage. As they picked up speed, the sleigh runners cut through the snow, taking Darius smoothly into the lead.

"Is that your brother?" Cara asked, as cheers erupted from the crowd around them.

"Yes." Tay clenched her hands into fists, the slightly sick, nervous sensation increasing as she watched the racers chase across the snow.

They approached the first turn, Darius still in the lead, with Kail in second place. Darius slowed to take the bend, but the right runner still left the ground. Tay bit her lip as the sledge landed heavily in the snow. The horses floundered slightly, the shifting weight putting them off balance. Kail's horses seemed better trained, as he took the corner in his stride. As Darius' horses struggled, Kail drew level, and then pulled ahead. The snow was descending faster now, the thick white flakes obscuring her vision. Despite the almost blizzard-like conditions, Darius managed to draw level as they reached the second turn. This time, luck was on Darius' side, and his team of horses smoothly navigated the bend with barely a hitch. Once more he pushed into the lead. Excitement thrummed in Tay's veins, and she cheered, her voice mingling with the other screams for victory. Almost neck and neck, Darius and Kail reached the smoothed, earthen slipway that led down to the lake. To Tay's horror, they turned into the slipway and

headed down onto the surface of the lake.

"They're on the lake?" Tay turned to Amira, her fingers almost white with the pressure of squeezing them into fists. "Isn't that dangerous?" Visions of Darius disappearing beneath the ice began to play within her head.

"It's fine," Amira reassured her, as the horses' strides lengthened, and they began to gallop. "They test the thickness."

Six more sleighs joined them on the ice, and the race began in earnest. Out in front, Darius began to pull away from Kail, his team speeding like a train across the flat surface. Tay felt herself leaning forward, watching with her heart in her mouth, as they raced toward the far bank and the next checkpoint. There was a groan of disappointment from the crowd behind her as one of the other teams pulled to the side of the lake and retired, one of the horses limping as they drew to a stop. Darius reached the opposite bank first, and the horses pulled the sleigh to the top, their flanks steaming in the cold air. Behind him and to his left, Kail's sledge reached the slipway. Several applications of the whip drove his team of horses up the slipway, and they plunged forward after Darius. Tay could barely see the racers, the falling snow so thick that it turned the racing teams into a grey blur. Neck and neck, the two leading sleighs reached the checkpoint. Darius' team effortlessly managed the tight turn. Kail was falling behind, with Darius poised to take the trophy, when it happened.

The first horse pitched forward, stumbling into some unseen hole, and it landed on its knees with an agonised whinny. As the first horse fell, the second horse shied and bucked, dragging the sleigh erratically to the side, as it tried to free itself. Darius flew forward, his body somersaulting over the front of the sledge to land in the churned-up snow with a sickening crack. The cheers stopped instantly, and an eerie silence fell over the spectators. One shocked moment passed as Tay stared at the wreckage of the sleigh that had been racing only moments ago. A scream rent the unnatural stillness and people began to run forward, Tay among them.

One of the other racers reached it first and took hold of the thrashing horse, releasing it from the chassis, and it plunged away from the tangled wreck with prancing, agitated steps. Tay raced forward, her legs carrying her through the snow as though it were nothing and her heart pounded painfully in her chest.

"Lyana." Amira ran with her, her long legs quickly covering the distance from the wall to the lake. "Wait." Her hand caught hold of Tay's arm and pulled her to a stop. "Let them handle it."

"But..." The blood pounded painfully in her ears as she tried to calm down. All she could see was him falling. "It's Darius..." Confusion burned through her as she sought to analyse her reaction. It hadn't been a calculated move or an effort to project sisterly concern; she genuinely was afraid. "I've got to..." She pushed away from Amira and staggered onto the smooth, slick surface of the lake. Several paces in, she skidded forward

and fell. Her knees slammed painfully into the cold ice
of the lake, and she gasped in pain. Gritting her teeth,
she pulled herself upright and kept going, slipping and
sliding over the frozen surface as she staggered toward
Darius and the wreckage of his sleigh.

"Darius." She reached the bank and pulled herself
up, before beginning to run. Her feet sank into the
snow, and she staggered through the deep drifts until
she reached the tracks made by the sleigh runners.
Placing her feet into the furrows she began to run,
aiming for the crash with a single-mindedness that she
could not quite understand. Flakes of feathery, soft
snow melted against her cheeks until they felt like tears
running down her face. Several of the racers reached the
mangled mess of metal and wood and began to fashion
a stretcher.

"Darius?" She pushed through the crowd and
stopped, frozen by the sight of his pale, unmoving
form. A bright bloom of red spattered the snow, and
she gasped, heart pounding painfully at the sight.
"Darius?" She made herself keep going, to push through
the crowd and kneel at his side. His face was ashen,
blood trickling from a wound to his head, and his arm
was bent at an odd angle. She could see the bone
sticking through the skin and bile rose in her throat.

"Is he...?" She couldn't finish the sentence, her fears
rising to choke her. "He's so still..." The whisper passed
her lips, and one of the men in front turned to look at
her.

"He's unconscious but breathing," he answered, as

more people arrived; called from the Palace to assist. "Back away now." An arm pushed her to one side as they gathered around Darius' still form and lifted him from the churned-up snow. Tay stepped back as the group pushed him onto the stretcher and began to move away. Brushing away the tears that she told herself were melting snowflakes, Tay followed the crowd toward the Palace and the warmth of the infirmary.

"Will he be alright?" She started at the sound of Kail's voice and turned to face him.

"I don't know," she answered honestly, as they walked through the main doors and turned left. "It looks like he broke his arm."

"And his head," Kail clarified, in his cool, emotionless voice. "Will you be alright?" His voice was mild, and despite the words, she could detect no matching sentiment. The question sounded formulaic, spoken by one who maintained the forms of society but did not truly feel. Her thoughts flashed back to that morning and Darius' insistence that Kail was investigating him. Part of her wondered if this were some elaborate ruse, but she could not for the life of her determine what that could be.

"I'll be fine," she answered, as she followed Darius' still body through a set of double doors and into a small infirmary. It was unlike any hospital that she had ever seen. The scent of antiseptic still laced the air, but the décor and furnishings were far more luxurious. They placed Darius' body onto one of the beds, and several doctors moved in to attend him. Tay was gently

pushed out of the way as they began to cut away at the clothes that covered his body. One of the nurses pushed her backward and told her to sit on the chair near the door. As the rest of the crowd moved back through the large doors, Tay sat on one of the comfortable chairs and waited, gnawing at a hangnail as the doctors worked on Darius.

"Lyana." She turned at the sound of her phony name and watched as Amira and the other girls walked through the infirmary. "Is your brother alright?" They reached her side, and Amira gave her a brief hug. Tay glanced back toward the working physicians and shrugged.

"They haven't told me anything," she said, aware of the anguish in her voice as she spoke. "He's broken his arm and hit his head. That's all I know."

Cara sat down in one of the chairs and gave her shoulder a reassuring squeeze. Annetta and Amira moved to sit opposite, and she could see Linnett still standing behind them.

"We'll wait with you," Amira said, as the small group gathered about her.

"Thank you." Tay felt a lump rise in her throat as she stared at them. She had only met them the previous night, yet they all seemed genuinely concerned. For a brief moment, she forgot her reasons for being in the Palace, and revelled in the feeling of warm friendship.

"Miss James?" She stood up as a tall doctor with a pair of spectacles perched on his nose, called her name.

"Yes?" She walked forward, conscious of the eyes of

the women around her.

"Your brother has a compound fracture to his right arm and a severe case of concussion." Tay felt relief run through her as he spoke. "He's conscious but unable to take visitors, and we'll have to keep him in overnight."

"Overnight?" A lead weight settled in her stomach, as his words penetrated her thoughts. "He won't be able to make the ball?"

"No, I 'm afraid not."

Her mind stuttered at those words. She would have to attend the betrothal ball alone. The one night where she would have to perfectly play Lyana James, and she would have to work it out on her own. Panic began to build deep within her, thoughts of navigating that morass alone paramount in her mind.

"If all goes well overnight, he should be out tomorrow," the doctor continued, mistaking her stunned silence for concern. With those words, he left her side and moved back to Darius' bedside.

Tay cast her eyes over the room. There were six beds in the ward and Darius was laying on the last one on the left. Propped up against snowy-white pillows, with skin as pale as the cotton beneath him, Darius was awake and talking to the nurse. His eyes flickered in her direction, and he beckoned her forward. The nurse shook her head, in disagreement with Darius' words. Tay waited, self-conscious and nervous, for the conversation to finish. After a few moments of quiet discussion, the nurse reluctantly nodded and beckoned Tay forward.

"You can speak to him for a few moments," the nurse announced, professional disapproval radiating from every pore.

Tay hurried forward and stared down at Darius' pale form. His arm and head were bandaged, and a sheen of sweat clung to his skin. For a brief moment her heart skipped a beat, troubled by the sight before her. Darius raised his good arm and crooked his finger, drawing her closer. She bent down to listen as his whispering tones filled her ears.

"Go to the ball tonight and dance." She moved to ask a question, but he waved his hand for silence. "At eleven they will open the register." His voice was wavering and slow, the medicine that coursed through his body bringing him closer to sleep. Tay leaned closer to hear, his voice barely audible with the onset of sleep. "Just sign." She nodded, as his eyes began to drift shut. "Remember to watch out for Kail." The lids fell over his blue eyes, but he wrenched them open. "Try the recorder during the ball." The words slurred, as he drifted off into a drug-induced sleep.

"He's sleeping now." The nurse said unnecessarily, as Tay stepped back away from him.

"Thanks." Tay moved back from the bed as the nurse drew a curtain about Darius' sleeping form. With slow steps, she walked back to the group of waiting girls.

"Is he alright?" Amira asked first, concern in her dark eyes.

"He's broken his arm, and he has concussion." Tay reported the doctor's findings as she tried to hide the

fear that was running through her veins. With Darius in the hospital, there was no one to keep an eye out for any potential mistakes. The night before had been difficult enough, but tonight she would be in a room filled with genuine nobility. The knowledge drummed into her by Darius and his sister would not be enough. Fear-induced sweat began to cover her hands as she focused on all the disasters that could occur.

"Come on." Amira looped an arm through hers and led her back toward the main hall. "Let's get some chocolate and pastries."

Unable to resist the coaxing smile of the other girl, Tay allowed Amira to lead her toward one of the smaller studies that branched off from the main hall. As they divested themselves of their outer clothing, a tray of sweet and savoury snacks was placed on one of the tables.

"He'll be alright." Linnett reached out and gave her hand an encouraging squeeze. "They can work miracles in that infirmary."

"Oh?" Cara raised an eyebrow. "Was he that badly injured?"

"No, but," Linnett continued, pushing a strand of hair away from her face, "they'll certainly be able to fix a broken arm."

"Surely any hospital can do that," Annetta interrupted, her voice packed with scorn.

"Not as fast as here," Linnett corrected her, leaning across the table in her eagerness to prove the point. "I heard my mother say that they have medicine that will

heal it like"—she snapped her fingers—"that."

"Don't be ridiculous," Cara interrupted. "I haven't heard anything of the sort."

"I think she's right." Amira added her voice to the discussion. "One of the minor nobles at last year's ball was injured too." She creased her forehead in thought. "Now, I don't know what his injuries were, but they were severe enough for a trip to the infirmary. They gave him something, and he was cured almost immediately."

"Oh, come on," Cara argued, "surely if they could do that here, we'd all have access."

"What's your rating?" Annetta asked, and Tay came to attention. This was the first time she had heard of the rating system being applied to the noble class.

"Four," Cara replied.

"Same as me," Annetta nodded, as she reached for the last pastry. "I'd say most of us are fours."

"Not Talia," Amira clarified. "She's Clockwork Temple. That has to be a rating two or higher."

Tay listened to the conversation with interest. She had always assumed that the nobility was not subject to the rating system, but the idea that there were different levels even in the upper classes was a strangely enjoyable one.

"Which proves the point," Annetta continued. "Talia would know about the medicine, but none of us would."

"I don't understand that," Cara argued. "We all have responsibility for the rabble" — Tay bristled at the

remark but managed to hide it behind a smile — " so why would that be restricted to twos and above?"

"I don't know." Annetta shook her head, and took a bite out of the pastry.

"They want control." The group turned to stare at Tay, who flushed as she realised she had spoken her thoughts aloud. Looking down at the cup of hot chocolate, she continued. "We may get ideas about running things if we had the same tools." Her voice trailed off into silence, as they continued to stare at her.

"Good point," Annetta said finally, reaching out for a cup of her own. "That's why the betrothal system is so rigged."

"Keep your voice down," Cara hissed, in an undertone as she leant across the table. "Talk like that will draw a penalty."

Tay felt the familiar sensation of fear trickle down her spine. It seemed that even here, talk was dangerous.

"I don't know why it's so dangerous," Annetta grumbled, as she lifted the cup to her lips. "It's not as though I mentioned the Clockwork Temple's hunt through the forest."

"Annetta." Cara's voice was a strangled plea. "Don't say another word."

"Or anything about the Coils." There was a thump as someone kicked her beneath the table. "What?" She looked around the table. "You're all thinking it."

"You're going to get yourself arrested," Amira hissed, as she caught hold of her fingers. "And probably us too, so shut the hell up and drink your tea."

Annetta fell silent as the impact of Amira's words finally sank in. Taking a generous sip of her hot chocolate, she turned the conversation back to the ball, and safer topics.

It was much later, when Tay finally left their company, that she realised what Annetta had divulged. Whatever the realities of her situation, it would appear that the Coils were a definite concern. Far from being the myth she had believed, they seemed to actually matter.

Chapter 20

Tay was sitting by the fire, a hefty book resting on her lap, when a loud knock sounded on the door. Moving to answer it, she was stopped by Beth's upraised hand.

"This is my job, remember?" Tay sank back into the chair as Beth headed back into the main study. From her place by the fire, she could hear the sounds of conversation, and she waited nervously. Beth returned to the room, and stood to attention, in marked contrast to her usual stance.

"There's a gentleman at the door for you, Miss," Beth intoned, even her voice altering to that of a submissive servant.

"Who is it?" She remembered to keep her voice cool, almost remote, wishing that she could just leave. The book slid to the edge of her lap, and she stopped it with an unconscious move of her hand.

"The gentleman gave his name as Kail, Miss," Beth

continued, not quite managing to mask the worry in her voice.

"I see." Tay took a deep breath, released it, and slowly got to her feet. "I should see him, I daresay" — she stopped at the minute shake that Beth cast in her direction — " but not now." Steeling herself, she continued. "I am here with only you as a chaperone." Tay took another breath, warming to the role. "It would not be appropriate." It was a calculated move, and one she hoped would not backfire. As Beth left the study, Tay returned her gaze to the flickering light of the fire, trying to lose herself in its ruddy glow.

Voices sounded once more from the other room, and Tay resisted the urge to move closer to the door. Setting the book onto a small table, she focused on the fireplace, waiting.

"I am not to be denied entry." A harsh, angry tone jolted her from her reverie. Tay got to her feet, staring at Kail's face with a confidence she did not feel.

"What the hell do you think you're doing?" she snapped, finding a measure of anger in amongst the fear. "This is my room."

"I don't care if it's the room belonging to the King," Kail retaliated, anger glacially clear in his voice. "I'm here on official business."

Another movement at the door caught her eye, and she watched a guard sidle into the room behind him. A swell of fear slid up her spine, but she controlled it, finding confidence from the role she was playing.

"Get on with it then." She sank back into the chair,

unsure of the steadiness of her feet. The fire's heat licked her skin, and she welcomed it, seizing the sensation as though it were a lifeline.

"I understand you were speaking with Annetta Chanlin earlier today."

Beth watched Tay straighten in her chair, and she mentally congratulated her. Despite the pressure, she was giving little away. Regret for her deception still ate at her, but she had to admit that Tay was managing to live the part.

"Yes." There was a moment's pause before Tay replied to the question, her voice full of scorn. "You know I did; we were at the race." Beth marvelled at the contempt Tay managed to pack into her voice. Despite the fear she had to be feeling, the façade did not fall.

"I mean after."

Tay took a breath, the action calming the raging thoughts inside her head. Behind Kail, the windows showed a vista of falling snow, and she wished she could leave this conversation, and lose herself in the drifting flakes.

"We had pastries and chocolate." Beth had to rein in a smile. Tay's response was simple and declared with an incredulous tone, as though she could not believe the question.

"What did you talk about?" A line creased Kail's forehead as he tried to hold onto his temper.

"The ball, my brother's accident." Tay gave an airy toss of her head. "Why is that important?"

"My informant," Kail began, his voice sounding

ragged, "stated that criticism of the betrothal system was declared."

"Is that all?" Tay affected a bored tone, though her mind was going a mile a minute. Why had the silly conversation warranted a visit from Kail? She recalled the worried looks on the faces of the other girls. "I mean to say," she clarified, as he opened his mouth, "that it wasn't particularly a criticism." A mental crossing of the fingers, and she plunged ahead. "I think she was concerned about the identity of her betrothed, I don't recall any criticism?"

"I see." Kail took a step forward, and Tay held up her hand.

"Please stay there," she demanded, infusing her words with as much steel as she could. "I may have to answer your questions, but you have no right to be so close." As he stared down at her, another idea flashed into her mind. "If you do not withdraw, I will inform Matron Caline of your conduct." Kail stopped moving and took a minute step back. By the door, Beth was trying to keep the smile of triumph from showing on her face. "That's better." Tay got to her feet. "Is that all?" She stared him full in the face and waited for him to flinch.

A moment passed, and Kail took a couple of steps away. "That's all," he replied. With a brisk nod of his head, he turned and headed out of the room. Beth followed him to the corridor and shut the door on his back. One click of the lock and they were alone again.

"I don't understand," Tay finally said, sinking back into her chair. "Why would he be questioning me about

a silly little comment?"

"Because there's more to it than the comment," Beth replied, as she took the seat opposite. "The Chanlins are very outspoken advocates of reducing ration control." She picked up the discarded book and turned it over in her hands. "They've incurred penalties for paying their staff more than the intended ration, and spoken about injustices in the system openly."

"How come I've never heard of this?"

"You've never been to the City before," Beth replied, as she returned the book to its place on the table. "It's information that's not told outside of court circles." She leant forward. "I don't know how much Darius told you about the court rules." Tay shrugged, disturbed by how little she knew. "Rating exists here as well." She reached into a pocket and drew forth the familiar stream of paper. "See." A finger prodded at the first line of numbers. "That's the rating number. I'm a twelve rating." She returned the tape to her pocket. "The King, his family, and some members of the Clockwork Temple would be rank one."

"And if they do anything wrong," Tay mused, "they can lose rating?"

"Not as easily as we can," Beth clarified, as she ran her finger across the polished surface of the table. "But" — the finger stopped moving, and Tay raised her eyes back to Beth's face — " it has been known to happen."

Tay rested her head in her hands, thoughts boiling within her like acid. Snow drifted against the window,

and she watched as it slowly began to melt. "Beth?" Tay lifted her gaze from the thin trickle of melting snow. "Why can't they talk about the Coils here?"

Beth tilted her head, a thoughtful expression crossing her features. The fire popped and hissed in the sudden silence. Tay waited patiently for the other girl to answer.

"I don't know." She shook her head. "It's never been spoken of in my presence."

Tay ran the tip of her tongue across her lips as she returned her gaze to the window. "Maybe Darius will know." The burnt orange sky was darkening to brown as the evening drew in.

"Maybe." Beth glanced at the clock, and an oath burst from her lips. "But we don't have time." Tay whirled round as Beth hurried across the room toward Tay. "The ball's in two hours and we need to get you ready."

Beth's fingers curled about her upper arm as she rushed past and dragged her toward her bedchamber.

Chapter 21

The dress was floor length, lace and a deep, midnight blue. Silver embroidery covered every inch of the fantastic creation, and tiny crystals sewn into the fabric caught the light as she walked. Sleeves of delicate lace covered her arms, and she stared down at the exquisite patterns in wonder.

"Just remember," Beth said, as she finished fastening the last button on the back of the dress, "the library will be in use, so if you try to get into the offices that way..."

"They may see me," Tay interrupted, trying not to think too deeply about all of the things that could go wrong. "I know."

"Just be careful." Beth gave her a quick hug before handing her the mask she was to wear.

Tay took hold of the mask and regarded it carefully. In the same blue as the dress, it was a delicate creation of lace and silver, designed to mimic butterfly wings.

Gingerly, she tied the mask to her face and stood before the mirror. The dress hugged the curves of her body and fell in waves of embroidered lace to the ground. When Beth had drawn the dress from the wardrobe, she was unsure, but her reflection vindicated Beth's choice. The dark colour seemed sombre, but the crystals and lacework made it beautiful. A pair of matching shoes finished off the ensemble, and she admired the sight as Beth handed her a matching bag. She started as she felt its weight, and raised an eyebrow.

"It had to go somewhere," the other girl explained, as she drew a plain stole from another hanger. "Try not to leave it anywhere."

Tay opened the bag and stared down at the recorder in thought. At some point this evening, she would have to find her way into the office and copy the records for Lars. The prospect filled her with terror. Now she knew that Kail was keeping an eye on her, it seemed unthinkable that he would leave her alone for the time it would take.

"It'll be fine." Beth fixed a stray hair at the back of her head and patted her on the shoulder. "Just go downstairs, play nice and don't make a scene."

"Easy for you to say." Tay drew the stole about her shoulders, and walked toward the door.

"Just try not to appear too guilty." Beth opened the door to the sitting room. "If you look as though you belong there, no one's going to question you."

"Hmm." A disbelieving snort left Tay's lips as they covered the space to the door in several short strides.

They entered the main sitting area, and Tay stared about the room with longing. If she could spend the rest of the night in this room, she would.

Before she pulled open the final door, Beth stopped and placed her arms around her. "Try not to get caught." And with those words, she stepped back and opened the door to the hall.

The sound of music drifted along the hallway and mingled with the noise of distant conversation. All of the lamps were lit, and as she walked along the hall, she passed other ballgoers dressed in their resplendent finest. Moving through the chattering crowd, she began to relax. Her dress was fine, but not a patch on some of the creations that she saw around her. Worries that her dress would mark her out in the crowd began to fade, as she followed a trio of chattering ladies to the staircase.

She descended the stairs, moving slowly to accommodate the length of her skirt. The staircase swept her down into the grand hallway and into fairyland. Strings of coloured lights crisscrossed the ceiling and walls, leaving pools of shadow in between. The music swelled in volume as she moved through the chattering throng. She had not realised how many people were in attendance, and the sheer numbers took her breath away. The men were as finely dressed as the women, and for a moment she wished that she could see Darius in this setting.

The doors to the main ballroom hung open and the music issued from beyond. She walked past several small groups of people, catching snippets of gossip as she did

so. Most of the talk revolved around Darius' accident, and she moved away in disgust. They treated his injuries as salacious fodder with no empathy for him.

The ballroom beckoned, and she walked forward into the chamber. The magnificence of the scene almost took her breath away. Beneath the lights of a grand chandelier, couples were dancing, a riot of colour in an already opulent room. The large doors on the left-hand side were open to the outside, the chill air making little difference to the packed room. Golden light spilt from the open doors, changing the colour of the fallen snow outside. Some couples even braved the frosty night air, seeking relief from the stuffy heat of the ballroom.

At the far end of the room was a large dais with three ornate chairs, one of which was occupied. A woman sat on the right-hand chair, an elegant crown of gold resting on her jet-black hair. Realising that she was staring at the queen, Tay turned away and returned to her perusal of the room. Several small tables were arranged on either side of the door, and at each one sat an individual dressed in black and white. Taking a step forward, Tay saw that a thick ledger laid before each of them. Realising that this was the famed register, she swallowed nervously and turned from the scene. Out in the main hall, the crowd had lessened, easing some of the claustrophobic tension. The clock chimed the hour, the deep notes lost in the noise from the ballroom. It was ten o'clock, and she had an hour before registration. Glancing at the crowd, she steeled herself and walked in the direction of the library, taking a glass

of strong-smelling spirits as she did so. As she moved across the hallway, she took a sip of the foul-tasting liquid and kept going.

People lined the corridors, and she moved past them, forcing herself to stay at a measured and unhurried pace. Lights blazed in the library, and there were people in there too, she could hear the conversations as she moved past and approached the door to the records room. As expected, the door was shut. Moving with a confidence she did not feel, Tay pushed open the door to the office with what she hoped was a drunken laugh. A young man in the uniform of a guard looked up as she almost fell across the threshold.

"Oh, I'm sorry," she blurted out, slurring her tones as she did so. "I was looking for..." She broke off and stared at the ceiling as though lost in thought. "The gallery."

"I'm afraid you're in the wrong place, Miss." The guard spoke with some respect, and she marvelled at the difference an expensive dress made to attitudes. "I can direct you to the right door."

"That's quite alright, I think I'd like to have a look at this instead." With a lurching gait, she staggered over to the archival unit and peered at it. "What does this do?" She waved her glass as she spoke, the liquid sloshing close to the top as she gestured. The guard stood up and walked forward.

"This room is off limits, Miss." He began to walk toward her.

"But I'm interested... oops..." She waved the glass

vigorously, and the spirits splashed across the table, narrowly missing the machine. "I'm so sorry," she giggled, as she ineffectually waved at the spreading pool of liquid with a handkerchief. The guard walked forward, frustration on his face as he stared at the spill.

"Here." He reached her side and began to wipe down the surface. Taking advantage of his distraction, Tay stepped backward and moved around to the other machine. Carefully, she drew the recorder from her bag, and placed it into the slot, the noise from the library covering the sound of the recorder connecting. She then made a big show of opening the drawer marked with the codes that Lars had drilled into her.

"Miss." The guard whirled round and caught hold of her hand as she picked out a random disc. "You have to leave, Miss."

"Or what?" The words slurred sufficiently as she continued to speak. "Do you know who I am?" For one moment, she was glad of her exposure to Talia's toxic personality, as she impersonated her snobbish, domineering tones precisely. Her fingers unwrapped the stole from around her neck and draped it over the machine behind her in a seemingly careless gesture. "All I want to see is one of these in operation." Her eyes quickly located the batch number of discs as she waved down at the drawer. "Not state secrets."

"I can't, Miss." The guard was sweating now, and she felt marginally sorry for the man.

"What about this?" She picked up a disc labelled 'lumber production'. "I'm certain there's nothing on

this disc I can't see." A softer, more cajoling tone left her lips. "I only want to see the pictures on the screen, and then I'll go."

The guard hesitated for the briefest of instants, clearly weighing up his options. "Alright." His fingers took hold of the disc, and he turned back to the machine. As soon as his back was turned, Tay reached downward and picked up the record she needed. Quickly, she placed it behind her back. As the guard switched on the machine, Tay used the noise to cover the sound of feeding the disc into the apparatus behind her. With her fingers crossed, she turned on the contraption and the recorder, hoping that the sound would be covered by the guard's machine and the muffling effect of the wrapped stole. A clacking emanated from the device before her, and she prayed it would be enough. The guard pressed several buttons, and the tell-tale reading noise sounded across the archive room. Behind her, the machine began to record, in muffled but still audible tones.

"Miss." She froze, almost expecting the guard to arrest her on the spot. Memories of the Ration Centre played through her mind as she realised that there would be no reprieve if she were caught. "It's ready, Miss." Masking the sense of relief, she stepped forward and made a show of staring at the tiny images that raced across the screen.

"How can you make sense of them?" she asked, unsure of just how much time was needed to copy the contents of the disc.

"Practice," the guard replied, looking at the machine with some pride. "It takes training to read this."

"Tell me more." She leant forward, ensuring that the front of her dress stretched downward, exposing the top of her cleavage. "I've always wanted to know how these things work." Another shuffle forward and she reached in close, pointing at the screen with a delicate finger. "How can anyone read anything that small?"

The guard glanced downward, eyes fixed on the swell of her breasts as she leant in close. Tay saw him swallow, but he continued to talk, his voice slighter faster than it had been. From behind she could hear the muffled clacking of the recorder.

"The images can't be read on the screen," he explained, a strangely patronising note to his tone. "There is an image code or stream of codes, which are known beforehand." He pointed at the plainly visible numbers. "You select the number" — his fingers tapped out a sequence on the typewriter and one of the images centred in the middle of the page — " and it tells the machine to type out the information." He pointed at the familiar paper spool.

"That's amazing." She purred her voice and leant in to stare at the fuzzy image. The clicking behind her ceased, and she breathed a little easier. "What's that speck in the corner?" She pointed at the screen and stepped back, allowing him to go in for a closer look. As he leant forward, she reached out behind her back and retrieved the disc.

"I can't see anything." He turned back to her, and

she gave a vapid smile. "I must have imagined it." With a kittenish laugh, she moved toward him again, placing the disc back in the drawer as she did so. "Thank you." A finger touched his face. "I..." She made a great show of glancing at the watch on her wrist. "I'd better go." She whirled round and made to remove the stole, turning off the machine as she did so. "My stole's stuck," she muttered, as she returned to the other side of the apparatus, carefully removing the recorder as she pretended to free the lacy fabric.

"May I help?" The guard reached forward, but Tay slapped his at his fingers.

"Keep your clumsy fingers away," she retorted, as she pretended to remove the last of the fabric. With a seemingly drunken lurch, she pulled away from the machine, the device concealed within her hand. "There." She wrapped the stole about her neck. "Thank you so much." With a brilliant smile, she reached out and bestowed a kiss on his cheek. "This has been the most entertaining bit of my night." She backed out of the room and into the hallway. A group of people pushed past her as they left the library, leaving a room that was clear of people. As the door to the records room fastened behind her, she ducked into the library and slid the recorder deep into her bag.

"The library again?" She turned, heart pounding, to face the speaker. Talon stepped in front of her, his face uncovered and the mask he should have been wearing dangling around his neck.

"I didn't think we were supposed to take those off."

She pointed at the mask, hoping that he hadn't seen her place the recorder in the bag.

"I must have missed the memo," he replied, with a shrug.

Tay watched him lean against the wall, her curiosity piqued by his nonchalance. "How did you know it was me?"

"I guessed," came the answer. "Not many of the ladies would come here during the ball, so I assumed."

"And if you had been wrong?" The weight of the recorder played heavily on her mind, but there was no opening to leave his company.

"I would have apologised." A fine-boned hand reached out toward her. "Care to dance?"

"What, here?" She gazed about her in confusion. Whilst the library was extensive, there was no space to speak of.

"Why not?" His fingers hovered before her. "I don't fancy dancing in the main hall, and as a fellow nightly researcher, I thought you'd appreciate this room more."

"Alright." Tay reached out her hand and slowly took hold of his. The music could still be heard from the main hall, but it was faint, the notes almost inaudible. With a gentle tug, he drew her closer and then took her other hand.

"I'm not good at dancing," he noted, with a wry smile, "but I can wave my arms around with absolute perfection."

A chuckle escaped Tay's lips at his words, and she followed his arm movements as he began to weave them

through the air. "You're crazy." Her laughter surprised her, as did her behaviour. It was the worst possible time to flirt, and yet, here she was. She could have left, made some excuse and returned to the packed cattle market in the main hall, but she felt strangely comfortable in his company.

"So, did you find what you were looking for?"

"Hmm?" She finished copying his latest arm movement and stared at him.

"The other night," Talon clarified, as he lifted his right arm, and moved her into a spin. "You were looking at history."

"Bits and pieces," she replied, her mind drifting back to the books she had read the night before. Most of the information had been similar to the information they had been given in school, but some of it...

"Like?" he pressed, and she looked back at him, drawn out of her reverie.

"Well," she murmured, as he spun her around for the second time, "I found out that the Clockwork Temple is the oldest industry."

"Really?" A thoughtful look slid over his features. "I suppose it makes sense."

"How so?" His fingers felt pleasantly warm against hers as they moved through a couple more steps.

"Well before the Factory can build anything, it has to be invented."

"I suppose," she hedged. "I always thought the Mine was first."

"No," Talon replied, as he danced them closer to the

bookshelves and let go of her hand. "This is one of the earliest accounts of the Clockwork Temple." A thick tome, bound in red leather, was drawn out of the bookcase. Tay glanced greedily at the title, wondering if Talon would hand it to her. "It states that the Mine and Factory were created by the Temple."

Tay's eyes followed the book in his hand as he placed it back on the shelf.

"What about the forest?" Talon almost stopped dancing, as a guarded look drifted into his eyes.

"What about the forest?" He threw the question back at her, and Tay was surprised at the forced levity to his tone.

"Are there really monsters?" Concerned by his reaction, she decided to stick with the popular rumour.

"Oh yes." It was Tay's turn to almost freeze, she had almost convinced herself that the gossip was false. "You can hear them from the windows of the Summer Palace."

"Really?" Talon caught hold of her hand again and continued to dance. "I thought..."

"You thought it was a story?" He gave a small chuckle. "Well it's not." They danced closer to the fireplace, and he pointed at the engraving on the lintel. "That isn't someone's fancy." Tay glanced up at the mantel and swallowed. Several fanged and demonic-looking faces stared down at her. "Whenever the Clockwork Temple go into the forest, they take a full complement of guards and go via the river."

Tay fell silent as she digested his words, a theory

working its way through her mind as she tore her gaze away from the monstrous depictions.

"Sorry to bring down the mood."

"That's fine." With a shake of her head, she tried to dismiss the fear that the faces on the mantel produced. "Let's talk about something else..."

"Sire." They stopped moving as one of the footmen walked into the room. Tay froze and stared at Talon in shock. "Your father requires your presence," the man stated. Talon gave a small, wry grin and released her hands.

"Very well." He nodded to the older man and replaced his mask. "I'll be right there."

"You're..." Tay couldn't finish the sentence, stunned by the revelation.

"Disappointed?" he asked, with a bite to his tones.

"I just..." Tay whirled away from Talon and headed for the door, the desire to run flooded her veins. "I'll see you in the main hall." Without waiting for him to speak, Tay raced out of the library and rushed down the corridor. Panic seared through her as she moved past the crowds of people heading for the ballroom. How could she not have known? The guard from the night before had been deferential and compliant. She should have realised that he was more than a regular noble.

She pushed past a couple of girls in the doorway to the ballroom and raced inside, looking for a corner to hide in. Talon was the prince, she shook her head and reached for a glass of something from a nearby tray, downing it in an instant.

"Lyana?" She glanced up and cast her eyes around the room. The masks, and noise of the orchestra made it difficult to identify the speaker. "It's me, Linnett." Dressed in garnet and jet, the taller girl walked toward her. Even with the mask that covered her face, Tay had to admit that Linnett looked good. The jewel tones of the dress expertly matched the caramel colour of her skin.

"You're looking good."

"Thanks." Linnett reached her side and leant closer. "Did you hear about Annetta?"

Tay froze, remembering the visit from Kail. "No." She shook her head and allowed the other girl to lead her to one side.

"She's gone." Linnett's voice dropped lower, as though afraid that someone would hear. "Her name's been wiped from the betrothal books." Her voice caught, but she controlled herself. "I don't know whether she's gone home, or..." Her voice trailed away.

"I don't..." Tay stammered, unsure of how to comfort the other girl. Disappearances were common in the Factory, but she had never expected them to happen here.

"Just don't ask questions," Linnett continued, her voice spilling rapidly from her lips. "Sign the damned books and go home." For a moment, Tay thought that Linnett was about to cry, but the other girl composed herself and started to walk away from her. "It's show time." Before Tay could formulate a question, the sound of a gong echoed through the crowded space. The hall

fell silent, and everyone stared up at the dais.

Shaken by Linnett's words, Tay cast her eyes toward the stage as a man walked out from the wings and crossed the platform. As he reached the podium, the ballgoers dipped into reverential bows. As Tay hurriedly moved to follow suit, she followed the movements of the man, who could only be the King. Shorter than she anticipated, but with the lithe movements of a skilled athlete, he approached the podium.

"Welcome." Light bounced off his greying hair as his voice echoed loudly about the room. "We shall start the proceedings directly." Behind him, Tay could see Talon, and she looked to her feet, the wall, anywhere but in his direction. "My son will sign the register first."

Talon pushed himself away from the wall and picked up a pen from its place on the table. The large ledger was open before him, and he signed his name. As he finished, he almost threw the pen back to the table in a casual, yet somewhat mocking gesture.

"Corlan Talon Chandar." His father's voice boomed out across the room. "Is betrothed to Talia Cassia Winnick." There was an audible groan of disappointment from the ladies within as Talia sashayed up the steps, a triumphant look on her face, and Tay felt nothing but pity for Talon's, no, Corlan's future. "Henna Melona Farley." A girl with a river of blonde hair ascended the steps to the stage and signed her name. It proceeded like this for some time, and it soon became apparent that only the girls' names were being called in order of familial importance. As such, Tay was

unsurprised to find herself as one of the last.

"Lyana Brialle James." Taking a deep breath, she walked across the room and climbed the set of the stairs. As she walked past Corlan, she studiously avoided looking in his direction. The man behind the desk handed her a pen, which slipped in her nervous fingers.

"Just here." A finger pointed at an elegant rendering of her name, and she reached forward to sign.

"Kail Rosen Tanton." Tay nearly dropped the pen as the name seared into her mind. Turning back from the table, she scanned the hall, looking for him as she began to walk down the stairs. Behind her, a herald continued to call out names, yet she paid it no mind. The thought of her, no, Lyana being married to that man flooded her mind, and she almost tripped as she reached the floor. In a daze, she crossed the floor and found a pillar to rest against.

"Congratulations." She started at the words and turned to stare at Amira. "You look as pleased with your match as I am at mine."

"He's..." She couldn't finish the thought, overcome by the need to talk to Darius about this unexpected turn of events. "I'm not particularly thrilled with it," she finished lamely, aware that she was giving far too much away.

"Well, I'll swap you," Amira continued, as she nodded toward a portly man on the other side of the room. "That's my betrothed, he lives on the coast, at least two days' travel away from my home." She bowed her head. "So not only do I have to leave my home to

live with a stranger, I have to live so far away that I don't have anyone to talk to."

"I'm sorry." Tay felt a swell of pity for the other girl as she struggled to keep her own emotions in check. "Look, I've got to tell my brother." A quick glance around the room revealed no trace of her 'betrothed'. "Will you be okay here?"

"Sure." Amira gave a grim smile from beneath her mask. "I've got to enjoy my last bits of freedom."

Tay nodded and moved toward the main doors, at the edge of her vision she caught sight of the rail-thin form of Kail and shuddered slightly as she picked up speed and almost raced from the room.

Moving past revellers, she headed for the main staircase and away from the noise of the ball. Reaching the first floor, she turned right and headed toward the infirmary.

Darius was lying in the end bed, dozing in the dim light. As Tay reached his side, his eyes opened, and he stared at her in mild shock. Tay was breathing fast, and her eyes were wide with barely suppressed panic.

"What's wrong?" He pushed himself up on his elbow and reached out his hand toward her.

"It's Kail." She knew she was being obtuse, but she couldn't help it, panic was flooding through her veins, and she could barely think.

Darius' face froze. "Kail what?" he asked, his eyes ran over her body, almost as though he feared that she had been physically harmed.

"He's marrying L..." She stopped just in time and

continued. "Me. He's my betrothed."

The colour drained from Darius' face at her words, and he reached forward to grasp her trembling hands.

"And he's seen me." She began to babble, thoughts crowding through her head, demanding to be set free. "He'll realise, and..." In agitation, she pushed the mask from her face. "And..." She couldn't finish, the fear seized her voice.

"I promised I would keep you safe," Darius finally answered, his voice weak but reassuring. "And I intend to do just that."

"But how?" A door at the back of the room opened as one of the nurses responded to the agitated volume of Tay's voice. "Is everything alright?" Professional concern echoed across the ward, bringing Tay and Darius back to their roles.

"Everything's fine," Darius replied. "My sister's just a little upset."

The nurse took a step into the room, eyes fixed on the tears that streaked down Tay's cheeks. Understanding softened her features and she gave a small nod. "Very well, just a few more minutes."

"Thank you." Darius flashed a quick, grateful smile.

"I won't stay long," Tay reassured, with a watery smile. "I'll try not to tire him out."

The nurse nodded in agreement and withdrew, leaving the pair alone once again.

As the door closed, Darius returned his attention to Tay and the problem she had just presented him with.

"What do we do?" Her voice was hushed, fearful and

close to tears. "How can we swap back easily? He'll know." Silence stretched across the room at her words and Tay bowed her head, tears pricking the back of her eyelids. "When he meets the real Lyana, he'll realise."

"It may not be as bad as you think," Darius responded. "He's only met you the once..."

"Not the once," Tay replied, misery coating her words. "He came to our rooms and asked about one of the girls from dinner."

Darius closed his eyes and took a breath. Tay watched him carefully, her heart rate increasing with each passing second. "The ceremony will be many months away."

"He may forget," Tay breathed, clinging to that bit of hope like a life raft.

"Exactly." Pain creased his features as he shifted position, and Tay reached out a steadying hand. Her fingers connected with the bare skin of his shoulder, and she carefully moved him back onto the pillows. "Thank you," he muttered, his voice a tired whisper as he laid back, closing his eyes as sleep once again caught up with him. The sheet shifted, and her eyes flicked down to his bare chest. Tay took a breath, momentarily distracted by the lean, muscular torso before her. His skin was warm, the muscles taut beneath her fingers and she let them linger for longer than she meant to. "You can let go now." Reddening slightly, she removed her hand and stepped back.

"I'll leave you to sleep," she babbled, embarrassed and somewhat confused by her actions. "I'll talk to you

later." With rapid footsteps, she backed away from the bed. Darius called something, but she did not hear as she rushed from the infirmary and out into the corridor. As the door shut behind her, she stopped and backed up to the nearest wall, cursing herself for being an idiot. What had she been thinking? Darius was the son of the mine Overseer, a member of the nobility and the person who had gotten her into this mess. Of all the people she could have fondled, he was definitely one of the worst choices. With a sigh, she rested the back of her head against the wall and closed her eyes. She could still remember the feel of his skin against her hand, and she gave a hiss of annoyance, frustrated with the wanderings of her mind.

The music swelled in volume from the end of the hallway, and she pushed herself off the wall. She should return to the ball and let herself be seen. There was little point in hiding in the corner. Casting an almost furtive glance back at the infirmary door, Tay strode along the corridor and returned to the ball, reattaching her mask as she did so. The dance was in full swing now, and virtually every member of the court was on the dance floor. Hesitant to join the throng, she waited at the side of the room, watching.

"Lyana." Kail's cold voice broke into her thoughts, and she turned to face him, heart pounding slightly in her chest.

"Kail." She returned his nod of greeting as her stomach plummeted through the floor. If possible, his eyes seemed even colder than they had been that

morning.

"Let's take a walk." He held out his arm and, for lack of any other options, Tay stretched out her hand and allowed him to lead her into the hall.

The other partygoers whirled past in a flurry of colour and sound, yet Tay ignored them, her focus completely on the ominously silent man at her side. They reached the staircase, and he began to walk upstairs, jolting Tay out of her frightened complacency. At the third step, she came to a halt and let go of his arm.

"Where are we going?" Thankful that her voice didn't quaver, she faced him down.

"We need to discuss something," he replied, in the same dead tone as before. A girl in a dress the colour of late summer roses pushed between them and headed up the stairs. Kail waited for her to leave before he leant forward and whispered. "Or I can arrest you here."

For a moment, time stopped. Music, laughter and talk still reached her ears, but faintly, as though she was underwater. Her legs buckled and he caught her before she fell.

"This way." A hand reached around her back and helped her upright. An iron-like grip clamped about her waist, and he pushed her forward and up the stairs.

Tay climbed in halting, jerky movements; the shock of his words turning her limbs to jelly. In desperation, she glanced over the railings and her gaze landed on Talon. The Prince glanced toward her, but Kail dragged her up the last steps before she could silently plea for

help. He led her to the upper landing and into a small room. With little finesse, he dropped her into a chair and closed the door, shutting out the sounds of the ball. As he turned the key in the lock, Tay took the opportunity to look around at her surroundings. The room was a study, several shelves of books lined the walls and a single lamp illuminated the large desk that dominated the room. Much of the room was in shadow, but a glance into the corners revealed two guards, one of whom she recognised from the records room. A cold spike of fear raced down her spine, and she clenched her hands into fists, trying to control her shaking fingers. Kail settled into the chair on the other side of the desk, and smiled pleasantly at her.

"Hand it over." He pointed at her bag. "I know you've still got it on you."

"I don't know what you mean," Tay replied, trying to brazen it out, the weight of the recorder heavy against her leg.

"Don't take me for a fool." At his nod, both guards moved to stand on either side of her.

"What are you doing?" She gave a shriek as one of the men pinned her to the chair. "How dare you?" There was a pained grunt as she landed a kick on one of the men. "Get off me." A stinging slap echoed through the room, and her head slammed into the back of the chair. Blood filled her mouth from where she had bitten her cheek. Kail took possession of the bag and looked inside, revealing the small recorder.

"You really should have gotten rid of this." A slow,

malicious smile spread across his lips as he drew the copper device into the light. Kail leant back against the table, the small recorder grasped between his thumb and forefinger. Tay stared at the device in his hand, frozen in place by fear. "Did you honestly think that the guard wouldn't report you?"

"I..." she stammered, her voice trailing into nothing as she imagined her future: the Mine or execution.

"Especially when you know your brother is under surveillance." Tay's head lifted slightly, her cover seemed to be intact. "Asking you to spy was stupidity."

"I didn't," Tay said finally, her voice a breathless whisper. "I just wanted to see how the recorder worked." She chanced a look at the men holding her and gave a small sob. "I won't ever do it again."

Silence fell over the small group, and Tay prayed that her nascent talent for lying wouldn't fail her. Caught in this company, with her whole future and that of her family at risk, she couldn't afford for her lies to fail.

"Hmm..." Kail twirled the recorder in his fingers. "I'm not sure I believe you." Tay felt her heart sink. "Perhaps we should..." He stopped at a knock on the door. "This room is occupied," he called out, irritation in his voice.

"And it's my study." A grimace creased Kail's features as Talon's voice sounded from beyond the door. "So you can open the door."

Kail gestured, and both guards removed their hands. Tay felt a rush of gratitude as Kail strode to the door and unlocked it with ill grace.

"Your Highness." He gave a perfunctory nod as the other man entered the room.

"Stop your toadying Tanton," Talon's voice snapped out, his gaze hardening as it fell on Tay's bruised face. "You've graduated to hitting women now?" A distinctly icy tone rippled through his voice. "How manly of you." The guards stepped back and moved deeper into the shadows, trying to escape the Prince's gaze. "I may take this as a reason to end your betrothal."

"She removed information from the archive," Kail continued, a note of panic entering his voice, "with this." He held the recorder aloft. "She plugged this into one of the machines downstairs."

Talon's gaze slid over her features, and she sagged deeper into her chair, knowing that he was thinking of the night before. A long, low whistle issued from Talon's lips as he reached out to the recorder. A look of assured triumph crossed Kail's features as Talon took hold of the instrument. Talon turned the object over in his hands and glanced down at Tay's white, distraught face.

"I gave that to her." Tay gave a start, and Kail's mouth dropped in shock. "Last night."

"Sire?" Kail stepped forward, his eyes blazing with barely contained fury. "My guard informed me that she used that device to copy information."

"Of course she did," Talon replied, as he slid the recorder into his pocket. "I asked her to."

"Sire?" Tay could understand Kail's confusion, she could barely understand it herself.

"I know the archive is usually off limits, but I wanted to test the efficiency of your guards, and Lyana"—he waved down at her—"offered to help."

Kail spluttered incoherently as Talon reached out and took hold of Tay's hand.

"Excellent work though, Kail." Talon continued. "I commend you on your diligence." He gently tugged on Tay's fingers. "Shall we go?" Tay leapt to her feet, and almost tripped in her haste to follow Talon from the room.

They reached the door as Kail finally regained control of his voice. "I'll take this to my father," he threatened. Talon's hand fell from the door handle, and he turned to face the other man.

"Please do," he offered pleasantly, watching confusion replace triumph on Kail's face. "Though he may take some time to reply."

"What do you mean?"

"He's in the forest with my uncle for the next few months." Talon cocked his head to one side and continued. "Didn't you know?" Kail closed his mouth, shock clearly evident on his face. Talon gave a soft smile. "After all"—a faintly condescending note entered his voice—"the rest of his trusted"—Talon placed a slight emphasis on the last word—"advisors were informed."

Kail took a step forward, his face dark with fury. One of the guards placed a restraining hand on his arm as Talon opened the door.

"Come on." He led Tay out into the hall and closed

the door behind them. "This way." Tay almost tripped as he hurried her across the upper hallway and into another room. He shut the door behind them and held his fingers to his lips at the sound of hurrying footsteps from the hall.

They waited, nervous tension raising hairs on the back of Tay's neck, for the sounds of movement to cease.

"Well." Tay jumped as Talon finally spoke. "You're in the clear."

"I... I... well..." Tay stammered, stunned by the night's events. "Thank you..."

"Don't thank me." Talon walked past her and sat down. "I've only delayed your arrest." Tay stayed silent, the stress of the evening freezing her in place. Only her eyes were mobile, flicking from Talon to the door and back again. "I presume this" — he removed the recorder from his pocket and waved it at her — "is why you were in the library the other night."

"Then why did you help me?" Tay asked, bewildered almost to the point of tears. "If you knew what I was up to, why did you lie to Kail and to the guards?"

"Because I don't particularly like Kail," Talon replied, with a lazy chuckle. "And I don't like his tactics. You're a guest in my father's palace. If anyone is to be arrested, I decide whom and when."

"So are you going to have me arrested?" Tay asked, confused by the direction her evening had taken.

"For this?" He waved the recorder, and the chuckle died on his lips. "I should" — Tay felt cold fingers slide

down her spine — " but what purpose would that serve?"

"I don't understand." Thoroughly confused now, Tay stared at the man in bewilderment.

"You'd only inspire some other heroics if arrested. It's easier to keep an eye on your activities."

"I see."

"No, I don't think you do." Talon opened the back of the recorder and removed the disc from within. "You're a member of the nobility." He waved a careless hand at her dress and mask. "It's one thing for a bunch of unwashed peasants" — Tay bristled at his turn of phrase — " to shout for freedom and make demands, but when one of us does it" — he gave a low whistle — " it gives it a layer of legitimacy that cannot be ignored."

"Then why did Kail let me go?" she demanded, anger finally freeing her mind. "If it's such a problem, why would he?"

"Because he's desperate for a noble rank." Tay started at those words, wondering just what Lyana and Darius had failed to include in her education. "And he doesn't fully appreciate how arresting you as a rebel would be detrimental." The disc in his hand glinted in the lamplight as he turned it over in his fingers. "He doesn't understand how this could push for a change in government."

"And you don't want things to change?" Tay responded, finally moved to anger by Talon's casual

superiority. "What if it needs to?"

"But things can't change," Talon continued, a strangely frustrated look on his face.

"Why not?"

Silence greeted her question and Tay looked down at his fingers, watching as they fiddled with the golden disc. Tension stretched between them, and anger fuelled Tay's next words.

"So we just let people starve?" Talon took a step back, taken aback by the vehemence in her voice. "We leave them at the mercy of rating and your..." She stumbled, remembering her cover almost too late. "...our court?"

"You don't understand."

"No, I understand perfectly well." Tay whirled round and headed toward the door. "You don't want to lose all this." She seized hold of the handle and pulled open the door. "Thank you for saving me from Kail." And with that, she marched from the room.

Anger carried her across the landing and back toward the stairs. The dress rustled beneath her fingers as she raced up the steps and back toward her rooms.

Chapter 22

Tay slammed the door to her suite and crossed the room at a fast trot. "Beth." The door to her bedroom loomed, and she pushed it open, looking for her companion. "Beth?" she called out again, as she reached out and tried to undo her dress. "Are you in here?" She dropped her hand from the ties and pushed open the bathroom door. Puzzled by the empty room, she returned to the bedroom and reached for the bell pull that was hanging by the bed. One tug on the rope and she returned to struggling with the ties on the back of her dress. Unable to free the knots at the bottom of the bodice, she sank into a chair, the dress rustling like fallen leaves as she landed.

A dull headache began to build behind her eyes, and she reached out for the water jug on the side-table. Pouring herself a glass of water, she took a sip before closing her eyes. Visions of the evening flowed through her mind. Despite her fear, it had been an exhilarating

experience. Returning the glass to the table, she stood and headed back toward the mirror. In two days' time, she would be back in the Frazers' kitchen and as far away from this life as she could be. Her fingers slid across the rustling fabric of her gown, imprinting the richness of the material on her memories. There would never be anything as exquisite as this in her possession again.

"You called, Miss." Taya turned at the unfamiliar voice and stared at the strange maid with shock.

"Where's Beth?" She marvelled at her ability to sound so calm; visions of Beth being interrogated flooded her mind, and she desperately wished for Darius' presence.

"She's been transferred, Miss," the other girl answered, with a small bob. "I hope I can assist you."

A shiver of cold fear slid down the back of her neck as visions of her meeting with Kail passed through her mind. Anything could have happened to Beth. The girl waited with a nervous expression on her face, worried at her silence.

"If I'm not acceptable..." Tay's head snapped up as she heard the tremulous words. The fear on the girl's face was almost palpable, and Tay remembered the feeling of being in the presence of nobility. She was a fraud, but the girl didn't know that, and should she say that the maid was unacceptable, it could ruin this girl's career.

"You can untie the laces," she said finally, watching the look of relief cross the girl's face with a strangely

disconnected sensation. This girl could be her reflection, worried at angering the noble in the fancy dress. "So, why was Beth transferred?" she asked, forcing bright interest into her voice as the other girl moved to stand behind her. The fingers that had begun to unlace the bodice stilled and Tay was certain that the maid was trying to contain shivers of fear.

"I don't know Miss." Tay heard a frightened quality in the other girl's voice, and concern for Beth's well-being increased. The girl continued to undo the dress, her fingers still shaking.

"Well, I never had any complaints," Tay responded, fear sharpening her impersonation. The laces popped open, and Tay allowed the other girl to draw the dress from her shoulders, remembering that she was supposed to be undressed like a doll. "Do you know who transferred her?"

"Master Tanton." There was no mistaking the fear that infused the girl's voice.

Tay felt her heart sink like a stone. Kail had Beth. The sense of fear that had dogged her since the interrogation flamed into full-blown life.

"There you are Miss." Tay stepped out of the dress and walked toward the bathroom, her teeth nibbling at her lips in worry. "Would you like me to draw a bath?" She turned around, schooling her expression into one of unconcern.

"No that's fine," she replied. "Could you pack the dress away and lay out my nightclothes?" Her voice wavered slightly, and she hoped that the maid did not

notice. Stepping into the large bathroom, she closed and locked the door before sinking to the floor. The smooth tiles were cold and pressed uncomfortably against her knees. A thin, wavering whimper escaped her lips, and she pressed her fist to her mouth in an attempt to stifle the noise.

She did not know how long she knelt there, trying to still the frightened whimpers that threatened to overwhelm her. Shoulders shaking, she picked herself up and walked toward the mirror. Her reflection showed a pale, quivering girl with terrified eyes. A bead of blood flowed from where she had bitten her lip. Taking a deep breath, she reached forward and turned on the tap. Dipping her hands into the cold water, she splashed her face and tried to rally her thoughts.

"Come on girl," she whispered at her reflection. "You can do this." If she couldn't keep it together, she wouldn't be any help. Tears mingled with the water that slid down her face as she struggled to rein in her emotions. Another handful of water hit her skin, and she gripped the sides of the sink. *What would Darius do?* she found herself asking, as she tried once more to find some measure of calm. Darius would have a plan, she was sure of it. Her breathing slowed as she focused on memories of Darius and his calm, controlled mannerisms. Another breath and she reached out for a towel. Drying her face, she walked back out of the bathroom and smiled at the maid.

"Thank you." With swift steps, she crossed to the bed and began to dress. "You can go now." The maid

nodded and left the room, leaving her in peace.

The nightgown settled into place, and she let her hands fall to her sides, listless from all the worry. Dousing the lights, she got into the large bed and closed her eyes. She would wait until the palace was asleep and then she would find Darius and get his advice.

A knock sounded distantly from the other room, and she jolted upright. Climbing out of bed, she stepped into a pair of warm slippers before turning on the lights to her room. Opening the door to her sitting room, she hesitated as the knocking sounded again.

"Who is it?" she called, as she walked into the main suite and crossed to the door, where she stopped, hesitant with the late hour.

"It's Talon."

Tay's hand stilled on the key, nerves freezing her movements.

"Talon?" It was an unnecessary question, she was merely stalling for time. The air in the room seemed to grow thin, and she took several deep breaths.

"Yes." There was a bite of impatience to his voice. "Let me in please."

Hesitantly, she turned the key, moving the tumblers slowly into place. With careful movements, she pulled open the door. Talon stood in the hall, looking strangely awkward in the dim light.

"May I?" He took a small step forward. Swallowing her fear, Tay moved to the side and allowed him in. With several long strides, he crossed the room and came

to a stop beside one of the bookcases.

"Your Highness." Tay stepped back from the door, but did not shut it. Despite his aid to her earlier, she still could not fully trust him.

"Don't get all formal on me." Talon's exasperated tones whipped out across the space. "I'm still the same person you met in the library." Tay said nothing, thoughts churning in her head as she regarded him. "And I did get you out of Kail's clutches."

"What do you want?" The words snapped out with some vehemence, and she wished she could take them back.

"To talk." He settled into a chair and regarded her carefully.

"I barely know you," Tay snapped back, quickly forgetting that he was a prince. "I met you for the first time last night. Why do you presume I'd want to talk?"

"Because of this." He held up the golden token that she had recorded onto in the archive.

"I thought you were going to arrest me." Tay stared at the disc, hunger in her gaze. That information was her insurance. If she could return with it, then Lars would be far more likely to try to protect her and her family.

"No." He gave a small shrug.

"Why?" Tay wanted the disc but wasn't foolish enough to assume that it didn't come with a catch.

"Close the door." Tay slowly reached out a hand and pushed the door shut. For a moment, there was only the sound of the fire in the grate. Tay impatiently

tapped her foot on the floor as she waited for him to speak. Talon took a breath and released it slowly. "The rebellion is doomed." Tay jolted back as though she had been shot. "Kail has been investigating the mining sector for some time now." He waved a hand at her. "He knows about your brother, and he is clearly suspicious of you."

"Then why are we betrothed?"

"Because he wants the status that only a noble rating will bring, and marriage into nobility is the only way to get it." Tay opened her mouth as he continued to speak. "You're a hostage for good behaviour." Her stomach twisted unpleasantly as she contemplated her options. "Kail and his father can count on the support of Darius' father, but Darius himself..." He gave a shrug. "His family loyalty and sense of fair play is his weakness. With you in Kail's clutches, he may have to curtail some of his more extreme activities. And of course, he'll get the rank he wants with the benefit of keeping you two under control."

"Does my father know?" Tay pressed her fingers to her temples. She remembered the Frazers' party and Darius' father. What she had seen of that man's character chilled her to the bone.

"Not that I'm aware of." Talon leant forward in the chair and fixed her with an intense gaze. "But I do know your father's reputation. He's a loyalist, through and through, and even his own children will not be exempt from his punishment."

"So if we're doomed, why are telling me?" Anger

supplanted the fear in Tay's voice. "You don't know me."

"But I'd like to." Tay froze at those words. As though her life weren't complicated enough, Talon seemed determined to add to her problems. "And," he blithely continued to speak, ignoring the stunned look on her face, "you asked about the forest." He reached into a pocket and removed a slim book. "I know that the rebels are looking for the Coils." He stood up and walked across the room, stopping just before her. Tay looked up at him, mentally comparing his dark eyes to a pair of blue ones. "Give this to your brother." He handed her the book. Tay gripped the cover with nervous fingers, barely holding on to the soft leather. "You want the Coils?" Tay nodded at his question, staring down at the book in her hand. A flutter of excitement settled in her stomach, and she itched to read the words that laid within. "This'll help you to find them."

"Why?" She grasped the book a little more firmly as she lifted her head to stare at him. "I'm a rebel sympathiser."

"I have my reasons." Carefully, he reached forward and brushed a stray strand of hair from her face. "You're the first person to not treat me like a prince."

Stillness settled over the room as he stared down at her. His fingers moved to her chin and tilted her face upward. Tay's breath caught as he leant in.

"What is going on here?" They both jumped as Darius' voice echoed across the room. Talon's hand

dropped to his side as he turned to face the door.

"Darius." Shocked by his sudden appearance, and acutely aware of Talon's closeness, Tay took a sudden, guilty step back. "I thought you were supposed to be in the hospital."

"I can tell." Tay winced at the dry innuendo. "I'm feeling better, and I discharged myself." He walked past the pair of them to the wine cabinet and poured himself a drink. "Though I am surprised to see you here, Sire." Subtle notes of shocked condemnation flowed through his tones. "It's most inappropriate to be a lady's rooms unchaperoned at this hour."

"I completely agree," Talon replied, moving away from Tay as he spoke. "I haven't been here long, and I should be going." With casual steps, he walked back toward the door. "Enjoy the book," he called, as he walked out into the hall and closed the door behind him.

Darius took a long sip from his glass and regarded Tay carefully. Beneath the quiet scrutiny, Tay shuffled uncomfortably. It was as though he were her older brother, but at the same time, she was painfully aware that he wasn't.

"We weren't doing anything," she said finally, more to fill the space with some kind of sound. "He just loaned me this book."

"That's not quite what it looked like." Darius' soft tones slid between them, and she flushed, aware of the disapproval in his tones. "He's the prince, and you're engaged to another..."

"Lyana's engaged to another," she noted, wondering how this conversation seemed to be happening.

"Couldn't you find someone more appropriate to flirt with?"

"Who?" Tay responded, feeling a surge of defensive anger, he wasn't her brother and had no reason to act like one. "And I wasn't flirting."

"Then what were you doing?"

"Talking..." She recalled the feel of Talon's fingers against her cheek with a flush of embarrassment. "I wouldn't have let him kiss me or anything." Darius did not reply, but his eyebrows quirked upward, mocking her assertion. "And why would it be so bad if he did?" she continued, replacing the embarrassment with anger. "I'm not your sister."

"I'm very much aware of that." The answer whipped across the room, and he took a step forward. "But I would have thought that discretion would be a paramount concern for you." A flicker of what she took to be anger flashed through his eyes. "Flirting with the Crown Prince is not discreet."

"I didn't invite him here," Tay snapped back, aware that he was right and hating him for it. "He knocked on my door."

"You should have sent him away." Darius took another step forward. "What if he had been seen entering?"

"He helped me get away from Kail," she snapped back, taking a step toward him. "Kail knows that you're involved with the rebels and Talon rescued me." She

took another step forward, anger searing through her. "I didn't want to be here." She lifted her hands and indicated the room with a wave. "I damn near got arrested, and where were you?" Another step closer and she was within touching distance. "Talon saved my bacon, and you're taking me to task for it." He opened his mouth to speak, but she didn't give him the chance. "You're acting like my brother..." She took a breath, and another thought raced through her head. "Or are you just jealous?" She froze, stunned by the flood of words that had passed her lips. Brittle stillness surrounded them, and she wished she could retrieve those words.

"Why would you think that?" Mild, mocking tones laced the air, and she flinched slightly, lifting her head to stare directly into his eyes.

"I..." she stammered, wondering where she had found those words. "I..." Her words stilled, frozen by the look on his face.

"Don't stop on my account." Calm notes lowered dangerously and she flinched at their sound. "Carry on."

"I..."

"Don't be shy." He raised a hand and ran a finger across his lip. "Explain it to me."

"I didn't..." Hesitant, halting words filled the air. "I..." She stopped again, unable to think of a way out of this conversation.

"Do you wish me to be jealous?" He took a small step forward, and the tension between them ratcheted up a notch.

"No," she replied, answering too quickly to be believed.

"Then why did you say it?" He raised a hand and brought it a hairs-breadth away from her cheek. "Have you forgotten who you're supposed to be?" He stopped moving, though Tay could still feel the heat from his fingers.

"I haven't forgotten," she replied, her skin trembling slightly from the nearness of his fingers. The tension was suffocating, the desire to stretch across the distance and press the skin of her cheek against that hand almost too much to bear.

"Good." Darius took a deep breath and stepped back, the burning intensity of his gaze slowly vanished as he visibly reined in his emotions. "I will not have it whispered that my sister is enamoured with the Prince."

"No." Tay bowed her head, disappointment surging through her.

"And what about the rest?" He indicated the other chair, and she sat down, her knees shaking.

In halting, hesitant tones, she told him about Kail, his threats and Talon's rescue. As the words finally stuttered to a halt, she glanced up to stare at Darius, and a prickle of fear raced through her at the concerned look on his face.

"Luckily, we return tomorrow," Darius finally uttered, his voice as calm as it ever was. "And you'll be free of this."

"What about you and Lyana?"

"We'll manage." Slowly, Darius got to his feet. "This

is not your fight."

Tay watched him walk to the door to his rooms, and she got to her feet. "But, aren't I implicated?"

"How can you be?" With his hand on the door, he turned back to the rest of the room. "No one knows your identity." The door opened, and he stepped over the threshold.

"But..." She didn't know what to say. A mixture of emotions raced through her, relief at returning home warred with a desire to help.

"Be grateful." He threw the words back over his shoulder. "You get to be free from your debt."

"Wait," she called out, stepping forward to take him by the arm. "What about Beth?"

He stopped and turned back to face her. "What about her?"

"She's been transferred by Kail," Tay replied, appalled that she had failed to mention it before. "We'll have to help her."

"And you didn't think to mention this before?" Darius snapped.

"If you hadn't started..."

"Are you blaming me?" Darius interrupted, a definite snap to his voice. "You're the one who had the information."

"Okay." Tay held up her hand to forestall the impending argument. "Let's just focus on finding her."

"Fine." Darius leant against the door frame. "Are we safe to talk here?"

"Yes," Tay nodded, remembering almost too late that

they could no longer speak freely. "She's gone for the night."

"That's a blessing at least," Darius sighed with relief. "Now about Beth, what exactly were you told?"

"The new maid told me that she had been transferred." Fear made her trip over her words. "Do you think Kail's interrogating her?"

"I wouldn't have thought so," Darius replied, after a moment's thought. "After all, I didn't request her transfer to these rooms." Slender, elegant fingers reached up and rested against his chin. Tay followed the movement, wondering what he was thinking.

"I don't understand," she snapped back, abandoning all sense of calm as she began to pace. "Why would that have any bearing?" Thoughts of Beth in Kail's hands crowded through her mind. "She works for us." Darius raised an eyebrow, and she winced at her wording.

"Because Kail cannot guarantee that Beth is with the resistance."

"And if he interrogates her for no reason," Tay replied, with sudden awareness, "then he's irritated one of the nobility with little justification."

"Exactly," Darius replied, pushing himself free from the wall. "I would suggest that the new girl is a spy." Tay thought about the girl's petrified demeanour and doubted his assessment. "We'll know for certain if she accompanies us home."

"You're not going to look for Beth?" Tay took an involuntary step forward, anger building once more.

"If I do" — exasperation flowed through his voice

— "they will certainly know that she is involved."

"But..."

"However" — he interrupted her protest with a wave of his hand — "that doesn't mean I can't check through a proxy." Deep, blue eyes took in the concern on her face. "I'll make sure she's alright," he reassured in softer tones. "I won't let anything befall her."

"Thank you." Tay took a step back and headed for the exit.

"Tay." She turned back to face him. "I'm sorry for earlier."

"No, you were right." Tay stared down at her feet as she answered. "I'm here to be your sister." The carpet rippled as she dug her toes into the soft surface. "I almost forgot that." Biting her lip, she finally raised her eyes back to him.

"That's not what I meant." Darius did not move, but Tay took a step away from the seriousness of his gaze. "I shouldn't have reacted as I did." Tay felt tense, unnerved by his manner. "You are not my sister" — he took a deep breath — "nor my lover." The air about Tay felt close, suffocating as he continued to speak. "I had no right to act like one." Tay opened her mouth to speak and then closed it again, unsure of how to respond. Darius watched her from the door, eyes calmly fixed on her face. "Rest assured, it'll not happen again." He turned and headed into his bedroom. "I'll see you in the morning," he called back over his shoulder, before he closed the door behind him.

Amber Sky

The clock ticked quietly in the corner as Tay stared at the shut portal, unsure of what had just occurred.

Chapter 23

"I thought we were leaving today," Tay snapped across the breakfast table, "and now you say that we're staying until tomorrow,." Her fingers curled painfully about the handle of her fork. "I can't keep this charade going much longer."

"It's not my fault." Darius returned his cup to the table. "I was informed that the King wishes to hold a full conclave." A frustrated shrug rippled across his shoulders. "There's absolutely no way I can get out of this."

"But what am I supposed to do?" Tay slammed the fork down on the table. "I only just managed to make it through the last day and a half."

"You could stay in your rooms." A napkin landed beside his half-eaten breakfast. "I have no choice, I have to stay..."

"Then why can't I leave?"

An eyebrow arched almost to his hairline. "Is that a

serious question?"

"I just thought..." Tay ran a distracted hand through her hair.

"That would not be a good idea."

"Why not?" Tay snapped back, frustration making her voice sharp. "Why do I need to be here? I've done my job."

"Yes, you have," Darius replied, in his infuriatingly calm tones, "and you did it well, but we can't leave separately." Tay gave a sigh and sank back in her chair. "I'm not happy about this either." He picked up a piece of toast and slathered it with butter. "I'd much rather get out of here and away from Kail." Tay glanced back at her plate, she had almost forgotten her 'betrothed' with the shock of the news. "But we're stuck, and we're going to have to put up with it."

"Fine." Tay picked up her cup and took a small sip of her tea. "So, what happens now?"

"Conclaves are usually held in the afternoon." He took a bite of toast and chewed thoughtfully. "So, we stay low-key this morning."

"What about Beth?" Tay had slept little, concern over her friend had preyed on her mind."

"I..." He stopped speaking as a knock sounded at the door. "Yes?"

"It's Kail." The words echoed through the room, bringing more tension to the already fraught atmosphere. "May I enter?"

"A moment," Darius flicked his eyes toward the door to her suite, and Tay took the hint. Dropping her

napkin on the table, she raced across the floor and into her own rooms. Closing the door, she leant forward and pressed her ear against the keyhole.

"Two days in a row, Kail," Darius' languid tones drifted across her ears. "Should I be honoured?"

"I am going to be your future brother in law." Kail's voice reached her ears, as chilly as the night before. "I felt it a courtesy."

"Did you?" There was a chink, and Tay pictured the tea cup landing on the saucer. "Was it a courtesy last night?"

"What do you mean?"

"So, you threaten women so often that you don't remember?" A chilly note entered Darius' voice. "She did tell me."

"I was acting in my capacity as a guard." A hurried note of justification rippled through Kail's tones. "It wasn't personal, and I would never..."

"You still struck her." Tay bit her lip as Darius' voice turned deadly. "You understand, I could use this as a reason to end the betrothal."

"I apologise for any offence I caused." Kail's apology was stiff, yet grovelling. "I was acting within my remit."

"Strange." Darius' voice sounded close to the door. "Interrogations of the nobility usually require evidence and a writ, not removal from a betrothal ball and questions in a side room."

"I will apologise to your sister personally." Kail seemed torn between righteous justification and fear. "The Prince vouched for her actions." His voice was

hurried, and Tay thought she could detect panic in the tone. "Please understand, I would not have acted the way I did without a solid lead, and I had one."

Tay moved away from the door, and scrambled into a heavier gown, unwilling to meet Kail in her dressing gown.

"You will certainly apologise," Darius continued, his voice unrelenting. "And then I shall think about your betrothal; I doubt my Father wishes Lyana to be matched to someone who falsely accuses her of treason."

"It won't happen again, I promise." There was definitely panic to Kail's voice now, and Tay wondered at it. Why would the thought of losing the betrothal mean so much to him?

"It better not." There was a note of finality to Darius' tone. "Wait there, I'll see if she wants to see you." Tay retreated to the far side of the room and waited for the door to open.

"Lyana." Darius' voice increased in volume as he walked into the room. "Kail's here, and wants to apologise." Darius rolled his eyes, nearly making her laugh. "Do you want to see him?" A slight nod informed her that he wanted her to say yes.

"I'm not sure." Her voice wavered slightly, unwilling to agree immediately. "Is he alone?"

"No, he brought one of his guards." Darius moved into the room. "I understand you may not want to see him, but Father wouldn't be overly impressed if you didn't allow the man to apologise."

"Oh, okay." Tay walked forward and caught hold of

Darius' arm. As a pair, they stepped back into the sitting room.

Kail's fingers curled around the back of the chair; thin, elegant fingers that seemed at odds with his callous eyes and stiff demeanour. At his right elbow, the equally rigid form of a guard watched her approach. She swallowed back her nerves and faced the pair of them.

"Do you have something to say?" she asked, forcing strength into her voice from somewhere.

"I apologise for my appalling behaviour last night," Kail replied, his cold voice offering a hint of sincerity. "I was merely attending to my duty. I hope this will not affect our betrothal."

"We'll see," Tay replied, unwilling to allow Kail a sense of relief. "I'll think about it." She sat back down at the table, and picked up her knife. "Is that all?"

Kail hesitated, before nodding once and stepping back. "Once again, I apologise for last night, and I hope you will forgive me in time." He raised his eyes to Darius. "See you in the conclave."

The door shut behind the duo and silence descended. As the sound of retreating footsteps finally echoed through the room, Tay released a tense breath.

"Why is this betrothal so important to him?" She plucked a piece of toast from the rack and buttered it. "Particularly as he's investigating you."

"He wants noble rank." Darius returned to his seat. "Military rank doesn't provide the same privileges." He took another bite of toast and chewed thoughtfully. "If I had the power, I'd veto the pairing."

"Why can't you?"

"Father." Darius leant back in the chair. "I'm willing to bet that he pushed this through."

"But why?"

"Who knows." His fingers curled around the arms of his chair, Tay stared down at those hands, her mind feeding her images of the previous night. "I think it best if you stay here today."

"You won't get any argument from me," Tay replied, the thought of diving back into the morass of court life almost too much for her to bear. "What are you going to do about Beth?"

"I have some contacts." Darius lounged back against the chair. "Don't worry."

"I do worry." Tay pushed her chair back and stood. "I worry that she'll be hurt, I worry that she'll talk." Short, agitated steps carried her toward the fireplace. "I worry that they'll come for us..." Darius stood and joined her at the fire. A hesitant moment passed before his hand descended lightly onto her shoulder. Tay swallowed as he turned her to face him.

"I'll find her." His voice was soft, reassuring, and the weight of his hand sent shivers across her skin, bringing memories of the previous night to the fore yet again. "We will get away with this." Darius did not move, his other hand still hung by his side, but Tay felt herself drifting forward, captured by the gentle look in his eyes.

You are not my sister, nor my lover.

Words from the previous evening sang through her mind, and she struggled to stay focused. "But Kail..."

Her voice trailed off as the door opened behind them.

"May I clear?" The new maid entered the room with her head down.

"Yes." Darius' hand dropped from Tay's shoulder, and he stepped back. "I'd better get ready for the conclave." The kindness had fled his voice, the softness buried beneath cool, business-like tones.

Tay watched him walk to his rooms, warmth still tingling though her shoulder from the weight of his hand. The room seemed smaller, and she took a steadying breath.

"Do you wish me to draw a bath, Miss?" The maid drew her from her thoughts.

"Yes, please." She allowed the maid to lead her into her rooms, confused at the feelings that had begun to simmer within.

Chapter 24

A knock on the door drew her from the book that Talon had given her. Despite his insistence that it would assist them in searching for the Coils, it had so far seemed to be nothing more than a collection of fairy-tales, and while they were fascinating, she couldn't see the connection.

"Come in." She closed the slender, leather folio and placed it between the cushions of the chair.

"Lyana." Amira swept into the room like a small hurricane. "What are you doing moping in your room?"

"Everyone else is at the conclave." Pushing herself from the chair, she waved at the snow drifting past the window. "And it's freezing outside."

"That's nothing." Amira lifted her arm. A bag swung from her fingers, dark red and embroidered with white flowers. "We're going swimming."

"We?" Tay glanced at the door as Cara and Linnett poked their heads into the room.

"Come on." Linnett's dark hair was coiled back in an elaborate plait. "There's nothing else to do."

"And it's boring being stuck in your room." Cara's auburn curls bounced about her face as she spoke.

"Talia shouldn't be there," Amira said, with a cheeky grin, clearly feeling that this would be an inducement. "Come on." She reached out a hand and seized Tay's wrist. "We're never going to be here again..."

"So let's make the most of it," Cara finished, finally moving into the sitting room. "Please." Tay chuckled at the pout that creased her features.

"Alright." Tay pulled her hand away from Amira, and walked toward her bedroom. "Just give me a minute."

"Can I help you, Miss?" Tay jumped as the maid spoke from behind the door.

"Yes." Tay calmed her breathing. "I'm going swimming."

The maid nodded, and began to look through the chests. From the other room, the sounds of conversation continued, and for a moment, she forgot that this wasn't her life. As the maid packed a small bag, she stared out of the window. Snow drifted past, white flakes bright against the grey sky. On the far edge of the grounds, she could see a platoon of guards carrying what appeared to be a large crate through the boundary gates that led to the woods beyond. Tay moved closer to the glass, her breath fogging the cold surface as she strained to see more clearly. The crate was unwieldy and as the guards pulled it through the gate, it fell into the snow.

"Here you go, Miss." Her maid interrupted her contemplation.

"Thank you." She took the bag from the girl's hand. "What's your name?"

"Emma, Miss."

"Thank you, Emma." With one last look at the struggling guards, she left her room.

The water came up to her neck. The swimming pool was rectangular in shape and tiled in shades of blue. Square columns supported an arched ceiling made of glass. Snow blotted out the natural light, but steady, non-flickering lamps glowed from each alcove. Lifting her feet, she floated in the warm water, and her mind drifted away. Behind her she could hear the conversations of the other girls, but at this moment, she relaxed, forgetting her troubles as the water lapped around her.

"What did you think of the ball?" Amira swam to her, her voice low and barely audible amongst the babble of conversation. Above them, the metallic forms of the spiders scurried across the glass, clearing the snow from its surface.

"Enjoyable," Tay said. "Except for..." Her voice trailed off, unsure of what she could say.

"I know." Amira moved closer, her voice dropping to barely a whisper. "I heard that Annetta never made it home."

Tay jerked upright, water spraying into Amira's face.

"What?" She remembered to whisper, but she couldn't contain the outrage. "Do you think...?"

"I don't know." Amira moved closer, her voice almost a breath. "But the guard have been mobilised out to the forest." She glanced at the others, making sure they were out of earshot. "I think something big is going to happen."

"Why are you telling me?" Tay asked.

"Because I know that Kail is watching your brother, and he's watching you." Another sideways glance. "Be careful. It's not good to question too much."

Tay watched Amira swim away, confusion running through her head. She thought about Annetta, if one of the nobility could vanish, then what chance did Beth have? Returning to the others, she joined in the conversation, hiding the worry that surged through her.

Chapter 25

The route from the swimming pool took her past the library, and she drifted inside. She told herself she wasn't looking for Talon, but disappointment sliced through her when she realised he wasn't there. Turning back to the door, she started to leave, before Kail's familiar tones echoed along the corridor. Unwilling to be cornered alone, Tay raced over to the secret entrance and hid.

"Is there anyone in there?" Kail's voice drifted through the door, and Tay froze.

"No," a man answered, his voice gruff. "Looks like we're safe." From her hidey-hole, she heard the library door close. "Carl will tell us if anyone comes."

"Good." There was a creak of leather as Kail sat in the chair. "Now, what do you have for me?"

"The girl knows nothing." There was a pause. "Or she's very well trained. But regardless, I can see no reason to hold her. She has clearance and no record."

"I'm not willing to release her yet," Kail replied, the sound of something metallic hitting the wood. "Not when I'm this close to breaking James."

"I doubt you'll get him," the other replied. "And, you will certainly lose the rank through marriage."

"You think so?" Kail laughed in a strangely flat tone. "His Father makes the rules, not him. I think he'd throw his son to the wolves, particularly if I promise to keep it quiet."

"That's foolish," came the sharp response. "You can't accuse him without being open about it, and that will lose you the betrothal." The sound of footsteps paced across the floor. "You can arrest as many nobles for sedition as you like, but it'll never get you what you want. They won't allow it."

"Maybe you're right, but I do want something on him." Another creak as Kail vacated the chair. "Just let me try?"

"Very well." The library door opened. "We'll sort it out now, while the others are still in the conclave."

Tay waited for the duo to leave the library before she moved out of the passageway. Carefully, she moved over to the library door, sneaking out into the corridor. She had no doubt that Kail was talking about Beth. The backs of Kail and one of his guards could be seen in the far distance. Tay hesitated at the door. The corridors were devoid of other people, any attempt to follow would be easy to spot. The duo moved down another corridor and out of sight. Tay gritted her teeth and made up her mind. She couldn't wait for Darius.

Decision made, she moved out into the corridor and began to follow, always keeping them far ahead.

Kail led her deeper into the Palace, down corridors and halls that were unfamiliar. The windows were fewer here, the lighting gloomy and sporadic. Tay moved slower along the passageways, trying to calm the panic that was building within her as she counted the turns she had taken. Ahead, her quarry strode around another corner and out of sight.

"Alright, let's see if you'll talk now."

Tay flattened herself against a wall, coming to a stop as Kail's voice sounded from just ahead.

"I don't know what you want me to say." Tay's heart gave a lurch as Beth's voice sounded nearby. "I don't know anything." Anger began to burn within her at the scared note to Beth's voice.

"We can do better than that."

Tay crept closer to the open door, her heart thumping painfully in her chest as she plucked up the courage to peek through the entrance.

Both men were standing, facing a chair with Beth lashed to it. A bruise stood out livid on her cheek and blood oozed from a cut on her lip, but she otherwise looked unharmed. Beth, staring forward, caught sight of Tay, and swallowed the look of hope that had started to crease her features, clearly not expecting a rescue. Whatever plans Tay might have conceived of were discarded in that one, still moment. Fury seared through Tay's mind and obliterated rational thought. She stepped into the room, burying her fear of Kail

beneath scalding hot rage.

"What the hell do you think you're doing?" Both men whirled to face the door, startled by her sudden entrance. Stunned by her own actions, Tay continued to brazen it out, allowing the burning rage to drive her. "On what charge are you holding this girl?" Quick steps carried her closer to Kail and the strange man beside him. Tay's gaze raked his form. Where Kail was rake-thin and austere, he was rotund with a florid face. Small, watery-blue eyes scanned the scene with a disquieting interest.

"None of your concern." Kail snapped back, his face lost the startled look and in its place something ugly took hold. "I have the authority to question whoever I wish." He took a step toward her. "Leave now, or do I need to question your loyalties?"

"No." Memories of the previous night played through her mind, but Tay stood firm, secure that Kail had no real power. "You've already called my loyalties into question." Beth stared at her, hope burning in her eyes. "And as I was vindicated, you can't be so foolish as to attempt to strong-arm me a second time?" Kail took a step forward, his height towering over her small frame. "Don't come near me." The rage was beginning to fade, as fear of her situation began to increase. She was alone with two men, and at least one of them meant her ill. Swallowing nervously, she kept going, not willing to let them see her fear.

"One moment Kail," the other man said. "This is Lyana James?" The insincerity was well-hidden, but Tay

could see it was there, buried beneath the courtesy.

"And you are?" Tay acknowledged him with a brief nod, wondering if she should have heard of the name.

"Jackson Prentice." He extended a sweaty hand, which Tay took gingerly. "What brought you to this part of the Palace?"

"I was exploring." Tay shuddered at the slimy touch of his fingers. "Though some of the others are expecting me for lunch."

"I see." Jackson held Kail's gaze. "But I believe he is right, this is none of your concern."

"This was my maid," Tay continued, sweat building on her brow. "I was told she was transferred. There was no mention of interrogation." A line creased Jackson's forehead. "I thought you need cause to question people within the Palace," Tay continued, sensing victory. "You have made no accusation, and you didn't even declare that you were holding her." She folded her arms across her chest and crossed her fingers, hoping that sheer audacity would see her through. "You should have learned from last night." A triumphant note entered her voice at the awkward look on his face. "Perhaps I should ask Father to end our arrangement." Kail took a small pace back and she congratulated herself on pressing the right button.

"I have every right to question possible subversives," he blustered, frustration in every syllable, though he sounded less certain of himself.

"Without evidence?" A sneer settled on her lips. "I'm certain the Prince wouldn't look too kindly at that."

Tay's voice brightened, as though the idea had just occurred to her. "Why don't we ask him?"

"Miss James is quite right," Jackson noted, voice oily with obsequience. "Perhaps Mr. Tanton has been over-zealous in the application of his duties." Kail made to speak, but stopped at one look from the other man. "Please." He reached down and undid Beth's bindings. "Take her with you."

"Thank you." Tay helped Beth to her feet and they both started for the door.

Kail took another step forward, but Jackson took hold of his arm.

"We apologise for the misunderstanding." Tay reached the door and walked through it.

"Thank you," Beth whispered as they quickly walked down the corridor.

"Don't thank me," Tay replied, in her most imperious tone of voice. "The maid they sent to replace you was a disaster."

Chapter 26

"You could have been hurt." Darius' voice bounced off the papered walls. "You were alone there." Concern layered every syllable. "What if he had decided to dispense with the pleasantries?"

"Because he still needs the marriage," Tay replied, "I figured he couldn't just make me disappear."

"No?" Darius took a slug from the glass in his hand. "And what do you think happened to Annetta Chanlin?" Tay stared down at the carpet, shuffling her feet. "What you did was extremely risky."

"But I had to do something." In the background, Beth looked between the pair of them, following the argument without comment. "He could have..." Her voice trailed to a halt.

"I know." Darius moderated his tone, allowing a measure of gentleness to enter his voice. "But it was still dangerous."

"He may think that Father will continue the match,

but if I go missing..."

"There's no positive for him." Darius nodded and stepped closer. "Alright, I suppose it worked out, so I can't really complain." Tay felt a smile lift the corners of her mouth. Darius looked at the clock on the mantel. "I suggest we pack and get ready to leave first thing in the morning."

Darius reached the door of his room before Tay caught up with him. "Is it over?" she whispered, relieved, but strangely regretful at the thought.

"Looks like it." A soft smile lit his mouth. "You didn't do a bad job." He reached out a hand and ruffled her hair affectionately. "You even said Father." A chagrined smile crossed her features as he gave a small laugh. "Don't forget we still have the ride home." Darius glanced over at Beth and gave a small nod. "Now let's get some sleep and get out of here."

Beth walked up as the door closed behind him. "You like him," she noted, making Tay turn to face her in shock. "Don't even try to lie." Beth glanced at the closed door. "He's a decent guy."

Tay followed Beth into the suite. "Yes," she replied. "And who is he?" She began to remove her clothing. "Just because I'm not immune to his charms, doesn't mean I can do anything about it."

"I know." Beth folded the set of clothing. "But it would be nice to think about it, right?"

"Yeah." Tay clambered into bed and drew the covers up to her chin. "Are you returning with us tomorrow?"

"No." Beth sat on the edge of her bed. "I'm going

back with the other staff in three days' time." Beth reached out a hand and caught Tay's fingers. "Just be careful on the trip home. I know Kail won't be able to do anything, but" — her fingers pressed painfully down against Tay's skin — "people don't always make it home from every trip to the city. They say it's bandits, but..."

"I understand." Tay reached up and hugged the other woman. "We'll be careful." She released her hold. "And you too, I don't want my rescue to go to waste."

"It won't." Beth stood up from the bed and finished packing. "Now, get some sleep." Closing the first trunk, Beth walked across the room and left. Tay switched off the lamp and laid back against the pillows, thoughts full of the day's events. Despite her desire to go home, she would miss this life. The luxury in the Palace was excessive and unnecessary, but it had given her a perspective she hadn't thought of. The rating system tied more people into their positions than she had first thought. Tay rolled onto her side and dug her nails into the pillow. Her thoughts turned to Darius. Irrespective of Beth's words, that was a situation with no future. Darius would return to his life and Tay would return to hers, granted it would be a different life than before, but it was still incompatible. Her teeth nibbled her lower lip, and she screwed her eyes shut. The pillow moulded to her grasping arms as she forced herself to relax.

Tay woke with a start and stared blindly into the

darkness. The room was still, the quiet almost holy, but something caused the hairs on the back of her neck to stand on end. Carefully, she pushed the covers off the bed and stood in the centre of the room, listening. Other than the measured ticks of the clock, no sound drifted over her ears, yet she could not relax. Whatever had woken her still played on her mind, the prickling sensations of a nameless fear running through her. Hesitantly, she walked toward the windows and the panoramic view they afforded. Pushing the curtains aside, she stared out at the Palace gardens, and her mouth dropped in shock. The sky was a deep, jet black. Tiny lights sprinkled across its surface, and in the distance... she staggered back, stunned by the vision. In the far distance, she could see a tower, so tall it touched the sky. Stumbling back from the window, she ran from her room and raced toward Darius'.

"Darius!" She pushed open his bedroom door and slapped on the light. Darius' bed took up the middle of the room and he was lying within. Despite the light in the room, and her shout, he still slept. In a rush, she moved to the side of his bed.

"Darius." She reached out and shook his shoulder. With a grunt, he rolled onto his back, displacing the sheet tangled about his torso. A hiss of shock left her lips as she stared down at his naked chest. Bruising from the fall covered his upper body and she gently reached out to trace the dark blotches. Beneath her fingers, his chest was warm, the muscles taut beneath his skin. Darius flinched, and she removed her hand.

"Darius." She leant forward and caught hold of his shoulder. "Wake up."

"Tay?" Darius' eyes snapped open, their blue depths dark with sleep. He sat up, and the sheet slipped to his waist. Unbidden, Tay's eyes drifted across his chest. Toned rather than muscular, the smooth skin of his torso was dotted with a light sprinkling of hair that spread downward toward a flat stomach. She caught her breath, feeling her heart beat a little faster.

"Enjoying the view?" Heat flooded her cheeks.

"I..." She stammered and stepped back, removing her hand from his shoulder. Another step back and she bumped the back of her knees against the table behind her. "I... just..." Confusion flooded her mind, and she stammered to a halt, wondering what had just occurred. "Look, I just needed you to be awake." Tay traded confusion for anger as she tried to avoid looking at him.

"What's wrong?" He pushed aside the bedclothes as he turned to face her. "It's"—he picked up his timepiece and stared at it—"three a.m."

Tay tried not to stare as his nearly naked body rolled out of bed. Flushing an even deeper shade of red, she tried to return to the task at hand.

"Look out of the window," she uttered, returning to the reason for her panicked flight to his room.

Darius quirked an eyebrow and crossed the room. He drew the curtain aside and a long, low oath burst from his lips. Tay came to stand beside him, staring out at the deep black of the sky with fear running through

her.

"What is it?" she asked, staring out at the pale landscape in confusion. The tower was not visible from this window, but a silvery orb hung low in the sky, casting a ghostly beam over the landscape.

"I don't know." An awed whisper fell from his lips as he stared out at the strange sky.

For a moment, they fell silent, dwarfed by the sight before them. Unbidden, Tay's fingers reached out and closed about his upper arm. They stood quiet and fearful before the unfamiliar sky. It could have been moments or hours that they stood there staring at the shimmering orb casting its light across the landscape.

"Let's take a look." Darius turned from the scene and dragged on his outdoor clothing. "There's a coat in that cupboard." He pointed toward the door in the corner and Tay rushed toward it, scared but strangely excited by the prospect.

The thick coat reached to her ankles, and Darius' scent lingered about it. As she drew the heavy fabric closed, Darius' shout of surprise caused her to look around. From the direction of the forest, a spear of light arced high into the air. They both rushed to the window, craning their heads to watch the spectacle. It lit the surroundings in shades of amber and gold as it streaked toward the pale orb. Tay moved closer to the window as she tried to follow the building light.

"What is it?" Her voice came as a whisper, terrified by what was occurring in the far distance. Beside her, Darius shook his head, the power of speech stolen by

the sight.

The column of light reached its zenith and burst into a thousand strands as it spread across the sky. As they watched, the strands coalesced and solidified, leaving the familiar amber sky in its place.

Neither of them spoke, both far too shocked at what they had seen. They remained at the window for several moments, the noise of the clock marking time in the background as they struggled to find the words.

"That book Talon gave you," Darius said. "I think we'd better have a look at it."

"It's nothing but stories," Tay replied. "It doesn't mention..."

"Go get it," Darius insisted, his eyes not leaving the window.

"Alright." Tay reluctantly stepped away from the window, stopping every few paces to stare back through the glass at the vista that was no longer there.

Once through his bedroom door, Tay raced from Darius' quarters and into her own. The book was where she had left it, stuffed between the cushions, and innocuous in its blue leather binding. Picking it up, she turned and began to head back. Her fingers reached out for the door handle, only to still at the sound of movement from the main suite. Carefully, and with as little noise as possible, she opened the door. Something smashed in the room beyond, and the noise of several feet reached her ears. Heart in her mouth, she closed the door. She knew that sound; it was the night of father's arrest, and she was in the attic, listening to the

guards ransack their home.

"Fetch the girl." The voice drifted through the door, and Tay panicked. She backed up into the bedroom. Locking the door to the main suite, she dragged on a set of boots. Reaching into a drawer, she pulled a pair of gloves free as footsteps sounded from her living room. A blast of frigid air chilled her skin as she flung open the window and clambered onto the ledge. In her haste, her foot skidded on the frozen sill, and it was only thanks to her firm grip on the window-latch that she did not plummet to the ground below. The door to her room shuddered as several heavy blows slammed against it. Trying to control the fear that raced through her, she forced herself to start moving. Reaching out, she seized hold of the sill with her other hand, uttered a brief prayer, and then let go of the latch. For a moment, she hung in the air, kept safe by a tenuous grip. Her muscles screamed in pain as she dug her toes into the wall, trying to find a foothold. Scrabbling against the rough stone, a pained whimper escaped her lips as one of her fingernails tore and began to bleed. Thoroughly scared, she dug her ruined fingers into one of the tiny cracks on the wall. Her feet scrabbled uselessly against the stone, and her shoulder muscles screamed in agony as she tried to cling on. From above, she heard the door to her room smash open, and she pressed herself against the side of the wall.

"Where is she?" The voice was rough, menacing. Unable to move, she tried to flatten herself against the stone, fervently wishing that they would just leave.

"Here." The voice drifted from the window above her, and she clenched her eyes closed in anguish.

"So I see." The voice echoed in her ears. She tried to move, but her muscles were almost frozen as she struggled to hold onto the wall. "Do you require some help?" She chanced a glance upward. Jackson leant out of the window, his face mocking as it stared down at her.

Tay wanted to shake her head to deny him the satisfaction, but her body screamed out for relief. With her muscles shrieking in agony and Jackson watching her, her chances of escape were limited. Gritting her teeth, she nodded once.

His head retreated inside to be replaced by a guard. The man shuffled out onto the ledge and leant down.

"Give me your hand," he commanded, stretching his clumsy-looking fingers out toward her. Steeling herself, she reached out and gingerly took hold of his ample, calloused hand. His fingers curled about her wrist, and with a silent prayer, she let go of the ledge. Pain ripped through her right shoulder, the weight almost too much for one arm to support. With a grunt of pain, she reached out with her left hand to take hold of his wrist.

"I've got her, Sir." Exertion strained his words as he drew her closer to the open window. Another step and she would be back in the room and their clutches. In a panic, she looked back over her shoulder at the ground. A deep snowdrift laid piled against the side of the building, its height level with the windows below. Taking a deep breath, she tugged her hand free, falling

away from the window and into empty space.

Time sped up as she plummeted through the air toward the snow below. She slammed into the ground, the force of the landing driving the breath from her lungs. Pain seared through her legs and side, the freezing snow not quite deadening the sensations. She rolled over twice and came to a stop at the base of the drift. Pushing herself onto her back, she stared up at the window, watching as the guard disappeared. Scooting backward, she tried to stand, but she fell as her leg gave way beneath her. The guard poked his head through the window, watching as she struggled to get to her feet.

Her feet sank into the cold snow, the sensation almost painful as the bare skin of her calves touched the powdery substance. Conscious of the need to flee, she tried to run, her legs wobbling painfully as she moved around the corner of the Palace and toward one of the outer doors. Her feet slipped uncomfortably in the unlaced boots as she staggered to one of the library doors and tried the handle. The door was locked. Desperate, she reached down and closed her fingers round the lip of one of the stone planters by the door. Cradling the heavy urn in her hands, she aimed it at the door. Shards of crystal rain fell as the glass shattered.

Reaching through the jagged hole, and slicing her hand as she did so, Tay unlocked the door. The library was empty, but she could hear shouts from the corridor. Rapidly wiping her feet, she raced across the library toward the hidden door.

The secret passage opened easily and she dashed inside, closing the door just ahead of the guards' entrance. Hurrying rapidly along the passageway, she followed the route to the second floor. Reaching the exit, she came to a stop. The door to the upper floor laid before her, its solid bulk hiding her from view. Carefully, and as quietly as she could, Tay pushed the door open a fraction, leant forward and pressed her ear to the gap. Her breathing sounded loud in the small space, and she fancied that her pursuers could hear it.

As the pounding of her heart subsided, the pain in her leg reasserted itself, and she took a deep, steadying breath. From along the corridor, she could hear approaching footsteps, and she ducked back into the hidey hole.

"She can't have gotten far," Jackson's voice sounded from the other side of the door, and she shrank back even further against the wall. "She's probably headed back into the Palace, it's far too cold for her to still be in the grounds." There was a murmur of assent and Tay wondered how many were standing with him.

"What about her brother?" a female voice interjected. "You don't have any evidence to hold him."

"Oh, don't I?" There was mockery in that question.

"No." Tay stilled; the woman's voice was familiar. "Do you think the rest of the court will take kindly to an arrest purely on your whim?" A tense silence followed as Tay held her breath, trying to determine the speaker's identity.

"You forget your place," the voice retorted, his tone

sharp.

"And you're being over-eager." Tay pressed herself as close to the door as possible. "You have no solid evidence, no credible eye-witnesses and the girl is a close friend of the Prince."

"That's why I'm not arresting them," he continued smoothly. "Once we have them both, we'll clear out the suite and claim that they left as expected in the morning."

There was a hiss as the woman drew in a breath. "That's playing a dangerous game."

"But a necessary one." There was a creak, as though they had moved position. "They're looking for the Coils. It'll only be a matter of time before they find them, and with Kail too set on gaining access to the nobility..."

"He can't be trusted to deal with it." There was a sigh. "Alright, let's..." The sound of running feet interrupted the conversation.

"We've had a report of movement from on the ground floor."

"That'll be her." Tay slowly backed away from the door, hoping that Jackson did not know about the secret passage. "Come on."

Pressed against the passage wall, Tay waited for the group to leave. As the noise of the elevator sounded in the distance, she hesitantly approached the door. Taking a deep breath, she caught hold of the handle and stopped. In the still coolness of the passageway, her palms clammy with sweat, Tay waited to open the door.

Fear and adrenaline flowed through her body, shaking her fingers as she tried to build up the courage to leave her hiding place.

Come on.

With a mental shake of her head, she tried to push the fear behind her. Closing her eyes, she pressed down the handle and quietly stepped into the hallway. No shouts or cries of alarm assailed her. She opened her eyes and moved into the empty corridor. Pausing as she reached the centre of the hall, she glanced both ways, reassuring herself that the guards had left. Relaxing slightly at the sight of the empty landing, she took a few moments to think.

She couldn't leave Darius in their clutches, of that she was certain. For several minutes she dithered in place, constructing and discarding numerous scenarios. If she had any idea of where the Royal Apartments were, she would have woken Talon. Time weighed on her mind as she rejected scheme after scheme. Finally, driven by the necessity to move rather than anything else, she turned toward the main staircase. Her feet made no sound on the carpeted floor as she traversed the distance.

She reached the lift and stopped, listening for any sounds of movement from the small box. Satisfied with the apparent silence, she continued forward, heart pumping painfully in her chest as she tried to stifle any noise. The corridor widened out as she moved toward the central staircase. Stopping at the balcony's edge, she stared down into the dim hallway. The lamps were

barely lit and long shadows swallowed the edges of the room. Hoping that the lack of light meant that the hallway was safe, Tay slowly descended the stairs. The large window offered a clear view of the sky, and Tay paused, remembering the strange darkness that had replaced the sky not fifteen minutes ago. As she stepped quietly toward the first landing, she wondered if this event had anything to do with the Coils of Copper and Brass. Certainly, the invasion of their rooms was an indication of such. Taking the final steps to the floor, she headed for the racks of spiders mounted against the walls. Carefully, quietly, she pried three loose before hurrying back up the stairs. Diving once more into the passageway, she carefully examined the spiders, looking for any hints to their operation.

On the back of the spiders, and next to the key that wound them, was a small switch labelled:

Delay

Below that, she could see another lever. Tiny, elegant script marked each setting. She brought the spider closer to her face and read:

1. Windows.
2. Minor Maintenance.
3. Mouse Catching.

She raised her eyebrows at third option, and continued to read.

4. Snow Clearance.
5. Floor washing.

Tearing her eyes away from the list, she stared into space, tapping her toes on the floor as she tried to think.

After a moment, she reached down and flicked the lever to *3*, and glanced back toward the exit. There was still no sign of any movement. Gritting her teeth, she flicked the delay switch on.

Tay left the passage with three fully wound spiders in her hands. As fast as she dared, she headed back to her suite. The main door to the suite was closed, but she could hear people talking from within. Taking a deep breath, she flicked off the delay switch. The spiders in her arms began to twitch, but she didn't let it faze her. With a confidence she didn't feel, she threw open the door to the suite, dropping the spiders as she did so. Slamming the door shut, she waited for the chaos to begin.

The spiders hit the ground, their primitive sensors homing in on the moving sources of heat. Heading for the door, the first guard gave a yell of agony as a long scalpel sliced into the top of his foot, the spiders' blind programming not seeing the difference between mice and feet. With a powerful kick, the guard launched the spider into the air as another spider slashed at his other

foot. Protected by heavy boots, the man lunged for the crawling piece of metal, only to drag his hand back as a deep slash opened across his hand. The second guard charged forward, tripping over the third spider.

Outside of the room, Tay listened to the chaos, her hand on the door handle. As another yell punctuated the air, she pushed open the door. The room was in a frenzy, the nimble spiders zipping away from the grasping hands of the guards as though they were alive.

"Hey." One of the guards saw her in the doorway.

Tay ran, dodging past the first guard as she did so. One of the spiders loomed in front of her and she jumped back, hampered by the loosely tied boots. The blade skittered off the smooth leather and sliced into her ankle. A cry of pain escaped her lips as blood began to flow.

"Got you." A hand grabbed hold of her hair and pulled her backward. Fighting to be free, she reached for another of the spiders. Ignoring the whirling blade, she threw the metal contraption behind her, and was rewarded by the guard's scream. The pain in her head subsided as he let go. Tay scrambled forward and dove into the other room. Darius was tied to a chair, a purple-black bruise livid on his face.

"Are you alright?" She rushed forward, and began to undo the knots that kept him pinned.

"Not particularly," he answered, flexing his arms as the ropes fell free. "What did you do?" He nodded to the other door and the yells that punctuated the air.

"Spiders on a mouse-catcher setting," she replied

tersely, undoing the bonds on his legs. "Come on."

Darius stood, stretched slightly and then headed for the door. Beside him, Tay stared at the scene in shock. The nimble, mechanical spiders were whirring about the floor, still aiming for the legs of the guards. The trio were bleeding from numerous cuts, and at least one was sporting the beginnings of a black eye.

"Smart move," Darius murmured. "Though I'm a little disappointed in their ineptitude."

"I'm sure they would be desolated to hear that," Tay quipped, her spirits rising with each moment of freedom. "We'll have to be careful." She nodded at the spinning contraptions. "They're dangerous until the mechanism runs down."

One of the guards kicked out, flipping over one of the spiders with a hefty blow. The clacking limbs flailed madly in the air as it tried to right itself.

"Put them on their backs," the guard called, as he kicked the struggling spider away.

"Time to go." Darius strode into the room, balled his hand into a fist, and punched the guard in the stomach. As the man bent double, Darius seized hold of his belt and upper shoulder, and threw him into the path of another guard. Both guards hit the floor, the spiders slashing at their faces with razor sharp blades. "Come on." Darius held out a hand, and Tay ran to take it. Darius' fingers closed about hers, the warm pressure sending a thrill through her.

They ran for the door, and out into the corridor. "Where to?" Tay gasped out, as they sprinted away from

the room.

"Help." Darius responded tersely, as they raced along the upper landing past the hidden passageway. Tay gave it a momentary glance as he rushed them toward the lift.

"Wait." She pulled him to a stop as they reached the top of the stairs. "They went down toward the library."

Darius nodded, and began to slowly walk down the stairs. Tay followed, the sound of blood thumping in her ears. It was a surreal experience, sneaking through the corridors of the palace, clad in nightclothes and Darius' thick coat. The lace hem of the nightdress peeked out from beneath the heavy wool, its delicate tracery incongruous with the boots and coat.

"Wait." A thought flickered through her mind, and she caught hold of Darius' arm. "We just need to wake the Palace."

"What do you mean?" Their voices were soft, yet they seemed terribly loud in the quiet of the hallway.

"I heard them talking. They said that this wasn't an arrest, that he couldn't arrest us." Her mind began to whir as she considered the possibilities. "He was going to make it appear as thought we had left for home."

"And then arrange an accident or bandits," Darius finished, a grim look running across his features. "If that's the case..." With quick steps, he descended the rest of the staircase and raced across the hall. Reaching forward, he smashed a small square of glass and pulled down the lever that laid beneath. There was a momentary pause, and then a bell began to ring. "Fire

alarm." He smiled down at Tay's curious face. "Now we just have to wait until everyone evacuates."

Tay gave a small chuckle, which turned into a yelp of surprise as he pulled her into a small alcove, out of sight of the main hall. "Just in case," he muttered, as he moved them deeper into the shadows. The bell continued to sound, the noise jangling Tay's nerves. Darius' hands were wrapped about her upper arms and his chin brushed the top of her head. A small shudder rippled through her, and she wet her lips nervously.

"Thank you." His rich, warm tones surrounded her. He was so close that his breath stirred her hair, sending another ripple down her spine. She looked up straight into his eyes.

"For what?" It was difficult to breathe, his gaze rendering her tongue-tied with nameless anticipation.

"Saving my neck." He leant forward, lowering his voice. "You didn't have to."

"I..." Her voice stuttered to a halt, strangled by the rush of emotion that was swamping her. Those eyes moved closer, and she felt herself leaning forward.

"Tay..."

The sound of running feet drew their attention, and they snapped apart, both stunned but what had nearly occurred. Concealed in the small alcove, they watched the first of the Palace guests head past them and through the main doors.

"Come on." Darius took hold of her hand and led her out into the hall. They followed the small group out of the building and into the snow. Behind them, people

began to stream down the staircases, all fooled by the alarm.

"What's going on?" Darius stepped forward, the question ensuring that all eyes were on them. "Is there a fire?"

"I don't know." Confusion rippled through the crowd as they stared at the solid stone structure.

"Lyana." A shout caught her attention, and she looked up to see Amira stumbling across the snowy courtyard.

"Amira." Relieved to see the other girl, Tay left Darius' side to join her. "Exciting, isn't it?" She forced her voice to sound jovial, trying to push aside the fears of earlier. Out of the corner of her eye she could see Kail leaving the building, his face filled with confusion. Turning away from his stare, Tay threw herself into her role as Lyana. With such a large group it was impossible for Kail to drag them away. Thankful for Darius' quick thinking, she glanced across at him. He winked at her grateful smile and returned to his conversation, leaving Tay to stare after him. Memories of being cramped together in the alcove ran through her mind.

"Well, do you want to?"

Tay turned back to Amira, conscious that she had missed the entirety of the girl's conversation.

"Do I want to what?" she asked, reddening slightly with embarrassment.

"Stay at mine for a few days," Amira replied. "You can return with me, and go home later."

"I would love to," Tay began, wishing that she could

accept the invitation, "but I have to get home." Her thoughts roamed about for a plausible reason to refuse. "My Father's expecting me back."

"Shame." Amira turned back to look at the crowd. "I think you would have had fun."

They fell silent as more people left the confines of the Palace. The alarm still clanged loudly in the background, echoing across the frozen landscape. Tay's feet were cold, the boots not quite able to keep her toes warm. She stared up at the sky, comforted by the familiar orange tint.

"Amira." She turned to the other girl, a sudden inspiration striking her. "Did you see the sky earlier?" Amira froze and Tay wondered if she'd said something wrong. "Amira?" The other girl's eyes darted quickly to the left and right, as though searching for listeners, before she beckoned her closer.

"Yes." Amira's voice was low, conspiratorial. "I don't think we're supposed to talk about it."

"Why not?" Tay argued, in a voice just as quiet. "You couldn't miss it."

"But not everybody would have seen it," came the response, as Tay opened her mouth to ask. "Only those awake at that time, which would have just been a few people." Shuffling closer, she continued, "It's happened before." Tay's brain stuttered to a halt, as she tried to comprehend Amira's words.

"Then why?"

"Because any rumours of the sky changing colour are quickly put to rest by the authorities." Amira checked

around for the second time. "And it usually only occurs near the forest or the capital." Catching hold of her hand, she steered Lyana away from the growing throng. "You won't have seen it near the Mine."

"But what is..." She stopped speaking as Amira's fingers dug into her hand, the sudden pain stilling her voice.

"It's not good to ask."

"Lyana." They turned at the sound of Darius' voice. Amira turned to move away, but Tay caught hold of her hand.

"Tell me." Amira glanced down at her fingers, and then at Darius. "I won't rat on you."

"Father said it is the Coils." And with those words, she tugged her arm free and headed into the crowd, disappearing from view within moments.

Tay watched her vanish before she turned to face Darius. A curious gleam lit his eyes as he stared down at her. "Is everything alright?"

"Yes," she answered. "Amira just asked if I wished to go to her estate with her." She felt compelled to use some of the truth.

"Why did she run off like that?" Light, teasing tones filled the space between them. "Did I scare her?"

"No, I think she likes you." Tay got into the light-hearted conversation, but her heart wasn't quite in it. The revelation about the sky and its connection to the Coils troubled her. She desperately wanted to talk with Darius about Amira's words, but she couldn't, not here. Indulging in a bout of faux sibling teasing, she waited

for them to return to their rooms, hoping that Kail would leave them be for what remained of the night.

After what seemed like an age, they were allowed back into the building. The clock in the hall struck four thirty as they crossed the threshold. With their night disturbed, many of the guests chose to remain in the hall and talk. Darius and Tay stood beside the stairs, unwilling to leave the company of so many people. Kail was nowhere in sight, yet Talon walked amongst the crowd, friendly and approachable.

Confident that Kail would not attempt any abduction in the presence of such a crowd, Darius and Tay stayed in the hall, the ambiance felt like a mellower version of the ball. There was still the gossip and laughter, but it seemed quieter, more subdued.

"Good evening," Talon's voice sounded by her left ear, and she turned toward him. His hair was tousled from sleep and the trip outside, but his eyes were alert.

"More like morning," Tay replied.

"Yes." His voice was strangely terse and she gave him a searching look.

"Are you okay?"

"No." Tay stepped back slightly at the curtness in his voice.

"Am I bothering you?"

"No, I'm just..." Talon's eyes flickered about the room. Satisfied with whatever he saw, he continued, "Look, you're leaving in the morning, and I don't think I'll see you again." Tay felt her heart stop at the deathly serious note to his words. "So" — he reached out and

caught hold of her hand — "I just want" — Tay sucked in a breath as he moved closer — "you to be careful."

Tay's head snapped up, almost disappointed that he hadn't attempted to kiss her. "Thank you." From the corner of her eye she could see Darius watching them, and a strange sense of satisfaction drifted through her.

"This isn't an idle wish," Talon continued, checking his surroundings for the second time.

"Sire?"

"I think someone intends for you to not make it home." Tay stilled, the memory of her earlier frantic dash running through her mind.

"I agree," she replied, allowing her fears to bubble to the surface. "They've already tried."

"I thought they might have." Talon nodded at the crowd surrounding them. "He has some clout, doesn't he?"

"Can't you do anything?" She stepped closer to him, ensuring that her words wouldn't be overheard. "You're the Prince."

"That title doesn't have as much power as it should," Talon replied. "They are following Father's instructions, and looking for traitors." He gave a small snort. "And you have to admit that you and your brother are less than innocent in that regard."

"What can we do?" Tay's stomach sank unpleasantly with Talon's words.

"I've decided that I need to see parts of my future kingdom."

It took a moment for the implication of his words to

sink in. The conversation in the room ebbed and flowed behind them, as Tay's mouth dropped open.

"Do you mean...?"

"Yes." Talon gave a small smile at the look of shock on her face. "I'll return with you and your brother to the Mine." He continued to speak, but Tay heard none of it, stunned by his decision, and troubled by the potential issues.

"But why?" she stammered out eventually.

"Because" — he reached down and took hold of her hand — "I don't want you to disappear." Tay held her breath as he drew her hand to his lips.

"Sire."

Both turned at Darius' approach. Tay stepped back quickly, removing her hand from Talon's grip.

"You'd better tell him the good news." Talon turned away, and began to walk toward the stairs. "I'll see you at the station."

Darius waited until Talon had reached the second floor before he turned to Tay. He raised an eyebrow in query, watching as Tay shrugged her shoulders helplessly. "He's coming home with us," she blurted out, unable to keep the panic from her voice. "He thinks that they'll try to take the train."

"And he thinks it won't happen with him on it?" Darius replied with incredulity. "He's gambling on his safety."

"I don't." Tay felt her knees go weak, and she leant back against the balustrade in shock. "We're going to have to warn Lyana," she blurted out. "And I won't be

able to go home."

"I did say not to flirt with the Prince," Darius noted, with a wry smile. "Maybe his advisors will talk him out of it." Tay raised her head in hope. "But," Darius continued, the word striking down the flickering sensation in one fell swoop, "just in case, I'll let her know." Tay barely heard him, too preoccupied with thoughts of continuing with the charade. Moments ticked by as Darius stared down at her. "It'll be fine."

"I don't think it will," Tay whispered, her voice lost beneath the onslaught of emotions.

Darius watched her for a moment before, with a sigh, he reached out and drew her carefully into his arms. Startled, Tay froze for a moment, before relaxing and allowing him to hold her. It was a brotherly hug, at least that's what she told herself, as he wrapped his arms about her, holding her gently.

"It will be fine," he murmured against her hair. "I'll help you get through this."

Unable to answer, Tay rested her head against his shoulder, relaxing into his warm body with a strange sense of relief.

"Let's get sorted." He pulled back and handed her a handkerchief. "You're going to have to lie, and lie well."

Taking hold of the handkerchief, Tay dabbed her eyes, before she followed him back up the stairs. Thoughts of the trip home filled her mind, and she clamped down on the sensations they provoked. She could lie, she had managed it up until this point, it was purely a case of continuing the deception. As they

reached the landing, she raised her head to watch Darius' back, and the familiar, confused feelings began again. He had held her as though she were his sister, but Tay could not deny that he awoke other, less platonic sensations. There was also the issue of the Prince to consider, Talon had made no secret of his interest, which generated its own problems. The desire to be free of this hornets' nest raged through her, and she wished she had never agreed to this insanity. Biting her lip in frustration, she continued on to the landing and their room.

Chapter 27

The train seemed slower as they moved across the landscape. Tay, Darius and the Prince were sitting in the lounge. A strange, unsettled silence rested over them, and Tay constantly fought the urge to fidget. Several of Talon's guard stood at the entrances to the room, their demeanour rigid and humourless. Since the Prince's arrival on the station platform, the atmosphere had intensified and you could almost cut it with a knife. Talon seemed unwilling to talk, and Tay and Darius too hesitant.

"What did Amira say?" Talon finally spoke, the atmosphere shattering with his words.

"Sire?" Tay asked, her voice small.

Talon rolled his eyes and stood. "I've told you before," Darius shot her a look, but she ignored it. "Call me Talon."

"Alright, Talon." Clamping down on the nerves, she re-focused on the conversation. "What did you say?"

"What did Amira tell you?" he reiterated, with some patience. "I saw you talking to her."

"Oh that." Tay cast her mind back to the previous night. "She wanted to know if I could go and stay with her." Darius gave her a searching look, but she ignored it too, focusing in on Talon and his questions. Despite his assistance and friendly demeanour, she could not forget that he was royalty. Tay glanced at the guards positioned about the room, painfully aware that she could not speak freely.

"I would have gone." Tay tuned back to the conversation, wondering if she would ever be free of this feeling of dread. "It would have gotten you away from your betrothed."

Darius shifted in his seat, and Tay shot him a sympathetic glance. Once this assignment was over, she would be free, but Darius would still have to deal with Kail. Not for the first time, she wondered how he would handle the situation.

"That's true." Darius caught her eye and winked, the simple gesture reassuring her. "But it would have caused more problems." Talon turned his attention to the other side of the room.

"How so?"

"Surely you know that Amira's father is not held in particularly high regard," Darius replied, a strange mix of condescension and disappointment in his voice. Tay's eyes narrowed at his tone. "Particularly after his attempt to start archaeological excavations in the forest." Talon glared back at Darius, clearly infuriated by his manner.

"But I'm sure you knew that." With that, he picked up the cup that laid by his elbow and stood. "I'm going to my cabin."

With several long strides, he walked toward the back of the carriage. With his absence, the cabin felt smaller, more claustrophobic. Tay turned her head to stare at Talon. The young prince was watching her, curiosity in his gaze.

"What?" She couldn't help the touch of annoyance that tainted her voice.

"I'm just curious about your brother," Talon uttered. "He doesn't seem to like me." Tay struggled for a moment, wondering if he had discovered their lack of kinship. Glancing across the carriage at Talon, she dismissed the idea that had he realised her deception, she doubted he would be so calm.

"He thinks this is a stupid idea," Tay replied, conscious of the need to answer. "If Kail is determined to deal with us, why would he let you stop him?"

"I think your brother is overly paranoid," Talon replied, "and a little over-protective." He gave a small grin. "Is he like this with all your suitors?"

"No," Tay replied. "I don't have any suitors."

"That's not the Palace gossip." The words fell against her ears, like lead weights splashing into a pond.

"What do you mean?" Dread teased at the edges of her mind. Their entire plan rested on Lyana's anonymity. With that gone... she tried to resist the urge to panic.

"Did you think your dalliance had gone unnoticed?"

"I hoped." She tried to brazen it out, acutely aware of the gaps in her knowledge. Lyana had covered the basic details of how to act, but had been reticent on personal history, insistent that none at court would know her. Cynical and frustrated, Tay snorted inwardly at the girl's naïvety. Her brief exposure to the court revealed it for the nest of vipers it was. Lyana had sent her into this with barely enough information to survive.

"Of course you did," Talon continued, the interest still sparkling in his eyes. "So what happened?"

"Excuse me?"

"Did your father forbid the relationship?" Tay's mind began to whir as the questions started. "Did he leave you?"

Tay stayed silent. The answers were not available, and even if they were, the Prince's curiosity was in poor taste. The silence stretched between them, thick and uncomfortable, and the noise of steel wheels on tracks was loud in the quiet.

"If you'll excuse me," Tay stood and crossed to the door. She heard him apologise as she opened the door, but she paid it no mind. The door closed behind her, and she leant against it, wondering just how she had managed to get herself into this mess. Closing her eyes, she waited. The door at her back remained still, Talon clearly taking the hint and leaving her alone. The rocking motion of the train soothed her and she finally pushed away from the door.

A few short steps and she was outside her cabin door. Something made her hesitate, and her hand fell

away from the latch. Setting her jaw, she marched along the corridor to knock loudly on Darius' door. Following the muffled summons, she depressed the handle and walked in.

Darius was laid on his bunk, eyes closed, and hands folded across his chest.

"Come to chastise me?" he asked, eyes still firmly shut.

"What's with you?" She closed the door, and walked across the room. Sinking into a leather chair, she leant forward. "Could you be more antagonistic?"

"Probably." He opened his eyes and sat up. "His presence here is a very bad idea."

"So you've said," Tay retorted. "Several times."

"And I'll say it again." Rolling onto his side, he fixed her with an unwavering stare. "He's no protection, to us or to himself." Tay's eyes were once more drawn to his, captivated by their deep-blue depths. "Should our enemies decide to make us disappear, the presence of the Prince is more of an enticement."

"Why?" Tay was confused. "Why would Kail endanger the Prince, or risk exposure?"

"Because..." He didn't get to finish the sentence, as a loud explosion ripped through the carriage. The train buckled, and Tay pitched forward, slamming her head on the edge of the bunk as she fell. Stars flared before her vision, and a curtain of blood slid across her face. The carriage continued to roll, throwing both of them to the floor. Tay heard Darius scream in pain, as he slammed into the table. The train rolled once, twice,

and then fell still.

"Tay." Through a haze of pain and blood, Tay stared across at Darius. The table had splintered and a large, jagged piece of wood was sticking in his side.

"Darius." She tried to stand, but the pain in her head quickly put paid to that endeavour. With tortured, slow movements, she hauled herself across the wrecked carriage to his side. His blood dripped to the floor, and she took a breath. "I'm going to try to pull it free."

"Don't..." He caught hold of her hands and pushed her back. "If you do that, I'll keep bleeding." Swallowing convulsively, he pointed to the wood. "Try and break it off."

Swallowing back the fear, Tay gingerly took hold of the shredded timber. The splinters tore the skin of her palms, but she ignored them as she began to break the wood. In the distance, she could hear shouts and the sounds of weapons fire. Pushing aside the trepidation, she concentrated on the ragged wound before her. It didn't appear to be particularly deep, but she didn't have enough knowledge to correctly treat the problem. Darius winced with each minute motion, until Tay's nervous hands finally snapped the offending item in half. Dropping the remainder to the floor, she leant forward and tore the shirt away from the bloody stump.

"You seem to like my naked chest." The joking words slurred from between his lips.

"Not like this," Tay replied, missing the implication of his words, as she frantically began to tear strips from one of the pillowcases. "Two accidents within four

days." She wrapped the cotton tightly around his body, attempting to keep his torso still. "Are you trying to impress someone?"

"Is it working?" His voice drifted, and she glanced up at his face.

"Hey." She slapped his face, pulling him back to wakefulness. "Don't nod off." With rapid movements, she secured the makeshift bandage. The stake was still prominent, but at least it wouldn't shift position now. She covered him with a blanket. Finishing, she settled back and raised her fingers to the cut on her forehead. Flinching with the pain, she dipped a piece of cloth in the remaining drops of liquid from the base of a shattered china jug and cleaned the blood from her head. That done, she sat next to Darius and stared down at his pale, drawn features. With the wound bandaged, she was free to give in to worry. Blood stained the cotton bandages, and fear rose within her.

"The Prince?" Darius' fingers curled about her wrist.

"I don't know," she uttered, listening to the continuing sounds of combat from outside. "I can't leave you like this."

"If he dies, you can kiss the rebellion goodbye." Despite the pain, Darius' voice sounded strong. "Make sure." He let go of her hand, and sank back against the floor.

Tay stared at him for several moments, torn between the sense of his words and her concern for his well-being. Darius' injuries were severe, and thoughts of losing him began to seep through her mind.

"Go on." He pushed her gently toward the door. "I'll be fine."

Tay bit her lip, the wound in his side making his statement a lie. If she left him, he could...she didn't want to finish that thought. He pushed her again, the strength missing from his hands. With a nervous gulp, she stood and glanced toward the door. Shots still rang out on the other side, and she clenched her fists.

"Tay?" Her heart turned over at the pained note to his voice. "You have to." If she left, there was no telling if she would see him again. The thought burned through her like acid. Darius could not die, not when they hadn't worked out their feelings. He may not feel anything for her, but in that moment, with Darius bleeding on the floor, she finally acknowledged her feelings for him. Memories of his sardonic, yet caring nature flooded through her mind, and she came to a decision. A moment's hesitation, and she knelt at Darius' side.

"Just in case," she whispered, before she leant forward and gently brushed her lips against his. There was a stunned pause before, to her surprise, Darius responded. His fingers curled into her hair, trying to hold her with a strength he didn't have. His lips moved against hers with a passion that shocked her. Mindful of the damage to his side, she slid her arms about his neck, answering his kisses with ones of her own. The sounds of battle faded into the background as his lips explored hers, and she wished that the two of them were somewhere, anywhere, else.

"You were quite right, I was jealous," he uttered, as she finally, reluctantly, pulled away. "I've wanted to do that since..." His voice trailed off, as he drifted back toward sleep.

"Stay awake." Shaking his shoulder for the second time, Tay roused him once more. "We'll talk about it later," Tay replied, suddenly unsure of her actions. "I'd better..." She pointed at the door.

"Good luck," he whispered, as she shakily got to her feet and began to stagger across the room.

The door to the corridor opened with some difficulty, and she tottered out into the twisted mess of the train. The carriage was listing at an odd angle, and she pulled herself along using the wall. Periodically she could hear the sounds of gunfire from elsewhere in the wreck, and she began to creep along the corridor. Noises from up ahead stopped her, and she dove into her room. The luxurious cabin was a mess, filled with bits of shattered furniture. The clothing had spilled free from the wardrobe, and now laid in piles of glorious colour across the floor. Pressing back behind the door, she waited, praying that their attackers would pass her by unnoticed. The sound of the lounge door opening made her freeze, and she cowered against the wall.

"Check there." The command sounded from the hallway and she knelt, moving deeper into the shadows. A man dressed in a ragged mix of clothing entered the room. Tay held her breath, hoping that he wouldn't see her. The man crossed the room toward the nightstand. With a wrench he pulled open the shattered drawer, and

Tay cringed as he threw Talon's loaned book to the floor. Ignoring the thin hardback, the man rummaged through the drawer, dragging the jewellery from its box, and stuffing it into his pockets. Tay slid closer to the floor, as she took hold of the door's edge with her fingertip. Slowly, cautiously, she drew the door toward her, leaving only a crack for her to see.

"Come on." The man's head snapped up, and he turned back. Tay held her breath as the man moved closer. Nerves stretched to breaking-point, she watched him stride from the room with barely a glance in her direction.

Shaking with a mixture of fear and adrenalin, Tay waited. The sound of an outer carriage door echoed along the passage, and she relaxed. Carefully, she picked herself up, and walked over to the book. Securing it within an inner pocket, she headed back to the corridor, mindful of Darius' injuries, and the need to find the Prince. Checking the corridor for signs of life, she continued to move toward the lounge, and hopefully, a living Talon. The lounge door hung drunkenly on its hinges, and she moved faster, panic driving her forward.

"Have you found the others?" She stopped moving at the unfamiliar voice, and leant closer to the open door.

"Not yet." She approached as quietly as she could, nerves jangling with each step. Swallowing back the fear, she ducked her head through the door, and almost froze at the sight that met her.

Sprawled beside the door laid one of the Prince's guards, his limbs at unnatural angles and covered in

blood. She drew her hand to her mouth, and stifled the gasp that threatened to choke her. Before her, in the centre of the lounge, stood two men with weapons cradled in their arms. Tay drew back out of sight, and sank against the wall, heart pumping madly in her chest.

"Well, you'd better find them," the conversation continued, and Tay breathed a sigh of relief.

"They won't be able to go anywhere..." the other voice started to argue. Tay dropped to her knees and began to crawl forward. Glass cut her hands and knees as she slowly made her way across the floor. She crossed the threshold to the lounge, her heart thumping painfully in her chest as she prayed they would be too busy to see her.

"No, but I don't think we've got long before the Prince's guards mount a successful defence." Carefully, she raised her head and caught a peek at the two speakers. Dressed in a mixture of styles, they seemed to be rebels or bandits. Tay reached the bar and crawled out of sight behind it. Hiding with her back pressed up against the wood, she listened to the men talk, wondering about Talon.

"They won't be able to," the second man argued. "They're cut off, and with the City half a day away..."

"There's no chance."

Tay staggered back, stunned by the words she was hearing. Thoughts of Darius bleeding to death in the cabin flooded her mind. Slumping back against the wall of the bar, Tay felt her courage begin to fail. How could

she possibly hope to save Darius when she had no idea of where to begin. The conversation continued, but Tay shut it out, lost in her indecision.

It took the men walking from the lounge to galvanise her into action. Finally, alone behind the wrecked bar, she tried to pull herself together. Several deep breaths, and she stood. The lounge was a mess, bottles and glasses laid across the floor, and the heavy, acrid mix of alcohol and blood tainted the air. Shaking, she moved from her hiding place, looking for signs of the Prince. Distant sounds of combat still echoed through the air, but she heard nothing from the cabins behind her. The silence may not have meant anything, but Tay hoped that it signalled Darius' escape from the attackers.

"Lyana." Her head snapped up at the sound of her alias, and she looked around the empty lounge in confusion. "Up here." There was a shifting sound, and a ceiling panel slid open. Talon stared out of the newly revealed compartment, his face nervous. Relief rushed through her at the sight of his face.

"Talon." Keeping her voice as low as possible, she stood on one of the upended tables to talk to him. "How did you...?"

"My bodyguards," he replied shortly. "They hid me, and then went to fight."

"Come on." She reached out a hand. "We need to help my brother." The words felt strange on her lips, the memory of Darius' kiss looming large in her thoughts.

Talon ignored her outstretched hand, and lowered himself out of the crawlspace. He landed heavily on the

cabin floor, and Tay's head whipped round to the door, convinced that he had been heard. When no shouts were forthcoming, they carefully picked their way across the floor.

"Wait." Talon reached behind the bar and drew free a box. Tay stared at it carefully, confused at the slender object. Talon caught her gaze and smiled. "It's a first aid kit." He pressed a small button on the side, and it popped open. Several small packages laid within, and Tay reached out a curious finger to touch them. The parcels were bound in a slick, smooth wrapping, unlike any she had seen before. "Royals only," Talon noted, as he closed the box. Securing the package within his coat, he began heading toward the corridor. "Come on."

They left the lounge, shuffling quietly along the corridor. The door to Darius' wrecked room stood wide open, and Tay pushed past Talon to enter. Her heart dropped like a stone at the empty room.

"Where is he?" She rushed into the room. A smear of blood glistened on the floor where Darius had lain, but of him, there was no sign. Panic flooded through her mind as she began turning over the room. Cupboards, washroom, and under the bed; all were empty. Throwing the bloodied sheets to the floor, she felt the tears begin to flow. "They've got him" She turned her face toward Talon. "Haven't they?"

"We don't know that." Talon reached her side and awkwardly squeezed her shoulder. "Come on, let's get out of here."

Chapter 28

They hurried through the train, ducking into empty carriages whenever they heard movement. Sounds of combat still echoed through the train, but less frequently.

"I think they're winning," Talon noted, as he poked his head into yet another empty carriage. For the second time, they stared down at the body of a royal guard. "Which doesn't fill me with confidence."

"How long do you think we have?" Even speaking in whispers, Tay felt they were being overly loud. They closed the door and continued to move, stopping every few paces.

"I don't know." They reached the last door in the carriage. Listening at the door, they waited with baited breath for any signs of occupation. Satisfied with the seeming emptiness of the carriage, they pushed open the door.

"Darius." Tay rushed over the ground to the

slumped, semi-conscious form in the corner. "Talon." The prince rushed past her, tearing the lid from the kit as he did so.

"Hold him up." Tay drew Darius into her arms, revealing the jagged piece of wood embedded in his side. "Take that out." Talon nodded at the stake.

"But..." She looked down at the wound, remembering Darius' words.

"Do it." Talon drew a small tube from the box, and unscrewed the lid. "Now."

Hesitantly, Tay grabbed hold of the wood. Her fingers slipped on the bloody implement, but carefully, gently, she drew it free. The blood welled up from the wound and began to flow. Panicked, she reached her hands down to stem the crimson flood. "Wait." Talon reached forward, the tube ready in one hand, a square of meshed cloth in the other. Tay stared at the small square of fabric in distrust. The fabric glistened in the light, and as she watched, Talon smeared the tube's contents across its surface. With the square soaked in the sharp-smelling liquid, Talon pressed it to Darius' side.

Tay held her breath, her eyes fixed on the strange bandage. A gasp escaped her lips as the fabric began to glow. Strange, amber lights lit the mesh and radiated across Darius' skin. She reached out a curious finger, but Talon held her back.

"Don't." His fingers curled about her wrist. "It's doing what it's supposed to."

"What is it?" Her voice was hushed, the glow scaring

her more than she would have thought.

"It's closing the wound," Talon noted, as he reached back into the box and drew forth a small phial. "And this" — he scanned the printed label on the side, before pressing the tip of the item into Darius' arm — "will replenish any blood loss."

Tay looked down at the simple-looking mesh of fabric. The lights had dimmed, and the fabric had begun to curl at the edges. Darius' breathing grew stronger and easier with each passing second. As she watched, the fabric fell away, revealing a ragged, but definitely closed, wound. In shock, she reached down to pick up the disintegrating item. Flakes fell from its surface as her fingers took hold, until there were only splinters of wood and strangely coloured ash left in her hand. A sigh drew her attention, and she reached down. Darius woke slowly, his blue eyes blinking incoherently before they finally rested on her face.

"What happened?"

"Thank God." Tay reached out and wrapped her arms about his neck. For a long moment, she held him, holding back tears of joy.

"Steady on sis." Darius pulled out of her grasp, his eyes flashing a warning at her. "I'm fine."

"No pain?" Talon leaned into his field of vision, and looked down at the wound on his side.

"A dull ache, nothing more," Darius confirmed, staring down at the puckered flesh in wonder. "How did you...?"

"That's what I want to know?" The voice echoed

from the carriage door, and all three turned. Three of the attackers stood in the doorway with weapons trained on them. "Care to tell us, Your Highness?" The speaker walked forward, his eyes fixed on the small box.

"I don't know what it is, or where it comes from," Talon replied, his voice remarkably steady.

"Just for royalty, isn't it?" He walked closer, and without warning, smashed the butt of the weapon into Talon's face. Tay screamed as the blow sent the Prince to the floor, blood spurting from his broken nose. Darius held her back, his fingers gripping her upper arms almost painfully. The leader glared down at Talon, sneered, and slammed a boot into his side. Talon coughed, and curled into a ball.

"Leave him alone," Tay demanded, tears of anger sliding down her face.

"Or what?" The leader reached down and picked up the box. "People like you don't get to make demands."

"Reinforcements are on route." A head poked around the door and addressed the leader. "We need to move."

There was a whistle, and several hands pulled the trio upright. Tay struggled, her hands curling into fists as they flailed out at their assailants. Pained grunts sounded as her wild strikes landed on flesh, before two of the attackers pinned her arms to her sides, and a third raised his hand.

"Brave of you," Darius called. "Hitting someone who can't fight back."

The leader ignored him as the threatened blow cracked across Tay's face. Her head snapped back from

the force, eyes watering as her cheek reddened. Talon's book fell from her pocket and hit the ground.

"Behave." The leader called in a sing-song tone. "Or next time" — he glanced at the rough crowd about her — "I'll let them loose."

Tay settled down, her cheek burning from the blow. In quiet, simmering anger, she watched the leader pick up the book and pocket it. Two more men walked into the room, and picked up Talon's semi-conscious form. As a group, they were marched from the train and toward the side of the track. A set of self-rolling wagons waited near the ruins. The doors were flung wide and their captors pushed them inside, slamming the door behind them.

"Talon." Tay rushed to the Prince's side. Blood dribbled from his mouth and nose. His eyes were puffy and swollen. "Will he be okay?" Darius knelt down beside her and checked Talon's wrist.

"His pulse is strong," he replied, releasing the Prince's wrist as he leant back. "He'll have a pair of beautiful black eyes, but" — he nodded back at the prone form — "he'll be healthy for when they decide to shoot him." There was a jolt as the wagon began to move.

"What do they want?" Tay asked, trying hard not to pay attention to Darius' last words.

"I'm not sure," Darius replied, looking about with some interest. "They appear to be rebels."

"But aren't you," Tay stammered to a halt as Darius pressed his finger to his lips. "I mean," she continued, "how can you be sure?"

"The clothing, the attack. Take your pick," he replied, in his laziest tone, but Tay was watching his eyes. They were troubled and full of concern. "I'm sure they'll tell us eventually."

"I'd rather not wait for that to happen," Tay retorted, fear making her voice sharp. The wagon rocked violently to the side, and she cried out as her arm smacked against the wall. "Where are they taking us?"

"I don't know," Darius admitted finally, his voice hushed and regretful. "I'm as in the dark as you." He settled back against the wall, tilting his head toward the ceiling. "From here on in, we'll have to play it by ear." Closing his eyes, Darius relaxed against the wall. Jolted by the increasingly bumpy ride, Tay moved to sit beside him.

"How's your side?" Her fingers strayed to the puckered flesh, but hesitated before they could touch it.

"Sore, and slightly itchy." Darius opened his eyes and glanced downward. "But that's all." A sense of awe flowed through his voice. "That stake should have killed me." His voice was low, and Tay had to lean closer to hear. "The blood loss alone would have done it." He shook his head. "I don't understand why I'm alive."

"But surely you've used that medicine before?" Tay replied in the same, low tones.

"No." He nodded down at Talon. "It was meant for him." He reached out a hand, and caught hold of hers. "I never even knew that was there."

"But..." They fell silent as the door at the back of the wagon swung open to admit a man in the ragged garb

of the others. Over his shoulder, Tay caught a glimpse of rough scrubland before the door closed again. The man weaved across the floor, reached the side of the Prince and injected something into his neck. Tay almost moved, but Darius' fingers dug painfully into her wrist, and she stayed silent. The man threw them a nasty smile, before he sank to the wagon's floor and trained his gun at them both.

"That's what I like in a noble." His voice rasped out. "Silence." A barely audible sigh escaped Darius' lips. "Something to say?" the man asked, waving the gun in Darius' face. "Well, do you?" Darius stayed silent, his eyes following the gun with a strange intensity. The man waited, a sneer creasing his lips as the silence lengthened. "Shame," he muttered. "I was looking forward to shooting you."

"Sorry to disappoint," Darius replied, in a mild, flippant tone. Resting his head back against the wall, Darius closed his eyes and ignored the man.

As Darius retreated from the conversation, the guard turned his attention back to Tay. His tongue flickered out and ran across his upper lip. Taking a shuddering breath, Tay moved back and huddled against Darius' warm body. The guard gave a smile and mouthed slow, suggestive kisses in her direction. Unnerved, she wrapped an arm around Darius', and tried to emulate his nonchalance.

The wagon continued on its rattling journey. Neither Darius nor Tay spoke again, and the guard continued to mouth obscene gestures toward her. By the time they

came to a halt, she was almost glad. At no point during the journey had Talon woken. The back of the wagon was wrenched open, and several more of the roughly dressed 'bandits' entered.

"Get off!" she yelled, as several hands grabbed at her. In an instant, their guard pressed the nose of the weapon in her face.

"Play nice," he uttered, smirking at the pale cast to her face.

Stilling her movements, she allowed them to lead her from the wagon. Her feet landed in deep snow and a cold, fresh breeze hit her face. The scent of wood smoke tainted the air, and several tall branches arced above her head.

"Where?" She turned her head to face Darius, and worried at the bemused look on his face.

"Welcome to the Free People of the Forest." She stared up as the leader from the train walked into view. His arms were outstretched, indicating the space about him. Tay raised her head, taking in the scene around her with awe. The forest spread in every direction, and despite the path at their feet, there was no edge in sight. A snowflake drifted past the skeletal branches to melt against her cheek, as it began to snow again. She shivered as a cold breeze cut through the fabric of her dress. "We have been eager for your arrival."

"We had little choice in the matter." Darius spoke calmly, but Tay could hear the undercurrent of fear in his voice. "But thank you for your welcome." He took a step forward as their guard from the wagon waved his

gun at him. "I take it we don't get the welcome tour."

"Would my people get a tour of your home?" the leader asked. "Or more accurately, would you give a tour to those you sentence to slavery?" Tay felt sick, fear running through every vein.

"Why are we here?" In a shaking, fear-laden voice, Tay spoke up. "What do you want with us?"

"Not you," the leader answered with a snort, "but him..." He nodded at Talon's unconscious body. "He's worth a ransom. You on the other hand" — he raised his hand, and several hands caught hold of them — "are to be tried for your crimes." He closed his eyes for a moment. The silence that fell over the group was profound, and full of incipient dread. Shivering with each falling flake, Tay stared with the rest, wondering what was to come.

His eyes snapped open, and fixed on Tay and Darius. "Kill them." At those words, the guards began to pull them backward, away from Talon, and toward the dark, chilling emptiness of the forest.

"Wait." Tay tried to free herself from the arms holding her, but the grip was too strong. Her feet dug into the snow of the forest floor, yet she continued to be pulled backward. Fingers reached out to seize hold of something, anything that would stop them. The men continued to move, dragging them mercilessly across the snowy forest floor. "We're rebels too."

The leader held up a hand, and the guards stopped moving.

"I find that hard to believe," the leader said, staring

at her in distaste. "You wear all the trappings of the nobles."

"It's a disguise," Tay sobbed, adrenalin rushing through her. "My name's Taya Emerson, and I live in the Mine District."

"Emerson." The leader stopped and turned to face her. "Where precisely do you live?"

"Twelve Jarrow Street, Westford," Tay gasped out. "My father's in the Mine... I..." She stammered to a halt, and glanced over at Darius. A strangely calm expression had settled across his features. "And Darius is part of the resistance too."

The leader shot him a brief look, before holding up his hand for silence. "Very well," he noted. "We'll keep you alive while we check out your tale." He nodded once more and the guards' hands fell away. "But if you're lying..." He left the sentence hanging, as he stepped back to the front of the troupe.

The group of guards moved into formation around them as the leader led them through the bare trees. Tiny flakes of snow swirled about them as the group moved onward. Dressed for the warmth of a train, Tay soon began to shiver as the wind picked up, driving the snow into faster flurries. She wrapped her arms across her chest, trying to bring warmth back to her chilled hands.

"Here." A heavy jacket settled about her shoulders, and she shot Darius a grateful glance.

"Do you know these people?"

"No," Darius replied, after a moment's thought, "but, I have heard of them."

"Can they be trusted?" Their voices were mere whispers, yet Tay was certain that one of the guards glanced at them.

"I don't know." He stepped to her side, and wrapped an arm about her shoulders. "But we seem safe enough, for now." Tay leaned into his side, reassured by the warmth of his body.

"And Talon?"

"The Prince is our insurance." Tay stiffened as the guard beside them spoke. "He's fine for now."

They moved through the deepening gloom, the snow driving into their faces, chilling exposed skin. The forest was quiet, save for the rhythmic steps of their party. Befuddled by the cold and exhausted by the heavy pace, Tay stumbled over an exposed root, and fell into the snow with a yelp of surprise.

"Get up." The nearest guard poked the tip of his weapon into her shoulder. Tay flinched as the weapon dug into her flesh.

"Give me a minute," she snarled, as Darius reached forward.

"Hey." The guard motioned at Darius with the weapon, waving him away.

"What do you think I'm going to do?" Darius snapped, ignoring the threat. "I'm only helping her up."

"It's alright." Tay struggled to get to her feet, the long skirts making the simple movements difficult.

"For heaven's sake, Carlton," one of the older guards called. "Let him help her." Darius shot a withering glance at Carlton, before he reached out his hand again.

There was a brief moment of tension as Tay reached out to take Darius' hand. Carlton's grip on the gun wavered, the weapon shaking slightly as he watched the two.

Ignoring the guard, Tay took hold of Darius' arm, and pulled herself upright. She got to her feet. The small group of escorts stared at them in silence, before setting off once again. Carlton stayed still, a flush of embarrassed anger infusing his cheeks.

They continued walking through the densely-packed woodland, the snow falling ever faster, blurring the path ahead. Darius' footsteps faltered, his injured body succumbing to the cold.

"How much further?" Tay steadied his movements, concern sharpening her tone. Darius clung to her arm as she pulled him onward. Their guards did not answer as they continued to push ahead into the cold of a snowy night.

Tay's legs felt like cold planks of wood as they finally staggered into a small clearing. Through a haze of exhaustion, she made out several cabins, welcoming light shining from the windows. Beside her, Darius toppled to the floor, his legs finally giving way. She reached down for him, but the ground rushed up to meet her, as she too collapsed into an exhausted faint.

Chapter 29

Warmth cocooned her limbs, and the scent of cooking wafted across her nostrils. Waking in a warm bed, Tay pushed the covers from her body, and slowly looked about her. She was in a loft, the bed resting beneath the eaves sported blankets with cheerful and many-coloured designs. A hurricane lamp swung from the pitched ceiling, the light pleasant against the gloom.

Gingerly she got to her feet, and a heavy, cotton nightgown fell to brush her ankles. Swallowing back the sensation of fear, she stepped forward, looking around her prison with curiosity. A cabinet with one drawer stood against one wall, its wooden frame carved with beautiful, and strangely familiar, designs. On its satiny surface, there was a jug of water and a bowl. At the end of the bed and behind the door, there was a similarly carved wardrobe.

A sense of déjà vu slid once more through her thoughts, and she reached out with a curious hand to

trace the designs carefully. Each smoothly-carved line felt oddly recognisable to her fingers, and she stopped. A nervous, foreboding sensation raced through her as she carefully opened the cupboard, and stared at the clothes within. Reaching out, she slid her fingers across the garb, noting several different sets of uniforms, from guard uniforms to those of palace functionaries. Curious, she singled out the uniform of an upper housemaid, noting the similarity to those worn in the Palace. Closing the wardrobe, she stepped closer to the door, her sense of apprehension growing with each step. At the base of the bed, there was a chair. A pair of slippers and a folded robe laid waiting for her. Pulling on the robe and slippers, she moved to the door. To her surprise, it opened easily.

Another door faced her across the landing, and a set of steep stairs led downstairs. Hesitantly, she walked forward and tried the door in front of her. It was locked, the wooden portal fixed in place. Taking a deep breath, she turned to the stairs. From the floor below, she could hear the familiar, homey sounds of a kitchen at work. For a long moment, she stood in place, scared to take a step forward. A female voice cursed from somewhere below, and Tay froze, recognising the tones. Startled into movement, she dashed forward, heading for the ground floor at a rush.

The stairs led down to a single, large room. A seating area laid to the right side of the stairs, a door stood before her, and to the left... Tay took a step back, the sight sending waves of shock through her. The kitchen

laid to the left. Several pans bubbled on the large stove against the far wall, but it was the cook that startled her the most. Time seemed to freeze as she stared at the familiar, but impossible face before her.

"Mum?" Her voice was a disbelieving squeak as she tried to reconcile her memories with the face of the woman before her.

"Taya." Tarin Emerson walked toward her, arms outstretched in welcome. "I've missed you so much." Tay stiffened as her mother's arms reached around her back, and then she pulled away, retreating as she tried to think.

"I thought you were dead." Flat, hurt tones echoed through the kitchen as she shook her mother's hand from her arm. "How are you alive?" Numb from shock, she breathed the question, her voice almost strangled by her emotions. Tarin stared down at her, the same shock visible on her face.

"Why did you think that?" she asked, raising her hand back to Tay's arm. "Didn't your father tell you?"

"He told us that you'd died for the cause." The numbness was beginning to fade, and raw anger burned in its place. "That the cause" —contempt rippled around the word 'cause' — "was more important than your, or our, life." Tay felt tears of anger begin to prick at the back of her eyes, and she wiped them away with a hasty gesture.

"And you think it's not?" Similar heat rose in her mother's voice. "What did I teach you?" Incredulity fuelled her words. "Without the cause, we're slowly

dying." Her voice grew stronger, empowered by her belief. "How can you think that being a hostage to the rating system is any way to live?"

"Because you abandoned us to it," Tay snarled back, rage building her voice to a shout. "You left us there to starve."

"Your father..."

"Our father got himself arrested." Tay saw the look of pain that crossed her mother's face, but she did not care. "He got sent to the Mine." She took a pace forward, her rage making her mother take a step back. "I had to owe a favour to Darius, so that we wouldn't starve."

"Your father joined the rebellion?" Tarin asked, her mind unable to keep up with Tay's angry rants. "But he wouldn't..."

"He did," Tay snapped back. "Your 'friends' kept on at him to continue your work." Several angry tears fell down her cheeks, and soaked into her top. "He set up a petition to increase the ration size" — she took another step closer— "and your friends got him arrested." Tarin reached out a hand, but Tay slapped it down. "Didn't you care about us?" The tears were flowing freely, and she did nothing to stop them. "You were here and alive, all this time..." Choking sobs interrupted the flow of words, and she backed off.

"Tay," her mother called after her, as she raced back to the stairs. Pain exploded across her shin as Tay tripped up the steps, racing for the room. "Please..." Struggling to her feet, she limped up the last few steps,

before entering the attic room and slamming shut the door.

She threw herself across the bed, her breath coming in harsh, tortured gasps. Nothing made sense. The forest; the freedom fighters; Darius; all were parts of a strange world that she wished she had never heard of, and then there was her mother. A dull ache settled in her chest as she focused on the last five minutes. Anger at her mother's betrayal burned deep within her. She had always known that her mother had left them for the rebellion, but in her mind... A sigh escaped her lips. Throughout the last eight years, she had been convinced that her mother was dead. Father never spoke of her, and the loss was somehow easier for the assumption, but now...

Rolling onto her side, she balled up a fist and slammed it into the pillow. Blood trickled from the scratch on her leg, staining the sheets crimson. Raising herself from the bed, she reached for the jug of water. Gingerly, she bathed the wound, the blood turning the water pink. Satisfied that the wound had stopped bleeding, she returned to the bed, and buried herself in the blankets.

"Tay." The voice sounded from the other side of the door, and she raised her head. Even though the door was unlocked, Tarin remained on the other side of it. It was a consideration that made Tay even angrier. "I couldn't return." There was a pleading note to her voice that Tay tried desperately not to listen to. "They would have killed me."

Tay squeezed her eyes shut, willing her to be quiet. The pain in her chest increased, and a lump settled into her throat. "I never wanted to leave you." Tay's fist unclenched, and she swallowed back another round of hiccupping tears.

"Please Tay... Let me explain." Tay stared at the door, but said nothing. After a moment's silence, the sound of retreating footsteps echoed through the room as her mother walked back down the stairs. Burying her head in the pillow, Tay began to sob. Tears soaked into the fabric of the pillow, which muffled her cries. For an age, she seemed to lie there, releasing her hurt and anguish into the down-filled softness.

When the tears had finally dried, she remained buried in the fabric, feeling a pounding headache build behind her eyes. Exhausted with the emotional storm, she dropped into a haunted sleep.

"Tay." She woke with a start, staring at the door in shock. The lantern had burned itself out, and darkness shrouded the room. The scent of cooking had long faded, and she could hear no sounds from downstairs.

"Darius?" Pushing the covers away, she got to her feet and crossed the room. "Is that you?"

"Yes." Tay reached for the door handle and pulled open the portal. Darius stood on the other side, his hair mussed from sleep. "I've just woken and..." He stared at her red-rimmed eyes and pale features. "Are you alright?" The words brushed her still-raw nerves, and Tay rushed into his arms, tears flowing once more. Stunned, Darius wrapped his arms about her, and held

her to him. Memories of the kiss flowed through her thoughts, muddying her feelings. "What have they done to you?"

Tay heard the worry in his voice, and she pulled back. "Nothing," she said, her voice stuttering with emotion.

"Then what is it?" He led her to the bed, and sat her down, glancing at the bloody water with concern.

"My mother." Tears trickled down her face, and she brushed them back, angry at crying again. "She's downstairs."

"But I thought..." Shock rippled through Darius' voice, and Tay felt relieved that he did not appear to be aware that her mother was still alive. "Are you certain?" Tay nodded, unwilling to trust her voice through the tears. Darius took a deep breath, his hand stroking her back in a comforting motion.

"Have you spoken to her?"

"Not much," she muttered, trying to get a grip on her emotions. "She said..." Tay took another gulp of air. "She said she had to leave us." Darius said nothing, waiting for her to continue. "How could she?" Pushing herself to her feet, she paced the floor, agitation in every step.

"She must have had a reason," Darius noted, watching her pace with some unease. "Did you let her explain?" Tay stopped moving.

"No," she snapped back, allowing the rage to rule her. "I don't care why."

"I see." Darius got to his feet.

"You think I should ask her?" Tay rounded on Darius, her voice full of anger. "Why should I care why she left?"

"Because you clearly do, and..." He hesitated, unwilling to voice his thoughts.

"And what?" Tay stepped toward him, the anger aimed at him. "What else do you think?"

"I think, I don't deserve your anger," he uttered, in soft, reproachful tones. "I also think that you need to find out what they want."

"What do you mean?"

"She's with these rebels, and they have the Prince." A note of his old sardonic, mockery edged back into his voice. "We really should know what they want, and where we are."

Guilty realisation slid through her at his words. In the anguish of discovering her mother, she had forgotten about the Prince, and the reason for their capture. Her eyes drifted to the carved cabinet. The elegant designs made sense to her now; they had adorned the cupboards in her home. Thoughts of Lana and Roj tormented her. They were now alone in the City, abandoned once more.

"Alright," she replied, her voice still croaky from the storm of emotion. Reluctantly, she took a timid step toward the door, suddenly nervous at what laid beyond. "I'll talk to her." Despite the determination in her voice, she stopped moving, fear-laced anger still racing through her.

Darius read the stricken expression on her face,

hesitated, and then reached out a hand. "I can come with you if you like."

"Thanks." Gratitude swelled through her as she took hold of his hand and walked out of the room.

With slow, reluctant steps, she moved down the wooden staircase. At the bottom of the stairs, she turned her face to the sitting room, and her mother.

"Tay." Tarin's voice cracked, but to Tay's relief, she did not stand to greet her. "I..."

"This is Darius," Tay interrupted. "You know him?"

"I know of him." Tarin's hair was mussed and untidy, her face red with tears, yet she wrestled control from somewhere to ask, "How did you get my daughter into this?"

"Strictly speaking, I didn't." Darius took a seat, and Tay sat beside him, her fingers almost welded with his. "I asked her to pretend to be my sister." He shrugged. "The rebel angle was added by others..."

"Yes, by Lars and Cody," Tay interrupted, unwilling to let Darius speak for her. "They sent me to him."

"To release your father," Darius retorted. "Nothing more."

"And if you hadn't asked me to play as your sister..."

"You'd still be starving in the District," Darius continued, in his insufferably calm voice, "but this is beside the point." He glanced up and nodded at her mother. "Where are we? And why are we here?"

"You're in the Great Forest."

"That's not possible," Darius replied, leaning forward in shock. "The Great Forest is nowhere near our home."

"And that's where you were heading," Tarin replied. At the look of disbelief on Darius' face, she gave a sharp bark of laughter. "Honestly you nobles; stick you in a luxurious carriage, give you access to lots of pretty things, and you fail to notice the landscape."

"Why would we be heading for the Forest?" Tay asked, her voice wavering but strong.

"Because that's the route the Prince had detailed to the driver."

"Talon sent us this way?" Tay repeated the question, confused by her mother's words. "Why?"

"You'll have to ask him." Tarin got to her feet. "For now, I'll get you some food, and then you can attend the meeting."

"What meeting?"

"You'll see."

"Wait." Tay got to her feet, and faced her mother down. "Did Dad know?"

Tarin bowed her head, a glimmer of tears showing in her eyes. "No." Leaving an open-mouthed Tay to stare after her, Tarin headed into the kitchen and began to rattle some pots and pans. Once more, Darius and Tay sat alone, staring about the rustic, but strangely appealing, room. Tay moved and settled into her mother's vacant chair, and an awkward silence settled between them.

"About what happened on the train..." Tay closed her eyes. She had been hoping that Darius had forgotten.

"It was..." she stammered, struggling to find some words.

"I don't regret it." She opened her eyes. Darius was watching her from the other chair, his face gentle. The memory of the kiss still soared through her mind, and a flush of rose tinted her cheeks. "And" — he took a deep breath — "I would do it again." Tay's mouth dropped open, stunned by the words that fell from his lips. As she struggled to process what he had said, Darius got to his feet. A couple of steps, and he stopped just before her. "I know it's madness," he continued, his voice soft, "and it could have been a fear of dying kind of thing, but I don't feel sorry about it." His hands reached across and caught hold of her fingers.

"Darius, I..." Tay stumbled over the words, wondering if she had tripped into crazy-town. Was he mad? If, by some miracle, they managed to get out of this unscathed, there was no way they could pursue a relationship. But his fingers on her skin felt like fire, and dangerous, tempting thoughts tugged at her mind. It wouldn't take much to lean in and properly taste his lips. Indeed, without any of the court here, there would be no risk of exposure as a fraud, and yet, she couldn't. Despite his charms and his kind nature, the risk was too high. There was no way this could work, and it would be better if they never started. With some reluctance, she tugged her hand free, the skin still tingling from the contact. "I don't want to talk about this now." She ignored the small, internal voice that dared her to kiss him. "Not when we need to find out why we're here."

Darius nodded, and then stepped back, disappointment in his eyes. Tay almost rushed past him,

her feet sounding loud against the smooth wood of the cabin floor as she headed for the kitchen. Her thoughts flew into turmoil. He'd wanted to kiss her, and he would do it again. The flush to her cheeks deepened as she thought back to the feeling of his fingers, the look in his eyes, and she wished she'd had the guts to kiss him properly.

"Mum." She reached the kitchen, and stared at her mother questioningly. Tarin was sitting at the table, a small disc reader before her, and earphones over her ears. She waited for a short space of time before she moved to one of the empty chairs, drew it out, and sat. She heard Darius approach from the other room, and her fingers tightened into claws. As he sat down at the table, Tarin finally turned off the recorder, removed the earphones and looked at them.

"Your food." She pushed the chair back and stood up, agitation in every movement. Quickly, she opened the cupboards and emptied food and pans onto the nearest worktops. Silently, Tay stood and began to help.

"What's going on?" Darius asked, as the pair began to quietly make supper.

"I've had a report from the Palace." Tay gave a small start, wondering at the extent of her mother's influence. "Kail has left for the Western edge of the forest."

"That's in the direction of the Clockwork Temple," Darius noted, a thick vein of worry flowing through his voice. "He'll be out to warn his father."

"Reports are coming in about the King mobilising the guard." Tay picked up a kettle from the stove, and

poured a stream of boiling water into a pan. "They're heading this way."

"Well you did attack the train holding his son," Tay's voice whipped out, heavy with sarcasm. "Why on earth did you do that?" Tarin placed the kettle onto the side, and began to busy herself with a haunch of dried meat. "Mum?" Tay prodded.

"I'd like to know too," Darius interjected, from his place by the table. "Not that it hasn't been fun and informative, but you've done our enemies job for them. They don't even have to get their hands dirty."

"Because we needed to act," Tarin snapped back. "We can't go on like this, living in fear."

"And damn everyone else?" Tay's voice shook with pent-up emotion.

"When we find the Coi..."

"Don't say you're still looking for that fairy-tale?" Tarin winced at the raw anger in Tay's snarled words.

"It's not a tale," Tarin replied, with equal heat. "They're as real as you are." She reached beneath her coat a pulled a slender tome from her coat. "Or didn't you read this book?" Tay started at the sight of the Talon's book in her mother's fingers.

"I didn't get a chance to properly read it," she replied, staring at the leather-bound item with curiosity. "It just seemed to be a bunch of stories."

"This," her mother continued, "gives the location of the Coils."

"What?" Tay reached out and snatched the book from her mother's hand. With hasty, agitated motions,

she flipped open the cover, and began to flick through the pages. Rows of spindly writing covered each page, and she skimmed each line. "This isn't directions," she argued, turning sheet upon sheet. "It's a children's tale."

"Look closer." Her mother moved nearer, and pointed at a passage. "It states..." She cleared her throat, and spoke with the storytelling cadence that Tay remembered from so long ago. "They travelled to the forest's edge, and gazed upon the scene below. The world of copper and brass laid out before them, a mass of metal and clockwork."

"The Clockwork Temple," Darius interjected. "The Coils are there?"

"That's the start," Tarin confirmed. "They're somewhere in the Great Forest." She glanced back at her daughter. "The changes to the night sky prove it."

"You saw it too?" Tay said, excitement in her voice. "Amira said..."

She broke off as the door to the cabin burst open. The attackers from the train strode in, brushing the snow from their coats. A blast of frozen air cut through the warmth of the cabin.

"Are they ready Tarin?" the leader asked, as he strode toward them.

"Yes." Tarin stepped away from Tay and moved to sit at the table.

Tay watched the others file into the room without comment. Several faces, she recognised from the train, and at one, she took a sharp breath.

"Get him out of here," she snarled, as the guard

from the wagon stepped in from the cold.

"Tay?" Her mother turned to stare sharply at the group.

"I don't want him near me..."

"But I didn't..." the man protested, as the leader nodded at the door. "You can't keep me out of this." Anger flowed through his voice. "I didn't do anything to her!"

"Go out Lyle," the leader cut across his protests. Lyle was pushed out into the cold and the door shut in his face. "Better?" he asked, moving to take the seat beside her mother.

"A bit." Tay was only marginally mollified, the memories of her near-death on the orders of the man before her still played heavily on her mind.

"I'm Ander," he continued, seemingly unconcerned by her lack of enthusiasm. "I lead here." He glanced over at Tarin. "As does your mother." Another thought, even less appealing than Lyle, began to flow through Tay's mind, as Tarin reached over to squeeze his hand. "We founded this group in the hope of discovering the Coils of Copper and Brass."

"That seems a lofty goal." Darius' sardonic, mocking tones rippled through the crowd, causing many to scowl. "And why would that involve wrecking a train?"

"The Prince," Tarin continued. "We knew he'd be there."

"And he knows the Truth," Ander finished. "All the royal family does. When our spies in the Palace heard he was travelling with you to the Mine..."

"And that he had changed your route." A wide, brilliant smile spread across Tarin's face. "It was perfect."

"That's strange," Tay retorted. "I could have sworn you talked of ransoming his Highness.

"Of course," Ander replied, "When he's answered our questions."

"And you think they'll pay?" Darius cut into the conversation, an incredulous lilt to his voice. "What makes you think they won't just kill you?"

"They won't know where he is," Tarin replied. "None of the patrols come out this way."

"They have no clue that we're out here."

The door to the cabin burst open, and a young man rushed into the room. His breath came in short, sharp gasps, and his cheeks were red from exertion and cold. "The scouts have spotted movement," he choked out. "Half a mile away."

"Monsters?" Tarin asked, a serious note entering her voice.

"No." The scout shook his head violently. "Too organised and fast."

"How the...?" Ander rounded on Tay and Darius. "What did you do?"

Tay shot a confused glance at Darius. "Nothing." Another spike of fear shot through her. "We did nothing."

"Then how do they know our whereabouts?"

"I don't know..."

"Leave my daughter alone." Tarin stepped forward,

and laid a hand across Ander's arm. "We have to go."

"Alright." He jerked his head toward the stairs. "Get some warm clothing on and follow us."

Tay hesitated briefly, before heading toward the stairs, followed closely by Darius. The group filed out of the cabin, save for Tarin and Ander. As Tay reached the bottom of the staircase, she turned back to the room. Her mother was standing close to the other man, her hands wrapped about his arm. A hot feeling of resentment began to burn through Tay as she stared at the sight.

"Don't think about it." She started at the pressure of Darius' fingers on her upper arm. "That way madness lies." She gave a weak smile at his joke, and turned back to the stairs.

"I didn't realise she was..." Words failed her as she contemplated the nagging thoughts in her mind.

"Let's just get away from here first." They reached the top landing and their rooms. Darius moved toward his room. "See you in a moment."

Tay nodded and entered her room. Pulling open the drawers and wardrobe, she dragged on the clothing she found inside. The trousers were too long, and she had to roll them up to prevent them dragging on the ground. Pulling on her boots, she returned to the cupboard. A set of jumpers laid within the drawer. Several sizes too large, and moth-eaten, she drew them on regardless. Reluctantly, she left her 'Lyana' clothing on the bed, and headed back down the stairs.

The door was open, and snow blew in through the

gap. Tay glanced about at the empty rooms, the recently extinguished fireplace.

"Tay." She followed the shout outside. Her mother was standing with a small group, huddled against the freezing chill of the winter night. "You'll stick with me." An arm covered in thick wool coiled about her shoulders, and she resisted the urge to shake it off. "Where's the noble?"

"Right here." Darius walked out of the cabin, his frame wrapped in several layers of jumpers. "So where are we going?"

"Into hiding." Ander walked toward him. "Then we can deal with the Coils."

"I don't think..." Tay stammered to a halt, as the group stared at them. A tense silence passed, before she swallowed, and started again. "You have the Prince" — she noted the limp bundle held in the arms of one of the others— "but that won't help you."

"Explain." Ander stared down at her, his face hidden by a bulky scarf.

"If that's Jackson's men, then we're all dead," she explained, her voice becoming stronger as she spoke. "If they're the King's men, then we're still dead, but they won't give up." She nodded at the bundle. "Jackson wants Talon dead, and the King won't negotiate."

"You seem awfully sure," Ander retorted, peering down into her face.

"I am sure," Tay replied. "And if the Prince is killed by Jackson's men, we will have a real problem," Tay finished for him. "They will use it as an excuse to raid

the Factory District." She nodded at Darius. "They don't even have to reveal Darius' involvement, he'll just be a casualty." Volumes of anger flowed through her voice. "If they're the King's men, they'll stop at nothing to get the Prince back."

"What do you suggest?" Ander said, contempt flooding through his words. "Asking nicely before they fire?"

"Darius, Talon and myself should stay here. You guys hide, if it's the King's men, we'll leave with them, if they belong to Jackson, you can attack."

Ander considered for a moment, "We haven't questioned the Prince yet," he noted.

"Do you have time to question him?" Tay pressed, trying to keep anger from her voice. "Is he even conscious?"

"Tay's right." Tay glanced at her mother, feeling the familiar burn of anger against her mother's dedication to the cause simmer back into life. "We don't have time." Tarin laid her hand on Ander's arm. "Let them do it."

"Alright." Ander nodded at the two of them, and took a step back. "We'll go with this."

"Really?" Darius stepped forward and caught hold of Tarin's arm. "You're quite willing for your daughter to do this?"

"I trust my daughter's judgement," Tarin replied, pulling her arm free. "She's a fighter, and unlike you nobles, fully aware of the consequences of her actions."

"Tarin, come on." Ander gave a hand signal, and the

rebels moved out of sight, Tay's mother with them.

Left alone in the centre of the clearing, Tay turned to face Darius. "Let's get back inside." She refused to think of her mother, and the woman's devotion to the cause.

Darius nodded and picked up Talon's unconscious form. "And I thought I had the monopoly on disappointing parents," he muttered, as they both returned to the house.

Tay glanced at him but said nothing. Her mother's survival was not the miracle she wanted it to be. It seemed, even after all these years, Tarin still valued the cause over her family.

Despite the unlit fire, the house was significantly warmer than outside. Darius doused the lights, and they waited in near-darkness.

"Do you think we should have left?" Tay stared out of the window, looking out into the forest, her heart beating faster in anticipation.

"You're thinking this now?" Darius replied, coming to sit beside her. A jolt of electricity rippled up her arm as he brushed against her. Tay didn't move, resting against him in comfortable silence. "But, as it happens, you were right." He glanced across at her. "We would have been chased down."

"What if the King's guard try to kill us?" Tay shivered, more through fear than the cold, and Darius wrapped his arm about her shoulders. "We look like those rebels."

Darius swore and moved away from the window. "Get dressed in your other clothes," he ordered, as he

raced toward the stairs, taking them two at a time. Tay stared after him, bewildered by his words. As she made no move to follow, he turned back to face her. "You said it yourself, we look like rebels. The King's guard will shoot us wearing these clothes."

Understanding flashed through Tay's mind, and she ran for the stairs. The room was how she had left it, and she began to drag the warm clothing over her head. After the layered warmth of the jumpers, Lyana's day dress felt like gossamer, and the increasing cold of the cabin rushed through the thinner fabric. Shivering, she pulled a blanket from the bed, and wrapped it around her shoulders. Moving toward the window, she continued to stare out at the dark forest, worrying about her mother.

"Any sign?" Darius moved to stand beside her, and she shook her head, staring out at the dark forest in confusion.

"No."

"Are you warm enough?" Concern laced his words.

"No." She hesitated only briefly. Lying about the cold, would end in hypothermia, that she was all too aware of. Darius drew another blanket from the bed and wrapped it about her. Muttering brief thanks, she returned to her vigil, watching the darkened forest in apprehension.

They didn't have to wait long. A loud, rumbling sound filled the clearing, and a large vehicle crashed through the undergrowth. Tay jolted back from the window, fear racing through her veins at the sight.

Beside her, Darius kept watching as squads of guards moved into the village.

"King's Guard," he uttered, as the first of the soldiers came into view. With one hand, he pushed open the window. "Help," he shouted across the space. "We're up here." As the guards raced toward them, he drew his head back inside. "Sit there and look scared," he ordered, as he headed toward the door.

There was a crash from downstairs, as the main door flew open. Tay shrank back, seeking the comfort of Darius' arms. Outside, they heard shots ring out, and she glanced back out of the window. The guard were heading to the village outskirts, shooting as they went.

"I thought they were going to hide?" She tried to move, but Darius held her in place.

"You can't help them," he hissed frantically, as the sound of boots pounded on the steps.

"I have to..."

"Here's the Prince." They heard the words bellow from below, as the door to their room burst open. A small group of armed men entered the room. Darius moved himself away from Tay's embrace, and approached.

"I'm glad you're here." Tay marvelled at his ability to lie. "We were beginning to worry."

"Darius James?" The lead guard asked, his eyes moving past to rest on Tay. "Lyana James?"

"Yes." Tay summoned her courage and stood. "I'm glad you've come." She tried to ignore the sounds of combat.

"I'm glad we've found you Miss." The smile he gave did not match his eyes. "Come on." He held out his hand, and Tay took it gingerly, allowing him to lead her from the cabin.

The cold bit through her thin dress, even with the covering blanket, and she shuddered. The snow was falling heavily now, as they approached the large wagon. Shots and screams could be heard in the still night air. She almost halted, picturing her mother's death for the second time in her life.

"Go inside." The guard dropped her hand to open the back door. "We'll get you home."

"It's alright Lyana," Darius comforted, as he took hold of her hand. "I'm here."

"I know," she whispered, as she clambered into the back of the wagon, followed by Darius. Waiting for the Prince's body to be loaded, she was startled when the door slammed shut behind them.

"What the?" Darius moved to the door, hearing the locks click into place.

"Relax." They both turned in shock to stare at the speaker. Almost hidden by the gloom of the carriage, a man leant forward, his appearance sending waves of shock through both of them.

"Father."

Tay felt her stomach roil unpleasantly, as she stared across at Overseer James. He turned to face her, and a twisted smile creased his features. "Emerson's girl," he noted, with a nod. The blood drained from Tay's face, and shivers began to race down her spine as his cold

eyes regarded her.

"How?" To his credit, Darius seemed as cool and remote as before, but Tay could hear a quaver deep within his voice.

"I wondered why the daughter of Caleb Emerson was working for my neighbours."

"How do you know my father?" Tay's curiosity overcame fear and her question rang out in the still air.

"Come now, you think I don't meet all the agitators?" Carl glanced across at Darius. "I did find it strange that he was suddenly transferred." Darius shifted uncomfortably but his features remained still and watchful. "And then there was the query about this one's ration?" Carl jerked his thumb toward Tay. "So I looked into her file."

Tension stiffened Tay's back but she did not speak, almost entranced with fear. Distantly, she heard the sounds of gunfire, and for a moment she wished she were outside running for her life, far from the bone-numbing terror that was this conversation.

"Taya Emerson," Carl James continued. "Oldest daughter of Caleb Emerson; two siblings." He took a breath. "Rating" — his voice was slow, measured and merciless — " menial work only." He finished with an almost triumphant note. "I take it the rating increase was the reason you did this." Cold, pitiless eyes settled on Tay and she shivered, unwilling or unable to respond.

"Leave her alone Father." Darius' voice snapped across the wagon, drawing his father's attention. "The

deception was my idea." He gave a shrug. "She only asked me to transfer her father."

"And you agreed out of the goodness of your heart?" A leering tone entered his voice.

"Not totally." Darius' voice was crisp, curt with pent-up emotion. "But all this discussion is immaterial." He pushed himself upright. "You've found us out, so what are you going to do?"

"Nothing."

Tay and Darius started and stared across at him with disbelief. A small smirk played across his lips as he leant forward.

"I want you to continue playing my daughter," he noted at Tay, smirking at the confused look that crossed her face.

"Why?" she asked, shocked out of silence by the bizarre request. "I thought you'd turn us in or kill us."

"I only have one legitimate heir," Carl responded, with a sidelong look across at Darius, "and you," he glanced at Tay, "are doing a fine job of playing Lyana. There's no benefit to bringing you to the attention of the authorities."

"But..." Tay stammered, thoroughly confused. "I don't understand."

"Imagine how it would look if it came out that my son used his influence to remove your father from his rightful punishment." Tay felt a shudder race across her skin as he spoke. "I would be removed from my position for allowing it."

A thought began to burn behind Tay's eyes, an idea

born of desperation and fear. "If I reveal this charade, you'd be removed?"

"Don't get any ideas about blackmail girl," Carl retorted. "What do you think would happen to you and your family?"

A lead weight settled across her chest, and she glanced at Darius' pale body for support.

"What about Lyana?"

"What about her?" The casual indifference in his voice chilled Tay to the bone. "She made her choice." A cruel light danced in his eyes. "If she wishes to dally in the gutter, then that's where she she will stay."

"Where is she?" Darius sounded sick, but Tay could hear the steel tones that laid beneath his words.

"I moved her to the mine-head."

"She's your daughter." Tay somehow beat Darius to the punch, her words of protest echoed by his. "How can you do that?"

"Easily." Carl stepped back and shrugged on his cape. "So just think of how much feeling I have for you." Tay flinched beneath his gaze but did not drop her eyes, anger flaring into life beneath the surface.

"What do you want?" Her tones were flat, hatred rippling through every syllable.

"Just marry Kail and find me the Coils of Copper and Brass."

For a moment, time slowed within the wagon as both Darius and Tay stared up in surprise.

"The Coils?" Tay recovered her voice first. "Aren't they a myth told to children?"

"No." Carl fastened the clasp to his cloak. "They're quite real." He glanced over his shoulder and continued to speak. "Kail may know where they are."

It took a great deal of control for Tay to remain still. "Why would Kail know where they are?"

"One of the few benefits to being Head of Palace Security," Carl answered with a smirk. "Barely significant fiscal benefits, but the knowledge gained is priceless."

"What if I can't?" Tay asked, her voice a tenuous thread. "And what about Jackson, he's already tried to arrest us."

"Jackson's easy." He opened the door and beckoned someone over. Tay and Darius glanced at each other as Jackson walked up to the door. There was a loud bang and he fell to the ground, blood pouring from a hole in his shoulder. Carl moved back into place. "Problem dealt with," he announced, with a smile. "Do this" — he fixed his gaze on Tay — "or you may become an only child." Carl adjusted his scarf, and banged on the wall behind him. The door cracked open, and he stepped through. Darius lunged forward, but stopped at the gun pointed toward his head. "You have until tomorrow to agree." The words drifted toward them as the door swung closed, leaving them alone in the wagon.

"Darius..." Tay began, her voice strangled with emotion.

"I know." Darius closed his eyes, struggling with the emotions that his father had provoked.

"Lyana..." Tay's thoughts drifted to the friendly,

inoffensive young woman who had been sentenced, by her own father, to a lifetime of servitude.

"I know." Quiet despair rippled through Darius' voice. "I told you he was a monster."

"How did he..." A shake of her head and she dismissed the speculation as counter-productive. "Never mind, now what do we do?"

"What he says," Darius replied, with a lost note to his voice. "Find the Coils of Copper and Brass."

"And then what?" Tay whispered, scared beyond reason.

"Try to use them." Darius looked over at her, his face set like granite. "It's time to end this mockery of a system."

Tay nodded, staring down at her shaking hands. From outside of the wagon, the sounds of gunfire intensified, and the scent of burning thatch tainted the air. As she listened to the shouts of the fighters behind her, she thought of her siblings, her parents, and of Carl's threat to them. For the first time in her life, she gave voice to the roar of injustice that laid deep within her. She would find the Coils of Copper and Brass, discover the mysteries of that dark, silver-dotted sky, and then, she would tear this world apart.

About the Author

Claire was born in Peterborough Maternity unit, several weeks premature and the weight of a bag of sugar. Bad temper kept her alive through a bout of intensive care and she clung to this like a life raft. Not saying she's a grump but she doesn't really have zen levels of calm. She's worked as shop assistant, a butchers assistant and is now stuck in the admin ghetto of the UK civil service.

An avid creator of stories, she hit her teens and discovered roleplay. Yes she plays D&D, but so does Vin Diesel and no one says that he's sad. Playing and running games with her friends inspired her to return to her first love, fiction, and she started her first book in 2007.

Chapter Sneak Peeks

If you enjoyed this book, and can't wait for the next installment, check out these sample chapters from books one and two of Claire Warner's Night Flower trilogy.

The Black Lotus

15th June 1752

The floor was cold. That mundane thought floated through her mind as the deep dark of unconsciousness ebbed away. The unyielding surface sent small stabs of pain through her limbs as confusion set in. Her head felt heavy and somewhat hollow as she struggled to remember how she had fallen. She managed to blink; the simple task rendered difficult by the lassitude swamping her. As she struggled closer to full awareness, she became aware of something clasped in her hand. Its surface was smooth, shaped like a flower but, as she traced her fingers over it's surface, it seemed to spark a wary, almost sick sensation of worry.

"I think she's waking up,"

A voice, feminine and vaguely familiar, sounded close to her head. She tried to move, to turn her head to stare at the speaker but her body refused to cooperate, still caught in the spell of near insensibility.

"Yes, I can see that," Another voice, male and disapproving, spoke from further away. "You need not sound so thrilled; I doubt she will welcome you when she opens her eyes."

"Oh, Hugh darling, how can you say that?" Petulant yet teasing notes flowed through the woman's light lilting speech and she longed to see the face that it belonged to. Those tones invoked cautious recognition, a recognition which did not bring her any sense of peace.

"Because it is the truth," The man shifted position and walked closer to her prone figure. "Why on earth did you do it?" The voice dropped lower, becoming accusatory in tone and timbre. She wondered at this, struggling with tattered threads of memory that refused to make sense.

"It solved a problem,"

"I beg to differ," He was stood over her now; she felt the tips of his toes against her side. "Do you think that Justin will thank you?"

Justin, that name caught at her mind, dragging it free from the sludge her memory had become. She knew that name, the feelings it provoked were soft and wondrous. Once again the memories fluttered close to the surface yet she was still not awake enough to make sense of it all

"He should," The voice argued, louder and less teasing than before, "This solves all," She felt the woman move, the edge of a skirt brushed against her side, and she wondered how long they were going to stand and argue over her.

"Really?" There was a bark of incredulous laughter. "Our Justin, who promised never to curse another," Her eyelids opened slightly, and she focused blearily on the rich brocade silk that tickled her nose. "Do you honestly think he would be happy that you damned someone else?" From her position on the floor, she could see the man's calves and a pair of silver buckled shoes.

"Yes Hugh," The skirt rustled as the woman stepped away from her side to argue with the man before her. "The chit is now safe. John will not be able to hurt her," Another memory tugged at the edges of her mind and this one sent a thrill of fear through her. "And Justin..," The woman laughed shortly, bitterly, "Justin will not spend the next fifty years in depression because he had to leave her,"

"Don't try to claim that you did this for him," The man knelt down now and she felt his hand close about her wrist. Her limited vision took in a rose pink satin frock coat and embroidered lavender waistcoat. "You did it for yourself. You've always felt like the youngest, and now you're not," His other hand reached down and settled in the small of her back. "Come on now Melissa, let me help you up," She did not question her name, for she remembered that at least.

With sure movements, he helped her to her feet. Her eyes opened fully, and she took in her surroundings. She was in a parlour, mahogany wainscoting covered the walls, and a thick blue rug topped the parquet floor. Several chairs stood around a card table in the corner of the room, and a fire was burning brightly in the hearth. Behind her lay a closed door and she could hear conversation and music from beyond. As the man guided her to a cushioned chair, she glanced up, taking in the extravagant clothing that seemed totally at odds with the serious cast marred his features.

"You'll be a little disorientated at first," She could

see pity in his eyes, and she wondered at it. "It'll pass," He reached out to one of the small tables in the corner of the room and picked up a glass of amber liquid. "Take a snifter of that, it'll strengthen your nerves," The scent of brandy filled her nostrils, and she took a deep gulp. The liquid burned her throat as she swallowed and made her splutter. As she controlled her coughs, her eyes took in the form of the woman. Taller than her, the woman had blonde ringlets worn in an elaborate style and powdered. An expensive dress of dark blue brocade covered her form and blue eyes sparked with mischief or malice.

"What happened?" She asked, staring at the pair of them in confusion. "Did I faint?"

The man sighed and knelt down, staring at her with sorrowful eyes. "I'm sorry my dear, but," He held out his hand and she looked down at the small snuff box before her. Set into the lid was a black enamel locket in the shape of a lotus flower. The smooth planes of the bloom filled her vision, and she stared at it in utter shock. As horrified recognition raced through her; the man continued to speak. "You have one of these now and I'm so very sorry,"

It was then that she looked down, at the item clasped between her fingers. It was a lotus flower locket, a veritable twin to the one on the box. The sight of it finally sparked her memory and she remembered what it stood for. Her head snapped up and she stared at the blonde woman, hatred replacing shock as her mind finally filled in the gaps of her memory.

"You bitch."

Blood Orchid

Melissa sat before the fire, staring into the blaze without really seeing it. Her thoughts were miles and years away, back twenty years or more, when she was an innocent, thinking herself in love.

"This won't do," Marcus placed a large cup of tea at her right hand and interrupted her chain of thought. "You have to forgive,"

"If he hadn't..." She started to protest, but her brother held up his hand, stopping her in mid flow.

"Not him..." Marcus said softly, his green eyes searching her face. "You..."

"Marcus?" She stared up at him, confused by his words and sudden shift in conversation.

"It's not Justin you're upset with," Marcus did not remove his gaze from her face and she shifted uncomfortably under the direction of his stare.

"I..." She tried once more to protest, but Marcus broke in again, shattering her words with weighty truths of his own.

"You blame yourself, if you hadn't pushed for him to notice you," Marcus' fingers settled on hers and she swallowed back a burst of emotion. "Tell me I'm wrong,"

Melissa stayed silent, listening to the crackle of the fire in the background as she tried to process her brother's words. Her first instinct was to deny it, to loudly declare that he was wrong, but the words wouldn't come. Her mind was drifting back through the years to her first glimpse of Justin Lestrade.

"You did warn me," She whispered, her voice thick with unshed tears. "You tried to stop me and I didn't listen..." She bowed her head then, tears flowing down her cheeks like a river.

"Melly," He drew her into his arms and held her gently, letting her cry for the second time that day. "You weren't to know and neither was I," He rested his chin against the top of her head and stroked her hair. "So please...please try to forgive..."

"How touching," They pulled apart at the familiar voice and Marcus jumped to his feet and he stared at the source of the voice with something akin to hatred.

"Montjoy," Marcus pushed Melissa behind him and took a step forward. Melissa wiped the tears from her face and picked up a poker from beside the fire. She moved to stand beside her brother, poker held ready in her hands.